Nathen was recently diagnosed with autism, and he's a newly created vampire. His maker, a multinational corporation with its finger on the pulse of the technology industry, has recruited him to stop a terrorist plot. In the process, he meets Cameron, a telepath and psychologist, who has a troubled past he keeps locked up in the shadows of his psyche.

Nathen is confused by social cues and Cameron can barely block out the thoughts of others.

Together, they find common ground, and with the help of their friend Syn, they work out the secrets of the terrorist group and learn that the plot is far greater than they could have imagined.

I0583783

AWAKENING

Darklight, Book One

Sean Ian O'Meidhir &
Connal Braginsky

A NineStar Press Publication

Published by NineStar Press
P.O. Box 91792,
Albuquerque, New Mexico, 87199 USA.
www.ninestarpress.com

Awakening

Printed in the USA
First Edition
May, 2020

Print ISBN: 978-1-64890-010-5

Also available in eBook, ISBN: 978-1-64890-009-9

Warning: This book contains sexually explicit content, which may only be suitable for mature readers, violence, sexual assault, rape, racist language/imagery/slurs, and murder.

Connal: A dedication to the Vampire. Of the "classical" monsters, few have been as enduring as the Immortal Vampires. Their stories were whispered by our ancestors by night in every culture around the world (though they might have been cloaked in different cultural themes and myths). Of the monsters of our ancestors they are the most versatile and relevant to every century they inhabited. They have been villains, heroes, and everything in between in countless books and movies. They reflect and absorb the cultural zeitgeist they exist in and may reveal the hidden darker aspects of the author, or their heroic side, or repressed sexual desires that lay dormant in the shadows of their psyche. To gay men in particular, they take on the projections of the late twentieth century gay culture. Hidden, harbouring secrets, going out by night, and with the ever real and present danger of infecting, or getting infected by a disease that will change the life of the host. Their themes deal with existential issues that most shy away from dwelling too much about but are always brewing underneath. Life, Death, Mortality, Immortality, Divinity, Power, and Dark Beauty. The Vampire, to me, represents the quintessential mercurial archetype of Death, Change, and the Unchanging, and it will outlive us all.

Sean: This is our third published work. The first I dedicated to my parents who encouraged and fostered my writing. The second book was dedicated to David, my partner of 10+ years. This third book I'd like to dedicate to people who have shared love in this life.

Connal—next to David, my best friend whose love and encouragement have woken me up. Writing is like breathing, and he has brought me back to life. I have very much appreciated our journey into a wondrous land whose boundaries are that of imagination.

Angeles—my online partner and very closest confidant who knows absolutely everything about me (and has yet to run screaming). He rules with nonjudgmental kindness, acceptance, patience, quiet strength, creative dignity, and fosters and feeds my need for novelty, romance, and creation. A true dominant who wants everyone around him to grow and thrive, asking only trust in return.

Mark—a short lived whirlwind who will always remain in my heart. Our friendship grew out of play and will remain forever and a day despite the confines of the shells we reside in.

Daniel—my first partner of fifteen years who is on a separate path now. I grew up with him. I grew strong because of him. The most creative man I had ever met. I will always wish him joy.

Chapter One

NATHEN

Sterile. That was the name for a room like this. Brightly lit, the room had a mirrored wall reflecting the enormous, white, tempered glass-topped board table surrounded by at least forty, comfortable, white chairs. Sitting across from Nathen was a middle-aged, nondescript albeit impeccably dressed, man in a dark pin-striped suit that cost more than most people pay in monthly rent. He was sitting impossibly still with a demeanor of infinite patience and calm, observing Nathen with an unreadable expression. Behind him was a paper-thin monitor mounted on the wall that reflected the back of the man's balding head, and Nathen. They were alone in the room, and there were two doors leading out on the side of the room opposite the mirror. What looked like an original Pollock hung between them, the only color in the room.

"Oh good, Mr. Hale. You are with us. Welcome to your new...position." The man's voice was as boring as his appearance, though there was something strange about the way he spoke. Nathen couldn't quite put his finger on it. He even sounded blasé, as if he had given this speech a hundred times before. "It is good to have you as the newest member of the Impetus family."

Impetus? Nathen knew that company. He may have only been twenty-two years old and more concerned about playing World of Warcraft than following Fortune 500 companies, but he knew that corporation had its hands in just about everyone's pots. He became distracted by his reflection in the monitor and thought his raven hair, which was usually unkempt, looked uncharacteristically styled.

The man held up a finger as if to silence, though Nathen had not made a sound. "You have been recruited for an extraordinary purpose. And while I am certain you may have questions, please hold them until I am finished. Here is your on-boarding packet." He referenced a single sheet as he pushed a small pile of papers across the table, sitting a mahogany Montblanc pen atop them.

"I will need you to read through this stack of papers and sign where there is highlighted space..." Nathen considered the huge stack of papers, then shook his head. Wait...he had spaced out again. *How much* did the man just say he was going to be paid?

"...As long as you remain with the Company, we will see to all of your needs. Of course, you are welcome to hunt as you see fit, as long as it does not reflect poorly on the Company. But I'm getting ahead of myself. Please, read and sign, and we will move to the next step. I will explain everything you need to know about your first assignment. Oh, and what being a vampire means."

A whole slew of thoughts and emotions went through Nathen's mind as he adjusted his glasses. The sheer amount of information was overwhelming, and because he didn't have time to process it all. The only things he had paid attention to were the money figures and the fact they had mentioned benefits for his family. *How did I get here? I didn't sit for an interview, did I? Did I even apply for this job? And what is it about that man's speech?* He sat still for a long minute, sorting and retracing his steps after leaving the office of the psychologist. He had been there that morning after two days of testing the previous week, only to have the diagnosis of Autism confirmed, which he had not yet fully processed. The short of it was that he had a social communication deficit and didn't pick up on everything in social interactions. It explained why he was confused when people were supposedly being sarcastic, and he never had been able to tell if someone was flirting with him. His doctor had told him he saw things as black and white but missed the rainbow. It had made Nathen laugh at the time, though the doctor hadn't laughed with him, so he stopped. But he had found it funny that he was missing rainbows. Nathen's eyes darted as he was sorting his visual memory.

Finally, he admitted, "I'm sorry. I'm confused as to how I got here. And I don't remember applying for the position you are offering. Um...what is it that I'm getting hired to do?"

As the words left his mouth, he noticed something strange about how his teeth and tongue moved, as if there was something new, though he couldn't place what was different. He reached up to his chin feeling it for pain. Maybe he had been knocked out with a punch?

The man arched one eyebrow almost imperceptibly and stared at Nathen, speaking slowly, "You are being hired for your computer prowess, Mr. Hale. We are aware of your unique abilities to find your way into just about any system you attempt to enter, either legally or illegally. You will be putting your talents to work for us, and for the greater good if I may be so bold. Your first assignment will be to assist us in defeating those who are currently threatening children and their families, a story I am certain you have heard about. I will tell you more once you have officially accepted the position." The man tapped the on-boarding paperwork that he had pushed over moments before. "And, you did not apply. You are being drafted."

"I don't know what you mean by 'illegal,'" Nathen protested, his mind racing as he tried to figure out if he had done anything to worry about with his latest online endeavors.

Quickly trying to cover up, Nathen explained, "I'm paid to find vulnerabilities in systems, hired by companies to discover and report. And how did I get here? The last thing I remember before waking up here is leaving the doctor's office."

Nathen picked up the forms and started reading them, then glanced back up as his thoughts replayed what the man had been saying. It sometimes took him a few minutes to catch up if he wasn't paying strict attention. "And what do you mean by 'Vampire?' Is that the internal project name I'll be working on?"

The man fixed Nathen with a stern glare. "Do not play games, Mr. Hale. You are what is known by many as a 'hacker' and engage in a number of extracurricular activities I am certain you do not wish everyone to know about. But we do know. And that skill set makes you valuable. Please sign, and I will move forward with explaining everything else."

Nathen thought about it, reasoning that it was a competitive salary for California and appreciated that his family would be covered. Because his mother was an attorney, Nathen knew never to sign a contract without reading it first. Trying to be polite, Nathen asked, "Do you mind if I read over the contract so I know what I am getting into?"

The man waved his hand, a gesture of patient permission, with a slight inclination of his head as a way of acknowledgement. One of his hands gently came to rest on the other, both folded in front of him atop the leather portfolio as he stared ahead, returning to a state of perfect calm.

Nathen read through the documents, his eyes flying over the pages as he comprehended at a speed he was amazed by. It normally took him a long time to sludge through boring documents like this. He assumed everything was standard as nothing stuck out as concerning. Everything was as the man had suggested, a document that outlined the mundane tasks of bureaucracy. The emergency contact form was already filled out with his mother's information, including her cell phone. The position title was generically *Analyst*, which left room for a variety of tasks that were not actually spelled out in any way. Instead of a work schedule, the contract had *variable*.

"Oh, most of this is already filled out. That's good because my handwriting is horrendous." Nathen smiled at the man, picked up the pen, signed in his name on the marked locations, and pushed the stack back.

"Very good." The man opened the leather portfolio and pulled out a keycard that had Nathen's photograph on it.

"This will allow you access to this building and those sections of this building which you are authorized to be in. Your office is on the twentieth floor, office number 14A. Of course, with your assigned laptop you have the ability to work from home, or any other location of your choosing. We only ask that any work that you do with and for the Company is done on your assigned laptop and not your personal computer. Many of our associates never step a foot inside this building once hired. Either way, it is up to you."

Retrieving a black leather messenger bag, the man went on in a fairly monotone way, and Nathen focused in on his strange clipped way of talking, getting lost again. Wait. Did he say something was wrong with his thumbprint and he had a company phone now? He tried to focus. "...in it is my number. Do not call me unless there is an emergency, or you have completed an assignment. Should you have mundane questions, a text will do. Feel free to use this phone for any and all calls as you see..."

Nathen wondered what kind of phone it was and started going through the various types of phones that he had used, refocusing when the man said, "...Company's car service. You have unlimited access to this car service, and they are aware of your unique sun sensitivity, so once inside you will not have to worry about ultraviolet light."

Nathen sat quietly, listening without interruption. He tried paying attention so he would not miss anything, but internally struggled with so much information coming at him so quickly. Did that man say something about light sensitivity?

The man set the bag on the table next to him as he continued without pause, "With regard to your first assignment, you will find it in a folder on the desktop of your laptop, spelled out in detail. As mentioned, we are incredibly distraught about this group, the Sons of Discord, and what they are doing with the computer systems and data at the San Francisco Children's Hospital. We have had to move fast due to their imposed deadline, and thus you have been recruited. We need you to gather as much data as possible on this group and report back. I will expect you to read through all information available on this"—he patted the bag—"and work to gather and report data as you find it. Feel free to use anything and anyone at your disposal. We are aware that you have quite the extended group of acquaintances online and encourage you to reach out to them. The only thing I would like to impress upon you is to refrain from telling them that you have been elevated to your current physiological status by the Company. Indeed, vampires don't actually exist. Officially, you are an analyst, which you may tell them. However, the nondisclosure clause you have signed inhibits you from disclosing the specifics of things you are analyzing. That said, a person of your nature investigating this on his own would not be suspicious. Now, as to being a vampire. Please pay attention..."

Nathen listened to the man talk nonstop to him about dietary restrictions, being killed by the sun, and other strange information. When he finally asked if there were any questions, Nathen looked blankly and asked, "I'm sorry, am I expected to...uh...role play a vampire only while in the office or...I'm confused. I'm also still not sure how I got here. My memory is a blank starting from the psychologist's office up to waking up in this room. I am not sure where I am."

The man sighed, as if anticipating the questions but hoping for acceptance without question. "Mr. Hale, this is not a game. You are in the financial district of San Francisco at our office. You cannot remember the last eight hours because you have been undergoing a transformation. Your human blood needed to be removed and replaced with vampiric blood. Since that means you will have this countenance forever unless you choose to change it, we took the liberty of grooming you—nails, hair, etcetera. You will find you have fangs should you choose to use them, and they will likely extend automatically if you smell blood. At least until you get control of that. I can see this is going to be a challenge. Allow me."

The man called out to the room, "Agnes, please bring a glass in." He paused and stared at Nathen for a moment before one of the doors opened. A gorgeous brunette in a pencil skirt and blousy white shirt, with styled curls that bounced as she walked, entered carrying a wine glass of red liquid.

"Mr. Hale," she greeted Nathen warmly, sitting the glass in front of him. "Welcome!" After depositing the glass, she immediately turned and left through the way she entered.

It was the smell that hit Nathen first. Whatever was in the glass was unlike anything he had ever had, and yet so familiar. Coppery, but overlaid with something else. There was an odd sensation that Nathen had forgotten. An itch beneath his canine teeth but also slow movement. The itch itself was also mixed with an odd sense of sexual emotions: longing, yearning, overlaid with the disturbing need to devour. He shot up from the chair, causing it to fly backward and hit the floor. His left hand clasped over his mouth, as if he was using it to stop a word from coming out—in his case a scream—and he took a large step away. Nathen realized he didn't feel his heart catch up with the emotion he was feeling: anxiety, fear, and dismay. His hand went from his mouth to his chest, discerning no familiar pulse of life. Though he was feeling the emotions and breathing quickly, the rest of his body seemed abnormally calm. His right hand still on his chest, he started pacing, his left hand making odd repetitive motions and finger contortions, eyes wide with fear.

What's wrong with my teeth? Is this guy serious? He must be, why would he lie? What's wrong with my teeth!? He stabbed at his canines with his tongue, they were a lot longer and sharper. Rubbing at his chest, he searched for his pulse that was not there. *I can't feel my heart. It must be a heart attack! Hand in the wrong place?*

The man sat with his hands folded in front of him and watched Nathen move back and forth, his expression unchanged. After a few moments, he interrupted Nathen's internal dialogue. "May I answer any questions, Mr. Hale?"

Nathen snapped out of his thoughts, "This has to be a dream, right?" Talking was strange with his teeth in their new position. He sounded different, his tongue was not used to the new layout so his voice had a new twang. He stopped pacing, stood still and closed his eyes. He focused on calming himself and waking up. *Wake Up, Wake Up, WAKE UP*! repeating the words as a kind of ritual to snap his mind out of this dream. He opened his eyes and found himself still standing in the room with the man looking at him with a serene calm. "Is this a dream?" he asked the man again. "I mean, vampires are things you kill or play as in computer games. Or perhaps you have drugged me? Slipped LSD in my drink to see how I would react?"

"What you are experiencing is quite normal. Vampires are a thing of myth, legend. But they do exist, though are quite rare…"

Nathen's mind spun with what the man was saying and his strange stilted language. He shook his head when the man started talking about the San Francisco Children's Hospital. "I am certain you have heard of the hospital being hijacked by a terrorist group? Well, with your new gifts, you will be able to seek out information faster and with preternatural ability. So, no, Mr. Hale, this is not a dream and you have not been drugged. Nor is this a prank or a psychotic episode. Indeed, aside from Autism, you have no other mental health concerns."

Nathen wondered if that was true. *I'm being pranked.*

"Please let me know if you think you might want to speak with a therapist about this."

About what?

"We have one on staff who can certainly talk to you about your elevation, something that I know you would not be able to discuss with a regular therapist. That said, Mr. Hale, the clock is ticking, and we do need to focus on the assignment at hand. But please, working on the correct assumption that this is real, do you have any other questions that I may answer?"

Nathen quietly picked up the chair and slipped back into it, taking and releasing a deep breath. "Can I please have a few minutes to process this?" Nathen stared at the glass with the red liquid. He surmised it was blood and noticed he was salivating.

Silently, the man inclined his head in a subtle nod and made no other movement or sound, possibly to allow Nathen his request.

The Company seemed to be offering everything he could ask for: good pay, a nice bonus, insurance for his family, and new equipment. The car service was a really nice perk as well. Nathen hated taxies and ride-shares as the drivers usually wanted to talk, which he found awkward to do with people he didn't know. With his mind processing concerns about his routine being interrupted, Nathen picked up the glass and smelled the contents.

There was the familiar metallic smell, but also something else, something he hadn't noticed before. In his mind he had a blurry impression of a woman, maybe in her thirties. He smelled the blood again and focused. A light scent of beef tickled his senses, but no smoke or tobacco. With a sudden urge to drink it again, a lump formed in his throat which came with a mild sense of nausea. "May I drink this?"

The man inclined his head silently.

Nathen brought the glass to his lips and took a small sip of the warm liquid. The intense flavor accompanied fast-moving blurry impressions of events that were not his own. He blinked as if trying to clear his mind, but he wasn't sure if that was his imagination, or if that was imparted by the blood. It had a metallic taste, but the longer he kept it on his tongue he noticed it began to change and turn sweet. He swished it around and the flavor changed again to what he interpreted as a sweet orange taste, much like orange marmalade. Finally, he swallowed it, and something surprising occurred. Along with sense of taste, he was also overcome with emotions of excitement, sexual ecstasy, and a perverse sense of being used (and liking it). Were those the emotions of that woman? Nathen looked back at the man to see if he could get any reaction from him, but his face was blank. He took a bigger sip, then a gulp, and finally downed the glass. The taste of the marmalade was strong, and her blood ended up being incredibly sweet. He could feel it coat his throat and flow down to his stomach. He hesitated, waiting to be sick, though that didn't happen. In fact, he realized that he felt better. His mind calmed.

"That was incredibly weird," he said. "If I don't like it, you will change me back? And all I have to do is find information about the guys that installed the ransomware at the San Francisco Children's Hospital?" Nathen had learned when he was overwhelmed that the only logical course of action was to parse out the *known* from the *unknown*, as he did whenever he was working on the computer. In this case the *known* was that he didn't know how he got here, but he was here now. This company was offering him a ton of money for something he was already good at. And...he was a vampire. Having no frame of reference for this last bit, he shifted that to the side to worry about later.

"Mr. Hale, I am certain you will appreciate the new senses, strength, and abilities you will come to notice in time with your new being." For the first time, the man smiled, the gesture wolfen, almost predatory. "How did you find the drink?"

Chapter Two

CAMERON

Cameron sat in the Starbucks with his chai tea latte, surrounded by people talking about a horror that had hit. San Francisco Children's Hospital, the largest research, training, and practicing hospital in the country, had been hacked the day before by "cyber terrorists" who had taken control of the computer systems, threatening a data breach of protected health information, and were requiring a ransom? Cameron wasn't sure about this last piece because people's minds were clouded by their emotions. He *listened* to the thoughts of those around him. They heard, read, saw, imagined... He shut out their emotions, which would be a monstrous distraction if he let them. Sometimes sitting in a busy coffee shop could be soothing, like being at a rock concert or a symphony. He could simply tune into all the emotions around and let them flood his senses and wash over him, around him, through him. Today though, it was like being in a death metal concert. Or acid-jazz. Man, he hated jazz.

Cameron picked up that *something* had happened. People were outraged because a group calling themselves the Sons of Discord had decided that a *children's hospital* was the best way to get their point across. *Super creative, asshats.* They demanded some sum of money, but people's thoughts were too confused to get an accurate amount and various news agencies seemed to be reporting different things. One common thing was that there was a one-week time limit, and that the hospital was supposed to run normally. Something about if authorities interfered, other hospitals would be hit. *Well that's thinking ahead Sons of D's.* Cameron frowned. He and Syn had planned to take the following week off, though they hadn't planned on where they were going and sometimes chose staycations with marathon game nights.

Cameron's loud groan at the whole situation drew attention from nearby people who were glued to their phones and he smiled apologetically, feigned back pain and took his leave. An overall wave of anxiety permeated the city and it was enough to make him want to skip the gym entirely. But, then, pretty much anything could make him want to skip the gym. Cameron hated the gym and working out. It reminded him of junior high and high school PE classes in what he snarkily thought of as "small town/small mind USA," where he went from being the shortest and scrawniest to the tallest, and still scrawniest, with all the jocks being the quintessential dicks. But being a gay man in San Francisco pretty much granted him a gym membership. While he went through the litany of excuses to go directly to Trader Joe's and to not pass Go, to not collect a ton of sweat stained gym clothes, he got a text from Syn. He sighed, knowing gym it was.

Yes, Syn. I'm on my way. he texted back.

Though at least a foot shorter than his six-foot-four frame, Syn was at times more masculine than he was, and for as much as he liked boys, she liked girls. And though she claimed she was not a mage, Cameron swore to the gods and spirits that she had a kind of strange ESP, because she always seemed to know when he was going to skip the gym! It wasn't surprising since they had known each other since they were ten years old and Cameron and his mother had moved to the small town where Syn had been born and raised. They bonded almost immediately as Cameron was an outsider, and even though Syn was related to half the town she had always felt like an outsider too. He considered her a sister in every respect.

K was all he received in response, and Cameron laughed because he had been caught, and about-faced to Silver Stream.

Silver Stream was a small neighborhood gym but had all the requisite machines along a back mirrored wall that made way for the other two-thirds set up for kick boxing, yoga, and tai chi classes. In the basement was the real gem—two lanes of Olympic sized pool, a hot tub, and separate changing and steam rooms for men and women. Syn managed the place and taught kickboxing for "legit" funds but had never had trouble keeping them in the lifestyle they had become accustomed to due to her extra-curricular online activities. Cameron teased her that she had ruined him for marriage, and she teased that he needed to find himself a nice "real doctor" to settle down with. She often mused that his being a shrink at a nonprofit was a "phase."

After their individual workouts and showers, they met up in the small lobby. Cameron had opted to dress back in his work clothes, button-down shirt and slacks, rather than wear gym clothes out and about.

"Sad about the hospital," Syn remarked, knowing of course Cameron had heard about it.

"Yeah, fucking jerkwads," Cameron said aloud. Even though when they were together, he could open a channel to speak mentally with Syn, when in public they decided it was better to actually talk out loud so as not to draw attention to themselves by suddenly laughing for no apparent reason.

"Tell us how you really feel, carrot top," she jibed, ruffling Cameron's well-kempt ginger hair.

Cameron laughed and ducked away, running his hand through his hair to smooth it back into place as they dodged other city dwellers on their way to their favorite dim sum restaurant. It was cheap and good, right on the edge of Chinatown. The sky was a deep, clear blue with a cool, crisp, light wind that tickled across his skin and felt great after the workout. Cameron was often reminded that they lived in heaven and were blessed in so many ways.

"How was your day, dear?" Syn teased.

"Just a couple of CPS evals," he switched to speaking mentally so as not to divulge possible private information in public. *"One for a little kid who was removed from his home and is struggling. Probably exposed to meth in utero. The other was a mom who has mental health stuff, but surprisingly no drug problems. I don't think she should have custody, but definitely visitation. She's gotta stop having kids. Three kids in three years and she's eighteen? Come on."*

After they were seated, Syn ordered for the both of them when the waitress arrived and then openly checked her out as she walked away before returning her attention to Cameron. He loved Syn for her subtleness among other things. "Whackado sterilization program," she commented more than asked.

Cameron groaned. Syn had serious thoughts about who should and should not have children and was not open to people having the right to procreate without a license. Of course, considering where she came from, Cameron didn't argue. "What about you, *dear*?" he asked with a smirk, sipping the delicious jasmine tea the waitress had brought after she took their order.

"Well the Sons can lick my hairy nut sack," she started with a sweet innocent smile, summoning a wet choke from Cameron. "They're terrorists, that's all. They want to hold themselves out as these great revolutionaries, but seriously fuck, fuck, fuck them. And their sisters." She waggled her eyebrows.

They talked for a little while longer, and Cameron was grateful she waited until they were almost done until she started in on him. "So, Grindr?"

It was a constant discussion. Syn wanted Cameron to have a "rich and full" sex life, like she had; but he considered himself a hopeless romantic. Cameron often pondered on their gender role reversal. He had had two relationships in his life. The first was at sixteen with Tommy who had promised to visit "someday" after he moved back to New York after they had turned eighteen, but someday had not yet come and it had been five years. They were now Facebook friends, but nothing more. Cameron's other relationship had been with Frank, another doctoral student who was ten years his senior and never let him forget just how "young" he was. Cameron had been nineteen to Frank's twenty-nine when they first met. Frank had been working with his master's degree for several years before returning to school for his doctorate. Fundamentally they were different from the get, a strictly physical relationship. In the beginning, Cameron had enjoyed hanging out with Frank and studying together. He hadn't liked how Frank talked down to him and needed to put everyone down, reminiscent of the bullies in the backwater town of Texas Cameron grew up in. He also didn't like how resentful Frank was when Cameron finished his classes, then dissertation, then his degree before Frank did. Frank had broken off the relationship to "focus on me" with the promise to get back together once he was done with his degree. They used to occasionally get together for a slice and hookups. Frank got nastier and nastier after Cameron got licensed and the last time they were together was on Frank's birthday.

"No thanks, Syn-ister," Cameron said sarcastically and got the check. They switched off paying for meals, though Cameron knew Syn had entirely more money than he did.

"It's gonna shrivel up and fall off," she quipped, chucking him on the shoulder and he simply nodded at the game they played.

Their apartment was large for the city: a two-bedroom, two-bath, with a shared common area. A short hall with a coat closet greeted visitors. It led down to a sunken living room with three steps up to the dining room. An arch in the hall revealed the kitchen with an island that opened to the dining area. A door off the kitchen concealed the laundry area. There was a door to the left off of the dining room which was Cameron's room and bath, and a door to the right off the living room leading to Syn's room and master bath. Along the back of the living room was a floor to ceiling window with a sliding glass door to the balcony that overlooked the city. Both of their bedrooms also had private balconies. Cameron never asked how his friend had acquired the *rent-controlled* palace in the middle of San Francisco. Syn also had the place wired with every technological gizmo and doohickey imaginable: smart cameras, smart doorbell, smart vents, smart thermostat, cameras that allowed them to check on their cats from their phones during the day, and probably a dozen other things Cameron didn't know how to work.

The living room had a couch and lounge chair that faced a huge television and multiple gaming consoles. Of course, there was the cat tree in the corner next to a small table that held wine bottles below. One of the things Syn and Cameron bonded over as children were video games, and they had about every game console that could be imagined and spent many evenings engaged in some sort of play. Cameron often reflected on how ironic it was that Syn was such a technophile and he never actually *got* technology. While he could work a controller, and they played all the time, he was grateful he could bring his phone to her for basic updates.

Thumbing her phone, Syn crooned when it connected, "Sheeeeelah, how you doing girl?" She flopped onto the couch with one leg thrown back over the arm.

Cameron guessed where that would lead so he gathered Hansel and Gretel, their rescue Siamese siblings, and sequester himself in his room where he could do research. The cyberattack and data breech on Children's Hospital bothered him more than he'd consciously acknowledged, and he'd found himself drifting during dinner. While he didn't quite understand the whole thing about a cyberattack, there was an internal pull of annoyance. Why was he so upset? Cameron went back and forth with himself, finally realizing he related cyber terrorists with bullies, and that was something that always bothered him. He had been bullied, but once his abilities came online, he realized that bullying came from a place of weakness. People put other people down to make themselves feel important. Terrorists were bullies on a much greater scale and hid behind masks. And to be doing this at a children's hospital where families were already terrified of losing their children made Cameron feel like he was going to be ill. Maybe he could get in there and help to calm people? Maybe there was something else he could do?

Chapter Three

NATHEN

Nathen smiled at the man. Through his life, he had learned to smile back at people who smiled at him, though sometimes he forgot and looked at them blankly. What came instinctively to others, was something he had learned, like programming. "It tasted like blood at first, but then changed to be sweet, like a sweet orange? I thought I was going to be sick, but I actually feel good. But this whole thing is weird... I mean, I just drank blood."

Though the man was stoic and almost emotionless, he seemed a little more relaxed as he said, "Blood is life. You will find that every donor is different. That was blood type O from a young woman. You may find a preference for type, gender, or other..."

Nathen lost track again, nodding as he tried to process the weird images that had appeared in his mind as he'd swallowed the blood. Nathen had experienced a rush of arousal that was confusing. Along with the confusion and arousal was a rush of euphoria the likes of which Nathen had never experienced before.

He hesitated over whether to mention this to the man, but in the end decided he'd never get an answer to it unless he asked.

"I...uh...felt something. Like emotion that wasn't my own, as I was drinking. Is that...uh...normal? And, was the woman who brought the glass the same woman who gave the blood?"

"Indeed, it was. Her name is Agnes, and in addition to being an administrative assistant, she is also a donor. There are a few donors who work here and a few vampires, though for the most part there are humans with no knowledge of the rest. The blood you receive from the cafeteria will be from a private blood bank. The older the blood, the less likely you will be able to pick up anything about the donor. Agnes donated before you woke up. That is why you were able to pick up so much. If you hunt, you will find the emotional connection much stronger. If you disdain such, then utilize the blood we provide. If you wish to meet the other donors that work here, let Agnes or your floor administrative assistant know, and it will be arranged. Please do not ask other people who work here though; as I mentioned, they may not understand what you are talking about."

"Oh, that's good to know." Nathen started comparing all the knowledge he had about vampires from Hollywood movies and TV shows. "If I bite people will they remember that I bit them or feel pain?" As his canine teeth retracted, he brought his hand to his mouth again. The motion and the itching sensation were a bit jarring but also kind of pleasurable.

"It will depend on how you feed. If you do it in the course of a sexual act, you can usually disguise it and they will never know. In fact, they will extremely enjoy it. Of course, you can bite to inflict pain by tearing the vein open and leaving a wound that cannot be healed, if that is what you prefer."

Nathen blanched and changed the subject. "Can I see my office and look around the building? I won't lie, I've always wanted to know what was inside here. You guys have a lot of misinformation and honeypots on your network; it's hard to know what's real or made to look real."

"Of course. If we are done here, Agnes will show you around. Are there any other questions for me?"

"No, no other questions. I'm to find information on the terrorists and report to you. If I have other questions, I should text you or ask Agnes," he reiterated his understanding and received a nod of acknowledgement. "Fine. I'll start my digging later tonight. I have a few ideas already."

The man slid the laptop bag and leather portfolio over to Nathen. He noticed that *N. Hale* was engraved in a little nameplate on the leather portfolio. As the man stood, Agnes returned. Offering a big smile, she said, "Mr. Hale, I'm so happy you have accepted the offer. Please will you allow me to show you around?" She stood politely as the man exited.

After the man left, Agnes quietly shut the doors and walked slowly to the opposite side of the table from Nathen, standing with her hands clasped in front of her. She tilted her head, saying softly, "The answer is yes, in case you were interested in having me donate directly. I can also teach you how to do it without hurting someone. If you like?" She smiled broadly, having not moved.

Now that he was paying attention, Nathen could pick up much more about her. The first was the scent of the blood in the glass he had drank. He knew instinctively he could pick Agnes out of a crowd from her scent. He could also pick up a sexual tension that exuded from her though she stood in a completely professional manner. Underlying the libidinous energy was also a small wave of healthy apprehension like one would get when approaching a predator.

Nathen smiled nervously, "Um...thank you. I would love to see the building and the office. I would also like to learn to bite someone without hurting them, but that can wait till after the tour maybe?" He stood awkwardly, not sure where to put his hands, so he stuck them into his hoodie's pockets. He never knew how to respond to women, especially how to make it clear to them he was gay.

"Very good, Mr. Hale. Please remember your new bag and folder." She nodded toward the items on the table, and after Nathen collected them, ushered him out into the hallway that extended in both directions.

Another man, muscular with a crew cut, who was dressed in black loose-fitting pants, black tee-shirt, jacket, and combat boots, was in the hallway. The weight of the man's stare made the hairs on the back of his neck raise, but since Agnes didn't say anything, Nathen didn't either. She turned to the right and walked briskly down the hall, prattling information about the building and the location of Nathen's office, most of which Nathen didn't attend to.

As she showed him to the bank of elevators, she explained that there were over seventy other companies sharing the building. Nathen glanced at the man who had stepped onto the elevator with them, but then turned his attention politely back to Agnes. "The first stop is the cafeteria that only our company has access to. Also, it is on the other side of the underground garage, though most people do not have access to the garage from the cafeteria. Your card will work for it since you have garage privileges, in case you come in during the day. Incidentally, you're always on camera." She waved and smiled at the back mirrored wall of the elevator they had stepped into it. Nathen became distracted by his own reflection in the mirror and didn't hear the rest of what Agnes was saying. His blue eyes now seemed to have a subtle internal glow, and his dark curls were styled in a swept back way, instead of his usual messiness. He traced the edge of his chin as he noticed that his features were more defined, and his normally unshaven unkempt look was more refined. He thought he looked like an idealized version of himself.

Agnes continued as they stepped out into the cafeteria, "...all food is free for employees. Of course, if you bring guests they may be expected to pay." She led Nathen to the place where there was a sign for Order. "Hello John, this is Mr. Hale. Can we get him a sample of the Special A please? This is his first day."

There was a small Asian man behind the counter who looked from Agnes to Nathen. He adjusted his glasses and nodded, ducking out a back door. Nathen could smell him too: a combination of subtle human body odor and fried food. The man appeared a few moments later with a small plastic cup with a lid and straw and handed it to Nathen. "Thank you," Agnes called. "Now, for those important meetings or work you might want to do down here where there are several private rooms." She led Nathen to a bank of four doors along one wall. All the doors were open, and she went inside, shutting the door after Nathen. The room held a leather couch and small round table with four chairs. "You might want to use one of these rooms to meet a donor if it doesn't feel right to eat in your office. What I ordered you is blood type A. Mine is O. Go ahead, taste it. I'm curious what you think." Agnes smiled and slid onto the couch, looking at Nathen expectantly.

Nathen cleared his throat and nervously stuck the straw into his mouth to comply with Agnes' request. The blood was thick and cold. It didn't taste as metallic as he expected it to. Instead it took on the taste of something sour and he could not ascertain any other distinct flavors.

"It's like a tasteless lemonade. I liked the blood in the glass more." He smiled at her, realized his canines had extended and that his mouth was probably red and quickly closed it. "Sorry!"

"Well, it may be the type that tastes sour. I hear that different types have different flavors. The blood in the glass was fresh, never refrigerated." She giggled. "And there is the benefit, for some, of the things you can detect from fresh blood. Some others do not like the connection that comes with it. So, while that"—she nodded to the cup in Nathen's hand—"will definitely fulfill your need to eat, it seems like you probably have other preferences. If you like, I can get samples of the others for you to try?"

"Oh, thank you, but no. I'm full for now," Nathen considered, trying to detect his physical being. "At least I think I am. I don't feel hungry."

"Very well. When you come down here, tell the attendant you want Special A, B, or O. That's code," Agnes stood and took the cup from Nathen, opening the door and tossing it in a recycling bin before calling the elevator again. As they stepped in, the man who had been in the hallway followed. Nathen wondered who he was but had never been one to initiate contact unless he needed to. As they ascended, she told him more about each of the floors and pointed out that they had a fully functional gym with dry sauna.

On his floor, Nathen saw that behind the reception desk, studiously working on the computer, sat a small mousy looking man with large spectacles. "Bryan, this is Mr. Hale," Agnes called congenially.

The small man looked up from his desk with a slight grimace, stood, and nodded, "Ms. Katz. Mr. Hale, it's good to make your acquaintance." He was wearing a pressed, crisp-white shirt, blue tie, and black slacks.

"Bryan," Agnes began, "I've been showing Mr. Hale around. We've done a full tour except this floor and his office. Should I show—"

Bryan cut her off, "I can take it from here, Ms. Katz. You can go."

"Oh," Agnes looked affronted and stood up a bit taller. "Mr. Hale, will that be all, or did you want me to show you your office and go over the other procedures we were talking about?"

Nathen looked from Bryan to Agnes, considering the options. "Um, well Agnes began the tour. I'm okay with her finishing it, and we did have a few other things to talk about."

Agnes gave a Bryan a triumphant smile. "Very good, Mr. Hale, right this way."

Bryan eyed both of them and sat, resuming his work in silence. Nathen wondered why Bryan was being mean to Agnes but decided against asking. He was often confused by why people seemed mean to others and had learned long ago to steer clear of them because he didn't like confrontation.

Agnes led Nathen through a door that needed his keycard to open it, then down a hall to his office as she discussed the layout of the office floor. He was happy to note that the man from the elevator had stayed behind in the lobby. The only thing about the tour that Nathen paid attention to was the location of the restroom and breakroom, though he wondered if he would need the restroom now that he was…"undead"… He laughed at the absurdity of it. Agnes noticed and paused, looking at him questioningly. The thought was amusing, because of how absurd it sounded to him, but since he couldn't do anything about it, Nathan reasoned that he should move on. "Oh, sorry, I'm just…this whole thing is amusing. I'm a 'vampire,' and I'm getting a very polite, and seemingly routine office tour."

Nathen sat behind the desk and noticed a minifridge under it. He opened it and saw glass bottles with printed labels identifying specific blood types that made him frown for a moment, and then remembered it made sense that a vampire would have blood instead of sports drinks. He looked up, realizing Agnes had stopped talking and was standing by the door expectantly.

"Umm, I missed the last part," Nathen said, his patent response for when he had accidentally tuned someone out. He never meant to, but his mother had often yelled at him for not listening to her, which he realized was true.

"I was asking what you would like to do now, Mr. Hale. Get started on the project, or go over some of the…things we were talking about earlier?" Nathen noticed the sexual tension she had exuded earlier return, and he stared, realizing that if he concentrated, he could actually see the blood moving through her body now at a faster pace.

"Well, I don't want to hurt people when I bite them, and I figure if I am a 'vampire'"—he air-quoted—"I might as well embrace the nature of being one. I just think killing or hurting someone is rarely morally justified." He looked at her with an awkward smile, "If you wouldn't mind, I would appreciate if you could show me what I am supposed to do?"

"Of course, Mr. Hale. Please have a seat on the couch, and I'll be right back." She left for a few moments and returned with what turned out to be two white terrycloth towels and a package of wet disposable wipes. Despite what he assumed considering her physiological reaction was an attraction to him, Agnes maintained a pure air of professionalism as she took a seat next to him on the dark leather couch. Her tone was instructive and precise, "There are three types of blood vessels in the human body..."

Nathen became distracted by how close Agnes was sitting. He didn't like when people were close to him or touched him, though he had learned to tolerate it. Her scent was overpowering: a mixture of something floral combined with the tangy flavor of her blood rushing through her veins...or was that arteries, capillaries? He couldn't quite remember what she had said and blinked at her when she pulled her hair to the side and tilted her head, running her finger down the side of her neck. "And the femoral artery, here." Agnes stood and pulled the hem of her skirt up slowly, turning her leg to the side to show her inner thigh that she ran a finger up to indicate where the artery was. Nathen could see a thick river of blood under the skin running up her leg and beneath her skirt and looked away with embarrassment. He had no sexual attraction to her at all and didn't know how to handle knowing she was attracted to him and was now pulling up her skirt. What was even more disturbing was his canines extending. He could sense that if he were hungry, it would be difficult to resist biting her and was distracted for a moment with the thought of self-control as he was currently fighting a new internal instinct.

She began talking about "hunting," and Nathen reminded himself it was impolite to look at the floor when someone was talking to you, so he forced himself to look back at her face, purposefully ignoring that she had sat down with her skirt still raised so it was barely covering her, her legs left exposed. "...HIV, and pass it on to the next person you bite if you have not cycled out of all of your blood."

At the mention of the sexually transmitted disease, Nathen started and interrupted, "Is there a way of telling if someone has an STD or HIV before you bite him?"

Smiling apologetically, Agnes shook her head, "Only if you ask. If you do hunt, if I may make the respectful recommendation to come to me or Bryan and let us know. We will take a little sample of your blood and test it and let you know if you're safe. Much like if you were sexually active without protection. The good news is that if you do catch something, you simply refrain from biting for a few weeks, eat from the cafeteria, and it will be out of your system so you don't inadvertently pass it on to someone else. Now both the inner thigh and the neck are two of the most pleasurable places to be bitten, and with practice you can learn to drink a little. Extending it out will be incredibly pleasurable for both you and your donor or partner. And it does take practice because when you bite someone you might not actually want to stop. Which is why practicing when you are full is wise." She offered a big smile and gently touched Nathen's arm reassuringly. He inwardly cringed but mirrored her smile as she went on talking about blood vessels.

Nathen was reminded about a biology class he excelled at. He got lost in thought about how much he enjoyed learning about systems and how they connected with one another.

His eyes grew wide when Agnes rolled up her sleeve, holding her arm between them, "...biting my arm first and then quickly licking it?"

Anxiety tugged at Nathen's core. What had she been saying? Guess it didn't matter now, she was expecting him to...bite...her...arm. He stared at the proffered limb, then back up, forcing himself to make eye contact. "I have never actually bitten someone before..." He reached up to feel his jaw, his teeth were fully out now and making it awkward to talk. He put his hand on his lap again and looked down at her arm, "Should I lick the skin before biting?"

"Oh!" Agnes smiled compassionately, taking Nathen's hand. "Of course, you haven't bitten anyone! You were just awakened today. It's why I offered to practice with you, so you don't accidentally hurt anyone you love." She rolled her sleeve up further to reveal a bandage across her inner elbow where she had withdrawn blood earlier. "Just take my arm in your hands and bite here. When you're done, lick the bite, and it will heal. If you would like to lick my arm first, you may. The saliva has healing properties for wounds you make and slightly intoxicating effects if you were to say French kiss someone. It makes them more ingratiated to you, an aphrodisiac if you will. But on the skin without a wound it doesn't really do anything but make the skin wet." She smiled encouragingly at Nathen, holding her arm for him.

Nathen slowly took her arm with both hands and brought it to his mouth, opening it, and placing his canine teeth next to the vein. He momentarily lost control and unconsciously bit down, realizing what he had done after the blood was already flowing out of the wound and down his throat. He quickly looked up as a flood of emotion washed over him: that of compassion, anticipation, joy, sensual release. The emotions were hers, but he somehow owned them for the moment, owned her. The blood brought power, strength, and oddly a confidence he had not known before. Agnes shuddered with a controlled climax, biting off any sound with her eyes closed in ecstasy. "Lick the umm..." She swallowed, licking her lips and finally managed "wound."

Nathen withdrew his fangs and obediently licked the wound, marveling when he saw there was only a small streak of blood left behind which he dutifully wiped away with a towel and studied the unbroken skin. "That was neat! I felt your emotions. They were stronger than the glass of blood. Did I do it right? I am surprised of how fast that healed."

Agnes nodded with her eyes still closed, seeming to take a moment to collect herself. Finally, opening her eyes, she smiled and nodded again. "Yes," she breathed out. "Just like that. It's incredibly pleasurable for the donor, regardless of where you bite us. And I'm told you will always be able to learn things about us, especially emotion. I get the sense you will probably be much happier with a donor from the Company or a partner. I'm surprised by your self-control. Sometimes it's difficult to get yourself to stop, especially in the beginning, but you seem to have a great sense of self-discipline. That will be very good!"

Nathen frowned. "I did actually lose control right when I bit you, but afterward, I snapped out of it as soon as I started to feel your emotions."

"Interesting," Agnes said. "Did you want to try again? Perhaps an artery?"

He looked at her neck, and then down, and quickly up at her face, shaking his head mortified at where he could see all of the blood moving in her body.

Agnes smiled softly. "Mr. Hale, please don't be embarrassed. We also know that you are gay, which is why I was chosen to be your first donor. While the Company doesn't frown upon or have any rules against sex with donors, it's generally not good practice because it can lead to drama. Besides, my boyfriend might get jealous." She laughed lightly. "Though, we do have one gay donor here if you want to meet him sometime. I like being a donor, and while it's extremely pleasurable, it's actually just a benefit of working here."

Nathen loosened up a bit and relief flooded him. "Oh, that's good. I'm not sure it's a good idea to be biting someone at work that I might be attracted to." As soon as said that he quickly added, "Not that I think you are not attractive! But, yeah, I'm gay."

Agnes chuckled. "It's fine. I'm impressed that you're able to control yourself so well."

"It was when the emotions hit. I tend to shut down with too many of them," Nathen reflected on what his doctors had said about that being normal for him.

Agnes smiled and nodded. "Well, it looks like you won't get carried away or lose control if when someone's emotions hit you. You're able to stop. Do you want to continue practicing?"

Nathen shook his head. "I think I have enough examples to extrapolate to um...other parts. Thank you for helping me though and showing me around the building." He smiled at her. "I can probably start working immediately."

Agnes stood and righted her skirt and clothes. "I'll leave these here for you to put in your desk, but you can find more in the break room with other emergency kits," she said, laying the towels and package on his desk. "If you need more blood in the future, I'm usually in the gym by 7:00 p.m., then my hours are 8:00 p.m. to 5:00 a.m. Feel free to call my extension or drop by the sixth floor any time. There are always two donors in the building every weeknight. Weekends you're on your own with the cafeteria." She flashed a smile and opened the door. "Also, Bryan can get you anything you need. It was good to meet you Mr. Hale," she added over her shoulder.

Nathen waved at her. "Bye! It was nice to meet you as well!" As she left, his face relaxed to its usual emotionless state. After stashing the towels, he opened his computer and tried to unlock it before he remembered something about fingerprints and saw in the bag a small disk that opened with a black oiled pad. Placing his finger on the pad to moisten his finger so that his prints would show up, he then opened the computer and a browser. He next installed various software he knew he would need, mostly security tools and a chat client. He and his friends set up a chat server a few years ago, and they usually collaborated online, though not openly. A lot of code words and euphemisms were used to mean things other than what was being said. Chat was not a secure medium, but then if someone truly wanted to find you neither were Proxy Servers or VPNs. There was always a trail that could be followed that Nathen looked forward to seeking out for whoever was behind the cyber terrorist attack.

Nathen logged into their server and joined their usual room. The group often worked together on projects where outside intrusion attempts were required by the client.

Many large companies hired people like Nathen and his friends to try and break into their companies' systems to seek out holes in their security. Nathen and his friends enjoyed competing for rewards offered by companies for this service.

Nathen was excited to see that Syn was online. He had known her for almost five years, though they never met in person. While he knew other people online, Nathen knew Syn best, as they had worked together on other projects. She was always reliable and open to feedback, as well as having good ideas.

He messaged her, "Hey Syn! How's it going? Was wondering if you had time to discuss the ongoing issue at the Children's Hospital? Seems some hacker group has managed to cripple them...are you up to helping?"

"RU kidding?! Sign me the fuk up! Wuz doing research on my own, but wndr if it makes more sense to chat IRL?"

Chapter Four

CAMERON

Hey Cam, friends coming over 2nite 2 talk bout topics of interest. UR welcome 2 join. There may be Pizza in it for ya. ;)

> *Hawaiian with habanero sauce?????*
> *UR a sacrilegious heretic. You know this.*
> *=D What time?*
> *Mtg @ 8, but U know they won't show till 9.*
> *What time's the pizza showing up?*
> *............*
> *?*
> *I'll put the order in at 8.*
> *It's a date!*

Cameron put his phone back in his pocket. He wondered what the meeting on "topics of interest" meant but assumed it would likely have to do with one of Syn's social justice groups. He would be polite then quietly excuse himself. Of course, if the pizza beat them, he might be able to escape before the room was filled with lesbians. He was often the token male in the room, which wasn't all together bothersome. It was just that some of Syn's friends were rather antimale which could sometimes make things uncomfortable. Syn was fairly good at running interference, but he struggled with her standing up for him—still. She had been doing it their entire friendship. When they were kids, it was against her cousins. He laughed to himself with memories of little twelve-year-old Syn going off in Spanish to her much larger, older machismo male cousins and having them cow to her. She had always been a force of nature and he counted himself lucky to know her.

Cameron was almost finished with his day at the agency where he worked. Thursdays were training day for practicum students, and he loved it. Cameron had never thought he would be interested in supervising or training others but having the opportunity to mold untrained minds was rewarding in so many ways. Being one of the few licensed staff, Cameron had the joy of providing individual supervision to the slave labor paying their dues in the name of education. Several would make astounding doctors someday. Some trainees really should be choosing other fields. When Cameron came across those who would be doing more harm than good, he probed their thoughts to find out what their actual passion or ability was and slowly began mentally inserting a desire for *that* over the whole psychology business. Those were few and far between because ultimately Cameron did believe in free will.

Waving good-bye to the few stragglers, Cameron made his way grudgingly to the gym where he was happy to find the pool empty. Deciding to forgo any pretense at strength training, he hurriedly changed into the trunks he kept in his permanent locker (thank you, Syn) and dove in, getting in fifty laps before calling it a day and hitting the showers. He had never been a strong swimmer before they moved to San Francisco and Syn had found the gym. Now he swam whenever the pool was empty, which during business hours was rare considering there were only two lanes. Syn, however, had keys to the place and would let him swim after hours. Or use the steam rooms, which was nice late at night.

After showering, Cameron swung by the liquor store and picked up four bottles of red wine before returning home. In his experience, hanging out with Syn and her social justice band of merry lesbians, being the token gay dude he could go two ways with drunk lesbians—happy lesbians or mad lesbians. But either way, being the one who ingratiated yourself with the wine was usually the best way of staying on the good side of the mad ones.

"Hey, love," Syn called from the kitchen.

The delicious aromas of onions, garlic, cumin, and chili greeted Cameron as he entered the house and hung his coat on the antique hook Syn had installed on the back of the door. He brought the bottles in to see the island laden with homemade chips, guacamole, and three types of salsa. His mouth immediately began watering and, setting aside the bottles, he dove in. "Thought we were having pizza."

"What? You complaining?"

Cameron quickly shook his head and stuffed his mouth with another salsa covered chip, moaning in ecstasy to show he was doing the opposite of complaining.

Syn laughed. "I felt like cooking."

Cameron frowned. *Felt like cooking* meant anxiety. He peeked around Syn and noted the oven was on. That meant dessert, which was good for his belly, but something was up. "What's wrong?" he asked, trying to keep the alarm out of his tone.

Syn didn't try to put up any pretense. "Well, I've been talking with a few acquaintances online. We've decided we need to do something about this hospital thing."

Cameron had actually worked into the night doing his own research, which admittedly had gone nowhere. But that morning he had spoken with a colleague at Children's Hospital who had told him that his expertise would be more than welcome if he wanted to come for a few hours to host a training for the residents. The hospital was incredibly regimented about people providing services or volunteer work to the patients due to liability reasons, but free lecturers were always welcome. His friend had also said they were even more on alert due to the threats and had filled Cameron in on the group having *claimed* they could go in, change patient data, release sensitive information, and even begin shutting down necessary equipment during operations if their demands were not met. But they had agreed to meet up for lunch the next day at the hospital and talk about possible topics for the training and catch up. Cameron had already cleared his morning schedule to go in early and look around to see what he could pick up from people's thoughts.

"Wow. That's ironic." He filled her in on his conversation with his friend. "I just couldn't sit by and do nothing, Syn. This whole thing makes me a little...sick," he punctuated the statement by eating another chip with salsa. Nothing could make him too sick for Syn's salsa trio.

"Ooof," Cameron coughed as Syn unexpectedly threw her arms around him, forcing him back a bit.

"I am so glad you said that," Syn said, the sound of her voice muffled into Cameron's shoulder.

"Hey." Cameron hugged her, petting her head. "What's wrong?"

Syn seemed to reluctantly let go and turned abruptly, roughly grabbing one of the bottles Cameron had brought, snagging the corkscrew and pouring two glasses before turning back to him. Her eyes were rimmed in red which took Cameron's breath away. He thought for an instant and could not ever remember seeing Syn cry and before he realized it, he had read it...

Syn, a very little Syn, so so small, frightened and surrounded by big people in white, jabbing her with needles and tubes coming out of her...so cold. Her parents crying over her...her grandmother sitting at her bedside saying the rosary every night...cousins and aunts and uncles visiting. Everyone crying except nurses who were kind, but strangers. Her once long, beautiful hair, the pride of her father, gone. And then her father...gone. No longer visiting. Hushed arguments between her mother and grandmother. The internal knowledge, *no, it wasn't true*, but it was *her* truth that her father left because of her. And then her family happy, welcoming a frail and sickly Syn, cancer-free, home. A home that would never be the same.

"Goddamn it, Cam."

Cameron shook his head and blinked. Syn was staring at him with a mixture of annoyance and acquiescence. He realized tears were streaming down his face. He grabbed her and hugged her again. "Goddamn it," her voice defeated.

"It wasn't your fault," he whispered aloud, wanting desperately to take her pain away, knowing he *could...knowing* he could not. Her pain was her own; he had no right to it. It defined her, gave her strength. People are a sum of their experiences, Cameron had come to understand. Their thoughts and emotions, which were open books to him, helped to build their perspectives of the world. In some cases, the walls people built became inflexible and led to conflicts with people around them.

Cameron described this as "personality disorders" to people he was diagnosing. These walls, built from experiences from childhood, resulted in difficulty with others only because people needed to keep themselves safe. Everybody had a wall, and while Cameron had often wondered what had happened to affect Syn, he had never asked because people do not volunteer those deepest parts of themselves. He had assumed it was her alcoholic mother or the revolving doors of stepfathers. Syn was so healthy now, he would have never guessed.

Syn relaxed after a while and allowed Cameron to hold her until she had no more tears. When she gently pulled away, he said quietly again, "I'm sorry."

She nodded and took a deep breath. "We need to do something about these people. I want them all to hurt in a way that I can't describe."

"Okay," Cameron said, vowing to himself to help Syn in any way he could. She had saved him on more than one occasion, and he would do anything for her.

"It'd be easier if I were a mage or something more than a boring human." She pouted before forcing a smile. "Whatever, pizza's been ordered. Guess you're going to have to put more gym time in."

Cameron knew she was good at deflecting and loved that she used humor as a defense, so he laughed appropriately. "Habanero?"

"What's wrong with you? Honestly? Yes, habanero on your disgusting Hawaiian."

"My goodness—" he said with more joviality than he felt "—chips, guac, salsa, and pizza. You were buttering me up. I see now. You know the way to a man's heart."

Syn blew raspberries at him and pulled out a cake.

"Abuelita's tres leche?" Cameron asked, incredulously. "First off, yes. Yes, I will marry you. And second, what do you have in store for me? You haven't done this much buttering up since...since never."

Syn busied herself with the cake and spoke with her back to Cameron. "I want to make sure you are on board. I think we need your special abilities. I've, I've never actually asked..." she glanced over her shoulder not finishing the thought.

Cameron laughed, not able to keep himself from hitting the chips again. "What do you mean? I used my mad skills to get you laid more times than I can count in high school and at Leo's College!" Leo's was the early college that Cameron had escaped to when he was sixteen years old, and Syn had joined him at the following year.

Syn pursed her lips and faced him. "That's nothing. I never actually asked for anything important. Not like this."

"Ah, Syn," Cameron went over and took her by the shoulders, kissing her forehead. "You never have to be shy about asking me to use my abilities. Come on, you...you saved me," he took a deep steadying breath to keep himself from crying again, forcing the memories as to why they went to Leo's together out of his mind. "And remember, Mom said I have a responsibility. And this sort of thing with these cyber terrorists? This is not okay."

Syn nodded softly, taking the lid off a pot. "Well, I made refried-bean dip too."

"My goodness, ask me for my help more often, will ya?" Cameron dunked a chip into the pot, dragged the chip through the thick beans and scooped it up into his mouth, savoring the spicy flavor.

Syn spooned the dip into a bowl and together they moved the snacks to the living room coffee table. Cameron had just turned on the television to start up World of Warcraft when the doorbell rang.

"Probably pizzas," Syn said, turning to the door.

Chapter Five

CAMERON

Cameron was always mentally scanning. Since his mother had died, Cameron had a low level of paranoia and never wanted to be taken by surprise, and so he knew who was around at all times. It was the pizza guy at the door, but he didn't bother telling her that.

"Pizza and more," Syn returned, introducing happily, "Cameron, this is Nathen, Nathen, Cameron."

Cameron was busying himself with the television, having felt the delivery driver leave. He looked up confused, and fell out of the chair, crawling backward with his eyes wide. He looked from Syn to Nathen.

"Syn, get away from him," Cameron thought, opening a mental link between the two of them, his eyes locked on Nathen as he slowly stood. He could keep their link open for a while without a headache coming on.

"What's wrong?" Syn mentally asked, immediately moving away from Nathen.

"I can't feel him. It's like he isn't there. He's not a fae, I can read fae."

"Could he be another mage?"

"No, I could read my mom. I mean, I don't think so."

"Is it possible you can't read everyone?"

"Anything is possible. How do you know this guy?"

"I've known him for a long time, several years. Well, I've never met him in person, but he's white hat. He's a standup guy, Cam. And he's super upset about what's going on. He really wants to help."

Breaking eye contact with Nathen, Cameron chanced a look at Syn. "Cam, please. If he turns out to be a creeper, I'll shoot him."

"Go get your gun," he left no room for argument. "Have it nearby."

Syn laughed nervously, "Well, can you two studs feel the tension in the room? Never seen such love at first sight."

Nathen laughed uncomfortably, "Oh, um...ok." Cameron saw Nathen glance at Syn, then back to him.

"Umm, if you'll excuse me for just a second. Nathen, please help yourself. There's good pizza, then there's the stuff Cameron eats. Cam, maybe you could get our guest a glass of wine?"

Cameron nodded, skirting around the outside of the living room, keeping the couch between him and Nathen. "Nathen," Cameron said stiffly. "It's good to meet you." He picked up the bottle. "Red?"

Cameron studied the rather attractive and obviously shy man as he stared after him, then down at the floor, then back at him, then away before saying, "Oh, I don't drink. Thank you though."

Cameron focused, reaching out and purposefully, almost painfully tried to attack Nathen mentally and succeeded in giving himself a small headache. He was simply *not there*. Cameron had only once been surprised. But that time was because he had not been paying attention. Since then he had learned to *always* be aware. He was even a light sleeper because of it. After he had witnessed his mother die, it had taken him over a year to be able to sleep through the night. Having Tommy there had been a comfort. When Tommy left, Syn had unofficially moved in with him spending most nights in his small on-campus study playing video games and giving him a sense of comfort. Now that they had their own bedrooms, Cameron was comfortable since Syn had the entire home wired for any type of intrusion. She was also a sharpshooter, and he had learned to stop most people with his mind. Most...

Nathen looked normal, cute even. He was not as tall as Cameron, though most people weren't. It was obvious he worked out but wasn't a meathead. Cameron saw that he took care of himself, with well-kept nails, fresh haircut, neatly styled five o'clock shadow style designer stubble beard, thin glasses, jeans, gaming T-shirt, and hoodie. There was nothing at all out of the ordinary and on any other day Cameron might even find him attractive. But it was like he was a ghost, able to be seen, but not *sensed*. His mother had learned to block him from reading her thoughts, but her emotions were like perfume floating around her. Everyone's was. Nathen didn't have any that he could read. Was it possible that fae masked their thoughts and emotions until they struck? The thought made him feel sick, and he realized he had already poured a glass despite Nathen not drinking. Cameron brought the glass around to the chair he had been sitting in and lowered himself without taking his eyes off Nathen. He found himself draining the glass and was happy to see Syn positioning herself on a small mound of pillows she sat on the floor in anticipation of several people. She was closer to Cameron, but he felt naked without any ability to defend her except for the glass of wine. He frowned at the empty glass and set it down with the food.

Syn laughed, "Well, you're on time, huh Nathen? Perhaps you could tell Cam a little about what you were thinking of or found about this group? We can reiterate everything if anyone else shows. I put my feelers out, but only got a couple of people saying definite maybe. And that means no usually. You were the only one who said yes. Did you invite anyone else?"

Nathen seemed to force a smile at Syn as he sat on the couch. "I invited a few people, but they were noncommittal, probably anxiety about meeting in person. You know how nerds are, it's like herding cats." Cameron saw he sneaked a peek at him again and then looked past him, away, around, and down. "I didn't find out much. I know they installed the ransomware through an e-mail that one of the employees opened and it infected the rest of the computers on their network. It communicates back to a swarm of bots all using various IP addresses. The system has to be online to get the unlock signal, otherwise the data is lost past the date. It's similar to VirLock, in that it encrypts the data pretty quickly, but instead of RSA-2048 encryption it uses—"

Cameron blinked a few times, interjecting mentally to Syn, *"Is this guy for real? What the hell is he saying?"*

Syn snickered, mentally responding, *"I know what he's talking about."*

Nathen went on, having not seemed to pick up that Cameron's eyes had glazed over. "...RSA-4096. Similarly, they want payment via a Bitcoin address, 800USD or 0.28BTC. To figure out more, we will probably need to get access to the ransomware itself. This is a new group. I could not find much information on them, no Twitter account or anything else. They seem to like being in the shadows, which is strange for hackers."

Cameron sat, openly staring at Nathen. His mind raced with the whys? He extended his mind and could feel the incredibly familiar neighbors throughout the building. Over the last five years he had gotten better and better at knowing who was around. When he couldn't sleep at night, he would go floor by floor, so he knew all the neighbors by name and emotion, some more in depth with their issues. He had strived to slightly tweak people, sending them feelings of benevolence, love, and compassion. All the same people who lived in the building were there, nothing strange and no one suffering. He focused for a moment on what Nathen was saying. Hell, if he was a fae bent on harming Syn or him, Nathen was the most boring fae he had ever met.

What had he been saying about an R2D2? Cameron found himself drifting off, the same way he did whenever Syn started talking about technology; and leaned forward to attack the box of pizza. Stress eating was a real thing, and Cameron partook of it with abandon. Syn had often commented that his metabolism wasn't fair. He focused again on what they were talking about. Nathen was talking Syn-language. It would be as if Cameron went off about standard deviations, reliability and validity, and psychometric properties of IQ tests. All a different language. He glanced at Syn who had leaned forward, wine glass in hand, nodding like it all meant something. Cameron realized he was relaxing a bit and frowned. He didn't want to get too comfortable.

Syn listened intently. "Interesting, do you think it would be possible to decrypt the data ourselves?"

Nathen shook his head. "Not unless we can get the key. The encryption is pretty strong, even using a GPU farm. It would take longer than the countdown." Syn nodded and looked to be in thought.

Nathen glanced at Cameron. "Um, what's your handle? Are you going to help us with the hospital also?" Nathen seemed sheepishly nervous, his gaze not lasting long, darting to the floor and then back.

Cameron inwardly struggled with allowing himself to say anything. He didn't trust this guy and the thought that he had been playing with him in a video game online gave him the creeps.

Syn laughed. "He isn't great with technology."

Cameron let his guard down long enough to shoot Syn a look.

"He can help in other ways." Syn smiled kindly.

"Yeah," Cameron said, moodily standing. "Excuse me." He slid out through the patio door to think. Positioning himself so he could look into the room and watch, he leaned against the low wall separating Syn's balcony from the main balcony.

Cameron could hear Syn's side of the conversation through her thoughts as she spoke with Nathen. He watched from the balcony as she fetched her laptop, telling Nathen she was checking on the other people she had invited. Their link was still active and the mild pounding was beginning behind Cameron's eyes when Syn said, "*Cam, this guy is legit. He's got a great plan. But we need to physically go into the hospital to do it. Would you mind going in with him?*"

"*Seriously? I can't even talk to him?*"

Cameron saw Syn laughed out loud, pretending it was something on her screen to Nathen, then to Cameron she thought, "*Listen, I know this is bothering you, but it's also hilarious that with him you're like a regular person! Now you know how us little people feel.*"

Despite her teasing, Cameron could feel waves of concern, compassion, and empathy from her, caressing him like a hug. He looked out over the city, accepting her attempt at soothing, but still not happy that he had met the first person he couldn't read. At all. How many others were out there he had simply not "seen?" Had he gone through his life this whole time with an entire section of the population he had been "blind" to? Or was Nathen a mage too?

Chapter Six

NATHEN

Nathen had a wave of nervousness when Syn had sent him the apartment's address. He had never been overly comfortable in social situations that were in person. Nathen was a rock star online because he could connect with people's ideas. He liked that he could ignore interactions or join in as he saw fit. He also liked the fact that being online gave him a chance to think about how he would react. In person it was different. People expected immediate responses and their unpredictability was always a source of stress.

He had taken the car service back to his home and spent part of the day going over and over in his mind past conversations he had had with Syn online so he would remember specific interests as points of conversation. He knew she was a lesbian and motivated by social justice. He had also gone on many covert "missions" with her, hacking into various companies. He had shied away from the more questionable things Syn did, like hacking into big businesses and moving funds around to support causes she believed in. Nathen had always been afraid to go on those missions because he didn't want to get in trouble with the law.

From their interactions, Nathen knew Syn was strong willed and opinionated. He also knew she was loyal and had an admirable instinct to protect her friends, so when she had invited him, he hadn't hesitated at all. Now that he was in her home, he was having difficulty focusing on what she was saying as he looked out at the strange fiery haired man on the balcony. He didn't know what to think about him. He was cute, and the sapphire earring he wore matched his bright blue eyes. Nathen wondered if he had done something that might have upset Cameron. It seemed like in social situations he was apt to say something that annoyed someone, and so he started thinking back since he got to the apartment. He realized he hadn't said anything at all. In fact, Cameron had fallen out of his chair when he saw him. He had thought that was pretty strange but opted not to say anything at the time because he felt self-conscious.

Nathen inwardly groaned, realizing he had missed something. Syn was saying something, but he only started paying attention when she said, "Cameron is going in tomorrow. He's a doctor, a psychologist, and has a friend who works there. But maybe you could go in with him and steal away? Get into the system? Maybe you could go in as his assistant?" She glanced out the window. "He's pretty worked up about this whole thing. You know, being the super sensitive shrink type? I'm gonna see if anyone else is going to come tonight or if they would be willing to help in other ways. But I do understand the need for anonymity and the safety that *not* meeting in real life provides. You know, I was actually surprised even you showed up. I kinda thought it was going to be just me and Cam with a ton of food and the internet. Maybe you can talk to him and see about joining him?"

Nathen thought to himself, *I'd rather not.* He knew Syn from online, running missions, playing World of

Warcraft. He was comfortable with her. As far as he knew, he never met Cameron online, and he hated meeting new people. He never knew how to act, what to talk about, and besides, the man was already acting strange. Like he didn't like him. The inward debate was lost when Nathen reminded himself that he was a guest in her home and better do what she asked to be polite.

He thought back on all the times people had asked him to do things. Generally, if he didn't think it was an unreasonable request, Nathen would comply even if he wasn't interested. He was reminded of the last time he went along with his brother's request for him to go bowling with him. Nathen had spent the night staring at his phone and wondering what people found interesting about throwing a heavy ball at pins. The place was jarringly loud and as the night wore on his brother's friends were verged on intolerable. The night reached its pinnacle with Nathen driving all the drunkards back to their respective homes and then cleaning up the puke in the back of his brother's car. *Good times.*

Nathen silently stood and edged out onto the patio. The smell of Cameron's blood hit him again, clear as the bright morning. In moving through the city, Nathen had been inundated with the smells of people around him. Each human had his or her own scent and he was beginning to be able to tell similarities and differences. He had wondered if it was their blood types, but some people simply smelled sweeter or sourer to him. Syn had a more neutral smell to her, but Cameron... When Nathen had entered the apartment, he could immediately smell him. While he could smell the aroma of the food stuffs that had been laid out all over the table, when he saw Cameron he was taken aback, and his canines had begun to extend.

Cameron didn't smell like Agnes, Syn, or any of the people on the street. Nathen knew if he was hungry he might have been compelled to immediately try and taste Cameron. He was intoxicating, his blood was powerful, strong, and something else. And Cameron himself was beautiful. Nathen focused in on the scent: it reminded him of a juicy overripe peach that he could not wait to sink his teeth into. His mouth started watering, and his canines fully extended again and he got distracted for a moment willing them to stop and retract. He was thrilled to find he could control that.

Nathen focused and cleared his throat, "Hi Cameron, I was wondering if I could go with you to the hospital tomorrow? Also, um...did I do something wrong? You seem to be upset at me, and I usually have a hard time reading people."

Nathen stood against the door turning his phone over and over again in his hands. Instead of answering his question, Cameron posed one of his own. "Are you a mage?"

Smiling slightly, Nathen wondered why Cameron had decided to start talking about the online game. "Um...I play a Shadow Priest."

Nathen saw Cameron roll his eyes. "I don't mean in any game scenario. I mean right here, right now. What are you?"

Struggling with answering the question outright and telling Cameron he didn't know what he was talking about, Nathen stared at his shoes. He wondered if Cameron knew something about him being a vampire, and reasoned that it would be strange for him to know, so he asked, "Why?" He quickly followed up with, "And no, I am not a mage."

Cameron seemed to glare at him, sighing in frustration. Nathen knew that sigh as it was a sound that his brother often did when he was around and annoyed at him. Cameron asked, "Then what are you, if you're not a mage? Are you fae, then?"

Nathen gave an absurd half smile, going over the rules in the back of his mind. He wasn't supposed to be saying anything about the company, but here Cameron was asking strange questions. Odd paranoia crept over him and he had to remind himself there was no way Cameron could know he was a vampire. He opted to stick with the confusion. "I feel like we're LARPing. No, I am not a fae. Are you a 'fae' or a 'mage'?"

Cameron gave Nathen an even look and sounded intense as he said, "Yes, I'm a mage. No, I am not a fae."

Reasoning that Cameron wasn't talking about games, and since vampires existed, it followed that mages could exist, Nathen shrugged. Maybe he had used magic to see what Nathen was. "Oh, I didn't know there were mages and fae. I can't believe I missed all of that." *Damn psychologists, this all started in that office.*

"Really? *What are you,* then? I can't read you, can't pick up anything about you. So, if you're not a mage and able to block me, and not a fae here to hurt Syn or me, then what are you? And why are you able to block me entirely?"

Nathen shrugged and said, "A vampire?"

Chapter Seven

CAMERON

Does this guy think I'm joking? Cameron started to challenge him, because vampires didn't exist. But then he internally laughed because mages didn't exist either. *A vampire?* Cameron stared at him for a long time, trying to identify anything vampire-like. He looked normal, but then what did vampires look like? Fiction portrayed them from slavering, balding, undead beasts crawling from the graves; to unnatural fast blood-thirsty predators; to sparkly emos; to ridiculously gorgeous rock stars...the list did go on, didn't it? In fact, Cameron couldn't remember reading anything portraying just a guy. A handsome guy, to be sure. Kind of nerdy with glasses. Wasn't the unlife supposed to somehow correct nearsightedness? Or were those his secret disguise like Clark Kent? The whole line of questions was amusing, and Cameron found himself smiling.

"*Hey, Syn, know anything about vampires? I mean for-realz vampires?*" he thought.

He saw her look up from her monitor with a start. "*Umm, what now?*"

"*Your stand-up guy here says he's a vampire.*"

There was a long enough pause to make Cameron look back into the living room where Syn was staring out at Nathen. "*Do I need to worry?*"

"I don't know. But hell, get your grandmother's rosary, because I don't think you're thirty-eight will do it."

"You're not kidding."

"Nope, says he's a vampire."

"Fuckedy fuck, Cam!" Syn retreated to her bedroom, presumably to find her grandmother's rosary.

"Yeah, always loved you because even your thoughts are ladylike."

"No wonder he didn't want any food. All of it has tons of garlic in it."

"He probably didn't want food because he's a vampire. Heh, make him a Bloody Mary?"

"Nice joking, Cam," Syn returned and went into the kitchen. "Okay, all I got are chopsticks."

Cameron laughed loudly, then noticed that Nathen was standing and watching. "Sorry, bro. Had to arm ourselves with chopsticks and the like. You know, just in case you're here to slaughter us."

He shook his head at the absurdity of it all, rubbing his temples but not willing to shut off the link with Syn yet. Vampires!? First off, no wonder he couldn't sense him. He had never actually thought about it, but it would make sense that vampires, being dead, wouldn't be able to be sensed. He could sense animal emotion, human emotion, mage and fae emotion. But undead emotion? Nope. Okay, learn something new every day. And second, that meant there were normal everyday vampire dudes, and chicks (he supposed, no need to bring sexism into this) that were out there he had never sensed, because he couldn't read them. Then the idea occurred. He might not be able to read them, but he could read others' minds about them. Of course, that would mean having to sort out the sexual fantasies about being ravaged by a vampire versus reality. And considering most people Cameron read on any given day thought about sex, and some thought about sex all the time, he didn't necessarily want to go probing about that image. Though, now that *he* was thinking about it, he began to picture Nathen with fangs, less clothes...and then shook his head. "So, a vampire, huh?" he offered a half smile. "Tell me about it?"

"Oh, I have only been a vampire for a day. After leaving my psychological evaluation," Nathen explained, then laughed more to himself.

"All right," Cameron said slowly. Cameron's training took hold, and he started the decision tree of diagnosis in his mind. He had worked with many people who were psychotic either from methamphetamine or organically occurring psychosis. Nathen didn't seem like a meth-head, and besides, their psychosis ran the way of paranoia and visual illusions. But he could be delusional. "So, why were you getting a psychological evaluation?"

Nathen said with a monotone voice and no expression on his face. "'Cause I am crazy..." Then waited for an uncomfortable moment and smiled. "Actually, it was to rule out Autism Spectrum Disorder. They didn't rule it out."

"Mm-hmm," Cameron responded. "And how does that tie in to you now being a vampire?" Cameron considered, the guy could have schizophrenia, but that didn't explain the not being able to read him part. Cameron had completed training at Napa State Hospital, Haight-Ashbury Clinic, and neuropsychological assessment rotation at an outpatient clinic in Oakland. He *knew* crazy. This wasn't that.

"I was leaving the office and then I have a blank. Then I woke up in an office and was told I was a vampire. Weird, huh? Well, it seems every time I meet a psychologist I now discover something new. Vampires, mages, fae. I signed an NDA not to talk about the people that turned me. At first, I thought they were joking, but then..." He took a deep breath, and Cameron got the eerie feeling of being prey and his eyes grew wide when Nathen opened his mouth to show him his extended canines, which he pointed at with his left index finger. "See?"

Cameron blinked a few times and stepped closer, looking at Nathen's pointed teeth. What impressed him the most was the fact that they were *extending*. He wasn't kidding. A vampire? Cameron smiled. "Well, then. Yes, to answer your question. Incredibly weird. And the, umm, people who turned you into a vampire made you sign an agreement? Sure, that all makes sense." He snorted sarcastically, shaking his head. "I have never met a vampire. If all vampires are like you, I would have known. I can read people, emotions and thoughts. But you are completely closed off to me," he explained. "You're actually only here because you've been talking to Syn-ister for the last couple days and decided to keep the pizza date, despite a major life change last night?"

"I am not sure who Syn-ister is, but I got the invitation today from Syn. It was kind of stressful, but they told me it would be okay and I would like it. And I get to live indefinitely. That's kinda cool, unless maybe I get bored with life or something. I've always been confused about how people act, so I guess the Autism diagnosis explains that. But it also means I'm going to be this way forever—so perpetually confused? Though, I never lose interest in my passion for knowledge and technology, so that's gotta be a bonus for eternal life, right? As to your question, I did actually want to help the hospital though. What is happening is wrong."

"Syn-ister is Syn," Cameron explained. "Autism, huh? Can you tell me why these people turned you into a vampire? And, what they said you'd like about it?"

"They said they turned me due to my talents with computers. They gave me a bunch of money, and hardware, and free blood. But I can also bite people. Apparently, it feels good to be bitten," he shrugged.

Now that Cameron was paying attention, he could tell, of course, Nathen had Asperger's Disorder, aka Autism. He seemed quite literal and naïve in an endearing way. He was still standing by the door, rolling his phone back and forth between his hands, a self-soothing behavior that Cameron knew in psychological terms as *stimming*. But these people seemed to be using Nathen? That was alarming to Cameron, but it sounded like they had spun things just right to get someone with Autism to go along. One of the drawbacks to Autism was being so trusting, generally trusting blindly because they didn't know how to manipulate and didn't expect others to.

He nodded. "Listen, I don't know you or whatever arrangement you have with these people, but I do know Autism, or Asperger's Syndrome. And people with Asperger's, while brilliant and kind and incredibly talented a lot of the time, are also sometimes taken advantage of. This, um, deal seems a bit too good to be true. I'm just saying, you know, watch out. There are some jackasses out there and you might not pick up on their intentions." Cameron shrugged. He didn't like to see people being taken advantage of and somehow had a pull to get involved. He chalked it up to his mother's promise that he use his abilities responsibly to help.

Nathen frowned in confusion. "They were nice and gave a lot of perks to my family and me. What other thing could they want? They told me everything upfront. Well, I think they did anyway. I was kind of upset at first that they didn't ask me. But they're taking care of me. They said everything would be provide for my needs."

"Okay." Cameron smiled, holding his hands out in acquiescence.

There was an overwhelming urge to protect Nathen, even though he had just met him. He loathed the idea of anyone being taken advantage of but had a soft spot for anyone who was psychologically different. Cameron's mind went back to his mother and how she selflessly helped everyone she knew. She had instilled in him a deep sense of empathy, laying the groundwork for him to naturally navigate to the field of psychology. He tried to help every mind he touched in some subtle way. But Nathen...he couldn't even *feel* Nathen. And on top of that, a vampire? Part of him told himself he shouldn't be getting involved, but how could he not? And on top of that, Nathen was the first supernatural being he had ever met aside from his mother...

Cameron sat down on one of the two overstuffed patio chairs. It was a move he did instinctively that was born out of training. By sitting, he took the less powerful position, which was meant to deescalate and promote strength of the person standing. Cameron spoke with his head down. Eye contact could sometimes be challenging and individuals with Autism already struggled with eye contact. "Like I said, I don't know the situation. My concerns are that it seems like you were abducted, turned into a vampire by whatever process that takes and without your consent, and then they threw a bunch of stuff at you to make it okay. I would pose—would it have been okay for you to have said no?" He looked up briefly at the question, then away again. "My thought is no because otherwise they would have asked. So, they weren't up front. And why would they need you to be a vampire? If you're talented, how could being a vampire impact that?"

"Why would I say no though?" Nathen protested, with a confused shake of his head. Looking earnestly down at Cameron, he said, "They offered $50,000 as a bonus. And full health insurance to my mother, who has MS."

Cameron sympathized with Nathen's mother, but didn't want to become distracted. "That sounds like a wonderful deal, but I still don't get why you need to be a vampire. Couldn't you get the bonus and be human?"

Nathen considered it. "They also said that I could focus the blood to enhance my talents. I haven't tried that yet. Oh, and also do other stuff like blood magic. I have to remember to ask them what that is." He was staring past Cameron as he answered.

Then Nathen seemed to remember something else and brightened. "Oh! When I drink from a person, I can read their emotions, that's kinda cool. Though it was from a girl. I am into guys actually. They said they had a gay guy I could feed on, but I didn't think it was a good idea." He rushed through the last part, seemingly not concerned at all about revealing personal information to a stranger.

Cameron thought that whoever "they" were should keep a tighter leash on their vampires.

Then Nathen suddenly frowned and turned to Cameron with a worried expression. "I didn't consider the abduction part. Though I guess that I also actually died. They said the transformation took about eight hours. Do you think that means I'm dead?"

Cameron bit his lip and shook his head, letting it fall. "I don't know," he said quietly, reminding himself he didn't have all the pieces of the puzzle and it wasn't his problem anyway. Why was he getting involved with this? He internally groaned and put on his therapist cap. "Just be careful, okay? I don't know who did your testing, or if they explained it to you, but as part of the way your brain works you are less likely to see it when someone is trying to use you. And you might miss things. And you wouldn't know it."

Nathen stood quietly, his gaze having drifted back to the wall. The fact that he had stopped playing with his phone told Cameron that he was likely becoming overwhelmed.

Cameron gave Nathen a little time to process and then strategically chose to shift gears. He knew that when anyone started dwelling on something, *ruminating* was his five-dollar doctor word, that their anxiety built. "Hey, I'm sorry about your mom. Tell me about her."

Nathen shook his head, as if to snap himself out of a trance. "Oh, it's no problem, she's stable, but on a lot of medication. So, it's good that she's not getting worse, but she's not getting better either. I hope they find a cure. She was and still is a very strong, willful person."

Seeing Nathen was able to focus again, Cameron brought the conversation back to what especially bothered him. "Yeah, seems like a good deal if you need the money and your mom needs help. But"—he closed his eyes tightly taking a deep breath and choosing his words carefully—"If I wanted to take advantage of someone, I would choose to target what they value the most. And it seems like your mom might be important to you. So, looks like they had an in by saying they would help your mom?

I don't want you to be turned off by these people, or what I'm saying. It seems so suspicious to me is all."

"Oh...hmmm...they also actually had all of our information and already enrolled us in all the company's perks. But now that you mention it, I guess that is a bit weird." Cameron saw Nathen space out and stare into nothing. His thumb and index finger started to circle against each other, stimming again. His mind probably raced with insecurity and doubt.

Cameron remained quiet, having learned the importance of therapeutic silence. Nathen's entire description was bizarre. Not that he didn't believe him, just that whatever this group was and what they wanted was concerning.

"Syn, sometime ask Nathen where he works. They abducted him and turned him into a vampire, and they offered him a ton of money and benefits and made it seem like a good deal. But made him sign a nondisclosure and are feeding him blood. It's too strange! And on top of that he has Autism. This group, as he calls them, are up to something. I'm getting a tickle in my spidey senses. Think your friend here might need help."

Syn, who until now was standing rigidly nonchalant, armed with chopsticks, crosses, and a gun, relaxed. *"Spidey, huh? Okay otherwise?"*

"Yeah. If I hadn't known better, I'd have thought you were setting us up."

"Well," Nathen finally spoke up, "I'll keep an eye out, but if it's going to be hard for me to see their true intentions, I'm not sure what I can do." He changed the subject. "You know, you smell different from other humans. Your blood seems different somehow, and you smell like a ripe peach." He smiled and his canines were visibly larger again.

Cameron, rendered silent for other reasons, blinked, struggling to respond. "Umm, thank you?" he questioned. "I don't...I mean..." he blushed, stammering. "Peach?" He asked questioningly, having never been compared to a fruit before.

Nathen nodded, "Most people don't smell that strong. But your scent...." He grinned, eyes fluttering shut. "I really like peaches. Maybe it's because you are a mage? I've never met a mage before."

"Um, I guess?" Maybe it was the wine, but Cameron was suddenly incredibly warm. "I don't know anything about any of that," he tried to explain, feeling the need to stand, which he did. "I guess it has something to do with your new senses?" he offered moving away from Nathen to find himself sitting on the low half wall he had started against. What was it about Nathen? Aside from handsome and vulnerable in a way Cameron had never seen or sensed before. Hell, he couldn't sense him at all. Was that it? Was Syn right that this is what people felt? Totally confused and unclear and at a loss? Cameron had spent his adult life always knowing what to say and when, always knowing what people felt and how to help. This was beyond anything he had ever experienced, which was both maddening and curiously exhilarating.

Nathen considered that. "It could be. Maybe it's an odd form of synesthesia? The lady's blood reminded me of orange marmalade, and when I drank it, I could feel her emotions. It was pretty interesting. Normally I don't have the best control of my emotions, feeling someone else's was a bit jarring."

"Ah," Cameron said, lamely. "I'm different, a mage. And gay," he offered, his eyes opening at the admission. What was going on? He glanced in at Syn who had sat down with a slice of pizza and was alternating between whatever she was doing on her computer and making sure he was all right. He sent her a mental salute.

"Oh, that's cool. So am I," Nathen said, smiling. "Though, I think I already mentioned that. I didn't think I was all that different. Now, talking about it, I'm a gay Autistic vampire and in fact, saying it out loud makes me sound crazy." He laughed to himself.

Cameron laughed, too. "Sure. I guess being a vampire makes you different. This *is* very confusing."

Nathen lips curved up around his fangs again into a grin. "This is all super confusing for me as well. But that's life, right? I can't really change anything. I can't turn back into a human and apparently I have been oblivious to most *normal* things all my life."

Cameron acknowledged, "I'm sorry. I've evaluated many people, adults and children, who have Autism. I know how hard it is. On the other hand, you've been spared from a lot of the bad stuff that happens in life and between people, huh?" He found that he was sitting on the divider wall, kicking his feet slightly against it.

Nathen shrugged. "I don't know. I don't know how different life is for you, my perspective is the only one I've known. Until a few days ago, I didn't even know I was not 'neurotypical.' I don't understand why people do a lot of the bad stuff they do. Like this thing with the hospital. Why would anyone threaten children or anyone at all? I guess I get it intellectually. Just pure greed?"

Cameron snorted. "I don't know that I even get it intellectually. I have spent the last half of my life feeling other people's feelings, hearing their thoughts. I spend every moment of my waking life and a lot of my sleeping life, tuning them out. Making a concerted effort to tune them out. But it's easier sometimes to simply ride the wave of their emotions, or to hear their thoughts and help where I can. But most people are a combination of distortion, self-consciousness, and self-absorption." His voice quieted, "It's exhausting." He had never admitted that to anyone, even to himself. He loved his ability and how he helped so many people, but at times he had wished he could be alone on a deserted island without the burden of hearing and feeling everyone around him. He looked out at the city in quiet contemplation.

Nathen was also quiet for a while before offering, "It's not the same, but I kind of feel that way with sound, especially being in a large crowded room. I can hear everyone talking and can't filter it. It's like all of the talking is hitting me at once. If I can't focus on something, I feel like crying because it's so overwhelming. But I can always shut my ears or go out into nature. I cannot imagine what it would be like if I couldn't stop it. It would probably drive me mad."

Cameron laughed without humor. "It did drive me mad for a bit. I thank the spirts, ancestors, gods, whoever listens that I had my mom. She was a mage, too, and understood. I learned to filter. She had me start off with headphones, way back when, to help me try and block out the other kids in school until I got control and was able to start recognizing them as background noise. Had a special note for the school that excused me and allowed me to wear them allegedly for the migraines. But from where you were as a child to where you are now, you had to learn on your own, huh? Considering you were just evaluated? I mean, why were you just *now* evaluated?"

Nathen laughed. "An ex was a psychology major, went around diagnosing everyone, including me."

"Psych major, huh? I'm sensing that you have a type," he smiled softly. Wait! Was he flirting? He rolled his eyes at himself.

"Um, I like men with good hearts. Or at least that's what attracts me the most. Looks help, of course." He smiled bashfully and turned away.

Cameron chuckled. Asperger's. Literal. He reminded himself that people with Autism didn't catch nuance, innuendo, subtlety. But what was going on? Here's a guy who wanted to *eat* him. And Cameron was finding himself more and more attracted to him. After considering for a while, Cameron asked. "So, curious, are you doing some sort Dracula whammy thing on me now?"

Nathen looked confused. "What?"

"Well, you said, for all intents and purposes and please correct me if I'm wrong, but the line that 'I vant to suck your blood?' seems to be coming across. You're comparing me to a peach, which has many other connotations we needn't get into now, and, I don't know, I get the sense that you're flirting? Am I totally off here?"

"Well, I mean, I would not say no if you offered. I don't think I actually know how to flirt. I've not yet constructed a model in my mind of how I would do that. Like if I see a biologist, or psychologist explain how that works, or read it in the book, then I can synthesize a novel experience of flirting with someone, but it would be scripted. I haven't had that kind of exposure to learn how yet." He seemed to be looking anywhere but *at* Cameron and alternated to glancing up and then quickly away. Cameron saw him sway from side to side as he nervously explained, "The only person I have ever been with was really direct, which I liked, but there was not any flirting. He told me he liked me and we kind of went from there.

Would you mind if I flirted with you? Or am I being weird? I'm sorry," Nathen apologized with genuine confusion and embarrassment.

Cameron smiled again. "No. I wouldn't mind. And all things considered, I couldn't picture a stranger thing happening ever. Unless zombies, werewolves, ghosts, and all other supernatural beings existed. And at this point who the hell knows, right? But a mage and a vampire meet up because Syn in there invites you over for pizza? Honestly? To fight the bad guys?" He laughed at the ridiculousness of his life.

Wait, had Nathen said that he had a partner who was direct with him? Did that mean he had a boyfriend? Cameron frowned, feeling an unfamiliar pang of jealousy mixed with disappointment. He studied Nathen, the curve of his scruffy jaw, the brightness of his blue eyes, his thick mass of dark curls. Cameron had to admit that Nathen was completely his type if he had a type at all. He was hot, smart, and a computer nerd. And Cameron had always been attracted to the cute nerd types. The guys he could hold intelligent conversations with. And Nathen was direct. The fact that he wouldn't have to do the guessing game because Nathen would always be honest with him, was refreshing.

But he couldn't hear him. Or feel him. And that was still frustrating. Cameron mentally reached out again and again, trying to grasp hold of the man he *saw* in front of him. The fact that he couldn't sense him mentally at all was perplexing.

But why did he care? What? Was he thinking about asking the guy out? The *vampire*? The baby vampire who was mixed up with a strange organization that *made* vampires. The whole thing seemed absurd. He internally argued with himself. Seriously, he was thinking about asking a *vampire* on a date? Cameron chewed his lower lip thoughtfully, internally battling, but curiosity finally won out. "But, so, you're dating someone now?"

"Oh, no, I'm not actually. We broke up over a year ago. I have contemplated using Grindr, mostly because I wouldn't have to guess if someone is flirting with me or just being nice. Um...are you seeing anyone?"

Cameron glanced in at Syn, *"Syn, dammit, did you set this up? I mean, did you know he was gay and wanted to get us together? Vampire or not?"*

Syn looked up slowly from her computer monitor. *"Are you out of your fucking mind?"* she projected. It came across more of a yell to Cameron. *"Has this turned to some sort of...what the fuck, Cam? What the...seriously, what are you doing?"* She sat with her mouth hanging comically open, the slice of pizza she was holding drooping.

"K, just checking." Cameron smiled sweetly at her through the window and gave a little wave before answering Nathen out loud. "No. I broke up with my ex six months ago. I don't use Grindr, or any other dial-a-dick app. And I've learned I'm not actually interested in the whole casual scene at all." He shrugged nonchalantly.

Tuning back into Syn he kept his head down, hiding his smile at her tirade. *"You have got to be kidding me! Do I need to fucking excuse myself? I mean, you're out there about to get your kinky undead mage groove thing on?"*

"Oh, I actually like having an emotional connection as well! But I don't drink alcohol and I don't like loud places, so gay bars are out. And like I mentioned I can't tell when people are flirting with me unless they're direct.

Half the time I just smile and think they're being nice and do not say anything back because I'm horrible at small talk. Well, unless I know the person, then I can usually talk about something I know they're interested in," Nathen said smiling, his canines their normal size again.

Cameron flashed to the last obnoxious bar that Frank had dragged him to. It had been a cesspool of hormones, rejection, trepidation, and drunken abandon. Cameron liked going to places where people were having fun: concerts and plays, symphonies and shows, but most bars, while they had that pretense, were simply not fun. He found himself nodding in agreement. "Bars are so out," he murmured and then asked, "So, um, your...fangs? They're like, not there anymore?"

Nathen nodded. "Yeah, they extend and retract. It kind of feels like how your baby teeth were when they fell out. It's itchy, and you can feel movement, and it's kinda pleasurable at the same time."

"Why were they, um...out?" Cameron asked, sensing that he knew the answer but wanting to be sure.

"Oh, uh...um..." Nathen looked away uncomfortably. "Your scent was almost intoxicating. Thinking about it, focusing on it, made them come out. But I won't bite you or anything! I would never do that to someone...unless they wanted me to."

Cameron shook his head, saying quickly, "I don't want to be a vampire." Then he thought for a moment. "Well, who knows? I don't know if I would want to be a vampire. I already turn lobster red in the sun and avoid it at all costs. But, do you even know what biting someone would do?"

"Oh, it doesn't work like that. Me biting you, or anyone else, will not turn them into a vampire. Something else has to happen, but they didn't tell me what that is. I know that my saliva is an anesthetic and an anticoagulant, and if I apply it after a bite the wound heals as if nothing had happened. For humans, it's supposed to feel exceptionally sexual and pleasurable. The woman who let me bite her orgasmed."

Cameron was a little taken aback. Who was this woman who was letting Nathen bite her? Wait, was he jealous? Cameron sat up a bit straighter and thought about how ridiculously strange the entire situation was. Now he suddenly wanted to be bitten by a vampire? "All right, then." He laughed. Having never actually gone out on a *first* date in his life, Cameron was suddenly very shy. With Tommy, they had been in a class together and fell into the relationship. With Frank, there was no dating, just sex.

Cameron studied Nathen for a moment. He was sweet, like Tommy. Hot, Cameron had to admit. Finally, he shrugged. "So, I guess after tomorrow when we do whatever we're doing in the hospital, which I'm sure you and Syn will fill me in about, maybe you and I should go out on a date? Perhaps not for dinner, but maybe something else?"

Chapter Eight

NATHEN

With a combination of excitement and nervousness, Nathen said, "Sure, I'd like that! And technically I can eat normal food, but figure what's the point? It doesn't actually provide any nourishment anymore."

Nathen's regular track started planning. The *what-if's* that always seemed to plague him included this time *what if he doesn't like me, what if it doesn't go well, what if he takes me someplace that I don't like...* He preferred to have a plan and stick to the plan, but now he knew he would have to change his plans for tomorrow, which was okay, but still nerve wracking. He also liked to plan where he was going to go so he could look at the menu and know what he would order. Nathen was about to suggest against going on the date. He weighed chancing Cameron being mad at him versus all the *what-if's* that could happen, but was interrupted when he saw Cameron hop down off the wall.

"We should get back inside, talk to Syn and figure out the next step, huh?" He glanced at him as he passed through the sliding glass door. "Hey, Syn, any news on the home front?"

"I assume you told him everything about you?" Nathen realized Syn was staring at him and shrunk back for a moment before making his way into the room.

Cameron laughed, falling back onto the armchair and pulled out another piece of pizza. He had a strange habit of rubbing his temples, which Nathen found peculiar. Like he was in constant need of an aspirin. "Well, not 'everything.' I mean, I didn't tell him my favorite color is burgundy, or that I love butter pecan mixed with orange sherbet."

"You will find that your *new boyfriend* here has the absolute worst taste in food," Syn said, punctuating with an eyeroll.

Nathen lowered himself on the couch wondering, *He's not my boyfriend. Or...is he my boyfriend? I don't think so.* He tried to puzzle it out but wasn't sure how to respond. He eventually concluded that Syn must be joking. He realized when things people said didn't make sense at all, it often meant they were telling a joke.

"Hey, I like your cooking," Cameron retorted.

"Everybody loves my cooking," Syn responded, "Well, maybe not vampires?"

Nathen looked sharply at Syn. He wondered how *Syn* now knew he was a vampire. Maybe she had cooked for other vampires and they didn't like her cooking. "How did you know I was a vampire? Is the glass door thin or something?" He purposely picked up a chip and dipped it in salsa, scooping a hearty portion, and took a bite.

Syn laughed. "I thought you told him you were a mage."

"I don't think he believes me," Cameron said around a bite of the now cold pizza.

"Well, mages do enjoy fireballs. And I know you said you could feel other people's emotions and thoughts, but I didn't know Syn was a mage as well?" Nathen said, his attention shifting from one to the other.

Syn tapped her forehead and said, "He was talking to me when he was out there talking to you. He does everything telepathically."

Cameron sat up, saying with awe, "Syn, I've never actually told anyone but you that I'm a mage. This is wild."

"Oh, okay," Nathen said, wholly accepting the situation. "I like the salsa!"

Nathen was pleased when Syn grinned at the compliment. "Glad to hear vampires can still enjoy fine cuisine!"

Unsure of what else to do in any social situation, but certainly in this one, Nathen stayed quiet and listened politely. He reminded himself that people expect you to smile, so he made sure to do that even though he didn't actually understand the whole banter thing.

"You should try the habanero Hawaiian," Cameron pushed the pizza box closer to Nathen who had settled back onto the couch.

"You should NOT try the habanero Hawaiian," Syn corrected, pushing the box back at Cameron. "Nobody should ever try that, you sick, sick man."

"More for me," Cameron said.

*

Cameron stole surreptitious glances at Nathen, trying to analyze the many different emotions he was feeling. He was taken back to when he was a child, before his gifts had started manifesting. Puberty had hit him early, and so before he started getting bombarded by others' thoughts and feelings, he had begun lusting after a few of the other boys in his class. It was like that now with Nathen in that he could not sense anything from Nathen, which made Cameron feel at a loss, shy, excited, unsure. This was what normal people who could not read minds felt like. It was simultaneously exhilarating and maddening.

Cameron had come to rely on being able to tell exactly what his partner wanted; not by delving intrusively into their thoughts, a practice Cameron had curtailed early with everyone he was close to, but by accepting surface thoughts. People needed their privacy, but loud surface thoughts were like people screaming at him, and sometimes he couldn't filter those. Syn had come to notice and rely on those by mentally calling to him. It made things so much easier, like a constant intercom as long as they were in the same building. And with his partners, when in sexual situations, he could always identify what they wanted without being told.

Cameron was struck by the similarities between what he was going through right now with not being able to read Nathen and what Nathen must go through all the time. Nathen was emotionally blind, unable to read the nuances from others due to his brain. Cameron was now unable to read Nathen. He didn't know how this was going to work but was excited to see where it went.

Cameron had gotten used to the fact that people lie, though the ones who for no reason, or to hurt others, were the ones whom he struggled to deal with. As his eyes traced over Nathen's shoulders, chest, lap...he wondered what Nathen was into and hoped it wasn't like Frank who had been obsessed with toys. He sighed, and shook away the memories, hoping Nathen didn't also have a weird secret stash, but shrugging because he *could* get into pleasing someone the way they liked because he could ride the wave of their pleasure. But no, he reminded himself he couldn't with Nathen. Wow, how *was* this all going to work?

Cameron realized no one was talking and looked over at Syn, who was sitting with an unamused expression. He realized he had been staring at Nathen and deep in thought and blushed brightly, busying himself with another slice. "Um, so the plan?"

Syn gave a long-suffering look. "As I was saying, we need to get in there. Statix and Kat are going to try and sneak in in the morning and see what they can find from the inside. I was *saying* can you change your lunch date to an evening meeting so Nathen can go with you tomorrow?"

"Oh!" Cameron had missed the whole discussion in lusting after Nathen. He sat up and forced himself to get serious. "Yes, that would actually work out better I think for Matt." He turned to Nathen with an explanation. "Dr. Matt Keller is a friend of mine and works at Children's. I'm meeting him to talk about training his residents. Maybe you could join us as a subject matter expert on Autism? I had planned to go in early and start reading everyone. We had some back and forth about when to get together, but maybe I could ask to meet up with him at six? It starts getting dark around then. Umm, how does this whole vampire thing work? I'm super curious. I'm assuming no, heh, coffin? But maybe you could tell us about your restrictions or..." he stammered. Had he just asked a vampire to tell him all that stuff? "I mean, what we might need to know?" Quick save.

"Sorry Syn," Cameron shot her a sheepish glance and saw her smiling at him. He accepted her mental hug.

"Cam, I really like Nathen. I've known him for years online. Never knew he was a vampire, but hell, right? There are stranger things in real life than were ever written about in fiction."

"Heh, he's a baby vampire. One day old. But now that we're planning for a date, and wherever that might lead, I'm thinking all kinds of thoughts."

"Yeah, I can see your thoughts. You might want to put that pizza box in your lap."

Cameron's eyes widened, and he snatched the box and held it over the bulge in his pants, busying himself with the contents and swallowing hard, unable to hide his skin tone changing to match his hair.

"Uh huh," Syn projected. *"Well, baby vamp or not, he has always been cool. And no, I never knew he was gay. But I think you two will make a cute couple and I'm glad to hear you're going to take things a little slower this time. Frank was a douche."*

Cameron smiled, cut the connection with Syn before his head exploded, and focused on what Nathen was saying. The pressure behind his eyes was constant now, and he took a swig of wine to help with easing a small portion of the pain.

"...and I do not need to sleep. I can't let the UV of the sun hit me, though I'm curious what would happen if it did. I can die with decapitation and being burned to a crisp. If I don't feed on blood for a while, I'm not sure what will happen. I guess I'll pass out until someone feeds me blood?"

Cameron and Syn exchanged glances, both having the same thought projected at each other. Syn was the first to speak, "Nathen, honey. I know you were born yesterday..."

Cameron snickered mentally.

"And I know that it took a bit for you to actually share with Cam that you're a vampire. And thank you for sharing all of that information, that's definitely good to know. And we're cool, so you don't have to worry. Hell, I've kept Cam's secret about being a mage, and am sure he would be burned at the stake if anyone found out about him. But you can't be telling people how you can die. All of that, and being a vampire, you've got to keep to yourself, because in the wrong hands, you're putting yourself at danger." She threw a look at Cameron.

"That's pretty cool about not having to sleep," Cameron offered. Syn looked at him with mild annoyance and he shrugged. Cameron went on, "And if it's just a matter of the UVs, I'm wondering if covering you head to toe, like clothes, hat, blue blockers, gloves, and then tons of sunscreen? And an umbrella? Or like, hey, doesn't Children's have that covered walkway from the parking garage to the hospital? I mean, if it's only the direct sunlight, you might be cool to walk around outside if you take the right precautions?"

"Or not," Syn protested.

Cameron gave Nathen a grin, then laughed. There was something to be said for gender roles. Boys were often more likely risk takers and girls more often had common sense not to do stupid stuff like walk-outside-in-the-sunlight-when-you're-a-day-old-vampire stuff.

"Cam, call your friend! See if it's a go for tomorrow night."

*

Cameron shrugged and went into his bedroom, flopping down on the king-sized mattress on a frame. Both Hansel and Gretel darted out into the living room, having been stashed away for the meeting that seemed like it was ending. Cameron heard hissing from the living room and jumped up and ran in to see Syn capturing a cat and lobbing it gently through her bedroom door before going for the other. "Sorry," he called, and returned to the bed, quickly pulling up the comforter for some semblance of orderliness in case Nathen walked by. He had read somewhere that one shouldn't make their bed because it traps in dust mites, and that likely poorly done research study was enough justification for him. He had never actually purchased a headboard or bedroom set, namely because he had never felt the need. Since he had never had any guests, he had been content with his overstuffed purple bean bag which he used to read on, and small Ikea desk and chair which he used as storage for piles of miscellaneous papers and such. Looking around the room he felt more than a little self-conscious. White walls, litter box in one corner, laundry basket in the other, charger on the floor next to the bed that held his phone and iPad, and that was that. His childhood toys and everything he hadn't packed up and brought with him to college had been destroyed in the fire on the night his mother had died, and he had kept to a rather minimalist life since then. His room had a sliding glass door on one side going to the balcony and two doors on the other: one to a walk-in closet and the other to a small bathroom. Syn had gotten the master bedroom, which was larger with a nicer bathroom, but Cameron didn't mind.

"Cameron!" Matt answered on the first ring. "Don't tell me you're cancelling."

"No, no," Cameron said with a smile. Matt was a great guy, newly married with a new baby. He had told Cameron earlier that he would have liked to get together after work for a chance to hit the nearest bar and have a reason to "escape," but Cameron had begged off. In reconsidering, he figured he could always reschedule his last appointment, especially if it meant going on this mission with Nathen. "Actually, was wondering if we could move to the initial suggested time? I have a friend who might want to join, and he can only make it after work. Can you maybe do six? I'll get done with my case and get over there as fast as possible."

"Hell yeah," Matt's tone had a whoop in it, but then he quieted to an overly professional tone. "I mean, of course, Dr. Corazon, this will be a very important meeting, and I'm certain my wife will understand."

Cameron chuckled. "All right, Matt, I'll swing by the hospital around six with Nathen. Will bring a power point—we can meet in your office for a bit, then maybe move the discussion to that German pub you introduced me to?"

"Zum Wohl!"

"That's right." Cameron laughed, having no idea what Matt had said, but agreeing.

Chapter Nine

NATHEN

Nathen's gaze had followed Cameron as he left, darting from his broad shoulders down to his ass, to...was that a large amount of blood flow in the front? Nathen had the nagging idea that he was a perverted creeper as he stared at the gorgeous broad-shouldered ginger, but he had to admit to himself that it was a nice sight.

Nathen considered for a minute. He had never thought about anyone trying to kill him in his life. He used to joke around with friends and tell them "Make sure you don't die," but it had been a joke. The probability of people dying was generally low. And now Syn and Cameron were telling him that people might try and kill him. He furrowed his brow at the advice from Syn, "Why would anyone want to kill me though?"

Syn explained slowly, "We humans know how to kill other humans, but most of us, thankfully, are not out there decapitating and shooting each other. Though I've told Cam I'd kill any motherfucker who broke in here, I would never actually willfully hurt anyone. I feel guilty accidentally stepping on bugs. We've known each other for what, five years now?"

Nathen thought for a moment and nodded. He remembered the first time they met was online in a chat room dedicated to Linux based software engineering and security. He was impressed by the fact that she seemed to know how everything worked much more than other people. Shortly after that he learned she was into gaming too and they started teaming up to play in World of Warcraft together.

Syn was going on about something and Nathen leaned forward to try and pay attention and not tune her out. "What I know about you is that you're a seriously nice guy. And you're not the kind of guy who would purposefully hurt anyone, so you don't see where people hurt others. And I'll guess you probably have blinders to some of that stuff. But I'm certain if I ask how many real-life mages or vampires you knew before two days ago the answer would be none and you might laugh."

Nathen remained quiet. He wasn't sure if she wanted him to respond and still didn't understand how he would know if someone wanted to kill him.

"And now you're a vampire and you know Cam. I know from being with Cam for a long time that there are things out there that hunt mages. For sport or whatever, I don't know. You have to know that there have got to be a natural enemy of vampires. It just makes sense. So, yeah, while no one would particularly want to kill you personally, there might be vampire hunters. Goodness knows, we've played enough games about them. And considering all the white hat missions you and I have been on over the years, you can't be naïve enough to think we haven't gotten a few enemies that if they could find us they wouldn't take us out? That's why we're all so careful about our identities. I didn't actually expect you to even show up tonight. I didn't expect anyone to. But I'm glad you did. You need to stay safe."

Nathen listened to Syn. He could not imagine being killed for any of the hacking he had done. Jail time? Sure, maybe. Getting swatted, yeah, a possibility. But getting killed? He didn't want to argue with her, so he nodded when she finished. "Okay." He was not likely to talk about being a vampire with anyone else anyway.

Syn looked over past Nathen, and Nathen glanced over his shoulder to see the rather sparse bedroom with an unmade bed and Cameron sprawled across it. He saw the curious blood flow and an interesting pooling right where Cameron's legs met. Looking away quickly, Nathen realized he might have blushed if he were still alive. He chastised himself for lusting after someone who he had just met. He didn't want to linger too long because he didn't want to chance becoming aroused. Besides, it was disrespectful to be thinking perverted thoughts about a guy he had just met who might not even be into him. But...Cameron was into him? Right? He had asked him out. He considered that that might be something to look forward to if the date worked out.

"Listen," Syn was saying quietly, "I'm not going to play the irate big sister role. Cam's a big boy and can handle himself, but he's incredibly sensitive, and I'm not kidding. His ex was a piece of work and did a number on him. Anyway, I see the way you guys are looking at each other. Just go slow, will ya?"

When she brought up Cameron, Nathen self-consciously fidgeted in his seat. He didn't understand how to respond to uncomfortable situations like this. Syn seemed to be insinuating that he would purposefully hurt Cameron. Nathen emphasized, "I would never hurt him, or anyone else. I have actually only been in one relationship. It was kind of serious and we broke up on good terms. He moved out of state for a paid internship. Normally, it's hard for me to date, because I can't tell if someone likes me or not."

"Well, he likes you," Syn clarified, with a small smile. "I haven't seen him like this in a while. He's happy and excited, wanted to know if I had gotten you here to set you up. I would have if I had known," she added quickly, winking and hushing him.

*

Cameron swung out of bed, a little disappointed that Nathen had not followed him into the bedroom. It wasn't like he had expected it, but it wouldn't have been unwelcome. But then reminded himself of his role if this was going to develop into a relationship. He'd need to be explicit and not actually expect or hope for something. On the one hand, that seemed to be a great thing. No confusion. On the other, that seemed sad because it might mean no surprises? He quietly shut the door behind him, a little embarrassed at the sparseness anyway, and returned to grab more pizza; a piece of which he dunked in the bean dip earning cold stares from Syn.

"Guess we're set for tomorrow, then. I'm supposed to meet him at six, but sunset is shortly after six, according to the internet. How do you want to go there? I usually Uber everywhere, so I can meet you there? Or...?" He slipped onto the couch next to Nathen as Syn had taken his place in the armchair and had returned to her laptop vigil.

Nathen seemed to be nervous with Cameron so close, but he was still smiling at him, "I got a free car service that will drive me around, so I can use them. It's actually how I got here. I think so long as I'm not in direct sunlight I should be fine. My glasses are already treated with UV protection and I'll wear my hoodie too."

"I was going to ask if you wore glasses to see or for a particular reason. Is it only the UV protection?" Syn asked curiously.

"I think there's a way I can correct my vision. I guess I'd have to concentrate on it?"

"Well?" Syn looked at him expectantly.

Nathen took off his glasses and put his hand in front of his face, focusing on it and feeling the soreness associated with the strain. He moved his hand farther away from him, willing the blood to correct his vision in the same way he could enhance other senses if he focused on them. His vision cleared. Glancing at Syn, he noted she was blurry. Tilting his head, Nathen concentrated harder until the fuzziness around her resolved into crystalline clarity. He held that desire and moved back, keeping her in sight. When his back hit the wall, he glanced around the room, realizing that everything was in focus and grinned. "I think it worked."

"Dang," Syn said at the same time as Cameron smiled, nodding.

Back to the matter at hand, Nathen looked from Syn back to Cameron, "I have an idea of how to get a copy of the software."

Interrupted by Cameron's laughter, Nathen squirmed with self-consciousness and stared at him.

"Sorry, man, that was cool. Go on," Cameron said.

Nathen stretched his shoulders, causing himself to relax a bit. He never knew why people were laughing and often thought they were making fun of him. He realized Cameron must be laughing because he was impressed. "Oh...okay. Well, I can use a thumb drive with Linux, and boot it up on any of the infected computers and bit copy the primary hard drive to a different thumb drive and restart the computer. That way we will not only have the ransomware, but the encrypted data as well. Maybe we can figure something out? I'll need probably about thirty minutes with the computer. So, if either of you can keep people away, or create a diversion, that would be great."

Cameron nodded and smiled. "That sounds great, huh, Syn? If you can get there at six, then we can go in together. I'm pretty sure they won't have cameras in the psychology wing. You could use one of their computers to maybe pull up a presentation? I'll send you something tomorrow and you can put that on the drive and then you can play like you're fumbling around trying to find the slides, etc. I'll keep Matt talking."

Syn looked pensive. "Umm, Nathen. Did you say that you had a driving service actually bring you to this *address?*"

"No, not this address. I gave them the intersection and walked to the building. I have watched enough spy movies to know not to give strange free car services the actual address."

Syn sat back with relief and Cameron frowned looking from one to the other. "Oh yeah, the car service is from the group that..." Cameron seemed to fish for the term before settling on, "made you?" He looked back at Syn. "Should we be worried?"

"I'm a little worried," Syn admitted.

Nathen nodded again. "Yes, I get a free car service, so I don't need to use Uber ever again. I don't think we need to worry about anything though. I don't think they would want to turn you into vampires. But then again..."

Cameron glanced at Syn and gave her a quick mental recap of his earlier conversation with Nathen. "So, Nathen, this covert corporate agency turned you into a vampire. And has a car service for you. And...umm, Nathen. They didn't give you a phone, did they?"

Nathen took out an iPhone and his new MacBook Pro laptop, "Yes and my laptop. But most corporations do that, especially in tech."

Cameron stood and started pacing, picking up Syn's emotions of alarm. He was amazed that she was able to keep her voice so calm considering her internal state, "Please tell me that you have it in the off position."

Nathen nodded, "I turned it off after the car service dropped me off, but I do that with all communication devices, especially if I'm going into a den of other...like-minded people."

Cameron fell back onto the couch with the relief Syn felt. "You two are going to kill me. Syn, why is that important?"

Syn also visibly relaxed. "It's the same reason that I have jail broken your phone and altered it so that you can't use the recording devices. Conversely, no one can use your phone to listen in on you. It's why I asked that you always remember to turn it to the off position when you're not using it. People can track you using the phone. It's why I have you trade out phones every few months." She reached across and patted Cameron's knee lovingly. "Just keeping you safe."

Cameron looked back up at Nathen who apparently also knew about all the importance of stuff like this. "Okay, Syn. You'll have to excuse my noobness. I honestly am clueless."

Nathen smiled. "It's a learned paranoia. I didn't have it when I started but being around other 'security experts'"—he air quoted—"I have learned to ritually do stuff like that."

Cameron laughed, "Is that what you are, Syn? A"—he mirrored Nathen—"'security expert.'"

Syn gave a sage nod, but responded, "I'm a simple kickboxing instructor." She stood and started picking up food items and ferrying them into the kitchen.

"So." Cameron turned to Nathen. "I guess I'll see you at Children's tomorrow at six, then? Let's plan to meet at the Starbucks in the Hospital. Um, should we have our phones on? Do you have a noncompany phone? Maybe I should—"

Syn interrupted with a cough, dropping a phone into each of their laps. "Use these for tomorrow. They're programmed for each other. Give them to Nathen after. He'll pull the sims and dispose of them."

Cameron looked to Nathen for confirmation.

"I have the eject pins in my wallet. I'll meet you at the Hospital." Nathen started to look uncomfortable and got up. "Well, it was nice finally meeting you in person, Syn, and it was a real pleasure meeting you, Cameron." He seemed to be unsure about what to do next but ended up just reaching out his hand to shake.

Cameron blinked at the term "eject pins," then realized he must have missed something. He had an interesting bubbling of adoration for Nathen. He had always been so impressed with Syn's technological prowess. She seemed to effortlessly understand things that were still such a mystery to him. They magically had access to all television shows and movies, even before release, and to his knowledge they didn't have cable. She could fix his computer and phone in seconds after he had spent hours troubleshooting. And she could pick up new things and help him figure them out even though he had read the instruction manual back and forward. Syn was his sister for all intents and purposes and he loved her desperately in that way. But to meet someone else who had her same skills pulled up a strange sapiosexual feeling that Cameron hadn't ever considered before.

Syn deposited the pizza boxes on the kitchen island.

"Yeah," Cameron said, blushing again and accepting Nathen's hand. "I'll see you tomorrow, then."

Syn came around and hugged Nathen. "It was great to meet you too. And I hope we can get good information tomorrow. I'll shoot you a message in the VPN if I hear from Kat."

Nathen looked uncomfortable hugging Syn, though he didn't object.

Cameron watched as she saw him to the door. "You've got my numbers if you need to contact me. And seriously, Nathen, be careful. These people at the hospital are dangerous and don't think for a minute they won't kill you. As for your new 'group'—I wouldn't trust them either. There is such a thing as an offer that is too good to be true."

Nathen nodded, looking past her and smiling at Cameron. "I'll text you on our new 007 phones when I'm near the hospital." Then to Syn, he said, "Thanks, I'll be careful."

*

Syn watched with her eyes wide, then shook her head, shut the door, and enabled the security system. She took Cameron's hands with a serious look and tapped her head.

He opened a channel, and she said, *"Don't say anything. I need to sweep."*

Cameron frowned and began to extend his senses as he did when they were younger. It was an exercise they had done weekly, then monthly, then occasionally. But he couldn't recall the last time they did it here in their home. He sat quietly on the chair, his eyes closed as he sensed for anyone or anything living that wasn't supposed to be there, or who might have an interest in them. He was methodical in his search, going inch by inch through their apartment, out into the hall and to the neighbors, floor by floor. This exercise took no mental energy at all for him. It was like passively listening to a radio instead of actively using a CB radio or walkie-talkie.

Meanwhile he sensed that Syn brought out her devices that swept the room for listening or video recording. After Cameron came out of his trance, their eyes met and they shook their heads simultaneously. He could sense an elevated state of anxiety and paranoia from her. *"Are we in trouble?"* he asked.

"Yes. I made a mistake and shouldn't have given out our home address. I'm sorry."

"Wait, what? What's going on? Should we...?" He tapped his head, ready to switch to mental communication, though secretly relieved when she shook her head.

"I don't know, Cam. Vampires? This thing with Nathen was totally unexpected. I just thought he was a cool guy, but this whole him being a vampire thing with a strange secret organization... We should have met in a public place. I broke my own first rule by getting too comfortable with him." Cameron saw Syn's head drop as she rested her elbows on her knees.

Crestfallen, Cameron asked, "So, should I not keep the meeting tomorrow? Or...or beg off?"

She shook her head, "No, not at all. I'm still committed to figuring out what is going on and potentially stopping these jerks. But this has gotten more complicated, and Nathen is a lot more reckless than I would have ever guessed. At least he knew to turn off his phone!"

Syn edged over onto the couch next to Cameron, "No, no. Please, seriously, you should still go on the date with him. See if you like him. Cam, I haven't seen you so excited in so long. Fuck!" She took his hand in both of hers. "This life that we live... You're hunted and I may have done like a hundred or so things to get me hunted as well. So, we keep a low profile for a very important reason. Yeah?"

Cameron nodded, swallowing hard feeling Syn's attempts at emotional soothing. "This adds an extra element that we need to watch out for. I can control for a lot. You can control for a lot. Between us, we've got like ninety-eight percent covered. Nathen is that two percent. He's something you can't read and is working for someone I can't scan for. There's just too many unknowns and you know how I'm not super excited about that which I can't control."

Cameron scoffed. He had accepted that Syn was a control freak a long time ago.

"Did you see his eyes?" Cameron asked, a hint of wistfulness in his voice.

"No, I assumed he was blind."

Chapter Ten

CAMERON

After they said goodnight, Cameron retreated to his room with a piece of cake. His mind was racing with way too many thoughts and was still not clear about what he and Nathen were doing the next evening, but he planned on getting there early and scanning for what he could find. Surface scanning never picked up deep dark secrets. Proximity to a person or familiarity helped Cameron delve deeper into their thoughts, so if he did pick up on something, he could go seek that person out and potentially pick up more. He saw the whole idea of going into the hospital as a crap shoot, but with Nathen there working his magic on the computer network perhaps they would pick something. And then they could go out for drinks with Matt. Cameron frowned. He had heard Nathen say he didn't drink and assumed that was because he was a vampire, but wondered if it was an allergy, the taste, religion, or if he was morally opposed to drinking.

To quell the thoughts, Cameron pulled out his noise cancelling headphones, turned on Avenged Sevenfold at ear splitting volume, and started his mental exercises of focusing on his thoughts instead of everyone else's. He decided to shelf Syn's cancer until he could devote the emotion to it that it deserved. She was obviously fine now. Vampires existed. Cameron wondered if they were hunted by fae in the same way mages were. He wondered how many vampires were out there, where they came from, how they reproduced, and how they ate. His mind flashed to Nathen's fangs. It was disarming seeing something he knew should absolutely not exist. He purposefully pushed out darker memories from his childhood because he wanted to focus on Nathen. Cameron wondered if Nathen was interested in him, or just his blood. The thought disheartened him. It was like being wanted only for sex. He purposefully pushed that away too. It was a little like playing with fire, especially since he couldn't read Nathen at all. He had worked with people with Asperger's in many settings.

Cameron felt a vibration in his pocket and flew out of the bed, pulling headphones off and coming to rest on all fours as he clawed the phone Syn had given him out of his pocket, having totally forgotten it was in there. Nothing like having a mystery vibrator catch the side of your dick when you're unaware.

The text from Nathen read: *It was really nice meeting you. I look forward to the hospital and our date.*

After he caught his breath from the near-death experience, Cameron took off his clothes and tossed them into the basket, glancing down at the tighty whities and made a mental note to wear a pair of the Ralph Lauren's the next day. What the hell was he planning for? He fell back onto the beanbag with a smile.

Chapter Eleven

NATHEN

The giddiness from seeing and being with Cameron made Nathen feel on top of the world. He reflected on Cameron: nice, cute, and seemed like he had a very big heart. Being around him, Nathen had realized that he had been relaxed by his scent and wanted to melt into those big arms of his. After he had found himself at the bottom of the five-flight building in a matter of seconds, he had called the Town Car that had dropped him off. Once he was securely in the backseat, he worked up the nerve to text Cameron. Nathen was thrilled when a few seconds later Cameron responded.

Hey. It was great to meet you too, though more than a little strange. Matt's a great guy but will want to leave early, though he will squeeze out every second of 'freedom' that he can get. He has a new infant with his wife at home. So maybe if you're up to it, we could go for a walk in Golden Gate Park? It's down a bit from the Schnitzel House. But...why don't you drink? Just curious?

He read and re-read the text. What did "strange" mean? Nathen considered and thought it was likely because he was a vampire, so he replied.

It was interesting meeting another mythical creature, yes :). The only mages I know are in WoW. I can drink, but when I used to get drunk, I would lose control and do crazy things like get touchy feely with guys. Though I don't think that's going to be a problem anymore, I cannot get intoxicated by drugs or alcohol. Only by drinking a drugged person's blood.

Nathen waited, watching his phone for the sign that Cameron was responding. He had always been more comfortable writing than speaking. It allowed him to be more literal, more precise. He leaned his head against the back of the seat and closed his eyes picturing Cameron: his smile, his lips, his body; the way his button-down shirt hugged the curves of his chest and stomach; the way his slacks accentuated the curves of his butt. Nathen went over the images in his mind and tried to ignore the twinge of guilt at being a perverse creep. He focused back on Cameron's scent and how he wished he could taste him, every part of him...

See you tomorrow.

The buzz of his phone snapped him out of the fantasy, but the brevity of the message made him frown. Nathen began analyzing. Did he say something that upset him? Why was Cameron being obtuse? Nathen considered a dozen responses. At the forefront of his mind was an apology. He went back and read his text and concluded that an apology wasn't needed.

He thought of something simple to say, minus the neurotic ideas now spinning in his mind, *Ok, good night! :)*

Nathen went back to staring out of the car. He loved watching the streets and people go by without being seen. Ever since high school he had liked *"people watching,"* but the streets themselves at night also had their own personalities. From buildings, parks, and natural landscapes, all of it fascinated him and he could spend hours looking outside the car without saying a word; enthralled by the activity of everyday life of other people and things, while not being part of it. The car also offered protection from the noise Nathen often had difficulty filtering and at times found overbearing.

His mind returned to thoughts of his new *un*-life and what it meant. When he had run down the hall, his perspective had shifted and it was like everything had slowed down, but he had been moving at his normal pace. And once he had hit the street, he had automatically pulled up his hoodie knowing it would be cold outside, but upon reflection he realized the air had not had its usual bite.

The car pulled up outside of his mother's home and Nathen slowly made his way to the brown door with a large stained-glass window of red climbing roses in an arch. On summer evenings when the sun was going down, its red light would hit the window and scatter a rainbow of color across the floor. Nathen's room had not changed much from when he was a child. A few of the posters changed, but it was sparse. The mainstays were his computers and three monitors. As he didn't need to sleep, he decided to read more books on what it meant to be autistic. Nathen sat in his darkened room reading and realized that he had not bothered to turn on the light and that his eyesight had adjusted so he could read in complete darkness. He marveled for a moment at the strange phenomena before diving back into his book, allowing the further realization that he no longer needed to sleep to set in.

*

In the morning, Nathen met his seventeen-year-old brother, Jake, in the kitchen. A political science major and already attending UC Berkeley, it was their mother's hope that he would follow in her footsteps and become an attorney.

"Hey, how's it going? You didn't call last night and Mom was worried," Jake groused over a bowl of cereal.

Nathen stopped at the table. "Oh, yeah, sorry about that. Had work-related things, totally lost track of time."

"Okay, talk to her before you leave. She was doing her usual 'Nathen died face down in a ditch' thing again."

Nathen laughed. "Okay."

Jake finished and headed out and Nathen called the car service and waited until he heard the Lexus' honk outside. He quickly ducked into his mother's room. Andria Hale was lying in a grand four post bed, propped up on pillows, and watching her favorite chef yelling at a restaurant owner. The room was brightly lit with the morning sun and Nathen was perplexed by an odd tingling sensation on his skin, akin to having been sitting too long, though it was accompanied by a burning numbness. From the hallway, Nathen smiled at his mother. "See, I'm not dead!" which now was technically a lie. "I do have to go, though, as I have work to do today. Promise I'll call later!" He waved and ran without letting her get a word out.

Downstairs, Nathen put on his hoodie and held up a black jacket as an umbrella before opening the door and running to the car. He slammed the door closed, relieved that the windows were coated to filter the UV light. He asked the driver, the same from the previous night who he learned was named Julian, to take him to the office.

Nathen managed to find his way back to his office, ignoring the day receptionist. He spent a few hours creating his Live Linux USB Stick with a bunch of utilities that he might need. This would be something that he could use tonight at the Children's Hospital. The rest of the day he spent researching the Children's Hospital, Sons of Discord, and anything else he could think of that would point him in the right direction of who was behind the threat. He was frustrated that his search came up with one dead end after another, and he circled back to the fact that going into the hospital was likely the only course of action. Nathen was a little annoyed to learn that the hospital had reverted to a temporary hard-copy file system while their computers were on lock down and teams of experts worked on uncovering and neutralizing the cyber terrorists. But he could tell that their experts didn't have the same level of skills that Statix, he, and Syn had. He was fairly certain that once they went in and captured the information they needed, that they could trace it back to its source.

Chapter Twelve

CAMERON

The next day progressed too slowly for Cameron's taste. About noon he texted Syn for Nathen's e-mail and then e-mailed Nathen with a power point for the Autism presentation. It was a brief outline with borrowed slides from a dozen other trainings Cameron had been to, but would be good enough to show Matt. He spent the rest of the day fielding trainee questions and conducting his own evaluation, before bowing out at four thirty to make it over to the hospital.

Once there, Cameron found the Starbucks and sat. He received a text from Nathen indicating he would be there at the agreed time. He found medical literature and feigned deep interest in spinal cord injuries while mentally scanning. There was so much despair, hopelessness, prayers, fatigue, sadness, frustration; people's thoughts were on their own ailments or those of their children. Cameron usually blocked all of this when he had to go to a hospital for any reason, and sitting there opening himself to it was making him more than a little ill. The hour passed with Cameron feeling a welcome reprieve when he heard from Nathen.

I'm here, see you soon! :)

Cameron enjoyed a fluttering of anticipation, which he wasn't sure was due to the covert operations that they were about to engage in or Nathen's text. He realized he spent too much time in his head analyzing things, which, all things considered, was probably a good thing he was a shrink. Feeling an increasing headache from the last hour's endeavor, he ducked into the gift shop and purchased a travel sized bottle of aspirin, having just popped a couple from the small tube into his mouth for a dry swallow when he stepped out into the hallway, slamming squarely into Nathen. He let out a gag, dislodged the aspirin and said something to the effect of, "Gachky!" Because of his ability to sense everyone around him, Cameron had never run into anyone before. He simply stepped aside, around, or paused. To run into Nathen was shocking on several levels.

Nathen went from smiling to confused within a split second.

"Excuse me," Cameron said flustered, purposefully taking a step back, his face now matching the color of his hair. "I don't usually run into people." He struggled with composure, realizing suddenly that somehow Nathen was holding his phone. He patted his pockets to assure himself he wasn't crazy. "Um, is that mine?"

Nathen was quiet, staring straight ahead. Cameron gently caressed his upper arm. "Are you okay?"

"Oh, sorry, that was weird. Let's talk about this somewhere else. Oh, your phone, yeah, you dropped it. Here are your pills also," Nathen said, depositing the gooey aspirin in Cameron's hand.

Cameron's eyes grew wide as he stared at the sticky white pills that he flicked into the nearest trashcan. Headache forgotten, Cameron wasn't sure if he should be incredibly aroused or extremely confused. He assumed Nathen had used a vampiric ability to retrieve his items and wondered if he blinked and had missed it.

Realizing he couldn't focus on that, he stashed his phone in his pocket, and asked, "Are you ready to meet Dr. Keller?"

Nathen nodded and made passing eye contact. His eyes seemed an icier shade of blue and his face had a more distinctive pallor than a few seconds ago or the last time Cameron saw him in the apartment. Cameron was taken aback. He remembered Nathen having beautiful eyes, but now under the unforgiving florescent light, they practically shone.

"Well, as mentioned, I think you'll like Dr. Keller," Cameron pressed when Nathen was silent and led him toward the elevator bank. "He's been here for a while. I met him a couple years ago in my training at the UC Berkeley extension program where he was teaching in the neuropsychology track and we hit it off," he explained and smiled at Nathen, stepping onto the elevator and pushing the button for the third floor.

Nathen cocked his head to the side. "Sounds good. I actually read up on Autism and Asperger's Syndrome last night and read through all the slides you sent. So, I should be prepared, though, for some reason, I'm really hungry now."

The elevator doors closed, and Cameron realized too late that he had unconsciously taken a step away from Nathen and that his back was against the wall. His mind raced with suggestions or what subtext Nathen could be meaning. There were cameras throughout the hospital, but Nathen had proven to be much faster than Cameron could have imagined. In a voice much calmer than he felt, Cameron asked, "Do you need to perhaps not come to this meeting? I know that you have low blood sugar. Maybe go get dinner and meet up with us later?"

Nathen smiled. "I think I can power through it, but I feel like I have not had any...food...for a week. I'll need to feed after this though."

"Oh." Cameron was trying to think of something to suggest when the door opened. He let out a breath that he didn't realize he had been holding and quickly stepped out and started down the hall, keeping his eye on Nathen. He struggled with something more to say but was at a loss until they followed the corridor down to a wing that lead to the psych offices. They found Dr. Keller's office and Cameron tapped on the door, smiling when the huge man behind the desk swung around and said, "*Guten Tag*! Is someone ready for drinks!"

Cameron laughed and accepted the bear hug from his substantial friend, appearing dwarfed by the shorter, but burly man with a bushy salt and pepper beard and entirely bald head. "Matt, Dr. Keller," he corrected, "This is a friend of mine, Nathen." He swallowed hard, realizing suddenly he had no clue what Nathen's last name was, so he played it off. "Nathen was recently formally diagnosed with Autism, and I think might be great to include in the training. We have a slide deck to show you if we could use your computer."

Matt frowned. "Sorry, the computers are all off limits due to the security breech! It's been a pain to go paperless. The hospital is up in arms about this security threat. It's been a nightmare for us all. You never know how dependent you have grown on technology, huh?"

Cameron frowned and mentally caressed his friend's mind, making it perfectly normal to use the computer and inserted the suggestion that Matt give Nathen access. As he did it, he realized he had never done anything like this with someone he knew and felt a little slimy, but also challenged himself to accept that it was for the greater good.

"Yes, of course! I'd love to see! Please, use my computer." Matt gestured to the computer, seating himself in one of the overstuffed guest chairs. Cameron settled across from him, and spent time catching up with Matt, laughing and encouraging him to talk about his new daughter. The conversation led to the new research that Matt was doing, which Cameron genuinely found fascinating. Whenever Matt's mind began to slip to wonder what Nathen was doing, Cameron would gently pluck the thought away and bring him mentally back. It wasn't hard as Matt was a gregarious sort who was not naturally inclined to suspicion but *was* naturally inclined to verbosity.

Cameron noticed Nathen fiddling with the computer for about fifteen minutes before he stood and said, "Sorry, Dr. Keller, I didn't want to interrupt, but can you log into Windows? I still need to bring up the slides."

"Oh, oh yes! Of course!" Matt lumbered back around the desk and logged into the computer, nodded to Nathen, then returned to his discussion with Cameron.

*

Nathen had been backing up the hard drive on to the thumb drive and this time put a different thumb drive into the system and brought up the PowerPoint Cameron sent. While they continued to talk, he decided to snoop a bit. He looked at the task bars notification area and noticed an odd icon. Double clicking, it brought up an ominous window of the Ransomware which had a four plus-day countdown outlining the one-week window. Nathen instinctively focused on it and tried to use the new "power" he was supposed to have. The room around him darkened and Cameron's voice became an incomprehensible mumble. Nathen could still hear it, but the words lost all meaning. A few seconds later, there was no sound except for white noise, and the room became completely dark. All Nathen saw, or could focus on, was a tunnel in front of him with a projected display of what was previously on the computer screen. It was a multilayered user interface, beyond which was a very deep tunnel splintering into many other tunnels emanating out of it like branches.

Nathen was confused. He was not exactly sure where this was, but he saw the Ransomware application window send a long slender drop of silver white liquid with bits of glowing fast changing alphanumeric characters down the tunnel. He soon noticed that the closer branches of the tunnel also seemed to have the same drops of whatever that was flowing out of them and down into the main connecting intersection. He guessed he was interpreting what a ping going out to a central server or tracker must look like. He waited till he saw a new drop form and focused his will on it. His awareness fluctuated and shifted to become part of the data packet that was about to be sent. Nathen heard a sudden crescendo of white noise and swish! It was the fastest he had ever traveled. First, down a thick dark tunnel and then a litany of other tunnels and openings that all rushed past him. He went through many basin-like structures that collected the substance he was in; this conglomeration was then flushed and rerouted to other tunnels and pipes. Finally, he was thrown out into a large black space with a closed, thin, golden gate in front of him. It had thin filigree and a central Victorian aesthetic to it, something akin to what he imagined the gates to heaven might look like. He walked up to it but could not get past or go around it. It was as if there was an invisible force keeping him on a straight line toward it like a train track he could use to move closer or farther away. He looked through the gate and saw a large factory space that was completely abandoned. On the far right was a wall with one broken window; out of it, in the distance, he could see Coit Tower lit up in blue.

Nathen tried to move out of whatever space he was in but was unable to. Anxiety and panic started to creep in which caused his vision to blur and the white noise to get louder. There was a momentary blip in his awareness, and he realized he was facedown on the keyboard, back in Dr. Keller's office.

"Oh, shit!" Cameron said.

Nathen shrunk away with confusion and fear as Matt was up immediately upon him. He hated people touching him and this huge man was crowding him, had him by the shoulder and was poised with a penlight in front of his face.

"He's diabetic." He heard Cameron lie and noted it wasn't true in his mind. He thought about correcting him, but then realized that Cameron was making an excuse for him passing out and let it go. Cameron went on, "Said that he had missed lunch and had wanted to power through."

Nathen watched as Matt put the pen away and stepped back grinning with his hands on his hips. "Well, we should get the boy some lunch, then!" He laughed heartily, though with concern in his eyes. "Are you all right, Nathen? Could have one of the MD's look you over? Or, could get a pint of beer in ya! That will fix you up!"

Nathen turned his huge dilated pupils to Cameron who seemed to have a multi-colored chaotic aura that shone despite the fluorescently lit office. Dr. Keller's body remained the same, but Nathen saw through his skin the pulse of red that highlighted an excited human's heart. Nathen's fangs extended slowly and his mind was flooded by adrenalin as he was awash with predatory lust. Of the two, the scent of peaches was overpowering and infused his very being. He had a strong urge to jump on Cameron and ravage him, both for his blood and sexually. Instead he shot up, disoriented and laughing nervously, "Oh, I'm okay, really! I apologize." He looked down, but was sure Cameron's eyes widened when he saw his mouth.

"Hey Matt," Cameron said, swallowing and pulling the thumb drive out of the computer. "Let me e-mail you those slides. How about we catch up at the restaurant in like ten minutes. I'm going to get Nathen secured away and will meet you for that drink? Cool?"

"Sounds good!" Matt said.

Nathen realized he was being pulled out of the office by Cameron who had his hand against Nathen's lower back and was guiding him down the hall. "Call that car service of yours. You need to go back to whatever this group is so they can help you. You are *not* okay."

Nathen was not fully aware of his surroundings and instead could only focus on his hunger. He could hear Cameron and understand him, but he was fighting the urge to sink his teeth into his supple skin, covering his well-developed body. A few minutes passed, and he realized there was a tenuous grasp of control. "I used an ability they said I had in order to try to help with getting us more information. I think I know where one of their servers is. I saw it, but I think doing so cost me the reserve of blood. I'm really hungry and you look ...um...never mind. I just need blood."

Cameron shushed him and spoke in hushed tones, "Please call your car service so they can come get you."

Once out of the hospital, Cameron spoke in barely above a whisper directly into Nathen's ear. "You need to stop talking and texting about all of this stuff." The sun had set during their time in the hospital and there was a faint glow of sunset that at any other time might be beautiful and romantic, but Nathen was focused solely on Cameron at this point. He heard him say, "I'm sorry that you were so, umm, hungry when you got here and that whatever happened in there, happened. But it seems like you maybe need to plan better? Or take better care of yourself. Why don't you call me or send word to Syn when you're feeling better? Here—" Cameron slipped the burner phone into his pocket.

Nathen took out the thumb drives and gave them to Cameron. "I got what we came for. The password is the square root of the size of the image, plus our normal cypher. Syn knows what that means."

Cameron asked, "Are you okay? You're super pale. Also, your eyes are ...intense." He glanced around, asking for the third time. "Can you please call the service? I'll stay out here with you until they come."

Nathen pulled out his phone, turned it on, and after it booted, he called Julian. He became distracted by the fact that Cameron was standing there holding his arm. He didn't like being touched by strangers at all, but right then he had a confusing mix of arousal and yearning. He shivered when Cameron leaned in, saying, "You really worried me in there."

Nathen smiled weakly, with controlled lust and hunger. He was reminded of childhood meltdowns, which usually resulted in crying, but he had learned to control his emotions as he got older. "Sorry about that, but what happened was incredible. I went inside the computer, and I think the internet? I'm not sure exactly. I was inside a tunnel and came out the opposite end of a server that was getting traffic from the hackers' application. But unfortunately, I didn't know I use blood to power this ability. And I was already hungry."

"That sounds cool, definitely something Syn would like to hear about. But, why?" Cameron looked away, and Nathen could see the rush of blood to his face suggesting he was blushing. "Why hadn't you had lunch or something?"

Nathen realized that while he read about people blushing when they were embarrassed or aroused, he normally didn't pay attention to that and in this case was confused. He had never understood emotions and wasn't sure if Cameron was blushing because he was aroused, embarrassed, or upset.

He certainly didn't want Cameron angry at him, so he quickly explained, "I didn't become hungry until after I caught the pills and phone. I guess all the 'supernatural' abilities use my reserves of blood? I didn't know that. And I didn't plan to do that with the pills, I just reacted."

Nathen resisted the surge of discomfort when Cameron rested his forehead on his shoulder for a second, laughing. "I'm going to have to get used to that. If I wasn't touching you right now, I'd still wonder if you were real." Cameron pulled away and met Nathen's eyes. "It's both neat and frustrating not being able to read you at all."

Nathen was still, then spoke up, "I do not want to lie to you...well, actually my mother says I can't lie at all, I guess I'm horrible at it...but I need to tell you that right now you are glowing like a Christmas tree. I see a bright chaotic aura around you, and only you. Others don't have that. They look like they have a red pulse in them, but you are literally glowing. And your scent is so strong. I feel like I'm swimming in it and want a large gulp. I'm lucid enough to control myself. I feel strong lust and hunger toward you. If I get any hungrier, I feel like I might not be able to control myself and will both want to um...make love to you and drink from you."

Cameron's eyes opened wider with Nathen's admission and he slowly let go of him and took a small step back. "Woah, um, wow. That is not something you hear every day." His face reddened again. "I'm kind of at a loss. I don't, I mean I didn't mean to make you uncomfortable or potentially mess with your self-control. And I can't say that being bitten doesn't sound intriguing, considering how you described it. Though—" He glanced around as if to make sure they were alone and admitted softly. "—I don't like pain." Nathen saw Cameron look around again, and then away from him. "And what you described sounds like rape."

Nathen shifted with the hope that accompanied Cameron's admission that being bitten sounded intriguing and quickly said, "Apparently there is no pain with the bite." Then he remembered the second part of what Cameron said, and he assured him, "And I would never rape you, but then again, *I* may not be in control at that point. I feel like something else is churning inside me, something animalistic."

"That sounds frightening. And I don't know how to help, aside from maybe to stay away?" Cameron asked. "I don't want to cause more issues. Maybe this was a bad idea."

Feeling rejected, Nathen searched his mind to somehow make this right. He wasn't good at social interaction and part of him thought maybe he should just go and not bother. But the other part looked over the handsome ginger haired man who was eyeing him with such concern that it melted him. He tried to explain, "I think as long as I do not use anymore uh...powers, we should be fine. So as long as no one tries to mug us or something, I won't have to expend anymore blood. The car should be here soon. But here is something to think about. If I can see you like this, so can other vampires. Maybe mage blood is special somehow? I mean, if vampires are predators and when hungry our instinct to find prey increases, mages seem to be the easiest to find. I can see you through my closed eyelids."

Cameron looked around and Nathen could see a spike in his heart rate. "I have never met another vampire, but then I wouldn't know, would I? Syn has been keeping us safe for so long, but if you're right and there are a ton of vampires out there, I wonder why they haven't approached me before? Or maybe it's because I don't get out much?" he laughed without humor. "Maybe, it's you're attracted to me?" he offered a half smile. "Is that your car?" Cameron gestured down street as a darkened sedan inched forward.

"Yes. Listen, I'm sorry about this. I didn't mean to scare you, either with me passing out or...well. I hope we can go out on a date after I have recovered. I was looking forward to that." He waited for the car to come closer, opened the door, and got inside, instructing the driver to take him back to Impetus.

Chapter Thirteen

CAMERON

Cameron turned away, suddenly in desperate need of a Schwarzbier. He was happy to find Matt sitting in the pub already, nose buried in foam. "Figured if you didn't make it because of your boy toy, more for me," Matt said good-naturedly, sliding the second full glass over.

Cameron paused dead in his tracks, gawking at the statement.

"Saw you all cuddly outside, heh! More than just a friend, I'd say."

Cameron burned with embarrassment, sliding into the booth opposite Matt who occupied the entire opposite side. He had never been one to advertise his sexual preferences, nor was he in any way shy about taking a stand for everyone's rights to live their lives unencumbered by another's biases. He was grateful for his friend's open acceptance. Cameron recalled Matt's wife trying to play matchmaker with him and one of her friends at their wedding, and while he had danced with the woman, he had also gently planted disinterest in her mind so as to make sure nothing awkward would occur. He took a long swig, "Pivo Pils?" he asked.

Matt nodded with appreciation.

"We only met a little while ago," Cameron admitted, feeling an interesting twinge of emotion, which he didn't want to think about. He had been looking forward to the time learning more about Nathen but accepted that it was likely not a good idea. "We're actually thinking about going out after you invariably ditched us for Baby. Maybe another time. Tell me more about your sleep deprivation."

"Oh, don't get me started!" Matt punctuated the discussion with a swig. "The best and craziest thing I've ever done," he said. It was an old dance that many people Cameron knew who had children engaged in. Tired, exhausted, thrilled, in love, Matt was wrapped around his baby-girl's little finger and would be forever. Cameron basked in Matt's adoration for his child, reveling in the purity of love that a parent feels for their newborn. It soothed and relaxed him in the way he knew it calmed his daughter. He kept Matt talking about little Hanna and they worked on their second, and then third oversized ale.

Chapter Fourteen

NATHEN

The car drove Nathen to the office downtown, and Nathen made his way to the cafeteria. He ordered three Special O smoothies that turned out to be reminiscent of sweet vanilla and sat at a table drinking them one by one. By the third, he was no longer hungry. As the hunger subsided, his emotions once again returned to the perfect equanimous state that he was used to, though he started spinning on something Cameron had said. *Rape?* Nathen would never do anything like that or hoped he wouldn't. He had been on the verge of losing control and had had to stay mindful. Whatever he was now had a mind of its own and he feared if he was too hungry, he may have a meltdown like he did when he was younger. As a child his meltdowns had included occasionally throwing things or hitting walls, but more often, it was hitting himself in the head or scratching his arms because the emotions were so overwhelming, and everything was so overstimulating that he couldn't process anything at all. With the hunger, it was like balancing precariously on the edge of losing control. But he was sure that a hunger meltdown would not include throwing anything or hurting himself. He was pretty certain it would be to sate the thirst and as he thought about it, he felt the anxiety start welling. He made himself a pact to always carry blood with him just in case.

To that end, Nathen got another smoothie in a sealed container, put it in his backpack, and returned to the car, which was waiting, asking to return him to the hospital.

Nathen flipped through his texts and saw that they were originally supposed to meet at a German pub but wondered if that was actually where Cameron had ended up going. He focused on Cameron's scent at the location of where they had been standing barely an hour before and was pleasantly surprised to easily be able to pick up on his scent. He followed the aroma to the Schnitzel House, walked inside and saw Cameron sitting with the doctor in a booth in the back. "Hello, gentlemen!"

"Nathanial!" Matt exclaimed, causing Cameron to cough in surprise as he looked up and seemed caught totally off guard again by Nathen's sudden appearance. "You are looking much better! Here, let us order you one!" He winked conspicuously at Cameron, who scooted over to the corner of the booth to make room for Nathen. Matt waved the waitress over, asking Nathen, "Tell me you are a stout man and not a pale ale lover like your friend here."

Cameron laughed as Nathen looked at him and smiled. "I'll have whatever he is having."

Matt waved acquiescence, and the waitress nodded. Cameron drained the rest of his and waived at her for a refill as well. "Do you know, when I met this guy, he had never had a good German beer?" Matt continued.

Cameron shrugged, pointing out, "When you met me, I wasn't old enough to drink."

"Pish posh." Matt laughed. "So, Nathen, feeling better, then?" the burly man asked, leaning forward with concern. "Was a little worried you wouldn't make it back in time for the date."

Cameron's mouth fell open as he stared at Matt who smiled innocently.

Nathen grinned nervously. "Yeah, I ate and feel much better now, thank you! Cameron was a perfect gentleman and all but carried me to my car."

"Well, I, for one, think you two make a very handsome couple. Will make handsome babies someday!" Matt raised his glass as the waitress deposited steins in front of Cameron and Nathen.

"Oh, that is so not something to toast to!" Cameron laughed, toasting anyway. "You new dads are one track minded."

Matt guzzled the rest of his drink. "And on that note," he said sliding out of the booth and tossing a few bills on the table. "Let the date begin sans me."

"See ya, Matt," Cameron called. "You'll have what I'm having, huh?" Cameron asked, a slight slur creeping into his tone.

Nathen laughed and watched Matt walk away, then said to Cameron as his mind was still on what Matt had said. "Having babies would be great, but I assume I'm sterile and I think the technology for turning spermatozoa into an ovum is still in the testing and experimental stage."

Cameron, midsip, coughed violently into the sleeve of his shirt. He alternated between laughing and coughing, coughing more because he was laughing. He turned to Nathen, seeming serious. "You did *not* just suggest that I carry your baby?" He laughed at his own joke. "Sorry, sorry. Yeah, wait. What? You want kids? Or wanted? Someday?"

Nathen shrugged. "I thought about it. Having someone to raise and show the world to...I won't be able to have that now though. I was actually researching artificial wombs. They're close to making one. But imagine one day, gay people being able to have biological kids of their own grown an artificial womb and be able to watch the baby grow inside it."

Cameron smiled and agreed, "Yeah! That would be really cool! Syn and I have talked about having kids. But her fear of commitment makes it impossible because she sure as hell isn't carrying a baby," he said, as if mimicking something she had said several times. "Anyway." He shrugged. "If she ever did find the right woman, our plan was to have me donate sperm and viola. It's actually refreshing that you like kids too." He beamed at him. "And aren't afraid to talk about it."

Nathen thought about his future and had feelings of hope, saying more to himself than to Cameron, "Maybe adoption?"

On the drive over, he had been playing out over and over in his mind how to assure Cameron that he wasn't thinking about *rape*. The insinuation was something that had taken him by surprise, but at the time he hadn't been able to process at all. The discussion of the future and children was nice, but as with many things, Nathen couldn't focus on anything else than what was looping over and over in his mind, so he changed subjects abruptly. "But enough of that. Please let me explain myself with the um...food. I would never hurt you, but I think you should know the risk of hanging around me and us being together. I had never felt like that before. I think it's part of who I am now. Again, I would never hurt you on purpose, but the hunger in me might if it ever took full control."

"I understand. And thank you. I guess what that means is we should not let you starve." He pushed his shoulder against Nathen's playfully, drinking more of his beer. "How come you don't drink? Something about making out indiscriminately?" Cameron finished his glass and eyed the one in front of Nathen. That would make six. He tried to figure out how many ounces that had been, then thought about how funny it had been that he had not had dinner, but was almost dinner, and started giggling. Then shrugged with zero cares that he gave, reaching over and switching glasses and sipped.

"Oh, I meant I would become that guy in the party who loves everyone, and if I had a date, I would probably be all over them. You know, like there are angry drunks, there are sad drunks, and then you have drunks like me, who love everyone." Nathen smiled playfully, having turned slightly so he could look at Cameron.

Cameron nodded sagely, not focused on what Nathen had said, though imagining making out with him at a party. "You are gorgeous, aren't you?"

Nathen seemed confused by that. "Am I? I don't know. I mean people think I look cute, so I guess?"

Cameron grinned drunkenly. "I think you're cute."

"Thank you, I think you are gorgeous as well." He smiled again but looked away appearing embarrassed.

Chapter Fifteen

CAMERON

Fully intoxicated, knowing such, Cameron made the only logical and clear-headed decision he could possibly make at that moment and reached across, sliding his hand up to cup Nathen's face, playing through his beard and pulling him into a soft, tentative kiss. He was thrilled when Nathen returned the affection, his tongue moving into Cameron's mouth, rolling slowly around. Cameron ran his fingers up into the coarse curls, pulling him in to give him more access as he played the tip of his tongue over Nathen's.

But then Nathen pulled away, "Maybe we should take this slow? I promised Syn I would, and she knows how to kill me."

Cameron was overcome with the truth that that had just been the absolute best kiss he had ever experienced. He couldn't identify what, but it was on the tip of his fuzzy mind. Ignoring whatever Nathen had said about Syn, he pulled him back, kissing him more deeply. His taste. Cameron was fully aware that Nathen had a dinner of blood, which would normally taste like, well, blood, but instead Nathen *tasted* like something else. He played his tongue over Nathen's, one hand holding more tightly to his head while the other sought out his hand to hold. He was acutely aware that he could quietly happily stay in the booth of a German pub kissing Nathen forever if allowed.

His eyes closed, Nathen slowly moved his tongue in a wave-like pattern, circling it from time to time and humming. Pinpricks of Nathen's canines caught Cameron's tongue when they began to extend, and he found himself rolling his tongue over the fine razor edges. He had shifted in the booth, restricted by the confines and a little annoyed that he couldn't pull Nathen into his lap, or straddle him, or *something* for more contact.

Suddenly Nathen's pulled away, his eyes wide. "Cameron, I forgot to tell you, my saliva is an aphrodisiac! Please don't be angry!"

Cameron blinked in surprise and fascination at the fangs. Part of him thought he should probably care about what Nathen had said, but the larger part of him that was intoxicated on both ale and aphrodisiac did the opposite of care. "Does that mean you don't want to kiss me, then?" he teased with desire.

Nathen smiled anxiously. "I could continue kissing you all night, but I feel like we should do this when you are not so drunk. It doesn't feel right, especially considering my kiss is meant to pull you in more. I'm going to take you home and have Syn take care of you. I don't trust myself to be alone with you." Nathen pulled out his iPhone again and Cameron saw the Uber app.

"We're not alone," Cameron pointed out, whispering in Nathen's ear, suckling gently on his earlobe. "We're surrounded by people and a waitress that has come over a couple of times to see how we're doing, has seen we're doing jussssst fine, and has left us to discretely continue doing what we're doing." He spread small kisses down from Nathen's ear to his neck before pulling Nathen in again, kissing him lightly around the fangs. "And I'm pretty sure that you're in control now," he pointed out, punctuating the statement with another kiss. "And...you said I can trust you," he hummed with desire, running his hand into Nathen's hair and kissing him again. Cameron pulled back, laughing. "Besides, this table is *so* in my way." He stared again at Nathen's fangs now fully extended and said, "Those look wicked sharp." He reached out and ran his forefinger down one, poking his finger on it. "Ouch," he said with a smile, studying his finger which seemed fine, but then started pooling a pinprick of blood which he instinctively began to suck himself. "Okay, those *are* wicked sharp." He laughed again.

Nathen gasped and Cameron saw that his eyes had dilated. He gently took Cameron's hand, asking in a husky voice, "Let me show you something?" He tenderly guided Cameron's finger into this mouth and pressed his fang into it, just enough to draw more blood but not enough to cause more damage. Cameron saw his eyes flutter shut as he inhaled, seeming to savor. Then he suckled Cameron's finger, rolling his tongue around it.

Cameron's breath was shallow with arousal allowing Nathen to take his hand and watched closely, his pants tightening with excitement as his finger moved between Nathen's lips. The actual prick had not hurt at all, and Cameron realized that what had hurt was when he had initially pulled his finger away. He licked his lips, rapt with attention as he watched Nathen's response to his blood and once Nathen opened his eyes and allowed Cameron's finger to slip away, he examined the smooth, undamaged skin. He slowly smiled, "Now, that is magic. Did it..." he exhaled, somewhat nervously "...taste... okay?"

Nathen licked his lips. "Yes, it was really good, like biting into a ripe peach that explodes with flavor in your mouth. But there was something else in it that was different from the normal human blood."

Cameron's eyes sparkled with awe and adoration. He was flooded with the exhilaration that comes with the novel exploration of something new. "Can you tell me about you, Nathen? I want to know everything. What do you like? What is your favorite color? I know you play video games and are probably a wizard with technology, but where were you born and raised? Aside from your mom do you have any other family? What are your hopes and dreams?" he asked wistfully, turning sideways in the booth and resting his head in his hand.

Nathen was about to start answering when his iPhone pinged, letting him know the Uber had arrived. "I...The car is here. Let's go." He smiled at Cameron, put down enough money to cover the bill, and picked Cameron up out of the booth. Cameron laughed, holding onto Nathen, muttering something about his strength as he was set down onto his feet.

They walked out to the car with Cameron holding unsteadily to Nathen's arm. Once the car started moving, Nathen took hold of Cameron's hand and began caressing small circles in his palm. He smiled softly at Cameron who rested his head against his shoulder, alternating between stealing glances up at him and down at their hands. They rode in silence until the car came to rest near the intersection where Cameron's building was. As they got out, Nathen took Cameron's hand and brought it to his lips and kissed it, walking Cameron back to his apartment building. Cameron laced his fingers with Nathen's and walked slowly in, waving at the security guard. After they entered the elevator, Cameron pushed Nathen against the back wall. "Mind if I kiss you again?"

Nathen looked shyly into his eyes as he wrapped his arms gently around Cameron's waist. "I don't mind at all."

Cameron's breath caught as he was pulled closer to Nathen, his arms naturally found their way around Nathen's shoulders, tracing the back of his neck and into his hair. A little taller than Nathen, Cameron's head inclined to kiss him softly, plying his lips over his. He was happy to find that at some point Nathen's fangs had retracted, making it easier to slip his tongue between Nathen's lips. An aphrodisiac, Nathen had said? Cameron didn't think he needed much more than this closeness to be turned on by Nathen. He had already been at half-mast from the moment Nathen showed up at the bar and had remained that way throughout the night, with periods of full arousal now revisited as Nathen held him tight against himself, his hands moving up under Cameron's shirt to feel the smoothness of his back. Cameron pulled back and searched Nathen's liquid blue eyes, realizing he could get lost in them. Was that a vampiric thing too? In this moment, Cameron didn't mind. He did, however, lose track of where he was, and when they arrived at his floor, the ding of the elevator made him jump. He fell into a fit of drunken giggles, grabbing Nathen's hand and pulling him out of the elevator and down the hall.

Once at his door he fumbled for his keys and teased, "Last chance for another kiss. Syn's probably in there playing Diablo and waiting for our report."

Nathen pulled Cameron to him once more. This time, keeping one hand on his abs as he planted small kisses on his lips followed by deeper and deeper ones, until their tongues were again entwined. The hall and door melted out of mind for both of them.

Cameron quickly unbuttoned his restrictive shirt which had somehow come untucked, allowing Nathen more access. Suddenly, he was especially happy that Syn had insisted he work out with her. While he wasn't as ripped as the guys who lived at the gym, Cameron's natural metabolism resulted in a lean physique. Coupled with the workouts that he did do, Cameron had built tone to his arms, chest, and abs as his body matured. He matched Nathen's kisses with equal intensity, pulling up Nathen's shirt and being happily surprised as his fingers explored Nathen's well-toned back. Realizing he still had his keys hooked around his finger, he pushed them into Nathen's pocket to free up his hands to roam, tracing Nathen's sides and back again. Cameron distantly noticed how cool Nathen was to the touch and filed that away for later.

Nathen kissed the side of Cameron's mouth, trailing down his chin, and finally to the side of his neck, where suckled the skin, causing Cameron to sigh, grinding gently against Nathen. His hands were exploring Cameron's body, feeling the ripple of his abs, and the soft hairs going down under his waistband. Cameron was thrilled to find that Nathen was as stiff as he was and ground a little harder.

Nathen pulled himself off Cameron's neck and cleared his throat. "We should probably stop before we end up doing something we regret in hindsight."

Cameron staggered a little. "What?" he asked breathlessly. He glanced around, realizing that they were still standing in the hallway and laughed, feeling around in his pants for his keys and frowning. He vaguely remembered having keys. He shrugged and rang the doorbell.

Syn answered with a judging look. "Thought you two would never get done."

Cameron straightened up. "Lost my keys," he said with aplomb. Feigning sobriety he walked in, sideways, utilizing walls for support.

Syn stared at Nathen with her lips pursed. "Well, you coming?"

Cameron was in the kitchen, clumsily pulling out the box of pizza leftovers and getting a big glass of water. He made his way to the living room where he gently set the box and glass on the ottoman before falling onto the couch, having to adjust himself for comfort. Somewhere between kitchen and living room he lost his shirt. He scratched his head, looking around, forgot what he was looking for and realized there was pizza in front of him and he was hungry.

Nathen sat down, and Cameron saw him reach in his back pocket to pull out a set of keys. "I think I found your keys, Cameron."

At his name, Cameron straightened. "You had the keys!" He laughed merrily, putting the keys back in his pants.

He saw Nathen was wistfully looking at him, his eyes on his shirtless chest. Then he saw that Syn was observing them both with a stink eye.

Nathen said with an uncomfortable smile. "We got what we were looking for and more. Cameron has the USB sticks with the data, but I also saw one of the servers in an abandoned building somewhere around Coit Tower."

"Do you have my shirt, too?" Cameron stage-whispered and was rewarded by being hit in the head with it as Syn came from the other room. USB? What? Cameron began fumbling in his pants and pulled out a set of keys he was sure he had lost. He put them on the ottoman and laid back a bit to dig deeper and found the thumb drives Nathen had given him. He held them up triumphantly and Syn snatched them away.

"Cam!" She said, the sharpness voice caught his attention.

He sat up again, sobering a bit. "Was' up?"

Syn stared at him, and he was receptive to the mental discussion which was always faster and clearer than talking.

"*Are you all right?*"

"*Syn, I'm so happy! This was the best first date, and he is such a great kisser! And he could have totally killed me like three times, and he didn't!*"

Syn glared at Nathen.

"*What does that mean, Cam?*"

"*He was super hungry and got kinda shaky and his eyes turned a beautiful blue, and he said I smell like peaches, and he wanted to rape me. But he didn't!*"

Syn's eyes hardened at Nathen. Cameron saw her swallow before turning her attention back to him.

"*And, Syn, he left. I thought he was going to you know, not come back. So, Matt and I went drinking and Matt had a new baby girl! Her name is Hanna. And then Nathen came back and guess what, Syn? He wants kids! And he's so sweet. Kept saying he didn't want to take advantage of my drunken self!*"

Cameron laughed out loud, leaning back and finding himself against Nathen as he had turned to look at Syn. He glanced back, but then settled in grinning at Syn who had relaxed.

"Okay," she said to Nathen who had been watching Syn and Cameron staring at each other for a few seconds.

"Syn, it's like it was with Tommy!"

He sensed the tension melt out of Syn and watched her memories of his first love when they were sixteen play quickly through her mind, including the painful time when Tommy returned to New York after he finished his degree.

"Did you pick up anything, Cam?" she asked softly, changing the subject.

"A headache! Hospitals are so sad. But no." He grabbed a slice of cold pizza. "Nothing else," he said around a mouthful.

"All right, Nathen. Your turn." She slid the drives into a hub that was connected to a laptop that was itself connected to the large television monitor on the wall, then handed Nathen the wireless mouse and keyboard.

Chapter Sixteen

NATHEN

Nathen was perplexed by the long pauses where Syn and Cameron sat staring at each other. He knew they had to be speaking telepathically and was curious about what that would be like. He had learned that usually when people whispered to each other it was something private, or maybe critical. That was kind of like this. He wondered if they were talking about him and sighed with increasing self-consciousness.

Shaking that thought, Nathen booted into his Linux drive and ran a script that started the UI. He ran a few commands, entered a password that extracted the compressed image of the doctor's hard drive. While looking at the screen, he said out loud, "This is not connected to the network, nor to the Active Directory that was in their office, so it will not actually harm anything to reset his password."

Nathen mounted the image and ran a different script that renamed the system files in the System32 folder. When it completed, he unmounted the image and started a different tool that converted the raw data into a VirtualBox VM file. He then started VirtualBox and created a new Windows 7 Virtual Machine that was pointing to the VM file as its primary virtual hard drive. He started the virtual PC and pressed "Shift" a few times.

A new command prompt opened. He typed in "net user mkeller new-password" and then "FF120A!" as his new password. Finally, he stopped the virtual machine and used a different terminal to revert the changes he made to the system files, and then started the Virtual Machine again.

Syn had been watching the screen passively, leaning back in the armchair and sipping a Tutankhamun ale.

Cameron had polished off his first glass of water and Nathen noticed when Cameron offered pizza to Syn who whispered, "Infidel," and waved him off dismissively.

He glanced at the pair as they waited a few minutes for Windows to find and install all the generic virtual hardware that comes with VirtualBox and it loaded up into the familiar login screen that he saw while in the doctor's office. He typed in "FF120A!" and it logged him into the doctor's desktop, the background picture was Matt and his wife with their new baby. Nathen clicked on the notification area on the taskbar and brought up the Ransomware countdown. All of a sudden he yelled, "Tada!...Oh...Woot!"

"Something happen?" Cameron looked from one to the other.

Syn nodded, saluting Nathen. "Your boyfriend here has skills."

"I'll say," Cameron responded, standing and weaving into the kitchen.

Nathen had been focused on the screen and trying to think ahead on how they might be able to crack the encryption when he was hit by the now familiar scent of Cameron. His thoughts began to swirl with the interruption of the now stronger scent wafting around the room. He looked around and saw him walking from the kitchen with a Cheshire cat grin, holding a glass of something red that smelled like tomato juice, which Nathen knew was also infused with Cameron's blood. Nathen didn't need to be told what it was. The scent was overwhelming, and he could also smell the source: a small cut on Cameron's finger that was now hidden beneath a bright green bandage. His heart dropped. This was the nicest thing anyone had ever done for him. Also, probably the weirdest. A tear started to form and roll down from his eye.

"Dude!" Cameron yelped.

Confused, Nathen watched as Cameron seemed to be looking around frantically and then grabbed the blue shirt that he had worn during the day that was balled up on the couch. Nathen was surprised as Cameron came at him with the shirt and was startled when Cameron shouted, "You're bleeding from your eyes!"

Nathen reached up and touched his face, watching as Cameron held the shirt up to him showing the evidence of blood which he could smell was his own. "Oh, that's weird."

"Are you okay?" Cameron asked. "Was it the interwebs?"

Nathen looked embarrassed. "No, I was crying because what you did is the sweetest thing anyone has ever done for me." He picked up the glass and drained it all in one gulp. The first thing he noticed was a sudden ringing in his ears and the room seeming to get longer. He dropped the glass and collapsed into the couch.

He heard as if in the distance, Cameron say, "Oh." And then, "Fuck, I've killed him!"

Cameron's blood began to infuse every inch of Nathen's being, causing his skin to raise with goosebumps. An incredibly pleasurable rolling wave starting from the back of his head flowed alongside the rest of his body. Nathen closed his eyes to ride it out, but found that he was writhing on the couch, grabbing the cloth of the pillows and squeezing. His eyes rolled back, and he let go a loud sigh. He noticed that he was exceptionally lightheaded; like being drunk. Then he remembered that intoxicated blood would also make him intoxicated, and he felt it instantly. He noticed something weird in the corner of his closed eyelids. It was a faint light, about the size of a person. He turned his head toward it and it moved to the center of the black void. That startled him, so he opened his eyes to see what *it* was.

He saw that Syn had walked over and crouched down, picking up the ice cubes and grabbing Cameron's already stained shirt to mop up the mess.

"Oh...I don't...I don't think that's death," Cameron said watching Nathen on the couch.

As soon as Nathen's eyes popped open, Syn jumped back and shouted, "What the holy hell is going on now?!"

Cameron sat back, against the far side of the couch. "I don't know."

Nathen saw as Syn reached under the couch and pulled out a katana, and Nathen shrank back, his eyes wide with fear. He had no idea why she might be pulling out a sword, but his senses were dragged in various direction. On the one hand dulled by alcohol, but on the other his eyesight narrowed to hone in on the point of the blade, the movement of blood and breath through her body as she readied for an attack... He thought about moving, really knew he should, but things were just so...funny.

"Syn!" Cameron shouted.

Nathen saw her attention turn to Cameron, and assumed she said something telepathically because Cameron said her name again, this time in a chastising way, before turning to him. "Umm, Nathen," he said using a calming voice. "Are you okay?"

Nathen tore his attention from Cameron to Syn. "That was the best drink of my life." His speech sounded a bit slurred. He started blinking returning his attention to the shimmery man with a halo of firey hair about his head. "Woah, you look so beautiful, like that elf on Lord of the Rings, all glowy. Have you come to rescue me?" Nathen reached out and cupped Cameron's face. "You look so concerned! Is everything all right?"

Cameron giggled, grinning stupidly at Syn. "He's drunk!"

"You sound proud of that."

Cameron leaned forward and kissed Nathen quickly, pulling away and leaving Nathen wanting more. "You're drunk!" he said again, as if Nathen hadn't heard him the first time.

"Fuck me." Syn shook her head in disgust. "You two— in there." She thumbed to Cameron's room. "Let the grownups take over." He saw Syn pick the equipment up off the floor and returned to the armchair to start working on the encryption.

Nathen had trouble getting up, but with Cameron's help managed to right himself. As they walked, he started mumbling, "The HR guy said I would get intoxicated if I drank blood from a human who was drunk. Boy, he wasn't lying. I feel sooooo good! And you look so good..."

Cameron tripped with Nathen out of the living room and across to his bedroom, laughed uncontrollably for a second. Nathen plopped onto Cameron's unmade bed and spread his arms out. He heard music come on as he began making sheet angels and saw Cameron fall on the beanbag and laugh at him. "What kind of music do you want? I like a lot of different kinds."

"Um...I usually like songs that have a nice message, so any genre, so long as it's not about doing mean things. Oh, but not big into music that is simply noise to me...like metal. I have been listening to "Biscuits" by Kacey Musgraves on repeat for a few weeks. Is it hot in here? I feel hot!" He tried to pull off his T-shirt, but it got tangled and he forgot his new strength and started to rip it. "Oops...Mom will be angry, SHIT! I forgot to call her!" He started fumbling for his phone in his pockets.

Forgetting the music, Cameron dove onto the bed and wrestled the phone away from him, offering in a stage whisper, "Text her!" He nodded pointedly. "You so don't want to *talk* to her right now. Heh, unless she's used to talking to an intoxicated you." He offered the phone back and sat up, looking around for what he was doing.

Nathen watched Cameron tug off his shoes and let him, not caring about footwear, or any other clothing for that matter. He had seen Cameron kick his shoes off at the door when they entered and had wondered if he should have too.

Nathen had become distracted watching Cameron who was glowing beautifully, his scent filling the room, but shook his head finally and smiled, "You're so smart! I should text her." He turned on the company phone and started typing.

I am with a very sweet new friend, will be working late, will call in the morning.

He looked at Cameron with concern, "Should I tell her about the T-shirt?"

Looking up from the phone, he answered, "Um...I don't think so."

The only light in the room came from the open living room as the blackout curtains were already shut. Nathen listened to a song that tickled at his memory from when he younger and hummed along with the chorus to "I knew I loved you" and was thinking about how it was an interesting, pretty song when he was interrupted by Cameron blurting out, "Do you want to be my boyfriend?" He glanced at him and saw that Cameron looked like he was in shock with his hand clamped over his mouth. As he stared at the multicolored aura surrounded the beautiful man, he noticed again the movement of blood rushing to his lap and now up to his face suggesting excitement, arousal.

Nathen smiled again, his heart dropping for the second time in the last ten minutes. He pressed the send button and slowly put down the phone. "I didn't think you would want to be my boyfriend. I scared you, and I'm kinda weird, but if you would have me, yes, I would. I'm not that experienced though. I have only had one other boyfriend, and that was a few years ago."

Nathen was overcome with apprehension, being invited into a relationship he hadn't thought about. It was a huge answer to say yes or no, and Cameron didn't know much about him. He didn't know how inexperienced he was or that he might be a disappointment. Why would this gorgeous man want to be his boyfriend? Since his last boyfriend, Zane, had broken up with him to move to an internship out-of-state over two years ago, Nathen had been self-conscious. He had read a lot about people with Autism and had found some interesting threads that many others were like him in that they were hypersexual.

Once he had become involved with Zane, he had realized that he wanted to be sexual with him daily, more often if able. He had wondered if that might have been one of the reasons Zane had left, so he hadn't actively sought a new relationship, worried that his quirks would drive the person away. But here was Cameron, this red-haired man with the brightest blue eyes, looking at him with obvious lust and he found himself sympathetically becoming aroused. He was also a little overwhelmed with emotion and again asked himself why would Cameron want to be his boyfriend? He had assumed that he would be alone forever.

Cameron's mouth opened and closed several times before he admitted, "I know that part of it is your kiss. I can't stop thinking about kissing you. So, asking you to be my boyfriend, I do realize is fueled by that. But it's so much more than that. You're the first person I haven't been able to read. I can't tell you how refreshing it is. And how terrifying. Everyone else is an open book and that really just leads to misery. But you're just so smart and sexy and..." His eyes closed with yearning. "And honest. It's wonderful to meet someone who is so genuine and even if it is chemical, I don't care. I want to see where this might go? If you do?"

Nathen nodded happily. "I'm going to dirty your sheets with my blood if you make me cry again." He picked his head up to study Cameron with glowing eyes that may have been disconcerting in a dark alley. "You are all glowy again...so pretty. It smells nice in here, like a...a warm peach pie. With vanilla ice cream!" His voice was still slurred and a bit distant.

Cameron smiled as the song changed to Moody Blues "Wildest Dreams." "Your eyes are glowing, like supernaturally glowing. That's probably why you think I'm glowing." He laughed lightly. "And..." He moved to lay out across the bed on his belly next to Nathen. "I guess we should talk about this. I think I mentioned that I don't like the idea of casual sex, and so I've never done that. I've had two boyfriends, and we were both monogamous. At least, I think we were. My first love was Tommy, and we were together in college when we were sixteen. He went back to New York, and that was that. Then there was Frank who..." Cameron paused for a long time. When he spoke again, he had changed subjects, "I don't know what you mean by experienced. I guess based on my two boyfriends you could say I've had a lot of experience." He laughed, ducking his head away. "At least a lot of sex. I know what I don't like at least. What, umm, do you mean by experience? And what do you want out of a boyfriend?"

Nathen propped himself up on his hand. "Well, I have only had the one relationship, so don't have a lot of experience with living with someone else, etcetera. Sex wise, I mean we were nineteen and had lots of sex as well." He laughed, again growing a bit self-conscious about his constant demands on his ex-boyfriend. "I want someone to share my life with, share our interests, and make a better life for each other when working together. I've been taking care of my mother for a few years now, and she used to take care of me, a lot...more than I realized, in fact." He looked Cameron in the eyes, which was still rare for him. "What do you want?"

Cameron was quiet, seemingly thinking, for a long while, before he said shyly, "I want someone to fall in love with. Ultimately, someone to share my life with, maybe raise children?" He paused again as Don Henley's "End of the Innocence" came on. "I've actually given it a lot of thought and I need a partner who is equal. I don't do the whole scene, I don't like labels..." his brow furrowed. Cameron stood suddenly. "Be right back." Nathen heard Cameron in the bathroom. He heard the water come on and focused in on the sound of Cameron breathing deeply. He wondered what was going on and leaned up to stare at the shut door. After a while, Cameron emerged and turned on the recessed lights that cast a soft glow across the bed before he quietly shut the bedroom door.

As Nathen watched, Cameron turned to look at him in bed and he saw the movement of blood again, rushing to Cameron's lap and saw his pants growing tighter. A fluttering in his chest rolled south causing Nathen to grow almost painfully hard in response. Concrete Blonde's "Bloodletting" was playing and for a second Nathen was sure that Cameron was going to join him in bed. Instead, Cameron grabbed his laptop off the desk and opened it. He sat next to him on the bed and after tapping on the keyboard, turned the screen to Nathen. It was a clinic's secure website that showed blood test results that indicated that Cameron was free of any STDs and healthy.

Nathen examined the screen, noting six months of bi-weekly tests, all showing the same thing. "Oh, that's informative, but I can't actually get STDs. At least not permanently. When they awakened me, they said I was healthy, no STDs, or anything else. Apparently, I can spread disease around though, if I drink from someone that has something. But the blood will eventually destroy whatever it is I'm carrying within a few days." His mind went back to the "who is equal" part of what Cameron had been saying. Nathen had given this thought while he was waiting to get his psychological evaluation. Since he had only his own experience of reality, he assumed that he was seeing it like other people. To him, everything seemed "normal." Of course, that word was subjective and in psychological terms "normal" was just a consensus. The experience of reality by the majority of people was the "normal" way to experience it; deviating from it obviously was abnormal. During the doctor's feedback, Nathen found out that he had deficits with understanding social cues and being completely oblivious to others. This gave him reservations about dating. People could take advantage of him and he would not know it. The doctors told him that he had a trusting personality, which opened him up for a slew of interpersonal issues. "As for your talking about being *equal,* I think you will always be my better at certain things; for instance, social settings or really any kind of complex interpersonal interactions. I don't know if we will ever be 'equal' in that regard." Nathen was a little apprehensive about imparting all of this, but he logically realized that it was important to be honest now instead of getting his heart broken later.

Cameron shrugged. "I'm sort of trained in that anyway. And you're always going to be better at tech stuff. You and Syn are like wizards to me. Heh, though I'm the wizard." He rolled his eyes and put the computer away. "So, you can spread...things, if you're biting different people?" He unconsciously examined his green bandaged finger. "Umm, what about the girl you were biting? Do you know about her?"

Nathen had a twinge of concern for a second, but then relaxed again. "I don't, but she is a special donor, so I assume that means she is screened. I haven't actually fed on anyone since her though. The blood we get comes from blood banks and is all screened."

"Okay," he managed after a thoughtful pause. "So, um, if you do drink from someone else, could you like, tell me? So, I can go get tested?"

"I would never do that if I were in a relationship. I wouldn't want to put them, you, in danger. And besides, the bite is supposed to be especially sexual for humans. I would feel wrong doing that."

Cameron gave a small shy smile. "It, uh, looked like the blood was actually sexual for you too." He gestured toward the living room. "Like, *really* sexual..."

Nathen blushed. "I think it's your blood. But I have only had blood directly from two people, so I could be totally wrong. It felt like every cell in my body was being infused with you."

Cameron smirked. "Wow. That's cool. So, what else are you into aside from computer stuff and games? Oh, and how old are you? I'm twenty-four."

Nathen smiled, mocking himself. "I'm twenty-two years old. I like long hikes, the beach, and picnics." He laughed. "Really though, I do like going out into nature, walking amongst the trees or out in the desert, though those are usually outdoor activities. Will be interesting trying that at night. Besides that, I read and research a lot. Apparently, I can get incredibly obsessed with things. I like working out and do it almost every day. Well, I did. I don't have to now. My body is going to stay like this till I get destroyed."

Cameron was grinning at Nathen's description and he saw that he was relaxing. Cameron reclined onto his back, looking at the ceiling. "I love all of that, too, though it's been forever since I've done any of it. Tommy and I used to hike all the time. Our school was in the mountains and sex in the woods is awesome." He shot a glance at

Nathen. "I read a lot for my job, and I hate working out!" He groaned for emphasis. "But Syn makes me, more days than not. I swim at our gym down the street." Cameron rolled over. "I'm sorry about your T-shirt..." He ran his fingers under the hem of it, trailing across Nathen's abs. "And, all things considered, your body staying like this isn't a bad thing."

Nathen laughed. "It's okay. I was taken back almost a decade. I used to take the labels off my shirts. They were distracting and itchy. But in the process, I would sometimes rip holes in the shirt. My mom was not amused. I have also not been drunk for quite a while." Nathen followed Cameron's hand on his body. "And thanks!" He offered a half grin as he used both hands this time to take off the shirt.

Cameron watched as Nathen's shirt came off and propped himself up on one arm, resting his head on his hand as he began to trace the definition of Nathen's abs and chest. He smiled. "You know, aphrodisiac or not, you are the best kisser I've met."

"Oh, um, thanks. I do wonder how much of what is going on is organic though and how much of it's the vampiric traits influencing you and me."

Cameron laughed and shook his head. "No, there's technique. Frank used to stick his entire tongue down my throat like he was trying to fuck me with it. It was not something I ever looked forward to. But you..." He licked his lips unconsciously. "I could have stayed in that pub forever, I think."

Nathen blinked. "Um...is that supposed to be a cue for me to kiss you again?"

Cameron laughed, falling backward and stared at the ceiling fan above them. "Yeah, well, if you want to..."

Nathen rolled so he was leaning over Cameron and softly kissed his lips, then pressed deeper in and was rewarded when their tongues began to slowly dance with each other.

*

Falling. That was the first feeling Cameron could identify when Nathen's tongue touched his. He was cognizant of when the aphrodisiac hit and his back arched slightly, belly rising to meet Nathen's hand, which had started to circle the soft down just below his navel. His arms snaked up around Nathen, pulling him down as the kiss deepened. He moaned, his tongue rolling around Nathen's. His taste was intoxicating, and Cameron's need increased. All thoughts, all reservations, began to fall away.

Nathen pressed against him as he maneuvered atop Cameron, instinctively grinding into him as he continued the passionate kiss. Cameron enjoyed Nathen's weight atop him and allowed both hands to explore the defined muscles of Nathen's shoulders, then back, slowly running down the length of his sides until he could cup Nathen's cheeks, kneading the firmness. His kiss alternated between soft brushes of his lips over Nathen's, to deeper more intense probing as his tongue sought more. Nathen started downward, kissing Cameron's chin, then neck, moving to the side, and feeling the soft skin there, and Cameron stiffened slightly when Nathen kissed his neck, suckling gently.

Taking a deep breath, Cameron relaxed and whispered slowly, "It's okay...if you want to bite me."

Nathen looked up surprised. "Um, so it's okay for me think about biting you? Or do I have permission to bite you?"

Cameron's breath caught, and he swallowed hard, nodding tensely. "I...I think so."

Nathen nodded, ensuring. "I'll never hurt you..." Cameron watched in awe and became almost rigid with tension as Nathen slowly started to kiss his neck, and then with a tender kiss bit into the skin.

Cameron hadn't realized he had held his breath in anticipation of Nathen's bite, but his body responded immediately as Nathen's fangs sank into him. Exhaling a loud moan, one hand clenched Nathen's head, pulling him deeper into his throat as the other clamped against Nathen's shoulder. He came explosively, soiling his pants as his back arched off the bed. Cameron had never known such pleasure, and it threatened to overwhelm. And then he felt it: trepidation, desire, concern, attraction...not *his* emotions. Nathen's! *"There you are!"*

Cameron was inside Nathen's mind now, and he was awash with Nathen's feelings of sexual anticipation and concern. He could feel Nathen's desire not to hurt him, but also the overwhelming orgasmic release as his blood flowed into Nathen. Then shock when their minds touched.

Cameron tried to hold on to Nathen mentally, tried to hold on physically, but it was too much. The pleasure was all encompassing. Physically, his entire being was responding, his skin prickled everywhere, his body trembling, his genitals released for a second time, and unconscious groans of pleasure escaped him. Mentally he could *see* Nathen. He was there, he was real, he was present in the familiar way that Cameron realized he had grown to need. Emotionally, they were joined. Falling...it was too much, too fast, too intense. He fought the darkness, tried to hold on...

*

Nathen was carried away with the flow of Cameron's blood; submerged in a fast rushing river of pure light and energy. His body was being infused with it, inside and out. He could have continued drinking until the last drop and was fixated on the taste of the familiar peach, and sweet metallic that was Cameron. It was his essence he was drinking, he knew that now, and with it came something else, older and primal, like the lifeblood of creation itself. As Cameron's emotions had hit him, he was back in the room and in bed with him. The blood that was already inside him was like a hot rum, spreading through him, and keeping him warm. Its influence flowed to every tip of hair and appendage. And he realized that he was still drinking. Fear and anxiety set in as if someone had struck him. Cameron was not moving! He quickly released and licked the wound. Panicked, but not enough to lose control, Nathen gently patted Cameron on the face, saying his name into his ear, trying to wake him up. When he didn't respond, he moved to his legs and raised them, hoping that the blood would rush back to his head. Nathen didn't have to feel for a pulse. As he focused, he could see glowing red energy, Cameron's' life force he assumed, still surging through him and collecting in his chest. The glow that had been white was now a tranquil blue. As he focused on the aura, he could feel what he thought were Cameron's emotions. Mostly he seemed to be wrapped in oblivious contentment.

Nathen saw Cameron come to slowly, drunkenly, his eyes opening wider as he lifted his head, focusing on Nathen. "Do it again!" he begged, then, "Wait!" Nathen could hear Cameron's thoughts homed in on him. He could feel Cameron overcome with relief because he could sense him and hear that Cameron was thinking he wasn't a dream. Though not his own emotions, Nathen could feel that Cameron was filled with an enormous sense of joy, such that he had never experienced. Cameron was riding a wave of emotional ecstasy, fed by the rush of healthy emotions from Nathen. He fell back, eyes closing for a moment as he relished, sighing. He lifted his head again and stared deeply into Nathen's eyes.

"Nathen? Can you hear me?" he reached out mentally, caressing.

Nathen sighed, releasing the pent-up stress with the exhale...then froze, *"Wow, this is weird. Um, Hello? Can you hear me, I hear you talking...thinking in my mind?"* He spoke up, "Are you okay? You scared me, I thought I may have taken too much blood."

Cameron started laughing uncontrollably, overjoyed. *"Yes, I'm okay. I'm insanely okay. So THAT is what you were talking about, huh?"* Cameron reached out and gently caressed Nathen's bristly cheeks, leaning forward and kissing him softly, pressing lips before falling back and thinking, *"And yes, this is me. It's been me since I was fourteen. I can hear people's thoughts, feel what they feel. It was uncontrollable at first, but after practice, I was able to block it out like background noise. I can focus on certain people, or groups, who are within a block of me and pick up on surface thoughts. Or, if I focus, I can get deeper. If you're ever in the other room, and you mentally call out my name, I'll respond. It's like someone in a crowd shouting at you to get your attention. I'll open a direct channel and be able to talk, as if we're talking on the phone. Though I can only do this for a shorter period before I start getting a headache. But I swear to you,"* he thought, running the back of his fingers across Nathen's facial hair, *"I won't probe. And I try not to read surface thoughts of people I love. Sometimes it just happens. I also won't do what I did with Matt to you...unless I need to."* He chewed his lip and continued thinking, *"I mean, if you're out of control maybe. I do naturally tend to want people around me who are happy. Syn is normally happy, but when she is agitated, I do this..."* He reached out, and Nathen was emotionally embraced with contentment, joy, pure emotions of calm, positive love. "We call it our mental hugs. And she can do it back when there is a channel open."

The rush of positive emotions wrapped around Nathen like sunshine. His skin had another strong galvanic response, and he relaxed into the bed. "That feels nice...like being in a soft comforter." He could feel Cameron reveling in his ability to share this which he had never shared with someone so intimately. He continued wrapping Nathen in waves of emotional sensation as he gently turned to him and began kissing him again, their tongues rolling languidly.

"Tell me what you want, what brings you the most pleasure?" he whispered as he almost reluctantly pulled away and stared down into Nathen's eyes with a new hunger.

Nathen inwardly blushed, before admitting, "Well, I like oral sex, and sex-sex. I also like cuddling and lying in each other's embrace. Though I probably won't talk much unless there is something interesting on our minds." He began thinking of his first boyfriend and saw that Cameron got a strikingly vivid image of a younger naked Nathen in a strange dark room with another naked young man lying next to him. The man had short blond hair, blue-hazel eyes, a cute angular face and was about as tall as Nathen. Both of their hair was messy, yet they were smiling and holding each other.

Nathen's mind floated in a space that consisted of otherworldly joy as he focused on the almost tangible emotions that danced through his body. The intimate experience was like someone pouring honey on his soul.

Cameron received the image and smiled, sending one of his own: a boy of sixteen with two-toned hair, taller than Cameron, spooning him under a warm blanket. The air around them was frigid, but they both seemed content. They were on a twin-sized mattress pushed next to a second mattress on a cold tiled floor of a room that had posters of the Smiths, Morrissey, Evanescence, and Type O Negative taped to the walls. The room had two doors, one leading out of each side and a bank of windows behind built in desks. The room was a mess with empty pizza and cracker boxes, schoolbooks, papers, clothes, and condom boxes; though there was a specific trashcan set aside that seemed to be for actual trash. The feeling from the younger Cameron was elation, much like he was feeling now, overlaid with bittersweet loss.

Cameron slid to the side, pulling Nathen to him and curling behind him. He wrapped his arms around him, hugging him tightly and spreading small kisses across the back of Nathen's neck. "Like this?" he asked, with a smile in his tone. He pulled the comforter that was wadded up at the end of the unmade bed up around them. "I know you don't sleep, but maybe you could stay with me a while?"

Nathen shrunk into Cameron. "Yes, just like this. I would love to spend the night being held by you." He picked up Cameron's hand and kissed it.

Nathen's emotions fluctuated from joy and excitement, to peace and adoration. Having the comforter pulled over disturbed the air and added more of Cameron's scent. Nathen tried to send how he perceived the scent to Cameron, not knowing if that would work. The image of a peach orchard flashed into Cameron's mind, a row of pink flowers and their sweet smell. Then a warm peach pie. The emotion of simple joy radiated from both images, unencumbered by the plights of a grownup life. "Those were my grandmother's favorite trees. I used to go and visit them when I was younger."

"*Pretty*," Cameron thought, drifting off, exhausted. "Lights off," he called out and the lights in the room dimmed and flickered out. He reached around and turned off the music on his phone, cutting off Billy Joel singing about the times of his life.

As the night progressed, the alcohol from Cameron's blood burned off and Nathen began to feel like himself again. He could still see his lover's aura coalescing around him. He focused on his sense of vision and suppressed the effect. The aura slowly dispersed from view.

Chapter Seventeen

NATHEN

They spent that first night together, Cameron tangled around Nathen. At one point, he turned over without waking and Nathen turned with him, slipping his arms around him, which Cameron seemed to settle into naturally. He was elated by the intimacy and closeness, meditating through the night. Nathen caught feelings, like the touch of a breeze bubbling up from Cameron's dreams, mostly happy or neutral. In the morning Nathen could feel Cameron stirring and turned around in his arms, throwing a leg over his. It was still almost completely black in the room due to the curtains. Nathen heard Cameron's thoughts about this being the first night since he could remember that he had not had insomnia and had not had to sleep with music playing through his headphones. Cameron grinned broadly before his eyes opened, thinking, "*Good morning. Would this officially be our second date then?*"

Nathen frowned for a second. The connection was weak, liken to static over a radio. "I think you asked if this would be our second date...Or did you want me to leave?"

"*What?*" The question sounded like it was coming from a far distance. "What?" Cameron said aloud.

"I think that the blood is fading?" Nathen said, tracing his fingers through Cameron's ginger stubble. "You look so sad."

"Oh...I'm sorry." Cameron swung back up into a sitting position. "I kinda liked having the link. I can still sense your emotions. But, I guess now that you're pointing it out...your thoughts are a little far away."

"Maybe it was the blood?" Nathen offered.

He saw Cameron nod in the darkness. "Hey, want to shower with me?"

Nathen's squirmed with a stirring of lust and embarrassment at the prospect of being naked with him. "Yes, that sounds exceedingly hot. I'm actually surprised you didn't take one last night. I know you...um...in your pants."

Cameron laughed. "Yeah. Sorry about that. I must smell to high heaven," he rolled out of bed and began pulling off his socks, tossing them at the corner where the laundry basket was. "Honestly, I swear I've grown out of the slob stage that I showed you last night."

"I like the smell. It's kind of has a sexual connotation for me. You know, kinda like Pavlov's dogs. I like the usually musky smell of men and especially you."

Cameron pulled off his pants and underwear and emptied his pockets onto the desk before tossing pants and underwear toward the corner in the general basket direction. Nathen watched with adulation mixed with guilt and Cameron stood up straight. "Heh, you're a vampire. And...can see in the dark, can't you?" Nathen could see the blush rising to Cameron's cheeks when he realized he had just done an unintentional striptease.

Nathen imagined his own cheeks burning in the darkness. "Yes, I can see. Though I didn't know it was that dark, to me everything is visible in the room."

Cameron bowed his head in humorous surrender and said, "Gimme a second," as he quickly entered the bathroom and pulled the door shut. Nathen could hear as the shower started and Cameron attended to human needs in there. He laid out in bed, enjoying the anticipation of being naked with Cameron in the shower.

Cracking the door, Cameron asked with a smile. "Need some help?"

Nathen was confused at the question and said in a quiet voice, "Need help with what?"

Cameron opened the door, the light from the bathroom illuminating his naked form, including the member hanging between his legs. "Thought you were going to shower with me?" he said teasingly.

"Oh!" Nathen said. He tapped into his new vampiric abilities and stripped quickly, shooting past Cameron into the shower. He grinned when he saw Cameron turn in confusion and stare at his athletically slim body, taking in his own impressive package.

Cameron blinked. "Did you teleport?" he asked, stepping into the shower with Nathen.

Nathen laughed. "No, but I can move fast if I want to. Though it doesn't actually feel like I'm moving all that quickly. It seems like time has slowed around me, but I'm moving my normal speed."

Cameron stood for a moment openly admiring Nathen. Nathen saw that Cameron himself was clean shaven throughout his entire package and he noticed that Nathen was neatly trimmed. They were both lean, though Cameron was a little taller and broader. "And here I thought you were gorgeous wearing clothes." He stepped closer to Nathen, kissing his lips without tasting him.

Nathen slid to the side and wrapped his hands around Cameron's shoulders and started to knead under the hot water. Cameron leaned back against Nathen and adjusted the water so the extra-large showerhead with its enormous distribution that rained down on both of them was a little warmer. Nathen saw that there were also nine jets, three on each of the three walls that were currently off.

After some time, Nathen wrapped his arms around Cameron, giving him a hug while standing behind him and slid his hands down his body, stopping at his hardening cock, running his hand along his engorged length. "Wow, you are really big."

When Nathen mentioned his size, he felt Cameron bristled and mentally pull away, blushing and thinking simply. "*Yeah.*" Confused by Cameron's emotions of embarrassment, apology, and shame, he struggled to keep up when Cameron shunted them to the side and picked up the white bar of hypoallergenic soap and rubbed it over Nathen's arms.

Nathen smiled as emotions of gratitude and closeness started to flow through him. He kissed Cameron on the cheek, then his neck, working his way around to his lips as he backed up a bit to give him more room. Cameron turned as Nathen was kissing him, shivering when he kissed his neck, the memory of the night before like a jolt through him and playing into Nathen's mind causing their members to thrum. He lifted the washcloth off the hook and began to soap Nathen, alternating between massaging and scrubbing. He smiled and ran the soapy washcloth around Nathen's erection, gently cupping his soaped-up fingers around the sensitive sac below, kneading gently.

"Mind if I suck you off?" Cameron whispered, catching Nathen's earlobe between his teeth.

Nathen looked down, rippling with shyness. He hated confrontation and potentially disappointing someone, but also knew that now Cameron could read his mind. "My sense of touch is hyposensitive to some things and sensitive to others. So, for instance, I don't like very light touch, but like a lot of pressure, or touch that is more substantial. So, head has never done it for me, but I know a lot of guys like doing it. Personally, I like giving head though..." He shifted his weight from foot to foot, afraid it would disappoint Cameron.

While he did feel a filtering of disappointment from Cameron as he leaned back against the wall and resumed running the cloth over Nathen's arm, Cameron admitted with his eyes closed and a small tickling of trepidation, "I don't like receiving anal... It hurts too much."

Nathen smiled broadly. "That's actually one of the things I like best, especially because it's so intense. I also like the sense of pressure of the person on top. I don't normally like topping, though I have in the past."

Cameron settled against the wall, letting the water cascade over him. He had a myriad of emotions that he seemed to be filtering through that were confusing to Nathen. Nathen had never been able to read another person's emotions, but their new link seemed to allow him to sense them as easily as if they were talking, but they didn't make sense without context.

Nathen had waves of concern. "Are you okay? Did I say something wrong?"

Cameron's eyes fluttered open, and for a moment Nathen sensed sadness from him, "No...it's me. It's probably better you don't like oral. I've been told I don't know how to do it very well." He smiled and poured a dollop of shampoo into his hand before blatting it on

Nathen's head and massaging gently. "I'm also too big to be ridden." He shrugged, another wave a sadness washed over Nathen. "At least not comfortably. But I used to like sixty-nine a long time ago."

There was a long pause before Cameron went on, "It's just, I don't like labels: verse, tops and bottoms, BDSM, doms, subs, slaves, masters, safe words—" his laugh had an edge, as he said out loud "—CBT."

When Cameron pulled away, Nathen rinsed his hair, opening his eyes to see Cameron had begun washing his own hair. "I didn't know about any of that stuff before my ex, and I just wish there was a way to go back to before I knew about it. Things seemed easier when we could explore and talk without labels."

Nathen shrugged. "I don't know half of what you just said, besides the common ones. I want a normal life with someone I love. Going out to parks, eating ice cream together, watching TV, or playing a game, reading interesting book, going to movies. As for your size, I think the vampiric frame is resilient. I know I can probably heal myself faster than normal and probably regenerate things that are removed, besides my head. Please don't be sad."

Nathen's eyes opened wide in shock when he was hit by a wave of consternation verging on illness washed over Cameron, and he say aloud, "No!"

Cameron quickly rinsed the shampoo out of his eyes, shaking his head for emphasis and staring at him with a wave of concern.

Very confused, Nathen was unsure of what was going on and said, "I'm sorry, I didn't mean to upset you."

Cameron hastily rinsed off and stepped out of the shower, pulling a towel from under the sink and handing it to Nathen before beginning to dry off. "I would never..."

was all he said before leaving the bathroom. Nathen could feel a cacophony of emotion emanating from Cameron: guilt, shame, rage, grief. Suddenly he was frustrated that he couldn't read his thoughts.

He heard Cameron say, "Lights on" as he entered the bedroom.

Nathen focused and noticed the water drops slow midfall. This caused him to become fascinated, and he watched the water stream as drops slowed to a crawl. He became contemplative, his attention drawn to each of the prismatic droplets hanging before him and he focused on the hundred little beads all around him. Then he remembered that Cameron was upset, so he wiped himself off, put on his clothes, and was sitting in the bed before Cameron had taken more than a couple steps into the bedroom.

"Please don't feel ashamed of your body! And you don't need to feel guilt. I'm sorry I brought it up." Nathen was upset and angry at himself.

Cameron fell back against the wall that separated the closet and bath, his eyes wide at Nathen. He glanced back into the bathroom, then back at back at Nathen again. "What?" he asked in both awe and confusion.

Nathen frowned. "I can sense you are feeling ashamed. I assume of your body? And I can sense guilt, anger, and sadness. I'm not sure why and am confused, but I know I said something wrong. I'm sorry. I won't bring it up again."

Cameron slid down the wall slowly until he was sitting on the ground. Tears started pooling in his eyes. "How? I didn't have a channel open. And...I thought that the connection had been lost! How can you see, feel...any of that?"

Nathen's overall sense of confusion increased. "I...I don't know. I thought this was normal? I'm sorry I made you cry. Should I go?"

"No...I didn't have a channel open. I thought that I was guarding those feelings." Cameron buried his head as he hugged his knees. "You should know, I guess. And then you can choose to go or not."

Though slightly hazy, as if watching a drive-in movie, but sitting far away from the screen with a crackling of static for the sound, Nathen watched Cameron's projection. It was a memory of a birthday party with an older guy in his thirties who Nathen instinctively knew was Frank, Cameron's ex-boyfriend. He was average in every way: appearance, height, with light brown hair and dull brown eyes. There were twenty or so men in a small apartment, all obviously gay, drinking, smoking, eating, dancing, making out. Cameron kept to himself for the most part, happier one-on-one. During the party, the older guy talked to Cameron, "It's my birthday, Camisole! Come on, for me?" Cameron blanched at the nickname, but opened his mouth, knowing that Frank was feeding him ecstasy. The night sped up. Cameron was dancing with all the guys who kept handing him drinks. The party started dying out and Cameron was feeling more and more tired. Then they were in Frank's bedroom and Cameron was on the bed, feeling strangely leaden. He felt Frank behind him and wondered how he had gotten naked so fast. Frank's stale breath was on his neck, "You're going to love this!" Cameron could read fragmented in Frank's mind what he had been planning for months. Frank was verse, and it had been a contention throughout their relationship that Cameron didn't allow Frank to penetrate him. The scene shifted to include several points during their relationship: Frank presenting Cameron with anal trainers, which Cameron rejected to Frank's annoyance; Frank telling all of his friends about Cameron, his "twink boyfriend with the porn star dick" when Cameron and he had first started dating when Cameron was nineteen and Frank was twenty-nine; Frank becoming more and more resentful as Cameron surpassed him in their doctoral program... And then Frank was behind him, in him, tearing him. Cameron screamed silently, unable to make a sound as the Ketamine Frank had slipped him paralyzed not only his body, but his mind. "You'll thank me for popping your cherry, Cami," Frank had said, spanking Cameron thirty-four times, Frank's birthday age. When Cameron could move again, he realized he was bleeding and Frank had not worn a condom. He had taken himself in shame to a clinic in Berkeley, immediately started prophylactic treatment, and had been tested every two weeks for the last six months.

"I would never do that to you," Cameron thought, sickened.

Nathen choked on a mixture of sadness, disgust, and anger. "I'm sorry that happened to you. But you wouldn't be doing that to me. What happened to you was rape. You were not a willing participant. I don't see it in your character to do what happened to you to anyone."

"It was my fault. I shouldn't have taken the drug, shouldn't have stayed there that late. I should have read what Frank was planning. I knew he was so angry at me for graduating before him, but..." He shook his head, unable to make eye contact. "It's okay. A bit much to lay on someone after knowing them for a day, huh? I can remove that from your memory if you want?"

Nathen shook his head, *"Please don't. And none of that was your fault. The fault squarely lays with the person that chose to rape you. You didn't consent to being raped because you took a party drug or chose to stay there."* Nathen didn't know what to do but knew people usually liked being held when they were upset. He slowly kneeled next to Cameron, pulled him close and hugged him.

Cameron visibly and mentally flinched every time Nathen had said "rape." When Nathen came over and hugged him, Cameron stiffened for a moment then relaxed into his embrace. Then he felt the most curious thing. Cameron's emotions, the darkness that was around him started to shift, as if being put away in another area of his mind. His thoughts calmed. "So, do you still want to be my boyfriend?"

Nathen was again awash in confusion. "Why would any of that make me not want to be your boyfriend?"

Cameron smiled softly, shaking his head as he cupped Nathen's face and searched his eyes. "This is reality, isn't it? A beautiful, sweet, kind guy who wants long walks on the beach and ice cream? I think I know exactly what I need." He smiled broadly, feelings of hope and tentative joy reaching out to Nathen as he leaned forward. He kissed Nathen fully, pushing him back onto the floor and following so he could lie on top of him.

Nathen was surprised by the sudden shift, but he went along with it. Cameron was not crying anymore and that made him feel better. He returned the kiss, gently massaging Cameron's tongue with his own and feeling the kiss work to sooth Cameron's emotions as he instinctively traced down his back and massaged his bare butt; a wave of arousal springing forth.

As the kiss became deeper, more passionate, their tongues rolling around, Nathen enjoyed the feeling of Cameron's erection growing against him. The stimulation and having a naked and now aroused Cameron on top of him sympathetically started to make Nathen hard, though his mind kept going back and forth between feeling sad and angry for him, to being in the moment and incredibly turned on. He caressed the small of Cameron's back lightly, moving slowly up his spine.

Cameron growled as he rolled over, pulling Nathen atop him while holding him and not breaking the kiss. Nathen's emotional struggle was suddenly extinguished and he was vaguely aware that Cameron had emotionally engulfed him with feelings of arousal, a kindling of lust and hunger, leaving no room for anything else.

Feeling a rush of sexually charged emotion hit him, Nathen was wholly moved into the moment. He took off his shirt and reached down and grabbed hold of Cameron's now fully erect member, slowly stroking it and eliciting a deep groan. Bending down, Nathen returned to passionately kiss Cameron again before producing a stream of kisses down his chin, neck, chest, where he used his tongue to circle around and kiss each nipple, before proceeding further down to his abs where he spread small kisses on the path to his erect cock. He saw on the path above his pubis to the left was a small, intricate tattoo of a colorful butterfly and kissed it. Nathen could feel Cameron's emotions inside him, knowing that he was reveling in his touch. It was like a mirror that bounced off and magnified the experience. Cameron's member was long and thick and while Nathen couldn't be sure, he guessed at least nine inches, maybe bigger. It was the largest penis he had ever seen in real life and larger than most guys in porn; it seemed larger still since Cameron's entire package was shaved bare. He began by kissing, and then he nibbled his sack before sucking them both gently in his mouth, using this tongue to massage each orb, before taking both of them in fully.

Feeling Cameron's enjoyment, Nathen continued for a while until he finally moved up to use the edge of his tongue to thrill the shaft of his penis base to tip; licking around the glans and over and probing the slit at the top. Once the head was wet, he took him lightly in his mouth. Bobbing up and down, he slowly took in more with every thrust, managing to take about half of Cameron into his mouth before it hit the back of his throat, which almost triggered his gag reflex, but he managed to control it. Cameron writhed on the carpeted floor, his heels digging in. Nathen's technique sent shock waves of pleasure through Cameron, which he projected back to Nathen. He moaned softly when Nathen pulled him deeper into his throat, reflecting to Nathen that he had never experienced this much pleasure from someone using their mouth on him.

The emotional waves coming from Cameron helped Nathen connect on a much different level than he had ever felt in his life. Since he embraced Cameron's pleasure, he didn't have to ask if what he was doing was good, which allowed for an automatic positive feedback loop. Nathen continued to use his mouth and tongue to please his lover and grinned internally, enjoying the fact that Cameron was so enraptured. He removed Cameron from his mouth, looking at him, "Did you want me to bite you here?" He touched the area between his leg and his engorged cock. "I'm told it's supposed to feel even more intense…"

An anticipatory wave of absolute desire washed out of Cameron before he gathered his thoughts enough to say, "It actually takes me an embarrassingly long time to...finish. If you do"—he shivered both mentally and physically—"I know I'll immediately come. Like last night." He reached over under the bed and caught hold of a drawer, pulling out a soft white washcloth from a pile neatly stacked within beside lube, condoms, and two large silicone donuts. He handed the cloth to Nathen with an almost too eager nod.

Nathen smiled, and using his left hand continued to stroke Cameron, while his head went in between his legs and he started to lick, kiss, and suck on the area above the femoral artery. He focused on the skin and noticed the pulse of red beneath it. Opening his mouth, he almost consciously this time willed his canines out to their full length. He smiled at Cameron with his teeth exposed and gently brought his mouth down to the artery, first kissing the spot, then biting into the skin. He sensed Cameron watching with a silent wave of fear at Nathen's fangs, so close to his...

"Oh god!" Cameron called out, his back arching again in immediate release. His mouth was flooded with quintessential flavor of Cameron intermixed with an erotic tinge, like cinnamon. Nathen started to quickly lap up the flowing blood feeling a euphoria that to him was better than sex. Cameron's eyes closed and Nathen could feel as his entire body was wrought with the pleasure of Nathen's bite as he came explosively, spraying out over his chest and Nathen's fingers. Nathen could read that the intensity of having his hand stroking him, and the exhalation of the bite, sent shivers through Cameron as he remained bowed, his body rigid in an orgasm that Nathen knew he could potentially have continue for a long time.

Nathen could feel himself becoming full, and didn't want a repeat of Cameron passing out, so he willfully made himself stop and lick the wound, which closed it almost instantly. He looked up with a joyful smile, small lines of blood running down the sides of his chin. He scooted up and playfully licked the come that was glistening on Cameron's abs and chest, smiling up at him and then moving up farther. Nathen kissed Cameron's lips and cuddled up next to him as he used the washcloth to wipe the come off Cameron's stomach and chest. He let his hand rest on Cameron's chest and waited for him to recover.

"Nathen...Nathen...Nathen." Cameron seemed lost in the rapture still. He gathered Nathen to him, weakly holding him and still shuddering with aftershocks of orgasm. They lie together for a long time until Cameron finally found the energy to kiss the top of Nathen's head before lying back again.

Nathen sent emotions of contentment, happiness, and peace to Cameron. "I hope that was okay? The emotions I feel are a lot stronger than usual. It feels sensual, intimate, and close." He thought for a bit. "What do you like...sexually?"

The questions were received, and Nathen could feel Cameron sludging through the endorphins that had kept him from forming a coherent thought. "Okay? Jesus..." He was trying to move, and Nathen sensed from him feelings of a joyful obligation, responsibility. "Wait, what? What do I like? I need to get you off...Your turn..." He bent his head down to kiss Nathen reaching down between Nathen's legs, but then paused with confusion that washed over of him. "If you don't like oral, do you like hand jobs?"

Nathen smiled. "I don't mind getting head, though my skin is not especially sensitive and it tends to tickle more than feel sexual. I just... I get more enjoyment out of knowing the other person is feeling good when I'm giving them head. I also like getting a hand job, mostly because it's less about the stimulation of the glans and more about pressure."

Cameron gave a half smile and, keeping eye contact, reached down between them to unbutton Nathen's pants. Finding his way inside, he began to stroke him and Nathen's hips lifted as Cameron's almost expert hand applied more and more pressure, squeezing him tightly and working into a surprisingly perfect pace. He shivered slightly when Cameron leaned over and licked his chin, then kissed him, sharing the flavor of blood. The taste caused Nathen to reach up and grab Cameron's head, pulling him into a deeper kiss as he thrust up into Cameron's hand. The blood was better than orgasm, better than anything he had experienced, and he mentally shared this with his lover. Cameron's breath caught, making him hum into their kiss.

A wave of euphoric pleasure quaked through Nathen, and in that instance, he projected an image of him lying on his stomach while Cameron was on top and inside him. With that image he bucked, let out a loud exhale, and came all over his stomach and chest.

Cameron pulled away and gasped. Nathen looked down to see what could be thought of as an emergency of blood splattered across his belly and chest. Cameron quickly got the cloth and mopped up the worst of it before it dripped down to the carpet, while also quickly pushing Nathen's pants off so that he wouldn't bloody them.

Humor overwhelmed Nathen from Cameron, "So, want to shower with me?" he asked for the second time that morning.

Nathen was both fascinated and mortified by what had happened and let out an absurd laugh that was accompanied by a shy smile, "Sorry! I didn't know that was going to happen. Yes, a shower is probably in order."

Cameron held out a hand and helped Nathen up, and returned to Nathen's earlier question, "I like what you showed me." He smiled, with a silent promise being sent Nathen's way. "My two favorite positions have been sixty-nine and having my partner on top but have had mixed results from that because I was always afraid that I could go too deep. But I have something now that helps with that. I like pleasing my partner, maybe above all else before I met you. Now..." Arousal emanated from Cameron and he looked down bashfully. "Guess I have a new favorite... I suppose my last two partners have not been great. Neither has ever done anything like what you did with your mouth."

Nathen followed Cameron into the shower and smirked. "Probably because neither were vampires. I do actually like pleasing my partner before my considerations as well, we have that in common. As for the donuts, we may or may not need to use them. I have a super high pain threshold, so most things that would hurt others, feel good or do not hurt as badly for me...sexually. Though things like labels on shirts bug me to no end."

Cameron pulled the shower door closed behind them, offering a soft smile before he began washing Nathen again, this time starting behind him. "Oh," he thought, and Nathen could feel embarrassment from him. "I guess I know better than to assume things. I don't like the idea of hurting anyone, for obvious reasons... I'm sorry about the meltdown."

Wrapping his arms around Nathen, he rested his chin on his shoulder and massaged and scrubbed the blood off him, sending waves of adoration, kissing Nathen's head.

Nathen relished the stimulation of the hot water hitting his skin, Cameron's touch, and emotional projections. Working his way around, Cameron finished by washing Nathen's member and backing him up against the wall. He kissed Nathen again, dipping his tongue in briefly and Nathen could feel him relishing the shiver that it sent through him before he began washing himself again. "I definitely wish we could stay in bed all day, but Syn said a little while ago when we had had 'quite enough of that' we should join her and Vita for brunch. She found stuff out? Now, I could insist on breakfast in bed if you like...?" He flashed a grin as he scrubbed himself again.

"Brunch sounds nice, but I can't go into direct sunlight or if it's really bright in the room. I guess it depends on if it's away from the windows?" Nathen was watching Cameron from the wall and became distracted by the arousal he had watching as Cameron's muscles flexed under the glistening droplets of water.

Cameron pressed against Nathen, his erection still prominent from handling Nathen earlier. He kissed him deeply, sending several pornographic images of positions he would like to try before stepping back, smiling wickedly. "I'll ask her," he said aloud, as the cascade of water fell over him and he ran the soap absently up and down his belly.

Nathen noticed as Cameron became mentally quiet and assumed he was communicating telepathically with Syn. A wave of embarrassment swept across him from

Cameron and he wondered what was being said as his fair skin reddened. Then he lost hold of the soap, swallowing hard. His blush started midchest and ran upward to his ear tips. His eyes were huge, and he looked at Nathen, emanating mortification tinged with humor. "Syn... um...felt me. Last night. This morning." He finished up and got out, drying off and handing Nathen the towel again.

Nathen laughed. "You're a strong broadcaster. Imagine if you could give everyone in a few hundred miles an orgasm. It would probably lower the crime rate." Nathen accepted the towel and started to dry himself off. Once done, he approached Cameron and kissed him on the lips gently. "Thank you for letting me stay the night. I'll never treat you like Frank did. And I swear I'll do all I can to make you happy."

Cameron's breath caught at Frank's name and he nodded silently. Nathen read Cameron's emotions of guilt and shame, chased away by gratitude. Busying himself with shaving and other toiletries, Cameron said, "Please feel free to use any of my clothes. I think we're probably similar in size."

"Also," Cameron called walking out of the bathroom. "I liked you staying over. Would it be too much to ask you to stay tonight?"

Nathen grinned and opened the closet, pulling out a form fitting gray shirt. "I can stay over, but I want to check up on my mother and make sure she's doing okay. We have a live-in housekeeper and she also has a nurse that comes and checks on her." Nathen's mother had instilled a deep sense of guilt whenever he worried her. He knew that throughout his life, his mother had to watch out for him a lot more than his brother. Nathen had always been going off and getting lost in his own world, causing his mother to have to work twice as hard to keep track of him when he was young. He realized sometime in his teens that he had been programmed to "check in" whether it be via text, call, or in person. And while he preferred texting, he knew his mother preferred to see him in person as much as possible. He was also worried about her. In the last few years her health had declined more and the last thing he wanted was to add to her stress.

Chapter Eighteen

CAMERON

"Of course! I didn't mean to keep you." Cameron switched gears, smirking as he openly stared at Nathen. "Do you know the saying 'That shirt would look better on the floor?'" he asked, moving past Nathen to pull out sweats and a T-shirt.

Nathen thought about the question. "I assume it means that I would look better without the shirt on? Though when you asked me the immediate interpretation was literal."

Half-dressed, Cameron gathered Nathen to him, whispering, "It means that regardless of how hot you are in my clothes, that you're hotter naked." He kissed the side of Nathen's head. "I'm being summoned." Cameron pulled his own shirt over his head and opened the bedroom door to find Syn and a tall bleach blonde woman sitting at the dining room table snacking on chips.

The woman waved, "Hi. I hear that you're the best brunch maker and Syn has been assuring me for an hour that you'd be getting up soon, but were partying all night with your new boy toy, huh?" The woman had a heavy Bostonian accent. She was a pretty woman, well dressed even for the early morning. Syn liked "girly-girls" and Cameron smiled at Vita's forwardness.

"Good morning," he said. "I'm Cameron."

"I heard," Vita said. "It's good to know you." She looked past Cameron. "And you must be Nathen. They do make a cute couple," she said to Syn before proceeding to take a sip of a mimosa.

Cameron threw a smile over his shoulder at Nathen before heading to the kitchen where ingredients were already prepped for cooking. "Omelets, then?" he called to the group.

"Denver for me!" Vita called.

"You know what I like," Syn responded.

"Nathen? Want to join them or help in here?" Cameron asked.

Nathen smiled at Vita. "Hello." He inclined his head to her and moved to Cameron who could feel him trying to subdue the anxiety and apprehensiveness that always followed when meeting new people. "I'll help."

Vita seemed pleasant enough, resuming her conversation with Syn about her latest exploits in the South of France. Cameron wrapped his arm around Nathen with a side hug. "Do you cook?" he asked softly, readying four pans on the gourmet style six burner stove. He began mixing the ingredients for Syn's Spanish omelet and Vita's Denver.

Nathen nodded. "I can. I watch a lot of cooking shows."

Cameron grinned. "Should you stay away from the flames?" he whispered, asking louder for Vita's benefit, "What's your favorite thing to cook?"

Nathen caught on and whispered, "Oh, I won't burst into flames or anything. At least I don't think so." He answered the question about cooking audibly, "I can cook a mean chicken tikka masala. I usually like spicy food and I can follow instructions pretty well from recipes."

Syn projected to Cameron, *"She'll leave after breakfast. I'll share the stuff I found with you guys then."*

After their meal, Syn walked Vita to the door, kissed her briefly and promised to meet up for the Dikes on Bikes rally. She turned back to the group, "Well, boys. Let me tell you about what I found. The software has a slew of addresses it connects to, all pointing to a distributed botnet, one I have not heard of before, and it seems the IP addresses all belong to private ISP user pools. So probably some poor grandmother's email machine has been compromised and is being used to reroute traffic to other networks and locations." She took a sip of her coffee and continued. "Whoever these guys are, they know what they're doing and are not a random script kiddies. It's a professional shop, could even be a government run one with the sophistication of the actual software."

Nathen spoke up, "I followed the traffic to a remote terminal that is near Coit Tower. I was thinking Cameron and I could investigate the area today and see if we can find the building it was in. It was a large space, like an abandoned factory or something, with a high ceiling and dirty windows all around. One of them was broken and I could see the lit-up tower."

Cameron finished cleaning up the dishes and listened in. "Guess we have a plan. Is there anything else on the agenda for today?"

Syn shrugged. "Well, I'm going to the gym. And I'm assuming since it's daytime you two will not be?"

"We could go to the gym tonight if you give us the keys? Nathen loves exercise, and I love steam rooms." He projected to Nathen the image of the two of them in the steam room, naked. "Nathen? Didn't you need to go home?"

Nathen projected back an image of him giving Cameron head in the steam room and grinned when he *felt* Cameron's libidinous shudder. While he couldn't read emotional cues on people's faces, this link allowed him to feel Cameron's in such a curious way that was both exciting and a little overwhelming. "I can show you around my home. It's in Marin and I can get an Uber to take us there. Though, we would have to wait till sunset. Or I would have to wrap myself up and you would have to walk me to the car."

Syn left them to their own devises, calling out, "I won't be home until this afternoon."

They retreated to Cameron's closet where they dug through and chose extra layers to bundle Nathen in while Cameron changed out of his sweats into a pair of khakis and cobalt blue button-down long-sleeved shirt asking with a sense of curiosity mixed with nervousness, "Umm, am I going to meet your mom, or..."

Nathen nodded. "Yes, though you should know she is usually in her bed or else walking around with an aid of a walker because of the MS."

"Oh, well, you should let her know that I'm coming over now and ask her if she is up for visitors. If not, it's totally fine. I can make myself scarce or not come at all. But otherwise, I don't mind. I'm happy for you that your mom is still around, though I'm sorry about her condition." He tossed him a bottle of sunblock, something he had to use anytime he went into the sun unless he wanted to become a lobster.

Cameron finished getting dressed, stepping out of the bedroom to leave Nathen privacy to call his mother and work on the sunscreen. He busied himself with summoning an Uber and finding an umbrella, for good measure. Their apartment building had a large awning outside that would offer a little protection. He peeked outside the window, relaxing a little and relieved to see that the predictable San Francisco fog was still blanketing the city.

"So, you can feel him now, huh?" Syn came out dressed for the gym.

Cameron blushed and grinned, nodding. *"Syn, I know this is moving way too fast. I know you're worried about me. But hey, he was your friend first,"* he teased.

"Don't even try to pull that crap." Syn waggled a finger good-naturedly, draining the rest of her coffee and a handful of supplements. *"Listen, I want you to be happy, as corny as that might sound. And I haven't felt you like this since Tommy. You need someone and Nathen is sweet. Strange to be sure, but sweet."*

"He's got Autism," Cameron explained.

"And what does that mean?" Syn paused, perching on the edge of the couch.

"Socially awkward, doesn't pick up on social cues, naïve, but also sweet, kind, nonmanipulative."

"Everything Frank wasn't," Syn mused.

"Also, likely, emotionally unavailable. People with Autism often live in their head and have trouble with empathy." Cameron shrugged sadly.

"Geezuz, Cam. You go from emotionally unavailable abusive to emotionally unavailable clueless?" She shot a glance over her shoulder at the bedroom.

Cameron shrugged. *"I don't know about that. Because unlike everyone, even you Syn, he can feel and sense my emotions. Things I thought I was filtering! And...and he wasn't freaked out..."* Cameron hadn't told Syn about what Frank had done to him. In fact, he had gone to the great lengths to try and keep up all pretense of being all right, though he knew she could sense something was wrong. *"It'll be okay. I like him, a lot. And I may be jumping in, but it's an eyes-wide-open scenario. Besides, I already promised to go meet his mom today."*

"You have got to be kidding. I told him to go slow with you. Didn't realize in gay-man land that meant drunk and banging on the first date and meeting the rents on the second."

Cameron laughed. *"We haven't banged yet. Just some good-natured bloodletting is all."* He batted his eyelashes at her and was rewarded with a throw pillow lob. He caught it and stood, holding his arms out, and Syn rolled her eyes and stepped into the hug.

"Speaking thereof, I'm not kidding. I know you never walked in on your mom banging someone, but fuck Cam. There I was last night working on this encryption and..." She shook her head emanating a shiver of equal parts arousal and disgust. *"Yeah, no part of me needs to be feeling* that *again!"*

Cameron assured her, *"All right, Syn. Will make sure to let you know to make yourself scarce when he's here."*

She stuck out her tongue. *"Cam, it went on for like an hour. Even with my best vibrator I couldn't get that kind of play."*

"Wait, what? An hour?"

"Last night, less this morning. But heh." She winked, humming "All night long" by Lionel Richie.

Cameron blushed deeply, having no idea that he had been in the throes of orgasm for so long. No wonder he had passed out, a fact that he didn't share with Syn. Instead, he retorted, *"Jealous? Vita could only wish to last so long?"*

He earned a middle finger as Syn grabbed her wallet and keys and headed out.

Cameron sat in the armchair and began rocking softly, allowing himself a moment to reflect. A lot had happened in a short amount of time. He had gone from a normal life as a psychologist, well, and also as a mind mage able to affect almost an entire city block, living with his lesbian best friend...to having an autistic vampire boyfriend who had brought him to an hour-long orgasm, who knew one of his deepest secrets and hadn't rejected him, who was created by a secret government agency, who enjoyed long walks on the beach, ice cream, and oh yeah fighting cyber terrorists in his spare time. Sure, all of that made perfect sense. Cameron was a little freaked out that Nathen could read him. Nobody had ever been able to read him before and while yes, this gave him a whole new level of empathy for those he had affected by his magic, it also made him concerned because what if Nathen learned more about him and was sickened by what he saw? What if he learned the other things Cameron wasn't all that proud of...some of the things Frank had made him do? Cameron took a deep breath. He would have to cross those bridges later. And who knew, maybe it would all still work out.

Chapter Nineteen

NATHEN

"What's the verdict? Am I coming with or no?" Cameron asked as Nathen came out of the bedroom.

Nathen fidgeted awkwardly clad in a large winter coat, hoodie, and baseball cap, with every place covered except his hands and the lower part of his face. Cameron ran back into the bedroom and returned, tossing him a pair of black leather gloves.

"We're good to go. Mom said that she would love to meet you. I told her I'm having sensory issues and to close the shades in the house," he said, pulling the leather gloves onto his hands and enjoying the soft smooth texture of the lining.

The two of them made their way to the lobby and hung out until Cameron saw the car arrive. They safely made their way into the car without incident, though Nathen was engulfed by Cameron's waves of concern even as he held an oversized umbrella above him as they dashed to the car. He had ordered an SUV so they would have the extra room in the back to potentially stay away from the sun. Cameron relaxed a little in the back of the SUV, holding Nathen close in the middle of the back seat as they rode through the city, over the Golden Gate, and to Marin.

"Okay, so you can travel during the day. But this is crazy. I'm not convinced we should be going out like this often." He ran his hand over Nathen's back, keeping him pulled down. "Heh, besides. I have vague memories of making out with you in the back of a car and can't chance it with the sun out." He gave a mental playful pout and rested his head against Nathen's.

Nathen agreed, "Yeah, this is a bit awkward, huh? Maybe we should wait till sundown." He sent a mental image of them driving down the highway toward the mountains listening to "Always" by Erasure and holding hands. Cameron was in the driver's seat, the sky was a clear blue and red with the sun setting behind them.

Though he had his head buried against Cameron's chest, Nathen sensed a soft push of embarrassment as Cameron admitted, "I actually never learned to drive. The driver's safety class was offered in my high school the year after I left for Leo's—the college I went to when I was sixteen. And, well, I've lived in the city ever since. Maybe this?" Cameron projected the same image with Nathen driving and a questioning feeling.

Nathen smiled. "I can actually drive, but it took me a while to get over my anxiety. It only happened after I stopped seeing the cars as people. Now I see them as objects on the road that I need to avoid."

"Is there anything else I should know about your mom? And what did you tell her? Am I still just a coworker...?" Cameron asked, hesitantly.

"Oh, no, I told her I met you through a mutual friend I work with, and said we started dating. She seemed elated." He grinned shyly, tucked into Cameron's chest and sent him an emotional hug punctuated with feelings of joy and contentment. "She used to be a lawyer, defended corporations against other corporations: patent suits, intellectual property disputes, contract breaches, that sort of stuff. She raised my brother and me by herself. We don't know much about our father. He didn't stay long after Jake was born."

Cameron took a deep breath, enveloping Nathen in returned positivity. "I hadn't realized you had caught on so quickly to the emotional hugs," he nuzzled Nathen's head. "At least we still have that connection. I learned long ago that I'm fueled by other people's emotions. I've tried a lot of things through the years and found that loud concerts are great for energizing me, symphonies are nice for being mellow, comedy shows are great for feeling upbeat, and it doesn't matter who is performing—though it's nice when I like the show too. The point is that I find myself being able to sit and absorb the crowd, just ride the wave that becomes communal."

They rode for a while in silence, each lost in their own thoughts, before Cameron asked with a pang of jealousy, "Tell me more about your family?"

"Well, my great-grandparents came from Europe, and in the 1840s they settled in California during the 49er's gold rush. They capitalized on the need of the time and opened a chain of stores that sold to the gold miners and their families. Things like household goods, staple foods, that sort of stuff. Along with good investments they bequeathed a lot down the family line. Unfortunately, a lot of it is now tied up in nonliquid assets, mostly empty land and our family home, which is a Victorian that was built in 1855."

Cameron smiled, listening to Nathen's description of his family. "That's so cool that you know so much going back so far. But what about your immediate family? And

I don't know my dad either! But...do you and your brother share the same dad? And you haven't told me much about your brother. Also, I'm curious... When did you tell your mom you were gay? Or did you have to?"

Nathen fidgeted in the seat when asked about coming out to his mother. "I told her when I was fifteen, and she seemed disappointed. Asked me about family, carrying on the line, the usual mother-guilt stuff. But I think she has come to accept it now. I think being awkward and naïve most of my life, and then coming out on top of that, kind of took her out of her comfort zone of what she expected from me. On the other hand, I was fixing people's Windows ME machines when I was five."

Cameron frowned at Nathen's description of his mother's reaction. "I guess I was lucky. Syn told me that she went to my mother and asked something akin to 'You know your son is gay, right?' To which my mom said, 'Of course! Want another cookie?' That had alleviated all of my concern with having that talk with her and I noticed whenever my mom talked about me 'meeting someone nice someday,' she was always gender neutral."

Nathen laughed and answered Cameron's previous question about his brother. "My brother, Jake, and I were born five years apart. We do have the same father, though I only have a vague recollection of a man that would come around and stay with us. He was always nice to me, but I don't remember seeing him past six. Jake and I are way different though. He's social, is into sports, going out, and has lots of friends. I guess he is into all the "normal" things that I never understood and thought people were strange for liking. I still don't get the point of small talk, for instance. I would rather cuddle or talk about substantive things. Talking about the weather and things like that is harder than discussing quantum effects in biology or politics for me."

Cameron seemed to become lost in his own reverie for a while, but finally said, "I don't know about quantum physics and the like, but maybe you can teach me."

Nathen got excited at the prospect of discussing quantum biology, chancing a quick glance up before ducking his head again, cuddling into Cameron's embrace. He spent the rest of the ride discussing the paradigm of consciousness, which Cameron enjoyed listening to, interjecting when the discussion turned to psychologists. It seemed like they could go on longer, but the driver pulled up the drive that led to a huge Victorian house painted mostly indigo and sky blue. Cameron ogled the home, which was easily a multi-million-dollar home nestled on a large lot and surrounded by forest. He whispered, dually impressed, "That is your home?" Cameron grinned. "I'd like to make out under that forest canopy. Are there any nice walking paths you'd like to show me sometime?"

Nathen's pants tightened. He had never done anything sexual with a boyfriend so close to his home and had a slight tinge of rebelliousness as he smirked. "There is a rock that I used to visit when I was younger. It's large enough to put a blanket on and use as an especially hard mattress. I used to lie on it and listen to the sounds of wildlife. There are also paths that I think were made by animals because there is a lot of scat and other things around. I used to play and follow the paths till mom saw in the news that someone spotted a mountain lion, and I was not allowed to go as deep. Of course, that was years ago."

A curious wave of calm surrounded him, chasing away the mild anxiety Nathen had about going into the woods. Cameron said, "First off, no animal is going to get near you. Did you notice Hansel and Gretel's reaction? And second, if they did, I would simply make them calm and they would go away. Ready to make a run for it?" Then Cameron stiffened and said with a deep breath, "Wait...Umm, heh...what's your last name? And...your mom's?"

Nathen laughed. "Oh, yeah! Her name is Andria Hale. She is actually nice but tends to do a lot of guilt tripping. I would get long talks about how I'm at fault for making her miss sleep because I was playing World of Warcraft at a friend's house too long and neglected to call her. 'I thought you died face down in a ditch...' is her usual go-to."

"I'm sorry to hear that. I've met parents like that. Sometimes a mom's insecurity can actually lead to their own child becoming anxious too. Okay, ready?"

Cameron readied the umbrella and together they made a run for it, from the winding driveway to the front of the home in a direct path. They entered a small antechamber that included a mudroom with coat and umbrella stand. Cameron secured the door to make sure no direct sunlight was coming in from outside before he shut the umbrella, and muttered, "Bad luck be damned."

The room opened into a large foyer with live ferns, lilies, and hanging baskets with fuchsia, easily resembling something out of *Better Homes and Gardens*. Off that foyer was one large curving stairwell leading up and a hallway leading deeper into the home.

"Your mom is in the dining room, and there's a housekeeper, Alice, upstairs cleaning the bedroom,"

Cameron told Nathen who paused for a moment, wondering how he knew that, but then reminded himself that Cameron could read minds. He thought momentarily how handy that was, saving him the time of searching the home for his mom, and led Cameron down the hall on the main floor, past several closed doors, to an elaborate dining room with a table that could extend to seat twelve, but was currently set up for only eight.

Ms. Hale was sitting and sipping tea, reading a poetry book, and waiting for her son and Cameron. Nathen could feel Cameron's nervousness and paused. He understood his own anxiety in social situations but had never even considered other people's tension. The concept of other people's emotions was so foreign for him that it took him a moment to process it before he stepped to Cameron and placed a steadying hand on his back, gently massaging. "It's okay, she's really nice," he assured him.

"She's in so much pain, but she's worked so hard to set all of this up to meet me," Cameron whispered, and Nathen could feel his tension, both a desire to impress and a myriad of other emotions that left Nathen feeling a little overwhelmed.

When they entered the ornate room with the Persian carpet over period marble flooring, Nathen saw that his mom had set out the fine bone china tea set that he had rarely seen used through his life and was touched that she would try to impress his new boyfriend. She had honored his request and made sure all the shutters and blinds were closed in rooms that he might be entering, though he knew she would have much rather showed off her meticulous garden that could be seen from the many windows across one wall of the dining room.

"You need to introduce us," Cameron prompted quietly, smiling at her as they entered.

Ms. Hale remained sitting, her head held high, setting down her book as if she had only been disturbed. Nathen beamed from his mom to Cameron, "Mom, this is Cameron, Cameron, this is Andria. You didn't have to make tea. I wanted to check in and show you I am actually alive." He laughed and sat down at the table. Picking up a biscotto, Nathen poured himself a cup of tea, brought it to his nose and inhaled the rich Earl Grey before adding a teaspoon of honey, asking, "Jake's not home yet?" Before she could answer he went on, "Oh, and thanks for closing the shades. The light has been bugging me lately."

Cameron approached on the opposite side and reached his hand out, "Ms. Hale, it's very good to meet you. Thank you for inviting me over."

Nathen's mother accepted the handshake. Seeming used to being bombarded by random questions and pieces of information, she chose to welcome Cameron first before addressing her son's tangent. "Cameron, it's good to meet you too. Please, join us." She threw Nathen a long-suffering look. "No, your brother has his own schedule and comes and goes. It's posted in the kitchen and upstairs if you ever want to check in about where he might be."

Nathen remembered that his mother preferred to have paper copies of schedules posted throughout the house, though he knew that electronic schedules were more efficient and didn't require someone to come home to check on the wall. He wondered if his mother was being passive aggressive by reminding him of the paper schedules that he had known about his entire life but sipped his tea without saying anything.

Cameron sat down opposite Nathen, and he could tell he was feeling much more nervous than he wanted to. Nathen could actually feel when Cameron reigned in his own emotions and suddenly was hit with another curious wave of calm.

Ms. Hale said, "So, Cameron, tell me about yourself while my son pours *you* a cup, too." She looked pointedly at Nathen and then back congenially at Cameron.

Cameron swallowed. "Well," he started slowly, "I have to admit I'm a little nervous, Ms. Hale. I've never met a boyfriend's parents before, as I haven't been in many relationships. I'm a psychologist and work at the JP Agency in San Francisco."

Cameron seemed to quickly add, "I was born and raised south of San Diego, but had the opportunity to attend Leo's Creek College and got my undergrad in three years, skipped the master's degree, and got my doctorate in three years, graduating about a year ago and was just licensed."

"I've heard of Leo's Creek," Ms. Hale said. "That's a good college. For fifteen-sixteen-year-olds, right?"

Cameron nodded. "I went when I was sixteen, and I've been living in San Francisco with my best friend from high school since grad school."

He paused when Nathen pushed a cup across the table to him and added honey to the bitter tea.

"That is a great accomplishment, Cameron. So, is your family still back in San Diego?" Ms. Hale asked.

Nathen frowned, confused at the feeling of Cameron bristle. "No, ma'am. I was an only child, raised by a single mom and she died while I was in school. So, it's just me and my best friend, and work family, of course."

Nathen struggled for a moment. He knew that when you hear about someone's parent's death, you were expected to say something, but he also had apprehension about his own mother's death. This led him to a curious state of empathy for Cameron. "I am sorry to hear about your mom." He shot Cameron a sad look.

He knew that if his mom had died at an early age, he would have been lost. She had done so much for him growing up. The more he thought about it, the sadder he got and he projected an empathetic hug to Cameron through their link. Cameron seemed to withdraw from this, and so Nathen didn't actually get confirmation of any other emotion returned. It was as if he hugged a void. This had the effect of confusing him further and his mind went blank before he visually shook his head to snap out of it. He couldn't understand what was going on and stared at Cameron who seemed to be focused on his mom.

"Yes," Ms. Hale was saying, "So." She turned to Nathen to include him in the conversation. "How did you two meet?"

Nathen gave a nervous smile. He knew he was a bad liar but telling her about the Vampire thing was not going to happen anytime soon. He opted for the truth, "I met him through work; a mutual friend introduced us."

Cameron picked up on Nathen's nervousness and saved him, "Syn, my best friend from high school, moved out to join me at Leo's the year after I started. She has been working in the tech industry since, though don't ask me what they do." He laughed, shaking his head. "So not my strong suit. I'm in awe of both Nathen and Syn. Syn had Nathen over for a nerdy pow-wow on a work assignment and ordered pizza for us. I had planned on hiding in the bedroom all night, but Nathen and I got to talking and actually seemed to hit it off." He smiled genuinely at Nathen. "And then we went on a couple of dates and learned that we have a lot in common. We both like to cook, and talk about philosophy, and are both interested in staying active. You have a very impressive son, Ms. Hale."

Nathen's mother smiled and seemed appeased. She affectionately patted Nathen's hand. "We've always thought so."

Nathen smiled at his mom, but his emotions belied his expression. They were a mix of sentimental memories, joy at what she had said, and a mix of sadness, "Thanks, Mom...I always thought I was 'special' too." He air quoted and laughed at himself. "Cameron is a gifted psychologist. You remember the research I was doing on consciousness and Carl Jung? I think Cameron would like that. I wrote a bunch about it on my blog. Probably too much actually, but it was so interesting."

Cameron blushed, correcting, "I can't say that I'm a gifted psychologist. I'm incredibly interested in testing and teaching. It's almost as if your son can read my mind, sometimes."

Ms. Hale shifted, and said, "Well, I'm certain you two boys have something more important to do than sit with an old woman and drink tea. I have my book to finish anyway. So off with you."

Cameron rose immediately. "Thank you for the tea, Ms. Hale. I definitely appreciated the opportunity to meet Nathen's mother." He picked up both his and Nathen's cups, but set them down with a small bow when she waved him off.

Nathen rose and said, "I'm going to show Cameron around a bit and then we have some work to do. A project I am working on requires traveling around the city."

Ms. Hale nodded. "Sure, let me know when you are done for the night so I know you are all right."

Nathen smiled. "Deal."

Chapter Twenty

CAMERON

Cameron let out a deep sigh of relief as Nathen led him out of the dining room and began showing him around the first floor. He was saying something about his grandparents and fond memories of them through his childhood, but Cameron was inwardly distracted with thoughts of his own mother, her death, his childhood. He wondered at the prim and proper Ms. Hale and how it must have been like for Nathen growing up in this museum quality home. Nathen was telling him about when his grandparents had died when he was in his early teens, and how his grandmother had been the matriarch and commanded the affairs of the home until her death. Her will had instructed that there be a requirement for the upkeep of the home and for it to be kept in the family. It also set aside one room designated as a sort of historical shrine to the roots of their family in America, which Nathen led Cameron to on the second floor.

"Nathen, this is really awesome! It must be cool to have such a tie to your heritage," Cameron said, forcing himself into the moment as he kissed Nathen's cheek and walked around the small room, taking in the antiquity. Beyond his abuela, he didn't know anything about his great grandparents, their origins, or his "father's" side of the family at all. He wondered what it would be like to grow up with such strong family ties. Perhaps grounding? Perhaps stifling? There was something to be said for anonymity. "This is such an amazing home. It had to have been great to grow up here," he said, looking around.

Nathen shrugged. "I never thought about it much. I mean, it's nice to have this house, but the heritage part was never a huge draw for me. It's nice to know where you came from, but I think knowing where you are going is something that appeals more to me. The house was large enough for us to live here but having to keep it in the condition it is in was not so fun. I couldn't go into certain areas, or if I did, I had to be supervised to make sure to not spill or touch anything. I spent a lot of time in my room playing computer games. Or else outside in the woods."

Thinking about a young, and likely rambunctious, Nathen being scolded or oppressed by supervision of things off limits in his own home-made Cameron sad for him. He reflected on how different their upbringings must have been and how very different their mothers were. He allowed himself a few seconds to reflect on how his mom might greet a new boyfriend of his. She would have insisted on a big hug and instead of bitter tea; she would have invited him for Mexican cocoa and homemade pastries. He quickly shut down that line of thought as feelings of melancholic grief threatened to overwhelm. It was interesting, Cameron reflected, seeing a person's origins.

Nathen smiled and closed the door. "Speaking of my room, that is next on our grand tour of Hale Manor," he said in an almost mocking tone and proceeded up the hall. He pointed at a closed door at the end of the hall on the left wall, "That's Jake's room and next to it is the bathroom." He then turned and gestured to the other door at the end of the hall, "That's Mom's." He walked up to a door in the center, gesturing across the hall, "That's Alice's. She's the maid. And this, is mine," he said with a grand gesture, extending his arm, laughing, "Please ladies and gentlemen, we're in a rush."

Nathen's room was sparse with a large king-sized bed, a few renaissance prints including a picture of the School of Athens on one wall on the left, and a large print of the Vitruvian Man by Leonardo da Vinci hanging right on the opposite wall as one walks in. Beyond it, on the right was a large desk with three monitors, a large black keyboard, mouse, and a full tower computer case on the floor with wires running out of it. The windows above the desk were shuttered with blinds, so the only illumination came from an overhead light. Nathen closed the door. "This is where the magic happens."

Cameron tried to smile at Nathen's attempts at levity, but just wanted to hug him. It had to have been difficult being so different and yet having such expectations from his mother in such a cold home. He sensed the discomfort coming from Nathen who was trying so hard to hide that he really wasn't at home in this house. Cameron looked around the sparse room, was surprised that Nathen and his own rooms were both so minimal, and that both had large beds. Nathen had wall decorations, but otherwise neither of their rooms was overly personal. In a person's childhood bedroom, they usually had relics of their life: toys, trophies or certificates, pictures, something suggestive of the life they had lived and what led them to who they are now. Cameron had packed up a lot of his stuff and sent it ahead of him to college, giving more to Syn before he left to go to college.

Occasionally over the years, he wondered at what he had left behind that could have been used to hunt him, but as the years ticked by with no threat he had let go of his fears a bit, holding only onto the overarching paranoia that having to steal away like a thief in the night could bring. Once in college, he had given away or left behind many items, only keeping a few mementos over the years. He still had a few of Tommy's tee shirts and a few keepsakes from his mom tucked away in a bottom drawer. Syn generally bought him things for the kitchen or clothes. He wondered what kind of gifts Ms. Hale gave and how distant a mother she must have been. Though it was obvious to him from what he read in her that she loved her son very much. Perhaps she was not the best at always being able to show it?

Cameron smiled and entered as instructed, looking around the neat and dust-free room. Alice's doing, undoubtedly. He turned back to Nathen. "It's a great room. Seems like you and I may have a few other things in common."

Nathen walked up to the computer and touched a few keys, which turned on the screens mounted onto a single large stand. He then sat on the bed. "Oh?" he asked, intrigued.

Cameron stood, not knowing where to sit. Seeing Nathen so nonchalantly on the bed sent a brief flash of arousal through him. He quickly slid onto the desk chair, turning to face Nathen. "Huge bed, not a lot of stuff—" he shrugged and laughed, gesturing to the window for one more similarity "—black out blinds."

Cameron could feel Nathen's emotions switched to confusion when he sat in the chair. He patted at a spot on the bed next to him. "Did you want to sit on the bed? I locked the door, so no one will be barging in here. I can also take you on a tour outside. We have a few fruiting trees, an old sour cherry tree, a mulberry tree, and a few peach trees." He grinned at mentioning what had once been the peach orchard.

Now, awash with arousal, Cameron glanced nervously at the door and then shyly slid out of the chair and onto the bed beside Nathen. "The tour will need to wait a few hours," he reminded him as it was only noonish. "And your mother is downstairs with Alice. They're actually out on the patio enjoying the day. She plans to take her lunch out there. Has suggested that Alice bring us some sandwiches...which I've taken the liberty of cancelling from Alice's mind. I hope that's okay. I mean...I'm not hungry." He glanced at the floor, smiling sheepishly and turned his gaze sideways to Nathen.

Nathen nodded. "Yeah, I forgot. The sun..." He laughed. "It's going to take a while for me to remember that sun equals bad now. Before, my mother would go on about how I'm always locked inside the room, and I needed to get some sun. I'm not that hungry either. What did you want to do while we wait? I can bring up the chat channel Syn and I usually hang out in, or maybe we can play a game?" he paused thinking over something, "Or...um...we can cuddle or something? I sensed your emotions earlier."

Cameron blushed, having not felt a level of arousal from Nathen. "My first instinct is to totally make out with you. But I can tell I got the wrong idea. You locking the door, asking me to sit on the bed..." He shook his head, laughing. "The last time I was in a boyfriend's room, we barely came up for air. But, then, we had his house to ourselves for that spring break. Umm, we could play a game if you like. I don't know about chat channels, but I also know that you might need to do some prep before we go check out to these places Syn wants us to see tonight? I can always play on my phone."

At the mention of arousal, Nathen shifted, feeling the curious growing symbiotic link that sent small jolts of sensation through him and he adjusted slightly. "Well, we can cuddle if you want, or, umm, something else."

Cameron could read that Nathen was unsure of how he should proceed. There was hesitation and a mild sense of anxiety of the unknown. He grinned. "This is a struggle for me too. On the one hand, I did mention not wanting to leave the bed all day. And here we are, in another bed." He laughed nervously and stole another glance at Nathen, chewing on his lower lip. "But on the other, I don't want to dishonor your mom who is right downstairs. But, she's down there and has no intention of braving the stairs until after dinner unless she has to...so that kind of leaves us alone up here. I can sense your anxiety but don't know what it's from. And I don't want to probe, so can you tell me?"

Nathen smiled nervously. "I have never had anyone but friends and family in my room, and I'm not sure what I'm supposed to do with a boyfriend. I want to do something sexual, but not sure that it would be proper or if you would be okay with it."

"It would definitely not be proper, especially considering what I read about your mother. She seems to prize convention, but as you said, you threw that out the window a long time ago just by the nature of who you are. And she's happy that you're happy. I saw that too. Oh...and she thinks we're doing a lot more than we're doing right now already," he cut off the connection with

Ms. Hale and shivered wondering where she had come up with that image he wasn't going to share with Nathen.

"As for me being okay with it, there's my struggle. Oh god." Cameron fell back on the bed with a sigh, staring at the ceiling. "I've actually never been sooo turned on by anyone in my life. You are hands down the best lover I've ever had. Best kisser...best"—the memory of watching Nathen going down on him flashed to mind and he shared it with Nathen—"at other things. So as to being okay with it, let's make a pact right now—I am always okay with it. I love cuddling in private and public displays of affection and need a boyfriend who likes both too. Please, feel free to always touch me, or whatever. My first ex was like that and it was the way I thought it should always be," he shrugged, not wanting to remember how Frank had been in their relationship. "I've also never been able to communicate mentally with anyone but Syn. And to be able to share with you last night was crazy thrilling. And even though it takes me a long, long time sometimes to finish, I'm pretty sure that's my hang-up about feeling relaxed. And I never had a problem stopping when my partner was done and just, you know, waiting till my erection went away. So, when you're done, tell me that too. Though, seems I'm DONE when you bite me." He chuckled at the memory, having never had that experience either. "As for biting me, I don't have control over my...heh...broadcasting when you do. And, well, your Mom and Alice are probably too close and would be hit when I mentally lost control. Which, in my defense, is all your fault," he teased. Leaning up on his elbows, he studied Nathen, "I would be totally down with making out with you until both of us needed a year supply of ChapStick," he gave a lopsided grin. "But, as you put it, I don't know if you'd be okay with it... This is your room. So, your rules."

Nathen smiled, stood, and pulled back the covers, gesturing for Cameron to crawl in. "Let's cuddle and see where it goes from there."

Cameron grinned and nodded, kicking off his shoes and crawling into the bed. He turned to see that Nathen had taken off all of his clothes and was naked in bed. Renewed waves of arousal washed over Cameron, "Cuddle, huh?" he asked with his eyes wide.

Nathen turned and wrapped his legs and arms around Cameron, giving him a soft kiss. "If my mother knocks, would you mind if I dressed you very quickly?"

Being pulled into Nathen's embrace, Cameron laughed. "I'm not even undressed yet," he whispered, kissing Nathen again and stroking his hair. "And you worry too much. I can do a couple of things. One, I can plant the suggestion that they stay down there all day and two I can hear them coming well before they get up the stairs. Though, being dressed by you would be a unique experience. I think—" he stretched out under the covers "—maybe being undressed by you would be interesting too?" Cameron pulled the now naked Nathen atop him, smiling at the clothing reversal from the morning when he was naked. He ran his hands slowly down Nathen's back, cupping his ass cheek and kneading gently.

Waves of arousal emanated from Nathen and his pupils dilated as a result. His hands traced Cameron's body down to his khakis and he started to unbutton his shirt. Nathen crawled backward under the covers and did the same with his pants, pulling them off his legs followed by his underwear. Cameron watched as Nathen undressed him, smiling and accommodating as needed. Nathen flattened against the bed and took Cameron's member in his mouth, tracing the tip with his tongue. He cupped and gently squeezed his jewels, while letting Cameron's cock grow and expand inside his mouth.

Cameron gasped when Nathen began to play with his member, instantly becoming fully erect. He watched Nathen, gently running his fingers through his hair and sending a wave of sensual energy to him. This was one of the most erotic scenes that Cameron enjoyed, though his eyes fluttered closed with the sensation. After a while, he instructed, "Come here," pulling Nathen up and cupping his face. He searched his eyes before kissing him, at first softly but then more intensely as he fell under the spell of Nathen's kiss. Nathen returned the kiss, tasting Cameron while gingerly swirling his tongue against his. His hands ran up and down his sides, stopping to fondle his length. "Tell me what other things you enjoy," Cameron asked, his entire body surrendering to the power of Nathen's kiss. Cameron was vaguely aware that Nathen's kiss was affecting him, but he gave in willingly and with increased desire.

"I want to feel you inside me," Nathen whispered.

"Wow...that seems to be your favorite...Is that something you are used to doing, all the time? Or, something you want to do right now?" He pulled away to stare up at Nathen with adoration, playing his fingers down over his neck and shoulder.

Nathen shrugged, smiling. "Whenever the muse calls. I don't know if it's my 'favorite,' but that is when I feel the most aroused and intimate with my partner. Something about having the bodies pressed against each other and both feeling intense pleasure, or a near balance of pleasure and pain. What is your favorite thing to do?"

Smiling wickedly, Cameron pulled Nathen back down, kissing him without pretense and rolling over so that he was on top, his weight obligingly pinning Nathen into place. He pulled back for a moment, looked up into the ceiling concentrating as he planted thoughts into the minds downstairs. "We won't be disturbed for the rest of the day." He resumed kissing Nathen before biting his neck playfully. "I like all kinds of things, but this is good, if you want it? Where's your supplies?" Cameron asked as he reached down to playfully stroke Nathen's hardened length.

Nathen shook his head. "Umm...I've only had intimate contact with my ex and that was in his dorm. No lube or condoms here, though I can't actually get any STDs anymore...for long. And no need to worry about getting pregnant." He winked.

Cameron pulled away and chewed on his lip thoughtfully, concentrating again. "I have a condom," he offered a small smile. "And though totally contraindicated we could use the Vaseline in your mother's bathroom or the olive oil Alice cooks with, but those are terrible with condoms." Groaning with desire, he kissed Nathen again. "I don't have anything, I've been tested. But I've never... purposely...had sex without a condom. Regardless, we definitely need something to lubricate with. Unless you don't want to do it?"

Nathen thought for a moment, then said, "Give me a second." Cameron fell over. A rush of air accompanied a blur of Nathen doing something in the middle of the room for a second. Then the door opened, the blur passed through, and then almost instantly closed, and Nathen was back in the bed beside him with a huge bottle of olive oil, "I have always wanted to try this. People in ancient Greece used olive oil as lubricant as well!"

Cameron laughed, amazed by how different his life had changed in the span of only two days. "Wow," he breathed, reaching out to pull Nathen to him again with feelings of both absolute desire and mild amusement as he accepted the bottle of olive oil. It wasn't something to use because any oil-based lube broke down the condom, but he'd try it. He reached over the side of the bed where his pants had landed and pulled out his wallet and the condom within. Unable to get enough of Nathen's kiss, Cameron caught his head and placed a kiss softly over his lips before rolling the latex down his length.

Nathen reached for the torn T-shirt he had tossed on the bed and put it under himself in case the oil ran as Cameron proceeded to spread his legs wide apart to survey him. He locked eyes with Nathen, exuding feelings of desire with waves of calm. It was cheating, Cameron knew. Normally he relaxed his partner with a long make-out session, massages, or giving head until his partner had reached a point where he was ready for penetration, but Nathen seemed so eager, which in turn sent waves of need through Cameron. This emotional link was powerful, distracting, and somehow the most intimate thing Cameron had ever experienced. He slowly took Nathen in, his muscular arms, incredibly well-toned chest and abs that belonged in a magazine. Nathen was well endowed as well, trimmed and erect. Cameron spent a moment admiring that area of him, sending feelings of sensual appreciation to Nathen to remove any self-consciousness though excitement and embarrassment filtered through from him.

"You are so beautiful," he whispered, caressing Nathen mentally before allowing his gaze to move farther south to Nathen's awaiting opening. *This* was actually one of the most arousing things for Cameron, the moment just before his lover opened to him. A shiver of excitement coursed through him, which he shared, tempering it with mental brushes to relax. He could feel Nathen's anticipation and smirked as he squirmed under him. Cameron gently massaged Nathen's inner thighs and he looked back up to Nathen's eyes, fueled by Nathen's own desire.

Taking the bottle of olive oil in hand, Cameron shook his head slightly that he was even considering using it but smiled at the new experience for both of them. He poured a little into his hand and looked back at Nathen as he slowly stroked the oil over his throbbing cock, coating liberally. He rubbed the rest against Nathen's opening and positioned himself, slowly pushing forward while guiding himself with one hand. "Do you know the squeeze technique to relax your sphincter?"

At the question, there was a mild sense of confusion, to which Nathen shortly thought, *"No, what is that?"*

Cameron smiled softly, pausing and leaning down to kiss Nathen quickly before kneeling back. "I would say first breathe, but I'm not sure that matters for you. But it can't hurt. Deep breaths as you squeeze yourself closed as hard as you can, all the muscles internally and externally. I'm going to count for you to thirty and then release the hold and I'll enter slowly. When I feel you're in pain again I'm going to stop, and we'll do it again. Okay? It's an old dancer's technique to be more fluid in movement one needs to be thoroughly relaxed, but this will hopefully help negate the pain. Okay? Squeeze now, and I'll count."

Nathen listened and did as Cameron described holding on to his arm with his left hand, his right caressing Cameron's thigh. Cameron counted slowly in his mind, feeling Nathen tighten against him. The technique had been taught to him by his ex, who was a dancer and later he learned about progressive muscle relaxation for the entire body. While the sphincter relaxation wasn't a technique that had worked for him, personally, though he did only try it on that one occasion, it had worked for others. He knew that his lovers usually had minor pain, but also knew that with his size he could cause damage if not careful, and no matter what Nathen said about being able to regenerate, he struggled with the idea of causing damage like that. That feeling was also complicated by the fact that he could read in Nathen that he enjoyed the sensation. When Nathen relaxed, Cameron pushed forward into him, keeping his hand firmly wrapped around the middle of his cock. He studied Nathen's reactions, both physically and emotionally while keeping his own arousal and pleasure in check.

Cameron could feel in Nathen as the sharp pain gave way to the sense of pleasure when it hit him, and all the sensations became a blur. He read that to Nathen the pleasure and pain circled each other, together becoming momentarily greater than each on its own. A mental pang from Nathen swept over him and he paused to allow Nathen to acclimate to his size, momentarily paralyzed by the symbiotic link. In the past, he could read his partner's joy and discomfort, but not actually feel it. The pain that Nathen seemed to embrace was exactly what Cameron feared and rejected in himself. But Nathen's enjoyment of it was compelling. He knew that being penetrated was incredibly pleasurable for his partner but had never experienced it like this before. The emotional waves joined with the physical sensation of Nathen's tight hole pulsing and widening to welcome him, was a sensation he delved into, sharing in turn with Nathen. Through this, Cameron held fast to his own sense of responsibility and duty to his partner. He stroked himself a few times to get more of the oil to Nathen's awaiting channel. As Nathen relaxed, he noted that Nathen was in a different mind space, semi aware and focused on the sensation and the passion. He put his hands behind Cameron holding on to his cheeks and insistently pulled him forward.

Cameron gasped at Nathen's demand and the desire washing over him from Nathen spurred him. He obeyed Nathen's commands and entered, though slower than he could feel Nathen wanting. He kept his hand halfway up his shaft and when it hit Nathen, and he was pulled farther in, he relaxed his hand slightly to allow his hold to slip down to the base, giving Nathen more than half of his length. He paused again, knowing that Nathen had said he thought he could take all of him, but also knowing that was often wishful thinking. Cameron pulled out slowly, before slipping back in to the point where he had been before, his hand still securely in place as he observed Nathen, spreading a series of small kisses across his chest.

A stifled moan bubbled out of him as Nathen clawed Cameron to him and passionately kissed his lover, enjoying how every shift in their position changed the sensation inside. Cameron received the impression from Nathen, a loud wordless demand to move faster, punctuated almost immediately by an apologetic, *"...though I think I'll need to...practice... before I can take you fully."*

Falling again as the magic of Nathen's kiss encompassed Cameron when their tongues touched. He almost lost hold of himself and had to fight to remain in control. Keeping one hand between them and leaning on his elbow in order to keep from crushing Nathen, he kissed him deeply as he began to pull out slowly again, inch by inch, and return with practiced patience threatened by the intoxicating effect of Nathen's kiss and the maddening distraction of their joined emotions. Cameron began to increase his speed, leaning back up so he could stare down into his eyes, communicating a million pieces of emotional information that transcended words or even thoughts. Adoration, intimacy, desire, love on a level he had never known and was barely scratching the surface of understanding. His speed increased to match Nathen's silent requests, returning to kiss him again.

Nathen drug Cameron back down to his awaiting lips and began to moan louder, their lips locked against each other, the only thing that was muffling the sound. Cameron's cock-massaging from within filtered pleasure through Nathen which he projected to Cameron as fast as it came. In danger of being overwhelmed, Nathen's canines started to instinctively extend, and the pain and pleasure were blinding his rational thought. "Can I bite you?" he asked in a guttural whimper.

Swirling from Nathen, the emotions of yearning and rapture hit Cameron as he swam through the ecstasy of passion, better than any concert or crowd that he had empathetically surfed, Cameron received the request and almost immediately begged for Nathen to grant it. Sense took over and instead he pulled away, sending Nathen a caution as he slowed for a moment. He closed his eyes, struggling to focus on not losing rhythm while also sending the immediate, if somewhat forceful command to the minds downstairs to *sleep*. Growling as they drifted off, he dismissed them and focused solely on Nathen, kissing him again around his canines, dipping his tongue between them as he began to speed up, this time allowing himself to relax into the kiss, into the new world that Nathen had showed him. When he was once again on the verge of climax, he pulled away and presented his throat desperately searching for the new highs that only Nathen could bring.

Cameron exposing his neck was the final straw, and as Nathen began to come he bit deeply into Cameron, drinking in his essence with fervor. Nathen's hands forcefully pulled him deeper, the condom ripping as Cameron let loose. Cameron shuddered, falling fully onto Nathen and losing hold of his cock and reason as Nathen's bite sank into his flesh. Though in the very back part of his mind where that reason still lived he knew he should be pulling away because he felt the condom tear, but his hands were now wrapped around Nathen, one pulling his head deeper into his throat as the other had snaked around his back to pull him closer. All thoughts were lost on the torrent of pleasure as his hips continued to pound harder than Cameron had ever considered thrusting, spurred on by Nathen's fingers digging into his flesh and pulling him deeper. He was also vaguely aware of loud groans of passion and elation escaping him, something he always bit off to keep as quiet as possible, now deafening. Nathen's waves of climax engulfed him, the physical release from his body and the sensual, almost spiritual release that his own blood granted. Their connection renewed didn't allow them to know where one began and the other ended and the amplified feelings of euphoria, pain, pleasure and sated thirst bounced between them making each feel alive in a way that neither of them had ever imagined.

The bliss that Nathen's bite granted kept Cameron locked at the peak of orgasm and his body continued to drive into Nathen's with no refractory allowed. Cameron sent another stream deep into Nathen, but his body was not capable of stopping banging into Nathen, now almost exquisitely painfully. Part of him knew he could continue this forever, but then he began to fall again, the blackened tunnel. *"Nathen,"* he thought weakly, spent in every way, but unable and unwilling to stop.

As Cameron began to get weaker as the loss of blood, sexual release, and the magic of his bite were starting to overwhelm him, Nathen reluctantly let go, licking the wound closed. Kissing Cameron lightly, Nathen held him as he slowly collapsed from exhaustion, shaking off almost passing out again, but only barely. He held Nathen while he pulled out slowly, painfully; gasping for breath through parted lips and rested his head on Nathen's blood-soaked chest. *"Condom broke,"* he thought with mild apology as they knew that the olive oil would likely do that. He remained like that for a long time, holding onto Nathen weakly with no real ability or motivation to move. After his breath returned to something resembling normal, Cameron began to take stock of the state he was in. He rolled over and pulled off the pieces of condom, making sure they were all there, holding them briefly before setting them on the bed amidst the rest of the scene of the crime. The shirt that Nathen had put beneath him may have indeed caught a little of the oil, but it was nowhere to be found now and there was a large oil and semen stain that remained behind as evidence.

Cameron sensed that Nathen was energized, like he could run a marathon, or fly. The news about the condom didn't have any emotional impact, though Nathen sent back, *"It's okay. Oh! Hey! We can talk again!"*

Cameron nodded, elated but spent. *"Guess it's the blood. It's strange...I've never had sex without protection."* The unwanted image of the terrible night only a few months back flashed through his mind and was quickly dismissed. *"I've been tested a dozen times, so I know I'm okay. And, I guess it's okay to do it without, if you want? I don't know. It seems strange."*

"My ex and I usually used condoms, but sometimes if we were out we didn't. But we were monogamous," Nathen offered.

Cameron thought for a while, figuring that this should be something revisited in the future. He couldn't analyze what it was like without a condom because it happened when he was so enthralled with what Nathen was doing to him. A lot of guys insisted it was better because of the stimulation, so that was intriguing to Cameron. He glanced over with a half grin, saying playfully, *"So...that's your idea of cuddling, huh?"*

Nathen laughed. *"Well, we could cuddle now, no?"* He shifted and found his ripped T-shirt had ridden up to his shoulder, pulled it free and used it to wipe the blood covering his chest.

Cameron laughed weakly. Unable to do much more than cuddle, he gathered Nathen to him and kissed his head. *"My goodness...I...I didn't hurt you did I?"*

Nathen shook his head, wrapping his arm around Cameron, *"I still feel you inside me, but it does not hurt. It's just noticeable."*

Cameron bit his lip and nodded, relieved that he hadn't hurt Nathen, but also trying to stave off memories of his complete lack of control. After a time, he asked wearily, *"Well... Since I can sense you are up, could you do a couple things and then come back to bed? I need you to go make sure that your mother and Alice didn't spill anything. I sort of put them to sleep so they wouldn't...hear or feel anything. Though their collective dreams...They were both sitting and reading. Perhaps clean up and make it look like they both drifted off? I can keep them asleep for a while, but...it's already been almost an hour. So... I'll put the suggestion that they should still not come upstairs. Then, after I can move maybe in a bit we could shower?"*

"Sure, I can clean up and make it look like they fell asleep." Nathen slipped out of bed and was gone.

*

As Nathen left, Cameron started overthinking, a trait he was never fond of in himself but kept him out of trouble for the most part. He had completely lost control, but even more to his dismay, he had welcomed it, plunged in with abandon. But *why?* He couldn't understand it. In the span of two days he had gone from all but swearing off men for life to using olive oil for god's sake and riding bareback with a vampire. Before, he had been so careful about his partner, health, hygiene, control... A friend of his who worked with sex offenders had once told him that everything comes down to power and control. That everybody is searching for control over themselves, and those who do not have control over themselves take control from the external: their environments for neat freaks, to other people for individuals in domestic violence relationships or many sex offenders (barring the indigent guy who pees on the sidewalk and picks up an Indecent Exposure conviction, or other such cases). Cameron had spent a lot of time analyzing that theory. He realized that he likely had trouble with orgasms because he didn't want to lose control. Tommy had gotten bored with him taking so long and they had fallen into a habit of not minding that he didn't finish. With Frank, he didn't even try to put up pretense, if it happened it happened but he didn't try. How could Nathen have won him over so quickly, so effortlessly? A little voice in the back of his mind reminded him he was being drugged each time he kissed Nathen and like heroin addicts, he kept going back for more. And the scary thing was that was wholeheartedly true and Cameron didn't *care*. He wanted this, wanted Nathen. It wasn't just his kiss, or bite, it was the way he saw the world and his kindness. Nathen couldn't hurt anyone, not like Cameron could. It made him vulnerable, sweet.

To Cameron it seemed like Nathen had been gone only a few moments as Nathen materialized sitting on the edge of the bed, smiling and leaning forward to kiss him before handing over a wad of paper towels and water. *"Did you shower without me?"* he asked, looking at Nathen fully clothed and accepted the water, which he drank. He used the paper towels to get the worst of what was all over his chest, belly, and lap, but knew it was a losing battle, especially with the sheer amount of blood splatter all over him and the bed. He laughed, shaking his head and fell back against the pillows again.

Nathen shook his head. *"Oh, no, I wiped it off on my shirt. I'll need to burn it or something. Do not need vampire blood in the dumpster. Might turn the alley cats or rats into...something...Zombcats? Vamprats? Do those exist?"* he laughed, getting back into bed and reaching to hug Cameron as waves of contentment and peace moved through him.

Cameron reached out with his mind, gently rousing Alice first. She was embarrassed that she had fallen asleep, but happy that Ms. Hale hadn't noticed. She busied herself in the kitchen while Ms. Hale slept. He renewed the suggestion to stay downstairs while Nathen was busy divesting himself of clothing again and then welcomed him with an embrace. While he had expected this while still dressed, Cameron was definitely not complaining. He accepted the contentment and mentally pulled it around himself for a time. Nathen played his fingers through Cameron's ginger chest curls and after a while Cameron couldn't help but ask, *"So, I know we talked about this already, and I kind of have no right to ask, but, if we're going to continue to do what we just did, without protection and all...can I ask that you only actually bite me? I know you can't get diseases, or if you do, you can do something about that, but I can't..."* He had a sense of embarrassment and concern, tinged ever so slightly with jealousy.

Nathen smiled. *"Of course, I wouldn't bite anyone regardless of you asking me. Not just because of the concern of getting disease, but because of how intimate it is. Though, I worry that if I keep drinking your blood, you will become anemic. Maybe we need to figure out how to help you stay healthy if I am to feed on you?"*

Staying healthy was certainly on his mind, but anemia hadn't been until Nathen brought it up. Cameron made a mental note to snag a bottle of iron pills and spinach from Trader Joes. He tried to hide his feelings of happiness when Nathen promised to bite only him, but since Nathen could see through him, that was unsuccessful. He held Nathen, gently running his fingers through his hair. *"So, well, that was insanely good."* He laughed lightly, kissing the top of Nathen's head. *"You don't think this is moving too fast, right?"*

Nathen buried himself in Cameron, taking in his smell and emotions. *"I don't know if we're going too fast or not."* He laughed. *"Seems like we're progressing at the right speed to me. What do you think? I mean...maybe the vampire magic is speeding it up? I don't know."*

"Maybe. But my mom always told me to trust my instincts—about people, situations, everything. And this feels right on so many levels." Cameron turned on his side so he could wrap himself around Nathen, twining legs, hugging him and nuzzling his face in his hair. *"While being bitten is unimaginably amazing, and I know you said your kiss influences me, and, well, turns out you're a phenomenal lover,"* he chuckled with the memories of Nathen's kiss, his touch, his tongue circling his... *"I love the way you see things. You are so forthright, but also care about people. And you're so smart! I know I'm the one with the doctorate, but I often thought I probably faked my way through school. You know so much about all kinds of cool stuff. And there's something about your knowledge of technology. Do you know, I got hard when you talked about those whatever pins you keep in your wallet for sim cards? I don't even know what any of that means! And yeah, being a vampire you can..."* Cameron grew quiet, intense, a wave of deeply hidden fear bubbled up for a moment, before he shook it off *"...protect me physically, it's like Syn is able to protect us with her knowledge of technology. You can do that too. And did I mention how hot you are?"* Cameron laughed, rubbing his face back and forth in Nathen's hair, which smelled like his own shampoo. The memory of their shower time, which had not turned out to be nearly as sensual as Cameron had wanted came to mind. *"Should we maybe,*

shower? I can block the sound from Alice and your mom if you like."

Swinging his legs out of bed, Nathen nodded. *"Yeah, let's go wash off the blood."* Cameron could feel that he was delighted and embarrassed all the while that he had been complimenting him, and as they walked to the bathroom, Nathen took his hand. *"Thank you. I've never had anyone say those nice things before. And I do enjoy spending time with you. It does feel right."* Nathen kissed him gently, steadying Cameron who was a little lightheaded. *"And you are really good in bed as well."*

The black-and-white checkered tiled bathroom had a long white pillar sink with silver handles and faucet on the right and a beautiful antique large white clawfoot bathtub with a silver circular curtain stand and a large white curtain that was extended around the tub directly across from them with a large silver shower head extended above it. Once under the stream, Cameron gathered Nathen to him, kissing him again. *"You know, I honestly don't think I've come so much this last year as I've come in the last two days. You have successfully made my balls ache,"* he laughed, putting his head back so the water could start washing away the blood he had missed on his chest.

Nathen took the soap and began lathering Cameron's chest, following its contours and happy trail down to his member. He grinned. *"I feel like an incubus. I wonder of those exist as well?"* Using the soap on Cameron's back to make it slippery, he took him with both hands and started to knead his shoulders, kissing the side of his neck gently.

Cameron hummed happily. *"That is exactly what you are."* He glanced over his shoulder, a shiver running through him when Nathen kissed his neck. *"It's okay. I considered and have decided it's totally fine to get addicted to you."*

Chapter Twenty-One

NATHEN

After their shower, Nathen quickly changed the linens on his bed and bundled up the soiled clothes and sheets into a garbage bag. Cameron stretched out naked across the bed and quickly fell asleep. Nathen watched the chest of his lover rise and fall with pointed fascination for a while before turning his attention to researching how the program he obtained from the hospital was written.

Nathen's watch alarm dinged, interrupting his concentration and alerting him to the fact that it was almost sunset. He could often become lost in research that was interesting him for hours, often missing meals and appointments unless interrupted. He sensed before he turned and saw that Cameron was stirring. Nathen slid onto the bed. *"I learned that the program was written in Assembly,"* he told Cameron excitedly.

Cameron yawned from his nap, stretching and pulling Nathen down to hug him. "You sound so far away again... And what is assembly?"

"It's one step up from machine language. Nobody uses it. It's perplexing. And, it's almost time to go, though before we do, I need to stop at the office. Did you want to join me? I was apprehensive about having them know who you are, but after thinking about it, maybe you can scan what they're up to? Maybe how many other vampires there are? I don't want to put you in danger though, so it is ok if you don't want to do that."

Cameron chewed his lower lip in thought. "Yes," he finally said nodding, "First off, you're my boyfriend now and it's my duty to keep you safe." He offered a smile, projecting confidence and responsibility that surrounded Nathen. "Second—"

Nathen cut him off with a hug. "Thank you, that means a lot. If there is anything I can do for you, please let me know. I know I can sometimes miss things, but I'll always try my best to make you happy."

Cameron smiled and held Nathen, petting the back of his head and kissing his forehead. "Hey, hey. We'll figure this out. For example, if there are other vampires around, I'd like to know it. Maybe I can pick up something about them, I don't know. But what I do know is I can read those who aren't vampires, like this woman donor if you know how to find her, and perhaps learn what she knows? Finally, if they're tracking you, which Syn is convinced they are considering your phone, computer, and car service, then they know about me. It only makes sense, right? That they know what corner they're dropping you off on and maybe followed you? Perhaps they saw us together and certainly they saw us together when the car service picked you up at the hospital. Syn has a plan if we need to disappear. We've prepared for that for a long time." A sadness was cut off by a nod. "So, yes, of course. Let's see what we can see? But...Nathen? Do you think we should go in a little prepared?"

"What do you mean?"

"Well, I can't hear you right now. I can, but you seem way far away. So, I don't know if it's time or me sleeping that weakens the connection. Umm, did you want more of my blood?" Nathen could see the blood rush to Cameron's face as he burned with embarrassment.

"Yeah." Nathen smirked. He ran a hand through Cameron's thick ginger hair and leaned in to kiss him but remembered and sat up straight. "Umm, but first could you put mom and Alice back to sleep?"

Cameron's eyes popped open wide and he leaned into Nathen, laughing and nodding agreement.

*

Twilight had arrived and the couple enjoyed the ambiance until the car got there and they traveled back into the city. This time hand in hand, looking out at the world around them, Cameron marveled at the Golden Gate Bridge at night. Nathen was holding his hand throughout the ride, gently circling his thumb around Cameron's palm. Sometime in the afternoon the fog had burned away revealing a night for photographers with one side of the bay alight with dark blue skies that melted to navy and then black that outlined the twinkling lights of buildings in the East Bay. They could see ships out on the water and Alcatraz lit up.

Nathen became distracted at being able to feel Cameron's emotions, which were contagious. Joyous soaring that made Nathen grin. He commented, "When it's foggy, some of the islands stick out, and make me think of the mythical Avalon. A magical city floating in the clouds. The fog makes everything look that much more mysterious."

Cameron smiled. "Hey, since you still eat, maybe after we've done our covert ops for the night we can go for sushi? Do you like sushi?"

Nathen beamed. "I love sushi!"

Chapter Twenty-Two

CAMERON

Cameron asked the car to swing by the Silver Stream gym on the way to the office. He ran in with the bag of sheets and stashed them in his locker before pausing to watch Syn in her kickboxing class. In the hope of dashing out quickly, Cameron mentally shot the address of Nathen's job with, *"We're going in to look around. Send reinforcement if you don't hear from me."*

"What the fuck are you talking about?" Syn asked, not missing a beat as she punctuated her annoyance with increasingly stronger hits.

"We're going to go to the office—"

"You mean the same office that kidnaps people and turns them into vampires?" Syn shot him a look, rounding a kick up and watching her class follow suit.

"I hear you. I do, but we need to find out more information. Listen, I know the escape plan. I shoot you a text, voice mail, carrier pigeon, whatever, and we meet up in the apartment in Jack London Square. Right?"

"Fine, fine. Listen, I learned something too. I need you and Nathen to come with me at the Kitten Club at 1:00 a.m. I'm going to get info from a buddy of mine. We can meet up at home and go together. Deal?"

"Deal. I love you," he shot back.

"Yeah, yeah. Oh, and Cam, if you die I'll kill you," Syn snorted, jumping in the air to faux kick with one foot and snapping her other straight out at the imagined attacker.

Cameron ran out and jumped back into the car and grabbed Nathen's hand. "Let's go," he told the car, smiling at Nathen. *"Syn found something, too, so we have to meet her at the Kitten Club tonight after midnight. I know you're not into clubs, but it'll be quick."*

Nathen rested his head on Cameron's shoulder, *"I can go to clubs. Though staying there for too long does become overwhelming after a while."*

The car pulled in front of a large, modern building in the middle of the financial district and Cameron followed Nathen into the building, scanning with hypervigilance. There was nothing strange on the street, the regular din of people getting off work, a few homeless hoping for extra change, and night crews heading to their jobs. Inside, two security guards argued over the fate of the A's and gave a passing glance to Nathen who headed to the elevator bank.

Cameron's heart raced as they stepped into the elevator, or lion's den, and ascended. *"The guards seemed to be just guys. Rent-a-cops, not even associated with any one group here. I could probe them, but if I spend my energy going deep into reading their thoughts I'll get a headache fast and have to stop. May be better to have you ask people questions? Catching surface thoughts is like background noise for me. Only frustrating piece is when fantasy and reality mix up. That makes me have to take a minute and think. "*

Nathen took a step toward Cameron who could feel that Nathen wanted to reach out to him before he stepped away, looking at the floor. *"Okay. We'll head to my office first. Though, I need to warn you that they told me the whole place is under surveillance. The receptionist on my floor is a bit weird. See if there is something up with him. He was mean to Agnes for some reason."*

"And Agnes is the woman you bit? Do you think she's here? Since she's a...donor...I should probably meet her? Unless it would be too strange." Cameron took a deep breath saying out loud for the sake of the surveillance. "Wow, you work in an extremely nice place!" He pulled out his phone and started flipping through it. "So while you're finishing up your project, I'll find us that sushi restaurant. I've got a few great ideas, but maybe something in walking distance?"

The car stopped and Cameron followed Nathen into the lobby, pocketing his phone. The small rodent-like man with glasses sitting behind the desk studied both Nathen and Cameron as they approached. "Hello, Bryan, this is my friend Cameron."

"Hello, Bryan," Cameron said, reaching out with his mind and catching the surface thoughts: disinterest followed by requirement to note any visitors and bristling at his use of his first name. His absolute adherence to rules made Cameron immediately diagnose Obsessive Compulsive Personality Disorder and he glanced around quickly and noticed the name plaque that read *Bryan Holtzman*. He made a show of looking closely at it and followed up with an overt correction, "*Mr.* Holtzman." He immediately sensed satisfaction from Bryan.

"Mr. Hale, and guest." He gave a curt nod. Cameron guessed he would have likely addressed him by his last name if Nathen had introduced him more formally. "Do you need anything?"

"Ask him about Agnes, I'll see what I can pick up."

"Um, do you know where Agnes is?" Nathen dutifully asked.

"I can summon her if you wish, Mr. Hale," Bryan said.

"*Bryan is interesting. Very much someone who adheres to the rules above all—a by-the-books kind of guy. He is against anything informal and doesn't like Agnes because he sees her as informal and is also annoyed that she's a donor. He doesn't want to be a donor and doesn't think that should prevent him from being granted the...gift?*" Cameron relayed.

"What gift?" Nathen asked aloud.

Cameron blanched and pulled out his phone, "I know you have a lot to get done," he tried to cover. "*Shhh, don't say stuff out loud. The gift of being a vampire. He knows about vampires, though you'd have to ask him more to find out.*"

"Oh, what do you know about vampires?" Nathen asked.

Cameron dropped his phone and blinked at Nathen. "What?" he said aloud shocked that Nathen was blurting things out.

Bryan tilted his head, seeming to consider his words carefully and finally settling on, "Sir, do you need something?"

"*Holy...*" Cameron rubbed his temple as he was flooded with a myriad of too much information from Bryan's surface thoughts. Eight vampires that worked on the floor. Old movies of Dracula. Arranging blood deliveries from a Dr. Manchester who ran the XX/YY corporation. Bryan himself in black and white trying to seduce Lucy Westerna. A fantasy? Bryan spying on a handsome guy with Agnes bent back, drinking blood from her neck and then winking at Bryan through the open door.

Cameron shook his head, "Oh! Mr. Holtzman, you play Xbox too?" Cameron beamed at him.

"Sir?" Bryan asked, obviously more confused by the shift in discussion.

"Oh, never mind," Cameron accepted the phone that Nathen handed over, having totally missed that it never hit the floor again. *"Tell him you've got a lot of work to do."*

"I have a lot of work to do," Nathen relayed.

"Good to meet you," Cameron said. He ushered Nathen toward the side door and followed him back to his office. *"Dude, you can't blurt out what I say."*

"But—"

"Stop," Cameron sunk down onto the couch. *"You said this place is under surveillance, right? That means when you talk to me you've got to be silent. Also, if you say weird stuff about vampires, people are going to think something is up."*

Nathen nodded and pulled out his laptop, *"Okay. Got it."*

"I'll find a restaurant while you work," Cameron settled on the couch and opened an app that allowed him to search for restaurants in the area. He felt a headache starting that had nothing to do with using his abilities. He relayed, *"Bryan is a lackey. He knows admin stuff and how to get vampires blood. But it's really stuck up and thinks that everyone should go by last names as a sign of respect."*

Nathen looked up and frowned, then turned his attention back to his computer screen. *"I don't understand. Agnes introduced him to me as Bryan. Was she trying to get me in trouble?"*

"No, no!" Cameron found himself leaning forward, though he kept his eyes focused on his screen. *"She actually seems to be genuinely nice, even from Bryan's surface thoughts. He doesn't make friends at work. He seems like a rather miserable guy."* Cameron reached out and mentally hugged Nathen. People with Autism often struggled with social interaction like this one and if Cameron hadn't spelled out everything he saw in Bryan's memories, and interpreted through his own lens, Nathen likely would have had the luxury of never seeing this side of things. *"Honestly, none of this matters. You asked what was going on with him and that's all it was. Office personalities. Let me scan the rest of the floor."*

Nathen shrugged and frowned at his screen. *"All of this is seems so unnecessarily complicated. People should be nice to each other."*

Cameron sent empathic warmth to Nathen, knowing there was no way he could explain the intricacies of human interaction because Nathen would become more confused. People had various personality defenses, went out of their way to psychologically protect themselves, played games of manipulation, all of which Nathen would likely never even pick up on. It was why Cameron didn't conduct therapy. He could see inside people, their emotions and thoughts, their anxieties and neurosis. He could see it every day in every interaction he had with every person. It was exhausting. To have the emotional blindness that Nathen had seemed like a blessing and for a moment Cameron felt a pang of jealousy. But then he was reminded when he could not feel Nathen and shook his head. He could never give up his gift.

"I'll start with the floor below us and go from there." Cameron looked up smiling. "There's Sushi Ship a few

blocks away. It's got good reviews," he looked back down at his phone.

Cameron spent time scanning various floors and while it was as interesting as it always was for him to read people, there was nothing of note regarding terrorism, vampires, or the hospital. He sat up when he came to the fourteenth floor where he found the gym. "*You guys have a gym? Oh, and I found Agnes! Whoa, her boyfriend's a cop!*"

He found that Agnes and her boyfriend were working out and her boyfriend was strutting around trying to impress her because another man was there. Cameron realized quickly that the other person who was working out was invisible to him and frowned. "*I'm vampire blind,*" he admitted with a tinge of fear and annoyance. "*So, a vampire just left the gym. So, if we go and talk with Agnes, I could probably pick up some information.*"

"Ok," Nathen stood and Cameron inwardly groaned.

"*Say, 'let's go check out the gym,'*" Cameron instructed.

"Oh yeah, let's go check out the gym."

Cameron stood. "Cool. Can I use it too?"

"*Wait—you actually want to work out?*" Nathen asked.

"*No, gorgeous. I'm covering.*" He chuckled and linked arms with Nathen.

"*This is kinda complicated.*"

"*I'm sorry, it doesn't have to be. It makes it easier if you ask questions and I pick up on the person's surface thoughts.*"

They headed back out and down to the gym floor. The small lobby had one frosted glass wall with double doors that lead into the gym area and separate men's and women's changing areas off to either side.

There were only two people making use of the lavish gym. "Hi Agnes," Nathen called. When he greeted the attractive receptionist, she slowed down her jog on the treadmill and hopped off.

Cameron picked up immediate arousal from her, and memories of how Agnes had kept everything "professional," and wouldn't have forced Nathen into anything, but certainly knew how to avail herself. Cameron inwardly laughed. After being bitten by Nathen, he totally understood her attraction.

"Mr. Hale!" Agnes grinned. "This is my boyfriend Phil."

Mild annoyance subsumed to friendliness. Phil was still trying to get over the other attractive man that had been working out next to Agnes. Cameron wondered idly if Phil could somehow unconsciously pick up on the fact that both were vampires who had bitten Agnes.

"It's nice to meet you," Nathen said, a programmed response as he held out his hand to shake Phil's.

"Mr. Hale just started here. How are you liking everything?" Agnes asked.

"It's good. I'm still researching stuff right now."

"Ask her if she likes her job," Cameron prompted and sighed with relief when Nathen asked just that.

As Agnes assured him that she did, Cameron saw the surface thoughts that outlined that Agnes' was one that was mostly administrative, processing paperwork for HR who was someone Agnes both admired and was terrified of.

"Who's HR?" Cameron asked.

"HR is the man who hired me," Nathen said aloud.

Cameron choked, but then sighed with relief when Agnes nodded, seemingly unaware that the response was not for her. Cameron picked up that she was thinking of Nathen as someone who was a bit slow. She responded kindly in a way that one might respond to someone who didn't quite get things. "That's right, Mr. Hale. HR is the person who met with you and had you sign all those forms."

Cameron picked up that Agnes didn't know if HR was a vampire or not. He had never bitten her; she didn't know *what* he was and didn't think that he was human. Cameron's breath was shallow as he began to flick through Agnes' surface thoughts of HR. Older, balding, well-dressed man; he was soft-spoken and direct. Fear and confusion? No. Wariness. HR had never given Agnes any reason to fear him, but there was something about his eyes and the way he was...cold. Then, as with all surface thoughts, a hodgepodge hit Cameron. A boardroom. New vampires. Agnes sitting at her desk watching through a monitor. Bringing a glass of her own blood which she had drawn with a syringe. A flickering of people who refused to accept they were vampires. The men who came into the room and murdered the vampires.

Cameron swallowed hard, glancing fearfully at Nathen.

Cameron shifted his mind to probe deeper. He could tell that Agnes was good at compartmentalizing. Overall, she was a nice person. He could feel her dismay when an "asset" had to be "terminated" and she drank a bit too much alcohol and smoked too much weed on nights that happened. She didn't know anything about how people were recruited or the process by which they were turned into vampires. And she tried not to think too much about when they became distraught, or what followed after that.

Then he realized that everyone was staring at him. What had he missed?

"I'm sorry, I spaced out. Low blood sugar. What were you saying?" he asked.

"I do that too," Nathen said.

"Do what?" Cameron asked, struggling to keep up.

"Space out," Nathen said. "Usually when I get to thinking about quantum physics or Eastern philosophies."

Agnes laughed lightly. "I was just introducing myself."

"Oh! I'm Cameron," he said.

"I told them that," Nathen relayed and Cameron groaned.

"We gotta get out of here, gorgeous. My head hurts."

Nathen caught Cameron's hand. "Oh, maybe Agnes has aspirin?"

Cameron's head spun. He wasn't sure if he was saying things out loud or not. By the look that Agnes was giving them, probably not.

"Of course!" Agnes said. "Hang out here, I'll go get some."

"Hey fellas, it was nice meeting you two but I gotta get going. My shift starts in about half an hour," Phil was saying, pumping both of their hands quickly before taking off.

Since he still had the link open with Nathen, he caught Nathen's surface thoughts that included a healthy appreciation for Phil's ass combined with something having to do with the Mandelbrot. Cameron tried to make sense of the non sequiturs as Nathen said, "I like Agnes. We should go for sushi soon. You must be famished. I can also show you the cafeteria we have before we go, in case you want a snack or something."

"I know you've got more work to do. Thanks for showing me the gym, it's cool. Let's get the rest of your stuff done, then we can go?"

Cameron caught the e-mail draft to HR that Nathen started mentally composing detailing his discovery of the Ransomware, and how he had used his vampiric power to access the server and building as Agnes returned and gave him the aspirin and a glass of water.

"Thanks," he accepted with a smile.

They said their farewells and returned to Nathen's office. On the way, Cameron thought, "*I want to scan the other floors and see if there's anyone that we should talk to?*"

"*Okay,*" Nathen said, this time silently as he slid an arm around Cameron's shoulders. "Sorry about your head."

Cameron snorted and nodded. Surface thoughts were nothing, but keeping a channel open for lengthy discussions was fatiguing. He lounged back onto the leather couch and pulled out his earbuds, plugged them in and cranked Killswitch Engage, casting a small smile at Nathen. Music helped to center him and unlike others who needed quiet with a headache, for Cameron the louder it was the more it drowned out the din of thoughts that belonged to everyone around him. Sinking lower, he closed his eyes and rested his phone on his chest moving his mind to the floor above them. He found the gay donor and probed, reading all about his antics and having to pull a throw pillow into his lap at the sympathetic arousal. He relayed information about the corporation having been around for a long time.

But soon the pull to probe became too strong and Cameron had the desire for *more*. It happened sometime, used to happen all the time when he was a teenager. But as an adult he had monitored this and used the meditative practice to sleep, going floor by floor with surface thoughts and then just a little more, probing a little deeper into each of his neighbor's psyches. He had learned that he could blanket-sweep entire floors for surface thoughts, scanning his entire building in a matter of minutes for overt thoughts of violence or maleficence. It had become a nightly ritual and he had rid his building of the few domestic violence relationships, rapists, and child abusers. But he had never actually done what he was doing now, sweeping whole floors for specific information, probing individuals deeper and deeper still. His breathing became trance like as he found himself becoming more comfortable on the couch, pillow falling to the floor forgotten as he began to expand again. He *wanted* more.

He flitted from one mind to another picking up pieces that he mentally filed away until he came to one who was reading a file with his name on it. He started digging into that man, Todd Jack's, mind and suddenly found himself standing.

"Nathen, we have to go. Now!" His eyes were wide with fear and he took Nathen's arm, gripping a bit too tight. He all but pulled Nathen out into the hall and down to the lobby, scanning frantically, probing minds—only Bryan and Nathen on this floor...and there was someone else...Cameron began trembling as the elevator door opened. He couldn't help himself from scanning, then trying to probe the average, balding, well-dressed man who accompanied Agnes out of the elevator. Curiosity, extreme interest, but no malevolence. His thoughts were simple—he knew who Cameron was, but as he tried to look deeper into who HR was, what he knew, why...he was blocked. He was blocked in a way that he had never experienced before. HR observed Cameron, his head tilted to the side ever so slightly, before he turned to Nathen.

"Mr. Hale, I trust that everything is going as planned and will expect an update soon. Mr. Molina." He looked at Cameron, who was now deathly pale, and pulled out a solid black silver embossed card with only a phone number and HR printed on it. "I trust I will be hearing from *you* very soon."

Cameron couldn't speak. He couldn't think. He accepted the card automatically. And then the man was gone. He had barely been aware of Agnes greeting Nathen and wishing them a good night, had not turned to see HR and Agnes disappearing into the door leading to the inner offices. He woodenly followed Nathen into the elevator, and everything went black.

Overwhelmed by the overuse of his abilities coupled with the information, Cameron slumped against Nathen who steadied him. Gently cupping his face, he quietly said, "Cameron, are you okay, what happened?"

Cameron came to slowly, weakly clinging to Nathen until the door opened and Nathen led him to the street. Tears were streaming from Cameron's eyes as he groggily looked at the card he had somehow managed to hold on to and stuffed in his pocket. "Take me to Syn?" he asked, trembling as Nathen used his phone to call an Uber.

Cameron's knees buckled and he sat on the curb, holding his head in his hands. He knew Nathen was holding him and trying to get through, but he couldn't think. And he sure as hell couldn't let Nathen know everything. Not until he had support.

The car pulled up and Nathen helped Cameron in. They rode in silence and when they arrived, Cameron grabbed Nathen's hand and walked numbly into the gym where Syn was in the middle of a class.

"Syn..." Cameron reached out.

Something about his "tone" made Syn turn and seeing her drawn, pale, and sickly friend she summoned one of her seconds to take over and bustled them into a back office shutting the door. She poured him a cup of water from a dispenser, handed it to him and instructed, "Drink."

She fixed Nathen with a look. "What happened?"

Nathen shrugged helplessly. "He hasn't said anything. He was scanning the floors and then all of a sudden said we had to go."

"They know everything..." Cameron sobbed, resting his head in his hands. "They know I'm a mage because they recorded the conversation we had on the balcony. They know Syn is a hacker and had a secret file that I couldn't access. They...they have cameras all over your house. Recorded and watched everything we did this afternoon." As the information came pouring out of him, Cameron found that he couldn't stop disclosing, coughing, and shuddering with too many emotions he couldn't control, above all staving back the feral need for escape of an animal trapped. "They kill vampires who do not comply, who try to leave the company. They have a task force specially designed to torture and slaughter you."

"What?" Nathen gasped, looking from Syn to Cameron as if there was a shared joke that he was missing.

"I'm sorry! I didn't realize they could hear us on the balcony. And they know about me. My real name. Gave me this card," he managed through his tears as he turned the card over and over in his hand.

Syn sighed. "Stop apologizing," she said aloud, firmly, making Cameron hiccup. She tossed him a box of tissue. "Let's see the card." Cameron handed the black card with silver characters to Syn who started plugging in the information into her private network of searches. After a few minutes, she grunted.

"Well, on the bright side, you two now have a boner-fied sex tape," she smiled, laughing lightly. Cameron looked up in horror as she turned to Nathen, "Okay, lover-vamp. What do you have to say?"

Nathen shook his head. "I don't have anything that Cameron hasn't told you. They seemed so nice. I didn't think they would...kill me or put cameras in my house." He slipped his hand in Cameron's. "Please don't cry, I'll protect you."

Cameron pulled Nathen to him, rested his face atop his head and looked helplessly at Syn. She sighed again and rolled her eyes, leaning back in her antique wooden desk chair behind the beaten-up second-hand desk. "Let me think... So, we have one of the top-five world-wide companies doing intensive background checks on newly recruited employees—not strange. Intensive backgrounds include illegal wiretaps and surveillance. Strange but not unheard of. Oh, and they turn some of those employees into vampires who they either kill off when they resist being turned into a vampire, and if not, they continue to follow to keep them in line and *then* kill them off if they fall out of line? Okay, little stranger." She put her feet up on the desk and reached over to a candy dish holding a colorful mixture of Skittles and started popping a few in her mouth while talking to the ceiling. "They know about mages," she nodded sideways to Cameron, "And they have a wicked IT group." She chuckled then shook her head. "There's no way, Cam. They must be mages or fae or something. Something else has to be going on. There is *no way* they found out who you are."

Cameron said in a strained voice, speaking barely above a whisper as he absently stroked Nathen's arm with his free hand, "He said 'Mr. Molina, I trust I'll be hearing from you very soon.' No mistake. And... And I could only pick up surface thoughts and feelings. *Something* stopped me from scanning deeper."

"Vampire blood?" Syn asked, looking at Nathen. "Could that do it? If he was maybe like some Blade type of motherfucking half-breed or something?"

Cameron nodded slowly. "Maybe? I don't know. And...there's more."

Both Nathen and Syn paused and looked at him expectantly. Rubbing his temples, Cameron admitted, "I *think* that Impetus might have something to do with the stuff at Children's."

"What?" both Nathen and Syn said in unison.

"Well, the guy who I was reading, he'd been there in the hospital. I became so distracted that he had files on us that I started probing his mind. I didn't get far. He was the one that set up cameras at Nathen's house. Had seen..." Heat radiated off his face. "But not just that. He had been monitoring when Nathen and I went into the hospital. They have to be involved, right?"

"You know...the first day I was there, when I woke up, there was this guy. He was dressed in all black and looked kinda menacing. He followed Agnes and me around while she gave a tour, and he didn't say anything at all. Do you think that was him?"

"Yeah," Cameron said. "Probably. I mean, the guy I was reading was a military guy who wore all black. So..."

"Okay, there seems to be a big ass elephant in the room." Cameron frowned, confused as Syn looked directly at Nathen, swinging back so she was sitting and could lean forward, "Nathen, what the hell did they hire you to *do?*"

Nathen glanced up bashfully, then away. "I'm not allowed to say. But it's nothing unusual, nothing that would make me pause. In fact, I think it's actually being helpful." He tapped his head, and when Cameron opened a channel sent an image of him hacking the Hospital computers to figure out who was behind the ransomware attack to Cameron.

Cameron sat up suddenly, eyeing Nathen with confusion and suspicion, as he passed on the image to Syn who also blinked in surprise, narrowing her eyes.

Syn said, "Lemme get this straight. They turned Nathen into a vampire on Thursday...after I reached out to him and several others on the same day after this whole thing went down? Fuck! Wait, no, no—they had six months of files on him." Syn fell back and laughed with relief, letting a few Skittles fall into her mouth. "Okay, what the fuck would this group care about what's going on at the hospital? Unless..." Syn sat up and started typing on her computer with focus.

Cameron took a deep breath, realizing how everything must be for Nathen and feeling his lover's emotions spinning to the point of shutting down. He spread a few kisses across Nathen's head with gentle strokes of his hair. "This is fucked up. There's stuff about me you don't know, a lot actually. One of the reasons you freaked me out so much when we first met was because Syn and I have been on the run since we were kids. I've always been so careful. But now they know about Syn and me and while they may have known before, but I don't think so... Don't worry, Syn will have a plan." A wave of admiration and absolute love for her flowed from him. "She always does."

Syn shook her head, "Nope. They don't seem to have anything to do with the Sons of Discord as far as I can find. Okay then. Well, we know they know about Cam and yet they didn't stop you from leaving. They can't actually hear in here." She laughed. "Unless they can, in which case my glass is raised to you asshats." She saluted the air. "But let's work on the assumption that my protections actually work. They knew you were reading them and let you go, even gave you a card and called you out. So that must mean they want you to call them. Let us hold off on *that*. What interests me is that their interests and mine align, which is curious. The question is why? And that might be answered tonight. I know you two still want to check out that warehouse which might give us a bit more info. So, this is what we do. Let's go on as if this whole knowing your secret identity and hot porn tape is not out there..."

Cameron groaned as another wave of embarrassment clutched him.

"Go splash some water on your faces, or fuck, better yet let me close the pool and you two can go for a swim? It'll piss off a few people, but maybe I can up sell and have them pay for private time in the future too. The place closes after this class which is ending soon anyway. You can stay as long as you like, then check out that warehouse when you've calmed down some. Then meet me tonight? Sound like a plan?'

"So...you don't want to leave town?"

"And go where, Cam? If these guys are as good as they seem to be, then they know about my other holdings and can track us? Plus, we still haven't figured out the whole thing with the hospital and Sons of Discord. And if, as you say, they might be connected, it's even more reason to stay and figure it out. Don't worry, we'll go with one of the other plans if we need to."

Cameron nodded, sliding away from Nathen to hug Syn. "Gettoff!" she protested, but gave him a quick hug and then grabbed a huge ring of keys off the wall. Cameron and Nathen followed.

The class had ended and most of the hall was empty. A few stragglers were on gym equipment, standing around talking, and a few were still down in the changing rooms. Syn called out as she walked, "Closing in fifteen!" As they entered the wet area, Syn made a grand gesture to the empty pool. "Thank goodness, it's always awkward standing there to catch someone's attention. I'll lock you guys in." She tossed Cameron an extra key from the ring. "Lock up when you're done?"

Cameron gave Syn a grateful look, which was returned with a pursed-lip no-nonsense from Syn who rolled her eyes again and left.

Cameron took a deep labored breath that burned after crying so much. "We don't have to swim. But I do want to put some water on my face. I, I'm still reeling a bit."

Nathen was feeling mildly violated and concerned for his and Cameron's safety. He nodded. "I usually like grabbing a floating device and just spacing out in the water. It's relaxing"

Cameron and Nathen changed into trunks that Cameron had in his locker and decided to swim. They passed Syn throwing towels in to wash for the night as they padded their way to the pool and Cameron waded into one lane and took off. He liked being underwater because it, like music, helped dampen some of the outside noise of all the people in the city. At night it was particularly nice as there were mostly businesses around and it meant even less chatter in his mind. He began to swim harder, hitting the edge, flipping and pushing off, challenging his lungs to burn.

"Syn, what do I do?" he reached out, feeling Syn upstairs.

"What do you want to do?"

"I don't know... I'm freaking out."

"Yeah, I get that. Listen, we have a plan. You spend time with your boyfriend. The two of you have been violated. That's the best word for it. And him more than you. Fuck, he got killed! And they've got his whole family on the line. You and me. We're solid. We can disappear tomorrow, tonight. Yeah, they might have my current holdings, and don't you fucking think I'm not digging into that shit tonight. But we're good. If we need to go, we can greyhound it, 'member?" She sent a wave of confidence and safety which slowed Cameron down in his swimming, and he turned over to float, breathless.

Cameron swallowed hard and nodded, starting a slower backstroke down the lane.

Syn continued, *"You need to do some soul searching about him... I'm with you whatever direction you want to go."*

"Okay. Thanks. Syn, stay safe."

"Heh." She sent a smirk, sending the image of her concealed thirty-eight special in her waistband, knife in her jacket, and twenty-two caliber in her steel-toed boot.

He sent back a wave of love and comfort, though it was tempered with just how fast Nathen could move and memories of fae. If they wanted to hurt her, there was nothing either of them could do—which contributed to ever increasing feelings of vulnerability and violation—that he tried to stave off by flipping back over and swimming hard again.

Nathen had found a floating pool noodle from when they held classes for children during the summer and bobbed weightless. He became motionless, and Cameron could feel him retreat into his mind, thinking about the past few days.

Independently the two took up their own lanes, Nathen floating on his side, Cameron power swimming across his lane, each lost in his own thoughts and emotions. Cameron lost track of the number of laps and finally collapsed against the side of the pool. He was drained but had come to a few conclusions. Wading over to Nathen, he reached out emotionally, stroking him with emphatic waves of love and concern. "This whole thing is overwhelming for me. I can only image what you're feeling." He floated a few feet away, not wanting to interrupt Nathen's process, but being present in case he wanted him.

Nathen turned to Cameron and smiled, though it was mixed with melancholy, "Yeah, I'm not sure what to think. And my emotions are all over the place. I don't know if I should be angry, afraid, or hurt. Mostly I feel confused and overwhelmed. Why did they pick me? Did I do something wrong? How can they get away with spying on me, or my family, or you...and how can they morally justify any of that? I mean, I think they killed me, right? Or maybe the awakening works differently. Should I be upset? I don't know. I'm still conscious, so I'm not actually dead."

Cameron waded closer, reaching out tentatively to gently cup Nathen's face. "I feel so insane too. Syn and I have been careful for so long, and now these people know about us. But yeah, this is so much more for you. I don't know why, but we will figure it out. Syn and I will help you, and your family. We're in this now and need to have each other's back. Yeah? I don't think this is a moral company at all. And I don't know how or why you were targeted. We need to be careful, learn what we can. I think we play nice until we figure out what exactly they want. It's okay to be upset, to be enraged, but also to be confused. I think maybe once we figure out what is going on with this assignment, or it reaches an end, that you and I talk to this HR guy together. He apparently expects me to talk to him... In any case, one thing at a time. That's all we can focus on, right?" Cameron took a halted deep breath and pulled his hand away, chewing on his lip.

Chapter Twenty-Three

NATHEN

Nathen struggled with a conflicted mix of strong emotions. He focused intently, staring past Cameron. On one hand, he wanted to be with Cameron, on the other hand, he started to realize that maybe them being with him put their lives in danger. Maybe he should walk away and not give Cameron the choice? He knew he could get out of here in mere seconds, and Cameron would not be able to stop him.

Cameron backed away, and Nathen could feel that he had a mixture of shock which flooded him with sadness and fear of losing something before it had started. Cameron said, "You do know it's too late for that, right? You don't have to be with me if you don't want to. But they already know about us, already know everything. Even my real name. So…" He shrugged sorrowfully.

Nathen calmed a bit and sighed heavily even though he realized that pushing the breath out didn't have the same effect that it used to. "I want to be with you, but I feel like I will mess up your life by staying, and that's selfish. Maybe if I leave, they will leave you guys alone? They only seem to be interested in me."

"They know I'm a mage. They know my identity, the identity that I've kept hidden for almost a decade. They've got files on Syn. They're not going to leave us alone… I'd feel safer with you than without you. And I don't think that this was your fault. They've been following you all this time, they likely knew about Syn before you. And if anyone messed up, it was me and my frustration with not being able to read you. And opening my mouth. All of us are blaming ourselves. Syn blamed herself, too. But blame is useless. This is where we are now, and it's just a matter of where we want to go and if we want to stay together."

Nathen considered that and couldn't find fault in the logic. "You're right. We probably would be stronger if we stuck together. But I want you to know that I'm sorry for getting you mixed up in all this. I didn't know they were tracking me or anything like that. I mean... I'm still not aware of what it means to be a vampire even...or hell, what having Autism really means. I literally got news of both just a few days ago. I don't want to hurt you more, so if you don't want anything to do with me, I won't blame you."

Cameron laughed. "I was the one who asked you if you wanted to be with me. And that hasn't changed. Come on, let's get out of here? Too much chlorine and all."

Nathen nodded and followed Cameron out of the pool. Their mutual feelings of vulnerability bounced back and forth and they paused, staring at one another until simultaneously they reached for each other and embraced. Leaning against the wall leading to the men's locker room, Cameron reached down and wrapped his arms around Nathen's waist gazing into his eyes. "Do you mind if I kiss you?" He gave a small smile. "A lot?"

Nathen's lips curved up into a lopsided grin. "No, I wouldn't mind that at all." He relaxed as shoulders dropped and he closed the distance again taking hold of Cameron's hips.

Cameron slowly traced the side of Nathen's face with his fingertips, and Nathen could feel his savoring the anticipatory flutter that suggested there would soon be no worries, no noise, only Nathen. His hand came to gently rest on the back of Nathen's head as he leaned down to tenderly brush his lips against Nathen's. Nathen shuddered as he recognized Cameron's heart rate increase before Cameron parted his lips with his tongue, his breath catching as the kiss intensified. Tumbling again into the brilliance of abandon, crushing Nathen to him as the darker emotions of the day melted away, Cameron moaned softly, his tongue rolling around and around in slow, almost tentative movements before he backed up, returning to less possessive kisses. Feelings of contentment, passion, desire and need emanated from Cameron like a warm inviting blanket, enveloping Nathen and pulling him in.

Nathen leaned in with a growing sense of arousal; his trunks showed what was running through his mind. Though he was afraid and unsure of the future, Cameron's touch had an odd effect on him. Momentarily he had forgotten his troubles and was just present from the sensations and the tactile feel of his boyfriend. He liked the warmth of Cameron's body against his. He circled his tongue around Cameron's, entwining them together, feeling at once whole and needed. Cameron turned, walking Nathen back through the swinging door into the locker room without breaking his kiss. Once inside he took off his trunks, kicking them to the side while hooking the back of Nathen's with his fingers and pushed them down and off, freeing him. Pulling him around to the counter of sinks, Cameron lifted Nathen so he was sitting on the counter, positioned between two of the basins.

Nathen thrilled as Cameron slid between his legs, Cameron's engorged cock pressed against his as he kissed him deeply and ran his hands over his back. Nathen could feel him tracking the lines of the muscles of his shoulders further down to cup his ass. He seemed content to kiss Nathen for a long time, before pulling away, breathless.

Giving a boyish and somewhat playful grin, Cameron asked, "So, what now?" his tone in part a challenge as he was clearly incredibly aroused.

Nathen was fully erect and ready for anything as he reached down and stroked Cameron's cock. He smiled at Cameron. "I would be happy to take you in again, or give you head. Which would you like?"

Nathen puzzled at the curious sensation of being able to feel Cameron's emotions as if they were his own, to know them in a way he had never been able to know what another was feeling. He sensed concern and assumed that was likely because Cameron was overly conscientious.

"Maybe I can bite your...meat?" Nathen offered with a laugh.

"Bite my...?" Cameron coughed with a mixture of curiosity and horror. "That might actually kill me, but what a way to go."

Cameron projected the image of the steam room and held out his hand, taking Nathen's and leading him to the teak door.

Nathen saw the small room that could hold maybe four or five guys and when the door opened, the steam roiled out. He could see that it was so cloudy in there that it might obscure people, but a deep inhalation told him that they were alone downstairs. He took a moment to reflect on his new vampiric senses but was interrupted when Cameron pulled him to him again, sighing as they kissed. Nathen could tell the instant that the kiss affected Cameron, not only did he relax into him, the kiss intensifying, but he could feel his heat pressing against his middle. Gently guiding Nathen to one of the benches, Cameron continued to kiss him, running his hands over Nathen's shoulders and back, before finally pulling away. "Please don't suggest us splitting up again, unless you're serious."

"I thought it would protect you from more harm. And...sometimes I say things without thinking first, especially if I'm emotional." As he slid to his knees on the teak floor, Nathen kissed Cameron's chest then punctuated his abs with small kisses, till he got to his happy trail, which he traced with his tongue down to Cameron's enormous member. He took on his head first, circling it with his tongue, then deeper until it hit the back of his throat. He relaxed his throat, trying to prevent his gag reflex. Using the tip of his tongue he traced the urethra underneath the shaft, and then played with the hole at the top, probing it with the tip of his tongue.

Nathen glanced up when Cameron's let out a low breath and their eyes locked. "You're so good at that."

Normally Nathen couldn't tolerate eye contact. It was usually uncomfortable and he didn't know what to do, but now he could feel the sensuous intimacy that sparked between them and for the first time wanted to continue staring into Cameron's deep blue pools as they almost disappeared into rings around huge ebony pupils. Nathen's cool smooth skin was a contrast to Cameron's perspiring with the heat of the steam and he found himself more and more turned on by Cameron's masculine presence.

Nathen caught a projected image of staring down at himself, his mouth sensually full as Cameron said, "That is, quite possibly, one of the hottest things I've ever seen."

Having Cameron's pulsing cock between his lips brought Nathen's attention to the blood flow just beneath the surface. He hummed his enjoyment through a smile before he pulled away and asked, "Did you want me to try biting you while I'm down here?"

He could feel Cameron shudder with both arousal and fear. "Oh, god. Every part of me is screaming no, you should never *want* someone to bite your dick...and yet." He laughed nervously, his eyes wide. "I'm pretty convinced this is one of those moments you don't talk about, think about...kind of like you just kind of do it and..." Cameron squirmed, unconsciously backing away toward the wall.

Nathen smiled releasing him to tease aloud, "Okay, I'll surprise you," and laughed in a stereotypical vampire way before diving back onto Cameron's cock, working it deep into his throat, moving up and down slowly, letting it stretch his mouth and jaw. Cameron's heart was pounding with both excitement and fear. Nathen focused on his canines, and they elongated a bit, enough to break the skin, but not go in too deep. With only one canine, Nathen carefully pierced the skin of the cap. The ecstasy was immediate. Cameron's back arched as he came, sending a small stream to accompany the trickle of blood down Nathen's throat. He cried out, his grip tightening involuntarily on Nathen's head as he seized the edge of the bench with the other hand.

Nathen lapped up both the blood and semen, sealing the wound. The taste of peach, and the normal nondescript taste of come brought forth a small laugh. "I think I just had my first taste of peaches and cream."

Watching Cameron pant the plumes of steam, Nathen stood to his full height and leaned down to clutch Cameron's head, forcing his tongue deep into his mouth. He stroked himself hard over Cameron's body, acutely aware that he had full control of Cameron. He leaned back to watch, glancing down at his hand working his dick until he shot his load, sending a crimson spray across Cameron's ginger-haired chest.

Cameron's eyes opened when Nathen came, both emotionally and physically. His mouth fell open in surprise and Nathen could feel a wave of shock colored with arousal emanating from him as he glanced down his body.

Nathen bent down and squeezed and licked the last of Cameron's seed from the tip of his cock. With a smile, he purred, "Everything about you tastes good."

Cameron laughed somewhat nervously. "Everything about you feels good." He fell back again, lying out on the bench. "I want this to never end," he breathed aloud, his eyes closing. Nathen reveled in Cameron's flood of the afterglow of release, adoration, and desire. "I can't...think." He laughed slightly.

Nathen gazed at Cameron's sated relaxed body, taking in the stark glow of his red trimmed pubes against his milk-white skin. "Well, I'll never age, and we can be together for a long time...or forever, if you ever decide to become a vampire also."

He sat up with a start. "I..." Cameron blinked at the notion and shifted around, finally saying, "I don't know. Let's figure out what all of this is... I don't think I would ever want to give up my abilities. Um...ask me again in a decade?" he offered with a small smile.

"Okay. I think I can actually bite you without drawing much blood, and it seemed just now that it still brings sexual pleasure. Agnes did say that was possible."

Cameron frowned. "But...you receive enjoyment too, from biting me? Right?"

Nathen nodded emphatically. "Yes, and the blood, and the sexual feeling, and intimacy."

Cameron smiled. "Yes, god yes. As long as you are enjoying it as well. You can bite me any time," he blushed. "But I'm not interested in just taking. Ever." He looked down at his blood splattered on his chest. "I'd love to cuddle with you here, but perhaps I should go rinse off?"

Nathen shrugged. "If you want, though I don't mind the blood."

Cameron shrugged too and leaned back with one leg dangling off the side, the other against the wall. He gestured to Nathen to sit against him, holding his arms out. "I hadn't realized how much I missed being close to someone. I so love touching you."

Nathen curled up in Cameron's embrace and hugged him, bringing his ear to his chest, listening to his heartbeat. He murmured, "I love being close you as well. I feel loved and safe."

Cameron ran his hand down Nathen's cool back and kissed the top of his head. "I'll try and keep you safe, I swear. And..." Cameron was quiet for a long time. He continued after a while, "And I think I could easily fall in love with you. I love being with you. You're the absolute best lover I've ever had. And I had forgotten how much I love kissing someone. And my god I love kissing you." He ran his hands down over Nathen's arms. "And I love that you don't seem to mind sleeping with me and cuddling with me."

Nathen was flattered but confused. "Why would I mind sleeping and cuddling with you?"

"My ex... He was obsessed with cleanliness. He wouldn't touch me unless we had showered, he had douched, and he was immediately in the shower afterward. If I stayed over, I slept on the couch because he didn't want to sleep with me. He was great in public and made a show of hugging me when people were around, but at home there wasn't anything like this. I mean, I had a lot of closeness with my first boyfriend. But I don't date, so since I was seventeen, nothing like this."

Nathen remembered Cameron talking about his ex before, the one who had raped him, and found himself growing protective. He glanced at Cameron. "Frank sounds like a piece of work. And he was learning to be a psychologist? He sounds crazy, like a psychopath to me."

Cameron tensed when he heard Frank's name, and Nathen could sense him trying to hide a wave of sadness and shame. "I don't want to think about him. I'm happy now. Though... I am getting hungry, and we do still need to find this factory and see what secrets it has before meeting Syn later. Plus, unlike you, I may turn into a prune if we stay in here too long."

Nathen nodded and laughed. "Well, let's get sushi?"

After they showered together, Nathen saw Cameron discretely examining his penis, glancing up with heat rushing to his face. "I'm amazed it's...fine. Considering a vampire having just bitten me *there.*"

Half-joking, Nathen said, "Yes, the curative power of saliva is here to heal your shaft whenever it gets too rigid."

Cameron grinned and finished pulling his pants on. After they were dressed, Cameron threw the sheets he had stashed in his locker, towels, and trunks in the washer, explaining that he would leave a note for the morning crew to dry them for him, before he shut off the lights and they headed out. As they exited the gym, Cameron locked up—immediately on the defensive.

Chapter Twenty-Four

CAMERON

It was easy this time to pick up Todd Jacks who was sitting over a block away in an SUV. Cameron would have normally missed the guy as his surface thoughts were on a burrito he was eating but having been in Jacks' mind earlier he knew how to pick him up again. *"We're being followed,"* he informed Nathen as a wave of nausea and fear passed through him with the memory that this guy had seen him and Nathen...in their most intimate moments. The feelings were replaced by rage and something darker. Cameron knew it would be so easy...but he needed to know more. He needed to know everything about this man. He forced his emotions down and grabbed Nathen's hand again, kissing the back of it. "Best sushi place in town is right up the road."

One of the best things about living in San Francisco was the food. It's difficult to find a bad restaurant. Space in the city is at a premium and as such, restaurants are constantly competing. Those that don't have good food, don't stay in business. But like everywhere else in the world, the best food is found in the little holes in the wall. One such place was found down an alley with a little hand-painted sign directing people in the know. There was always a line out the door and usually Syn and Cameron didn't mind waiting or got there early or late enough that it didn't matter. But Saturday night at nine was peak as it was gearing up for the late-night crowd. Mai's was a small family run joint sandwiched between two nightclubs. Club goers aplenty were there in all states of dress from the Lolitas who liked the club on one side that was dedicated to Strangelove, to the club on the other corner that hipsters called home. It didn't help that across the street was a biker bar. Good sushi transcends subculture, and Mai's knew that staying open till four was the best way to make big bucks on weekends. Indeed, the line was out to the main street and Cameron chewed his lip for a moment then shrugged, feeling like showing off a little. He wrapped his arm around Nathen. *"Stay close."*

They moved "invisibly" down the alley, dodging people who seemed to simply decide to step out of their way. Once at the front of the line, he mentally implanted in the mind of the people around that he and Nathen had always been "next." This was not a place that had a list, it was strictly first-come, first serve, and never allowed parties larger than four. Couples usually paired up so they could share tables, even if they had never met before. What better way to make friends? But Cameron didn't feel like sharing. There were ten tables and a bar with ten stools that wrapped around the station where the father and two sons were hard at work. People knew not to linger out of common courtesy. The next table that opened Cameron took Nathen's hand and slid into with a small smile. The daughter, dressed like she might be ready to hit the club herself with pink hair and an anime-short school-girl outfit, was prompt, wiping the table which had already been cleared of plates and set down two cups and a pitcher of steaming hot green tea. A plastic cup had a handful of chopsticks already on the table. The table was plastered with colorful notecards cut in shapes of fish with various specials under the plexiglass that served as the menu, though Cameron imparted, "You can order anything you like." The waitress looked expectantly at Nathen and Cameron.

As Nathen looked over the table menu and ordered, Cameron was still in Todd Jacks' mind. It had been an interesting challenge, staying there despite proximity as they had moved away from him over a block away. Jacks had spotted them and heard the discussion about sushi. Apparently, he had decided to forgo potentially losing his parking place (smart guy at this time of night) and decided to hoof it after them. He had kept a line of sight until Cameron and Nathen had turned the corner and Jacks made it half way down the alley before getting accosted by a rowdy bunch of bikers who didn't take to being cut in front of. He had talked his way around the group and had spotted Cameron and Nathen seated before making his way to the opposite end of the alley where he could theoretically keep his eye on the door. Cameron smiled, wondering how much fun it would be for those Hell's Angels wanna-be's to go kick the ass of an ex-navy seal. Only four on one? Probably not a fair fight... Cameron devoted one part of his mind to focusing on Jacks' surface thoughts and the other to staying engaged with Nathen. Nathen wouldn't notice his far away or mildly distracted look, and as long as Cameron could keep his emotions neutral or happy, Nathen wouldn't suspect a thing.

After they ordered, Cameron smiled at Nathen. "Can you tell me more about your interest in AI? What you were saying seemed interesting, but I don't understand much about it."

Nathen's eyes lit up at the mention of AI, "Well, I have been learning about Deep Learning and Neural Networks, which are the latest in AI research. There is also reinforced learning, which is what Google is doing, sometimes called Deep Q Learning. All of these have revolutionized the field and broke quite a long "AI Winter," but neither have touched on consciousness. Because a lot of scientists assume consciousness is an epiphenomenon of processing data. That it comes out solely out of the activity of the neural network. I think Neural Activity creates a construct of a world to be conscious of, and the more data you have the more "conscious" something feels. And so, in comes the "Hard Problem of Consciousness." What is it? How is matter, like us, conscious at all? There are many theories, as I brought up before, the overarching one is called Panpsychism, that "everything" is actually conscious on some level, think of it like a scale, an atom, compared to a thermometer, to a worm, to a cat, to a human, compared to...an alien maybe, or AI. Of course, there are also naysayers who say that we cannot know how to reproduce consciousness in a machine because of Gödel's incompleteness theorems, which basically say that something inside a system cannot fully know how it-itself works because it will never have access to the outside to know everything, or if it does have all the information, there will be a contradiction somewhere within it. I hope they're wrong. Because if true, it might mean that we will never reach other stars, due to the speed of light limit."

Cameron tried to stay focused, his mind in two places, but he listened on as Nathen, in a typical autistic way, went on. "But I digress. The reason AI interests me, is I think the system has gotten too complex for us to handle. We are a global economy with billions of moving parts and logistics are only going to get harder. Some people cannot handle truth or facts, we see that with people that support our current political structure, it has to be "others" that make their lives hard. Not the people they are voting for that want to take away their rights. AI would have access to all the world's knowledge via the internet. Think about this even now, if you don't know something you can take out a magical device we call a smart phone and look it up within seconds. It used to be that if you didn't know, you would have to go to the library and research it, or you might never actually learn the answer. Well, the AI would have the same thing. All studies, all books ever written, all accessible to it. Imagine how many discoveries it could help with, how many diseases it might cure. Nietzsche spoke about ubermench and eternal return, so have most religions, the three Eastern ones that talk about it a lot are Jainism, Hinduism and Buddhism. But Judaism, and Gnostic Christians also have "rebirth." So, if it's true, I would love to come back as a conscious artificially created brain that is attached to the internet. I fully support Transhumanism and Humanity+ due to that, which is another interesting subject..."

Todd Jacks was a forty-two-year-old Caucasian male with no ties. Annoyance at the crowd. Judgment at their clothes and revelry. Jacks loved his job. Preferred working. Curiosity about the food. Curiosity about how Cameron and Nathen had jumped the line. Interest in his phone. An e-mail from a coworker about the need to terminate specific "assets" overseas who were falling out of line. Jacks began answering the e-mail, citing safety protocol in what was obviously code language when he was bumped and looked up with annoyance.

Jacks was looking at a young Asian woman who was wearing a short form-fitting yellow dress and obviously dressed for a club. Cameron started with the images that flicked through Jacks' mind. A memory. Jacks in the military going into small towns in the Middle East. He was fighting for his country and this was *sanctioned*. Joyfully shooting "towel-head terrorists"—better them, than him. He exterminated their offspring with glee, the damn breeders. And then their women, well he had to see if they *were* women, right? Hidden under those full-body sheets, like dark ghosts in the desert? He tore off their clothes. Like unwrapping gifts - sometimes they were the unwanted socks, withered and old or fat and bloated. Presents not even worth regifting. Those women he shot outright, disgusted by their bodies. But sometimes he would find a pretty one, and the younger the better. Within reason after all. The look in their eyes as he tore into them. What was it, seventy-two virgins for Jacks? He must be in heaven! There was something so erotic about their screams as he fucked them. Knowing that he owned them. Afterward, he would exterminate them too.

Cameron snapped back in his chair, withdrawing from the man's mind. Jacks was a unique breed, and Cameron knew his kind immediately, having worked with criminals from time to time. A psychopath. He had no remorse for any of his sanctioned kills and had done a good job of finding a corporate home for himself. And now he was tracking Cameron and Nathen. But why? Cameron rubbed his temples and tried to focus exclusively on the man in front of him.

*

Nathen went on about AI, not noticing that Cameron had divided his attention. He could feel Nathen's emotions were a mix of love, passion, and an all-pervading sense of awe at what he was talking about. He saw that Nathen's expressions and hand gestures were a lot more animated than usual.

Cameron interjected only with nodding or smiling, as Nathen really didn't give pause for discussion. It was like sitting in a lecture in college and Nathen was touching on topics that Cameron didn't know much or have any opinions about. Images of old Twilight Zone episodes where artificial constructs took over the world played before Cameron's eyes and he couldn't understand how that would be a preferable existence, especially since it would not be existence at all for the subjugated humans, but he didn't voice these concerns. Weren't there a few movies where humans were used to feed the artificial construct mother ship or something? Cameron stifled a shudder and forced a smile. As Nathen bounced from topic to topic, covering science, politics, social justice, and religion in a period of a few minutes, Cameron realized it must be coming from a place of anxiety. He sensed Nathen's emotions were roiling, positive covering the negative of only a few hours ago. Cameron reached out and gently caressed Nathen's hand, interrupting his stream of consciousness.

Nathen paused and looked at Cameron. "I'm sorry, I have been talking about my interests! Tell me about yourself. Why did you become a psychologist?"

Cameron smiled softly. "You don't have to apologize. Everything you're talking about is interesting. Conversation usually entails back and forth though," he picked up Nathen's hand and kissed the back of it, rolling his thumb gently over his fingers. Caressing Nathen mentally, he said, "It's okay. I understand. People with Asperger's often struggle with the back and forth. It's also okay that you're still struggling with all the information you learned earlier. I am too. And I know it's hard to put up pretenses like this. The guy who is following us is outside on the corner. He's probably not listening to us because of the chatter from other customers and the fact that he couldn't follow us in here fast enough to plant a bug. And Syn scanned us already, so I know we're okay. I hope when we get on the other side of this I can take you on a date that doesn't include the intrigue." Cameron emotionally enveloped Nathen with feelings of calm and his own joy at being out with him, capturing what they could in the circumstances they had. "I have questions about a lot of what you said and don't know a lot of the rest of it. It seems like you have done a ton of research and come to a few conclusions about things."

They were interrupted as food arrived, and Cameron turned the conversation to the meal. He had lost all appetite having been in Jack's mind, and what would normally be scrumptious was like gooey cardboard in his mouth. Cameron was only slightly annoyed that he had to keep Jacks in "sight" and couldn't devote his entire attention to Nathen, but Nathen didn't seem to notice or mind. He was expounding the virtues of a world ran by AI and how he would like to be reborn as one since they didn't have to worry about human interaction, which Nathen struggled with. Cameron's heart went out to him. He had the opposite issue where he understood human interaction far too well and as much as Nathen wanted to shun it because it was foreign, Cameron wanted to shun it because it was familiar. He had to laugh that both of them found it overwhelming. He loved the way Nathen talked with passion about AI, though he didn't wholly agree with his conclusions. He found a few moments to reach across the table and gently stroke Nathen's hand as he talked and took joy in sharing his sushi eating prowess (which included a ton of wasabi and sriracha).

Cameron wondered if he should make Jacks blind to the fact that they were leaving. It was like a chess match. Jacks could have simply missed them, but he was too good for that. And since he was cataloging Nathen's whereabouts it was probably important that he take note of Nathen's attempts to follow the rules of what the company wanted. Though, Cameron would make sure to blind him when they went to meet up with Syn.

After they finished, Cameron paid and made a show of stepping out of the restaurant and kissing Nathen in the alley, in full view of Jacks who thought he was nicely hidden in the shadows, just another night crawler playing on his phone. He made the mistake of rolling his tongue against Nathen's and finding himself grasping Nathen to him, using sheer will to pull himself away. A few catcalls came from the line and Cameron blushed slightly, flashing a smile at Nathen and taking his hand. Cameron and Nathen walked past Jacks to the Uber they had called before leaving and Cameron smiled as he read Jacks cursing the need to go get his car. He mentally watched as Jacks passed by the Uber, affixing a tracking device.

The Uber carried the two to Coit tower and dropped them off. "So, which way from here?" Cameron took Nathen's hand.

"We're looking for a large building, an abandoned, or unused factory or warehouse perhaps, that has one of its walls facing directly at the tower. It was night, so I do not have a reference for where the sun was. But I do remember seeing it clearly lit up." He sent the image of Coit tower lit up blue showing through a break in a dirty glass window. The space had a high ceiling and dirty floors with loose cement, and mud covering it. The walls themselves were dirty and damaged, with light peeking through from damage in the foundation.

Nathen started walking away from the tower, toward the direction he thought mirrored how the tower would look like from a distance. Cameron saw that he was preoccupied, his eyes darting around to examine every detail as they continued down the street: graffiti, trash flying through the air, people walking by, the homeless moving about with bags... When they neared a homeless camp, which occupied part of a nearby park, Nathen paused with a mix of fear, aversion, and guilt. He turned to Cameron, "I'm not actually sure where I'm going. But I have an idea, though I am kind of afraid to use it again. Last time I think I passed out."

Cameron had a rush of concern at the memory of the Hospital and Nathen almost biting him. Though now in retrospect... "What do you want to do?"

Nathen gave a sheepish half smile. "I want to try that thing with the computers again. Maybe I can get a sense of where it is by seeing the traffic flow to one of these buildings."

Cameron had also seen the homeless encampment that had cropped up on the outskirts of Pioneer Park. While the city kept the popular tourist attraction free of the riffraff, the fact is that they couldn't always control where people en masse decided to lay their heads. Cameron had lived in San Francisco long enough to become desensitized to the homeless. Originally from

Texas where the homeless weren't quite so concentrated, Cameron's secretive move to California had been a culture shock at first. He had eased into his new identity and backstory of being from San Diego but never quite got used to people having to live on the streets. And while Cameron knew that most of them were harmless, his heart went out to most who struggled with mental health issues, substance abuse issues, or more likely a combination of the two. His abilities to read people's motives and change their minds had left Cameron with a sense of security, though now that he knew about vampires, he was doubly cautious. Cameron kept his mind expanded, chuckling to himself that Jacks was trying to keep his distance while keeping his eye on them. They sure weren't making it easy for him what with their walking and all. Other than Jacks, the homeless that would normally accost them kept their distance with simple mental suggestions to do so. He walked with his head held high, shoulders back, and close to Nathen just in case. "We could go back to my place and snag my laptop?" Cameron offered. "Do you want me to call an Uber?"

Nathen was confused momentarily. "Oh? No, I have a computer with me." He reached his hand into his pocket and took out his iPhone. "Our smartphones are computers. Most of the new phones are actually more powerful than computers were only five or ten years ago. I want to try to access whatever I did last time, but maybe less buried in it, because I was not conscious of what was going on in the room, or with my body."

"Oh! Sure, phone. Okay, let's either go to a Starbucks or maybe find a quiet place in case you collapse again? Which would you rather? Park bench or coffee shop?"

Nathen paused to consider, "I think probably outside. Starbucks might be too distracting or people might see something strange. Maybe an alley or something?" He had a fast change in emotion to nervousness, "Or maybe in the homeless camp?"

Cameron switched to transmitting thoughts, *"Let's sit on this bench over here in the park. I don't want to go into a homeless camp as that would add an element of distraction worse than Starbucks. And dark alleys aren't great either."* Cameron led Nathen to a bench on the outskirts of the park away from the homeless. It would allow him a vantage to sense and see anyone coming from any direction. Quickly scanning the area, he sensed only the residents of the camp, a few teenagers smoking pot over in the play area, and residents in their homes around the park. Nobody except Jacks was remotely interested in them. He sat and projected the image of making out with Nathen in the park to him, flashing a sly smile. "Maybe another time?" He pulled out his own phone and started sorting through e-mails.

Nathen smiled and leaned over and kissed Cameron softly. "Well, a small kiss won't hurt, right?"

Cameron returned the kiss, running his hand gently through Nathen's hair and gazing into his eyes, biting his lower lip. "I think my new favorite thing in the world is to kiss you." He groaned, *"The guy from your work is at the other end of the homeless group listening in on our conversation."* He switched to speaking out loud for the sake of their eavesdropper, "Let's see if you can't do your magic, and we can find this warehouse for Syn. I know she's not getting anywhere with this whole hospital thing. But if we can't find anything, I'm gonna propose maybe going back to my place for an evening in?"

Nathen nodded. "Yeah, that sounds like a good idea. I don't know what will happen with this ability. I never got training on how to use it, that my natural skills would be enhanced. If I pass out... Well, let's hope that doesn't happen again." He held up his iPhone, unlocked it, and opened the browser to Google. "Okay, I'm about to start."

As Nathen focused on the screen, his mind wavered, as if he was about to fall asleep. Cameron watched as Nathen's eyes glazed over when he stared at his phone. It looked as if he were deeply interested in whatever he was looking at, just another modern-day zombie. Cameron sighed, leaning against the back of the bench and mentally looked around. Nothing had changed for them except he noted he could no longer feel Nathen's emotions. Nathen usually had an undercurrent of anxiety, increasing whenever he was in social situations or more unknown situations like when they approached the park. Now Nathen was calm, even absent. Cameron could still sense him, but only just so. He relaxed a little, not realizing he had tensed when he couldn't feel Nathen. Cameron reflected on how reliant on his abilities he was. For Cameron, his ability to sense both emotionally and mentally was like any other sense. He looked around again, being mindful of possible vampires and relaxing when no bald, albino blood sucker was in sight. He glanced back at Nathen who seemed to be concentrating and turned his attention to his own phone.

As he feigned interest in his phone, Cameron began probing Jacks for more information. There was something on the edge of Jacks' awareness that Cameron couldn't quite grasp onto. He had never encountered it before he met Jacks. Something important that Jacks had forgotten. Forgetting is a natural part of memory. People are preprogrammed to forget irrelevant or extraneous information and only retain the most salient to survival. But this was something different that frustrated Cameron. Sometimes people forgot out of trauma, but that wasn't it either. Sometimes people forgot out of a difficulty with organic retrieval and with reminders, or cuing, the individual could dredge up that which they had forgotten. It was like how pictures reviewed later could remind someone of an event. But that wasn't it.

It was frustrating to Cameron who continued to mentally scratch and scratch at what Jacks had forgotten. He found it a personal challenge to try and get past the block and started to work around it. How long was the block for? No information? When did it start? Shortly after Jacks had come to work for Impetus! Cameron learned that Jacks had started working at Impetus shortly after he left the military, had been recruited in fact. Cameron saw HR himself going over the basics of employment. Jacks didn't immediately believe in vampires, but when HR left the room and the other door opened and a starved, slavering, wildly savage and terrified woman was pushed into the room and released, her eyes a brilliant blue, her features primal and desperate...Jacks didn't hesitate. He chose at first the Sig Sauer and plugged the woman's brain with six shots, immediately reaching for the survival knife, also set out on the table in front of him, and rolled onto the top of her still body, decapitating her with a few swift slices. Once the spinal cord was severed, the woman's body quickly began to dissolve into gore under Jacks' weight. Cameron saw as HR returned and congratulated Jacks on his abilities, reiterating the terms of employment. Jacks had such a rush, almost erotic, from the kill, that he immediately signed up. His training lasted for six months and was much like boot camp. He underwent extensive training on what vampires were and how to not only kill them, but effectively torture them for needed information. He learned that vampiric blood was valued by the Company and any kill that he made was more valued when he could successfully retrieve the blood.

That six months went by quickly. There was something about that time...missing time...Jacks had several episodes during that training period where he awoke with frustration. He had been regimented to sleep and wake at the same time, and since his time in the Middle East he had never overslept. But there were several times that he had overslept, and the first time he had chalked it up to excitement from the new assignments. After the third time he started a journal, but it never happened again. A few hours of oversleep...

Cameron knew Jacks was dangerous and as soon as Nathen had outlasted his usefulness he would be dispatched. The most important thing was for Nathen to meet the goals that HR and the group had set for him. Cameron frowned, though had renewed desire to help Nathen meet those goals.

*

For Nathen, the screen on his phone soon became the reality he was in. The normal Google screen took up the majority of his field of view, behind which was his mind's projection, Nathen assumed, of a seemingly infinite library, full of ceiling high shelves stocked full of books. The room was long and seemed to go on forever, fading into a dark tunnel. He stepped aside and moved past the holographic projection of the Google page toward the library. He focused on the space itself and shifted his mind toward the tunnel. The scene changed, and he saw an endless root system of an elder tree, with connections running through to other larger segments, which ran as far as he could see.

Through them he saw pulses of light traveling to and from large nexus segments. They were being routed and rerouted to other segments in a seemingly infinite system of wires. The first thought that came to Nathen was that of a brain, and in that instance that is what he saw. Neurons and their dendrites reaching and connecting to other cells, all pulsing almost endlessly with various impulses that Nathen instinctually knew were packets being sent across the internet to various endpoints and people's devices. Most of them were probably Netflix, YouTube, or porn videos being routed to someone's home. He focused on information that was sent to the Sons of Discord's server and soon the other impulses faded and disappeared. In the distance, he saw a neuron light up with the familiar feel. The impulse ran its length, was routed, and ended up in a neuron that didn't forward to any other connecting dendrites. This happened a few more times and he decided to focus on that cell. As he did so, he was carried away by a strong pull. There was no hesitation in the force of movement. It was sure and quickly carried him through various cells and their axons and dendrites to the location he hoped was the server he was looking for. As the movement stopped, he saw the familiar locked Golden Gate in an infinite black void. He assumed that projecting himself into that void would cause him to get stuck like he did in the hospital, so he decided against doing that. Instead he shifted his focus to just in front of him and visualized a browser window. One immediately materialized in his field of view, and with a thought he opened the Google Map's page. In the current location, he projected the image of him and Cameron on the park bench, the image morphed into coordinate numbers, which the program had resolved to the park. In the destination he projected the image of the Gate and the cell he was standing near. The image resolved into coordinates again and Google dropped a pin on a building in Lombard Street near the Embarcadero.

Nathen pushed away the projected display and visualized his phone. As his mind sent the thought, he was carried back to the path he came from. The white screen of his phone was the map he had created earlier. Elated, he turned away from the screen and the white noise faded. Nathen found himself staring at his phone, which had the Google Maps app now open with a path to an unknown location on Lombard Street.

Nathen return with feelings of joy and held his phone out to Cameron.

"Find it, then?" Cameron smiled, slipping his own phone back in his pocket.

Nathen nodded, his emotions were roiling with excitement. "I did! That was cool. I'm going to do that again later, but with other things. There is a whole world in there!" He gave his phone to Cameron.

With it opened up to Google Maps, with two pins being connected by a line of a suggested walking path about three blocks away, Cameron accepted the phone and said with a lopsided grin, "That's interesting, I guess. But yes, one thing at a time."

They left the park and walked down several alleyways to Montgomery where they turned down a few more alleys and made their way between buildings to Sansome.

Cameron smiled at Nathen, *"Heh, Jacks is cursing us trying to keep up."* Hanging a left on Sansome they found their way to Lombard where they turned right and followed it down the hill to the end of the street.

Standing on the street between a large red building and several white warehouses, Cameron looked back and forth, then out toward the Embarcadero. "It would be awesome to take a romantic walk with you down to the water later," he commented, stepping to one of the buildings and standing with his back to it. He began scanning the area. One of them was completely empty and the other had several offices with late night workers, two of whom were engaged in each other. Cameron laughed. "This one behind me is empty, the one across the way has several people working late or hanging out. None of them seem to be involved in this, but I can start probing deeper if you want. Where did you sense this?"

Nathen turned toward the obviously abandoned building and pointed. "I'm pretty sure it's this one." The painted white brick warehouse had seen better days. It had broken windows, structural damage, and graffiti all over it and was obviously not taken care of. The darkness within seemed foreboding.

"No one is in there. Do you want to go in and investigate?" Cameron asked.

Nathen nodded and proceeded to the entrance which was locked with a metal door with a chain around the handles. He frowned, "I can try breaking it, but I don't want to get in trouble."

"In trouble by who? A secret evil group who is trying to terrorize children?"

Nathen shrugged to that wisdom, focused and took hold of the new-looking chain forcefully yanking it. While the chain didn't break, the door handles did. He pushed the door away from them, which made a cracking warped noise as it swung open. A dark hall with a dirty floor and graffiti on both walls, lead to a single dusty receptionist desk next to an open door that lead into the building. Nathen could make out the details of the room even with the absence of light. He went ahead with Cameron following closely behind him. The door took them to a different hall with one solid wall on the right and half wall of a plexiglass viewing area on the left. This hall also had a door at the end on the left leading out to a large space.

Out of the plexiglass windows Nathen saw a brand-new small fridge-sized server cabinet with obvious hard drive and network activity. Next to it stood a table with a flat-screen monitor, keyboard, and mouse. He pointed it out to Cameron who was using his phone as a flashlight and led them to the door at the end of the hall. The space had not been cleaned for a while; yet the desk, screen and server seemed to be relatively dust free. They were plugged into an outlet drop, including an ethernet cable, which was plugged into the back of the server. Though there were no other lights in the area it seemed the building still had power. "I wonder who is paying for the power and the access to the internet?"

"Bad guys?" Cameron mused. "I'll see if Syn can't figure it out. Someone has to be paying, unless it is simply hijacked electricity, which wouldn't surprise me."

"Yeah, this whole thing is strange. Normally, hackers like these would be using computers of normal internet users that are infected with a botnet. Most hackers would not set up drops like this. This seems like something else." Nathen pressed a button on the keyboard and the screen came on with a Linux prompt blinking, requesting a username. "I can't crack this here. I'll have to disconnect it from the internet and use a secondary box to modify the filesystem. It will probably be encrypted, which means having to decrypt the data first." He examined the cabinet. "It's modular, so should be easy to remove the primary hard drive."

Cameron shrugged, at a loss for everything Nathen was saying, *"Jacks is outside the building, seeming to monitor us from afar, but he's not following us inside. I wonder why? Maybe he knows this building?"*

Nathen pulled the plug and opened the case, releasing two hinges on the sides which let him remove the blade. He put it on the desk and slowly unclipped the covering, removing the SSD drive and putting it into his pocket. Nathen turned to face Cameron and in that instant heard a loud pop. There was heat and a high-pitched noise in both ears as an invisible force hit him. Nathen stumbled back. Shock and fear triggered an impulse he didn't seem to be in control of.

Time stopped.

Nathen could see what he assumed were four explosions. There were balls of fire all around him with pieces of metal and cement suspended midair. Cameron was caught in midair—flying back with a gash on his chest and rivulets of blood suspended, having burst forth where something had hit and penetrated him. Nathen was struck by the intoxicating scent of his lover that was filling the room but was dulled by the chemicals that had started the fire. A part of his and Cameron's hair were singed and his once thick red hair was now missing where the flame of the explosion had licked him.

Nathen noticed something wet in his hand which he brought up to examine and became cognizant of the fact that shrapnel had hit him as well, though he had not registered the pain. He became transfixed by the hand that he held up in front of him. He knew it was his, but somehow the stump of an appendage that now only held three fingers and a thumb with visible tendon and sinew didn't seem like it should belong to him. There were also various pieces of metal stuck in his torso and he could feel a cold sting on the top of his head. He reached up and could feel something vaguely squishy and no hair. Part of him thought he should be horrified, but Nathen was emotionally numb, light headed, with a mild sense of awe as he watched the fireballs, the swarm of flying metal and cement, and realized they were all still moving, if only just.

There was a high-pitched sound and Nathen looked around to see where it was coming from but soon realized it was in his own head. He was moving too fast to hear anything specific that was going on around him, but if he focused, he could make out the snap of the flame.

Seeing Cameron's face, a mixture of confusion and fear snapped Nathen out of his stupor and he acted out of instinct. He grabbed Cameron by his waist and started to run, avoiding the fire and flying pieces as best he could. The door out of the building was engulfed with flame, but a new opening had been created by the explosion near the far-left corner of the building. He ran toward it and jumped shoulder first through the flame. It burned the cloth of his shirt and the heat of stinging cold fire ate away the top layer of his skin, though he was moving so quickly that the flames didn't have a chance to catch against his clothing. Nathen sprinted from the building to the alleyway far away from the flames and the street.

He gently laid Cameron down on the pavement. Cameron was in shock, his emotions a jumble. He was conscious, but covered in blood and burns on his face, head, and back. The wound on his chest was bleeding profusely. Nathen ripped off Cameron's ruined shirt and used it to apply pressure to the gash on his chest. Cameron winced, his face turning ashen as his eyes rolled back into his head and he lost consciousness. Nathen could no longer feel any emotions from him; though he could tell he was still alive, but fading. Nathen scrambled with what to do. Call for help? It would be too late, whatever had hit Cameron seemed to have damaged his heart and he could see his aura dimming as he focused on it. "Hold on!" was all he could manage through the tears, though he couldn't hear himself scream. The bleeding from Cameron's chest slowed, which caused Nathen to panic. Cameron was dying.

Nathen realized he was in shock as a sudden line of images of sappy vampire movies formed in his mind. Vampires bent over their hurt human lovers, slowly feeding them their blood. He let out an absurd laugh. Tipping Cameron's head back he opened his mouth. He bit his own wrist deeply and positioned the wound over Cameron's mouth allowing his blood to flow and disappear down his lover's throat. He didn't see any immediate change but did notice that Cameron's aura was now mixed with something else. Nathen licked his arm, sealed the wound and waited. This would either do nothing or maybe it would heal him...or turn him into a vampire. He hoped that if did turn Cameron into a vampire, he would forgive him.

Cameron didn't seem to get worse, but didn't look better either. Nathen bit himself again and brought his arm back to Cameron's mouth, forcing more of his blood into Cameron's throat. Suddenly and with a very weird spastic movement Cameron clenched hold of Nathen's arm and started to painfully gnaw and suck on his wound. He seemed to still be unconscious and Nathen startled, but didn't pull away. Nathen noticed that as Cameron drank, the burns on his head started to recede and normal skin was knitting back shut. A thin metal chunk caught his eye as it slowly withdrew from Cameron's chest and fell to the ground.

Nathen felt himself growing weaker and weaker, the bestial side of him screaming to be fed. Reluctantly he pulled his arm away from Cameron whose eyes snapped open, glowing a bright neon blue, though he was still human.

Cameron's screams were primal, feral, something from a cornered animal. Their link overwhelmed Nathen as he too could suddenly feel everybody's emotions nearby, perhaps in the entire city. Then Nathen saw it all. Experienced it all. As he was able to see and feel Cameron's emotions when he had his blood in him, when Cameron had Nathen's blood running through his veins Nathen suddenly could sense Cameron's thoughts, too. It was not simply hearing or seeing, but rather it was like he was in Cameron's mind.

Everybody's thoughts jumbled into a meaningless, garbled, symphony of gibberish. Cameron had no control, no conscious thought. He was on fire inside and out. He felt his flesh melting, his mind in flame. There was no beginning, no end of the pain. No escape. Cameron continued to scream, reaching out from the darkness for something familiar. Mentally searching desperately for something, something he could hold on to.

He found him, sequestered in the darkness searching for something. Searching for him!

Nathen slumped forward, overwhelmed with the same information Cameron was experiencing. The roar of thoughts and emotions from what seemed like millions of minds...and then just one. And Nathen saw him...

Todd Jacks.

A picture reel of memories assaulted Nathen as if he were Jacks himself.

*

Jacks, recruited by the Company. The perfect job. He went from killing monsters in the desert to real monsters in the US. Who knew that vampires existed? They offered such a thrilling challenge with their ability to move faster than he could. Their inhuman strength. The orientation that the Company had given had been a good one. Nathen saw the many videos of how Jacks was taught to successfully kill vampires, and what happened when a vampire won. Jacks was smart, a ruthless survivor, and always watched from far away, using his sniper rifle to incapacitate first. But once he got them alone... There were several places throughout the city that he brought vampires and their families if they had them and he had orders to take them out too. Usually if the vampire was stupid enough to tell his family about the Company in any way, the entire brood had to be exterminated. But if the vampire had kept the Company a secret, then the family could be left alone. It all depended.

The reel played on, showing Nathen:

Jacks' last kill—a young lesbian couple. The African American woman had been "recruited" for her linguistic skills. She was fluent in eight different languages and the

Company thought her a good acquisition to head their Overseas division and assist with foreign relations. She was in her fifties and her gorgeous Chinese wife was in her thirties. The woman had been with the Company only a couple of months but was bowing under pressure of her newfound abilities. Jacks had seen it happen in at least a dozen other cases where the vamp was too weak to embrace their new existence. Jacks himself had no interest in being a vampire. Sure, the speed and strength were enticing, but the bloodlust was a weakness Jacks had no interest in. The women were no problem to capture. He had overpowered the wife and got her into the back of his van, had shot the asset in the head as she sat in her car having exited the Wholefoods. He pulled the van up, transferred the undead into the back along with the groceries (waste not want not after all) and drove away. In the warehouse, he had tied the asset down and started the process of draining the blood out of it while its wife looked on in horror. Jacks reveled in the memory of how she had pleaded and begged. He allowed her to think that sucking him off might save her corpse-wife's unlife and was incredibly aroused at her gagging on him. As she saw her lover fall to gore when the last of the blood was removed, he broke her neck. Cleanup was easier with vampires—a simple hose down and done. Corpses were harder, but Jacks had a crematorium assistant paid off who looked the other way. He thought Jacks was a hitman and with his own meth addiction, the extra income was always welcome.

Nathen was privy to many other scenarios, each as horrifying as the last as the dispassionate Jacks slaughtered vampires and their families. He felt Cameron out of control, the blinding pain that his blood caused as

Cameron homed in on Jacks. Sensing Cameron's rage and a bubbling of old shame familiar now from their discussion of Frank, and all the pain both mental and physical that Cameron felt, along with the fear that he had for Nathen and Syn and his desire to protect them, Nathen witnessed Cameron pour all of that into Jacks. He saw in Jacks confusion and frustration as he had seen Nathen run from the building. Nathen wondered how was that possible? He had been running faster than the human eye could see. He then sensed as Jacks fell silent and heard a sharp scream of pain cut off quickly.

Cameron also fell unconscious, relieved, expelled of the pain. He lay in Nathen's lap breathing deeply, a look of serenity on his face. Only the ruined shirt and smears of blood across his newly healed skin betrayed the fact that he was not merely comfortably napping. Nathen heard shouts from the street as onlookers came out of their buildings and homes to watch the flames. Two men came into the ally, drawn by Cameron (and Nathen's own?) screams.

"Hey, are you guys all right?" one of them asked.

Nathen realized suddenly that he was famished. He looked up at the two men who were approaching. He could smell them, smell Cameron. He could see the blood flowing under the surface of the skin of all three of them.

The two men had stopped suddenly, about ten feet away. One asked the other, "Dude, what's going on with his eyes?"

Nathen was dazed and not fully in control of his senses. A large part of his mind was wracked with anxiety, fear, confusion, and disgust. He was overwhelmed and wanted to crawl into a ball in a silent room and go to sleep, or cry. With hunger gnawing at his remaining sanity, he began making justifications for biting Cameron, he had after all saved his life, to eyeing the hapless humans who would not know what happened and might even enjoy it.

Buried under all of that was also fear of Cameron, who had caused a person's brain to explode. Had actually killed someone.

Behind the two men he saw police lights, the familiar red and blue bouncing off the walls. He knew before long, one of the officers would be questioning him. No, that should not happen. He picked up Cameron and used the remaining magic of his blood to jump onto a roof of one of the buildings and run toward the Embarcadero. His hunger increased twofold and he was losing control. All he could hear was a loud high-pitched tone, so calling for help was out. Instead, he texted the car service and waited, forcing himself to be mindful of the moment, lest he accidentally bite Cameron. He took deep breaths, focusing solely on a point on the street next to him. Ten minutes later, the car pulled up and he gently placed Cameron into the back seat, settling himself in from the other side. His shirt in tatters, body covered in burns and gashes, jeans burnt and caked with blood, he stared off into the distance, crying.

He could hear the driver, Julian, immediately calling the office. Instead of dropping them off at the front, he drove into the well-lit underground garage where Nathen had never gone before. At this time of night on a Saturday, it wasn't surprising that there were no other cars in the area. There appeared to be multiple levels, though the driver moved the car through empty lanes directly to what appeared to be a service entrance. Standing by the door with a small cart was John, the cafeteria attendant he had met on his tour. On the cart were five containers. As

Nathen exited the backseat, he smelled the Type o blood "shakes" that were never preferable, but filling. Seeing Nathen, John clucked his tongue and turned, muttering something about needing to go get more.

Nathen took a cup and drank, not stopping till it was fully gone, and he was sucking air at the bottom. He repeated that and the blood coursed through him as he focused on his body. As the tinnitus faded, he realized he could hear again. Next, Nathen's attention was drawn to the sound of small metal bits as they emerged from his skin and skull, making tinkling noises when they hit the concrete. Reaching up, Nathen ran his hand through his hair that had returned, though seemed disheveled. It didn't feel the same, and he realized he was still missing half of his hand. It was something he knew, but was a shocking realization as he stood staring, transfixed at the itchy stumps where his fingers had once been, was now growing a new white...bone. The sight of it made him nauseated, but he didn't lose his blood, only produced dry heaving. He held on to his hand as suddenly the nerves began to send pain signals to his brain, and he held in a scream, crying blood and moaning behind parsed lips and gasped instead.

"You shouldn't do that," the small Asian man chastised, emerging with another cart that included ten containers. "Crying only wastes." He stood nearby, assessing the situation, snorted, then turned with the first cart, disappearing into the door to the kitchen again.

*

Cameron woke up in the back of the town car. He looked around confused, and remained still, quickly closing his eyes. He sensed tension, fear, confusion, but moreover

Nathen's hunger. Cameron took a quick self-assessment and realized he felt great. Better than he had ever felt? He had no aches or pains, his head was clear, even the fatigue he had from the incredibly pleasurable blood loss had faded. He thought hard. Where had they been? The last he could recall was going into an abandoned warehouse and seeing a black refrigerator thing with a glass door and a dozen blue lights on it. Then what? How did he get to here? And where was here?

Reaching out with his mind he sensed Nathen and Julian immediately. Julian was a driver for the Company. While he picked up various people, he was mostly assigned to pick up vampires. He worked all shifts and was currently assigned exclusively to pick up Nathen for the next month in order to monitor him, report his movements. Julian was a neutral fellow with no actual knowledge of the Company's more nefarious actions such as killing "assets." He had a family that included two kids and a wife with mental health issues. He liked working for the Company as it gave him benefits that included private school for his boys and a large enough salary that justified him leaving at any time day or night to pick people up. It also allowed for him to provide for his whole family. He had also been trained about vampires. Hence the unbreakable window between the backseat and front. He had seen vampires who were out of control with hunger at which point he had to call his service who dispatched someone with a tranquilizer gun. That happened so infrequently, though, that he was not worried. Most of the time it was taking people from one point to the other. Cameron delved deeper into Julian's memory pulling up images, names, and locations of where he took various vampires, repeating them for remembering later.

Cameron's reverie was interrupted with the arrival of John Lee, a cook in the kitchen. John was human and had worked for the Company for a long time. He read John's memories and learned that John had transferred several times, working initially for the Company in Japan in the 1970s. He had always worked in the position of a cook, food prep, and blood maintenance for the vampires. But that had come much later, in the 2000s. One of the managers had come to him as they had in the 1990s when they asked him if he would like to take part in a new program that was aimed at health and keeping people young. John was already feeling his age by that time and had agreed. Since then, he had not seemed to age a day. He had initially gone in for an injection and had returned weekly for blood monitoring. He had received another injection every ten years or so, but didn't know what they were injecting him with. It didn't matter to John as he didn't age or ever get sick. He was absolutely loyal to the Company and they rewarded him in kind. In the 2000s, they had taught him about vampires and told him that he would be asked to prepare meals for them as well. By then, John was more than happy with the Company and feeding the kyonshī was just another job duty. Cameron could read that this was all very routine and that he was bringing Nathen his preferred blood, making his way with a third trip.

How did Nathen get hurt? Then Cameron shook his head. How was he able to get so much information from John and Julian? He paused, anticipating the budding of a headache. Normally, he would have had to concentrate, purposefully focus to pull all of that information from someone. It would have been easy enough but would have come with a cost: a tension headache, a cluster headache, a migraine, then exhaustion. He was still great! Clear. No headache at all. Cameron thought he could probably delve further. Get more information. But...Nathen.

Cameron began reading Nathen...On the surface Nathen was horrified and watching his...hand grown back! Cameron sat up, feeling the need to go to him and hold him. He shouldn't be going through that, however mind-blowing it was, alone. The back door was open and while he sensed Julian's eyes on him, he didn't move to stop him. Cameron continued to read. There had been an explosion at the warehouse and Nathen had lost his hand there. Cameron had also been hurt and...

As he reached for Nathen, sending waves of concern and love and thinking, "*I'm so sorry, Nathen, are you all right?*" Cameron was hit by what Nathen had done and couldn't help but read deeper, seeing more. His eyes were wide in horror, mouth fell open, and he was momentarily paralyzed with the symbiotic memory of the pain that Nathen's blood had left him in, but moreover what he had done totally unconsciously to Jacks.

Cameron could feel how overwhelmed with pain and shock Nathen was, though he was automatically picking up another drink, downing it in a few seconds, then another, and another still. Cameron saw that Nathen's hunger was subsiding, and that he was healing. Cameron watched on as bone, sinew, and muscle weaved together and wrapped around the missing pieces of Nathen's hand. Nathen stared on as well, in both horror and fascination.

Cameron leaned against the side of the town car, his mind reeling from everything that had transpired from Nathen's perspective. But moreover, what Nathen's blood had done to him. Apparently, it had healed him. Cameron reached up and touched his now patchy hair where skin had healed, but his hair hadn't grown back yet. He looked down and even though he had blood smeared on him, he was not in pain. And... The blood had expanded his abilities, had allowed him (or compelled him) to do something he never knew possible. How had he channeled pain into Jacks...who was dead? From Nathen's perspective of being in Cameron's mind when he was out of control he was. And the act itself had horrified Nathen. Of course it had... Cameron stepped away slowly. He took a deep breath and nodded. Of course, Nathen wouldn't understand. How could he? Cameron was conflicted. Part of him desperately wanted to start removing the memories from Nathen, to keep him close and never let him know Cameron's secret. He was a monster, and Nathen didn't need to know that...they could go on as they had been! He could have Nathen, keep him clueless and... The other part of him that had vowed never to do that with someone he loved stayed his action.

Finally, the skin started to grow over the muscle and bone, and then the nail; growing like some kind of monster claw from the newly regenerated cuticle. Nathen continued drinking. Cameron sensed that Nathen's body was now whole and mind clear of the animalistic urge to feed. His mind clear and he wanted process.

Cameron read Nathen's surface thoughts and nodded. And then...Nathen was gone. Cameron didn't know how, but it was like when they first met and he could not sense Nathen at all. He was standing in front of him, staring into the distance and unwilling to look at Cameron. Cameron's mind reeled for a minute, desperately reaching out to mentally embrace Nathen and...nothing.

"Nathen?" Cameron took a few steps toward him. Had he done it on purpose? Shut him out?

When Nathen didn't respond, Cameron gently touched his shoulder. Nathen jerked away from him. "I need to be alone," he gritted out.

Cameron's breath caught, and he bowed his head in acceptance.

Stuffing his hands in his pockets, Cameron walked away and found his way up the ramp to the gated entrance. Cursing slightly, Cameron reached into Julian's mind and prompted him to hit the remote to open the garage. As the gate rose, Cameron ducked under it and went to the corner. Once figuring out what streets he was on, he called an Uber and hung out.

Chapter Twenty-Five

CAMERON

San Francisco downtown financial district at eleven on a Saturday is somewhat of a ghost town. There were a few people around, but it was not nearly as busy as it usually was during the day. Cameron leaned against the light post and started processing the events of the night. A lot had happened in twenty-four hours.

Cameron was lost in thought but noted the car that pulled up beside him. He slid into the Uber. He rode in silence, reading the driver's judgment of him being shirtless, disheveled, and mentally calmed him. Once home, he caused the security guard to ignore him and made his way to his apartment. Seeing Syn sitting on the couch with boxes of Chinese food, he began crying.

"You've looked better," Syn said alarmed as she came to him looking him over. "Come on."

She led Cameron to his bathroom and gently pushed him inside, shutting the door and then going to his closet to pull out clothes for him. "Bathe and then hugs. I'll hang here—you start spilling. What the hell happened? And where is Nathen?"

Cameron woodenly followed directions and peeled off the remains of his clothes. He started the shower and stood staring into the mirror, vaguely aware of Syn tossing fresh clothes into the room for him.

"I've got to shower. Will tell you when I'm done?" Cameron realized that the pressure that he usually experienced when opening a link wasn't actually there. It was like he could have his mental communication open forever without the headaches.

"Okay—I'll nuke the cold kung pow." Cameron accepted that, and even though he could continue talking to Syn, he went ahead and cut the connection.

The man in the mirror was vaguely familiar. Aside from being covered in gore and having missing hair, he looked great. Even the bags that were often under his eyes due to poor sleep were gone. Cameron began shaving, having always found it soothing. He shaved off the rest of the hair on his head and then began working on his face and then groin. With his first boyfriend, he had started shaving everywhere because it was Tommy's preference. But since he had been on his own, he stopped shaving his legs. Then when his chest hair started growing in, he didn't touch it and stopped shaving under his arms too. He stepped into the heated water, turning it a few degrees hotter than was comfortable and, sinking down to sit on the floor, he let the water cascade over him.

After about half an hour of tears where Cameron couldn't seem to get hold of his emotions, he reminded himself that he had to go with Syn to the Kitten Club to meet with her friend, and so he finished washing off. He looked at the clothes Syn had chosen and groaned a humorless laugh. Black on black? Well, he was going to be going to a club after all. He pulled on the old black Pink Floyd tee shirt with stylized rainbow prism and black jeans. Transferring his keys and wallet, he couldn't help but check his phone and was disappointed to see no texts waiting.

Coming out to the scene of newly warmed Chinese food, he found Syn sitting at the table waiting for him with a bottle of cold beer. He tried to smile, but faltered, as she had old 70s and 80s rock playing for him. Cameron sat down and ate in silence, grateful that Syn always knew exactly what he needed.

After finishing his beer, he began. *"We found a warehouse with a server in it. Nathen pulled it out, but it caused an explosion. I was knocked out, and Nathen pulled me out of there. We were both pretty tore up. I guess I was dying and Nathen gave me his blood."*

Syn's eyes opened wide in surprise and Cameron nodded and went to the fridge for another beer, pulling out a second for Syn as well. They moved to the living room and sunk onto the couch and Cameron continued with mental communication. It was faster, easier, and more natural. *"I don't remember any of it personally but read it from Nathen after I woke up. Apparently, I was in a lot of pain. Guess vampire blood gives indigestion."* Cameron offered a sarcastically sad smile. *"I woke up in the back of a car in the garage at Impetus. Got more info. They're keeping their human employees alive with some sort of injections. One guy has worked for the company since the seventies and hasn't aged in like thirty years. Anyway...the point is I killed a guy and Nathen saw it. He was the guy who has been following us: a psychopath, really bad guy. Would have killed Nathen if he got out of line, killed me, killed and raped you. I don't fucking know. Point is that when I wasn't in my right mind I mentally exploded dude's brain or something. Nathen doesn't want to be with me, and I don't blame him. I'm a murderer. And I don't feel bad about it at all."*

"Nor should you! Cam, fuck!" Syn reached out and grasped Cameron's forearm for emphasis. "First off you were under the influence of vampire jiz and in the second place, guy was evil it sounds like. You wouldn't hurt someone that didn't deserve it."

Cameron looked up sharply, narrowing his eyes. There was something in Syn's mental tone. "Come on...who do you think deletes your search history?" she asked.

Cameron frowned, his heart beginning to race.

Syn went on, "I know it started with Frank. And I know that there have been others. And it's okay, Cam. I know you would never hurt anyone who didn't deserve it. You're a protector, and a very, very good man." Syn ran her hand down to catch Cameron's hand.

Cameron ducked his head, dashing a tear from his eye and allowing Syn to pull him into her embrace. He laid out on the couch, resting his head in her lap. "Hey, hey," Syn pulled over a box of tissue. "Listen, if he can't deal with this, that's fine. You don't need to be with him, I don't care how good the fang was."

Cameron chuckled despite himself, wiping his eyes and then closing them. Syn clicked on a stand-up act and they watched in silence. Cameron was on an emotional roller coaster and struggled to remember another time in his life when he was quite so out of control. After a while, he sat back up so he could reach his beer and settled against the back of the couch, putting his feet up on the ottoman. "Maybe we should take off? I mean, after we figure out what your friend found? Maybe we should start over somewhere? Could always move to New York."

Syn groaned at him. They both knew that was where Tommy lived. They had talked about moving to New York and decided against it when Cameron got into the college in San Francisco.

"What about San Diego? No winters..." Syn countered.

Cameron smiled sadly, nodding.

Chapter Twenty-Six

CAMERON

Cameron was getting more and more restless. He had hoped that Nathen would have called, texted, or walked through the door, but his silence spoke volumes. Despite this, Cameron kept stealing glances of the dark screen of his phone, inwardly growing more and more despondent until he finally stood declaring, "We should go to the club. Get drunk, dance…"

Syn grinned. "Well, you are dressed for it."

The trip to South San Francisco took a while and they rode in silence, Syn mentally going over the plan. They would drink, dance, hang out, and at 1:00 a.m. she was supposed to come out to the parking lot where someone would hand her a flash drive from when Statix and Kat went into the hospital. The plan was for Cameron to already be out there and read everyone, protecting Syn should it get too dangerous. She didn't have to say it, but he knew she was disappointed that Nathen was not going to be there to protect both of them, considering what they were up against.

They got to the club shortly after midnight. Neither wanted to be too inebriated, and so only ordered beers. Both of them ended up leaving the cheap beer behind, having become beer snobs in the last few years. The club had overly loud dance music, which neither of them were enjoying or drunk enough to be into.

"I'm so not interested in clubbing right now," Cameron imparted morosely.

"Hey, I have an idea. We can hit Mai's," Syn offered excitedly.

"Fuck, Syn. I took Nathen there today!" Cameron looked miserable again and jumped when Syn punched his arm. "Okay, okay. Mai's it is!" He grinned sheepishly.

"That's more fucking like it!"

*

They headed out of the club and Cameron checked his Uber tracker. Being so far out of the city, Ubers were going to take a while, so he went ahead and ordered one. They hung out and Cameron began scanning. There were a group of people getting high at the end of the building, all interested in what they were doing. Otherwise, there was a full club of people in various stages of intoxication, sexual tension, sexual frustration. Cameron was reminded why he rarely went out dancing. Syn had her phone out and was working on something.

And then he sensed it. Two relatively handsome young men came out of the club and headed to a motorcycle. One was a purple and blue-haired enormous Samoan looking guy with his still tall, but dwarfed by comparison, dark-haired boyfriend. But there was something strange about both of them. He tried probing both more deeply and realized what was wrong. He was being blocked by rainbow hair! In the same way that he had been blocked by HR!

Cameron immediately tensed. "Something's wrong! I think that guy is from Impetus!" He began probing the dark-haired man. The couple had paused to make out, the Asian guy much more aggressive, but the dark-haired guy easily, if not shyly, following his lead. Delving into the man's mind, Cameron fell back against the car he was standing near. "He's a shape shifter," he said quietly, but out loud.

Though they were across the parking lot, and with the noise emanating from the club behind them no way they could have heard Cameron, but the big guy looked up, pushing his lover behind him and staring at Cameron with a challenge. He checked his watch, tapped it a couple of times. Syn looked up and saw as the man got on the motorcycle, pulling on his helmet and handing one to the other man who swung onto the seat and wrapped his arms around the chubby driver. Cameron wanted so much to talk to the man, but the fact that his boyfriend likely worked with the evil corporation gave Cameron pause.

Cameron's eyes grew wide as they drove by them and Syn bent over and picked up a thumb drive which they dropped in front of her. "How do you know these guys? Syn?"

"Just like Nathen. I've known them for years online!"

"He's blocking me, and I don't know how! But it feels like that guy from Nathen's work."

"Say hi before they're gone!" Syn demanded, whacking his shoulder.

Cameron reached out to the guy on the back and took a chance. *"Your boyfriend is blocking me, but I'm a telepath. I know you're a shape shifter, and it seems we're all working against the bad guys. But we don't know who to trust."*

Cameron saw the guys slow down and stop at the corner. There was a gentle, tentative caress of response.

"Theo says this is too much heat. He doesn't go up against big corporations or groups that are so corrupt and powerful. It's too dangerous. He's a mage and is blocking you that way. He says don't try contact him anymore as Statix, or online at all right now, and that the flash drive has a ton of information. He also says that you're interesting. We haven't met another mage in a long time. If you want, we should meet. Wednesday the Snake Pit is having a benefit and all three floors are participating. Midnight. We'll find you. After the benefit we're heading out of town, so it was nice to meet you if I never meet you again. I'm Robbie by the way."

They drove off.

Cameron relayed the information to Syn who suggested forgoing Mai's so she could get home and read the information on the flash, which Cameron agreed.

Chapter Twenty-Seven

CAMERON

Syn slept in, as she had spent the night pouring over information that she had obtained from her friend. Cameron hadn't slept at all. He lay staring at his phone all night, hoping against hope he would receive a message from Nathen and making himself sicker and sicker when nothing was forthcoming. Despite having taken the next week off from work, Cameron did not feel very much like a vacation and ended up sending a dozen or so work e-mails between 3:00 and 6:00 a.m., when he finally broke down and took an Ambien. He had gotten the prescription several years prior to help with insomnia when they had moved to the city. Too many minds and too much activity had resulted in Cameron not being able to sleep despite his music.

Waking up in the early afternoon, Cameron immediately grabbed his phone and was once again dismayed that he had not heard from Nathen. Tears were renewed, streaming down his cheeks before he went to splash water on his face.

It was over.

He berated himself for getting so close so fast. It was stupid. Syn had told him to go slow and instead of listening to her, he had jumped in. Trudging out, he found Syn playing WoW and took a deep stilted breath. "Hey."

Looking over her shoulder, Syn set the controller aside and took her best friend's hand. "I was waiting for you. This whole thing is too much. The information on the flash drive... I think we should go. Get out of town for a bit. I've rented an SUV. Let's go down to Carmel?"

Cameron didn't feel at all like going anywhere or doing anything but nodded anyway as Syn gave his shoulder an affectionate squeeze. They packed a few overnight bags, dropped the cats off at a kennel, and took off. Once on their way, Cameron purposefully shut the phone off and stopped monitoring it for signs of hope. It had been foolish to have wished for something he knew he didn't deserve.

Chapter Twenty-Eight

NATHEN

The bright glare of the fluorescents greeted Nathen as he groggily pulled himself out of a deep sleep. He squinted up at the tiled ceiling and terror momentarily slashed through him as he realized that that was not his bedroom ceiling, but as he looked around his office it slowly came back to him. He was in Impetus, but how did he get to his office? The last thing he remembered was sitting on the cement floor in the garage for a while, then pacing around... His mind and emotions had been unstable, jumping from one horrifying image to the next. His new red headed Adonis of a boyfriend had almost died in a fire, then the same boyfriend killed a man who had been following them—using only his mind, channeling pain and disgust into the man until he was no longer.

Nathen bolted upright with the memory.

Why would Cameron kill a man? It came back in a rush: Todd Jacks was following them on behalf of the Company. A sanctioned killer, Jacks was to terminate him and murder Cameron if they got out of line. Images of Jacks' other kills flickered through Nathen's mind, courtesy of Cameron's ability. Nathen doubled over, retching dryly and remembered vampires didn't puke. They did, however, cry, and soon the industrial carpeting below him was soaked with sanguine tears that fell freely down his face and dripped below as emotions of betrayal, disgust, fear, guilt, and confusion rolled over Nathen, causing his shoulders to convulse painfully.

Once he was emotionally in control, Nathen gathered up his phone, flipped it on and summoned a company car. On the way back home, he looked out the window, going over the events in his mind, visualizing them over and over, trying to figure out what he could have done differently. Perseveration, his shrink had called it.

There was no way to know that a bomb would go off if he turned off the server. There was no way to know that Cameron would kill someone if he had Nathen's blood in him. And as for Impetus, Nathen had no choice but to admit he had been kidnapped, murdered, and turned into a vampire.

He needed time to process and come up with a logical response, or some kind of conclusion he could rationalize.

At the time, Cameron had not been himself, and Nathen considered that maybe he had not been thinking clearly.

Jacks was a sick person and did evil things. He didn't feel anything for his death, but that made him feel guilty because they shared a common humanity. Well, maybe not, he was undead now. All of that contributed to his confusion, dejection, with a tinge of self-pity.

The car pulled into the driveway of Nathen's home and he thanked Julian and vacated the vehicle to trudge up the stairs to his room, grab a change of clothes and make his way to the bathroom. He stood under the hot water, the sensation from it flowed down his body, the heat and the sound relaxed him. His mind focused on that instead of the discordant emotions and thoughts. When he returned to his bedroom, Nathen blinked at the clock.

It was 8:00 p.m., but that couldn't be right. Exhausted, he put on meditation music and tried desperately to sleep before he remembered he no longer needed to. So instead he began to meditate, a practice he had begun over a decade before to keep his sanity and ground himself from the overstimulating outside world.

Chapter Twenty-Nine

CAMERON

Three days. An agonizing, horrible three days that Cameron would not be willing to repeat at any time, ever. He had to admit it. Nathen was gone for good, and in the most devastating way. Ghosting. If it hadn't been for Syn having hidden his phone, Cameron probably would have called him, or texted since Nathen would have preferred that. It didn't matter, if he had really wanted to contact him, he could have since he had read Syn's mind and knew the phone had been left out under the driver's seat in their rented SUV. But instead of going after the phone, he had indulged his best friend in her attempt to draw him out of his ever-deepening depression. He could feel it creeping in, the familiar darkness that he had first encountered in his adolescence when Cameron had started hearing everyone's thoughts. Cameron had only been with Nathen two days, he rationalized. Less than forty-eight hours! Some part of him reasoned that it had to have been the blood, because he had never been so out of control as the day after he had Nathen's blood.

Cameron played that last night over and over again in his mind. He had awakened in the backseat of the car. He had read Nathen's mind and learned that they had both almost died in a fire. Even though he was standing right there, somehow Nathen had severed their link entirely. It had been devastating to physically see his boyfriend, but not be able to *feel* him in any way.

Cameron had allowed Syn to drag him to the aquarium in Monterrey, eat amazing food, walk on the beach, and play a lot of board and video games. It wasn't much different from hanging out in their San Francisco apartment, but he appreciated the change of scenery and her attempts to take care of him and distract him. He cried himself to sleep each night, but each morning was a little stronger. A little more in control.

When they returned Tuesday night, Cameron and Syn talked about how to proceed. The Sons of Discord had given a one-week window, and the deadline was almost up. While they had wanted to do *something*, it was too dangerous. Besides, as far as he knew, Nathen was working on it now. Not to mention law enforcement. Agreeing to lay the entire matter to rest, they settled on sleeping and Cameron plodded to bed exhausted. So many things began catching up with him now that he was in his own bed...the bed that he had enjoyed waking up with Nathen in. A stab of pain caused him to curl up in a ball as he turned on Volbeat to ear splitting decibels through his earphones, implementing deep breathing techniques until he was finally able to drift off.

Chapter Thirty

NATHEN

Nathen came out of his meditation and momentarily the events of last night were not on his mind and he was cluelessly calm. Then slowly they crept back in and he was downtrodden and miserable, all within a matter of seconds. It was 5:12 a.m. He normally had his alarm clock set to 5:30 a.m. and his body was used to waking up around this time. He took out his iPhone and went through his morning ritual of catching up on the news. Politics, science, and advances in technology where his three main interests, though a recent new competitor came into the running: Autism itself. He had a newsfeed that displayed any new studies in psychology or genetics that shed more light on this...his..."disorder."

Nathen continued to read through various studies and reports until 6:47 a.m., at which point he decided to call Cameron. It went to voicemail and he hung up, reasoning that he was likely still asleep. He got up, went to the bathroom, took a shower, and brushed his teeth. Calling Cameron again at 7:25 a.m., Nathen frowned when it went to voicemail again, but this time he left a message. "Um, Hi Cameron. This is Nathen. Hope everything is okay. You are probably sleeping. I'll call back later. Bye!"

Nathen logged on to World of Warcraft and did daily quests and talked to his guild members who all missed him at their raids. He learned that they believed he had missed several days of quests which was disconcerting since he was only gone for a day. He assured them he would be back, but that his current work life balance was off skew and hoped it would stabilize soon. The game had been a ritual for him in the mornings and today it was a welcome distraction from thinking about Cameron, who was not picking up his phone.

At 8:10 a.m. he tried once more, voicemail again. He hung up and was starting to get worried. Had Cameron gotten upset at him? Maybe Cameron blamed him for almost dying, or feeding him his blood, which made him go insane and kill Jacks? Or maybe he was being insensitive when he left him in the car? Or maybe Syn talked him out of dating him? These questions started to circle around his mind, raising his anxiety levels. *Perseveration.* He groaned and logged off his game and started to pace his room, unable to keep himself from going over the events and what he did to upset Cameron. He decided to call him one last time. 8:55 a.m.: "Hi Cameron, this is Nathen. I hope you are not mad at me. I apologize if I did something wrong. I didn't know the explosion was going to happen and I didn't know what my blood would do. I'm not mad and hope we can talk again. Call me when you get this? Okay, bye."

Nathen crawled back into bed and put the phone next to him. He closed his eyes and tried to enter a meditative state again, lamenting the fact that he could no longer sleep.

Chapter Thirty-One

CAMERON

Sleeping in late the next morning, Cameron woke to the Siamese siblings crawling over him and Syn sitting on his bed holding out a large Chai from Starbucks and waggling a breakfast sandwich in a bag. He smiled and took off his earphones, cutting the music that had soothed him throughout the night.

"Breakfast in bed, sunshine?" Syn made herself at home at the end of the bed and sipped her coffee as Cameron set the sandwich aside and sipped the too-sweet tea. "Incidentally, I hate the hair. Skinhead is so yesterday. But the beard..." Cameron hadn't shaved since after the night Nathen had left, and he found himself reaching up and running his hand over his naked head.

He groaned, switching to speaking with her mentally. *"I'm going to have to tell my students it was to raise money for some movement."*

Syn laughed. *"So, I was thinking—"*

Cameron raised a finger and handed over the cup, switching to speaking aloud. "Nope, nope, not on a full bladder. No deep talks while one has to pee. Them are the rules." He swung out of bed and brushed past Syn.

"So, it was a Star Wars night," she commented on his Death Star pajama bottoms.

"I was letting the force be with me," he called from the bathroom.

Returning, he saw her nibbling on his sandwich and snatched it away from her. "How Rude!" he offered in his best Jar Jar voice, which earned him a groan.

"There are more where that came from." Syn laughed then added, "Or out on the table. There too."

Cameron snagged his phone as they moved breakfast onto the dining room table. His heart skipped a beat as he saw that Nathen had left two voicemails and had tried to call several times in the last three hours. He frowned, shaking his head in disbelief...hope...and the agony of hope he knew he should not have.

Syn growled, "I know that look!"

Cameron's gaze raised to meet hers, wearing his emotions on his sleeve as his eyes filled with tears. He chewed on his lip, silently begging Syn for permission, which she granted with a roll of her eyes. "Speaker please?"

Cameron nodded nervously, unconsciously trying to make his six-foot-four frame small as he slid into the chair, his legs tucked up under him. He took a sip of his chai and reached out with trembling fingers to hit play and speaker.

Syn sat with annoyance radiating off her. Cameron quietly held the tea with both hands, pensive. He played the second message.

Finally, Syn said, "Are you fucking kidding me?"

Cameron smiled stiffly at Syn.

"He doesn't fucking know yet not to talk about this motherfucking shit on the phone, in text, etcetera?" Syn ranted.

Cameron shrugged, happy that Nathen had finally called! He picked up the phone, quickly texting *You should come over* and hit send before Syn could stop him. He shrugged with mock apology.

*

Nathen opened his eyes from excitement at hearing his phone buzz with a new text message. It was from Cameron, though the message itself was nebulous and not exactly encouraging.

Nathen decided to ask for clarification, "Ok, but are you mad at me?"

In response, he received a simple "No."

Nathen lit up at the final message "Ok, I'll be there shortly."

He put the hard drive from the night before into his pocket and called the car service. When the car came, he used his supernatural speed to enter it as quickly as possible to avoid any sun exposure.

Thanking Julian again, he sped into Cameron's building. Fortunately, the city proved to be bathed in shadow thanks to the high rises. He still looked weird walking out in full-on winter regalia in October, but better safe than sorry. Nathen rode the elevator, and at the door knocked and waited.

Disheveled, clad in sweatpants and a T-shirt and unshaven, Cameron opened the door. Nathen shifted from one foot to the other with the rush of pity and sadness as it was obvious that Cameron was depressed and despondent. While he was incredibly happy to see him, Nathen was also beside himself with nervousness because he didn't know if Cameron was going to break up with him. He reasoned that if that was going to happen, it's better that it happens now than later.

But his scent...intoxicating. He wanted to touch him, taste him. And curiously, he missed the connection that they had. He could no longer sense Cameron's emotions, which had told him so much about what he had been feeling.

"Hi," Cameron said softly.

Nathen nodded. "Hello." He stood awkwardly at the threshold. "Um... can I come in?"

"Yeah." Cameron moved out of the way.

Syn stepped around the corner into view and sat on the end of the couch, eyeing Nathen with a world of judgment.

Nathen walked in and waved at Syn. He could sense there was something wrong but couldn't make out what. His first thought was that he *had done* something wrong. He worked his way around the couch and nervously slid onto the overstuffed chair and began to run through scenarios of why she might be mad at him.

Syn used a hand-held bug detector and as Nathen sat, she approached him and ran the machine over him. Once satisfied he was not transmitting or recording, she said, "First off, what the fuck for texting that bullshit this morning? And second off, what the fuck for giving Cameron your blood? And third off what the fuck for ditching Cameron when he had almost died? And finally, seriously, what the fuck—it's goddamned Wednesday! What the hell? You just leave a guy hanging for four days?" Her tone was even, though Nathen could see her heart rate had increased, suggesting that she was angry.

"Can I get you something to drink," Cameron offered, then winced at the statement, quickly amending, "Soda? Water?"

Nathen looked gloomy and in a monotone voice, answered each question in order. "About the message...I was nervous and upset and was not thinking straight. As for why I gave him my blood, he was about to die. Something had damaged his heart. He was bleeding and had passed out. He was slipping away. I didn't know what to do, so the only thing that came to mind...It was that or watch him die. I didn't ditch Cameron. He walked away while I was regrowing my pinky and part of my hand. I was too emotional to process or talk with anyone and needed time to calm down. And what do you mean? It's Sunday"—he looked at Cameron—"tea please, if you have some."

Cameron looked from Nathen to Syn. "It...it's Wednesday," Cameron said softly, a sob was caught in his throat and left quickly to the kitchen.

Syn clarified aggressively, "Yeah, it's fucking Wednesday. You've been gone since Saturday night. And while definitely, thank you for saving Cam's life, this is fucked up."

Cameron returned and handed a bottle of tea over. "Sorry I took off. I read everything you were thinking about. You cut off my ability to talk to you. I knew you didn't want to be around me. Figured you wouldn't want to see me again ever." He joined Syn who had turned around to face Nathen while sitting on the couch.

Nathen looked confused and checked his phone for the date. At Cameron's statement, he looked pained, but wanted to be truthful. "Honestly, how you...how you killed Jacks scared me. I didn't know you could do that. But after thinking about it, it was probably just my blood? I mean, I saw you were in pain while you were healing, and maybe the animalistic instinct in you was on overdrive. I mean

Jacks was more of a monster than I am, and I'm undead. You reacted, and he was there...?"

Cameron was shaking his head, looking at the ground. "I have no idea. The only memories that I have of that are yours. The last thing that I remember was going into a room with a refrigerator that you said had a server in it. Then waking up in the car. And reading everyone there. Picked up some interesting stuff from Julian the driver, and John, the guy from the kitchen. But then you...I hadn't even known I did that. Wouldn't even think I could do that. Interesting power if I could do it without being out of my mind in pain, if your memories of being in my head are right. But as for being able to do it. Nathen, I don't feel bad about it at all. I saw what that guy was capable of. I would do it again, especially if it meant saving you or Syn. I wouldn't hesitate, and I won't apologize. And I totally get if you don't want to date someone like that. Is that why you've been gone for so long?" Cameron glanced up, chewing on his lower lip.

Nathen saw Cameron look at Syn and realized they must be speaking telepathically because Cameron said aloud, "Syn, I think I need to talk with Nathen alone. Okay?"

Syn's glare swung from one to the other, then she stood and threw her arms up in the air. She shot Nathen a final look as she grabbed her keys and phone and stormed out of the apartment, seemingly purposefully slamming the door hard behind her.

"Sorry about that." Cameron turned back to Nathen. "She doesn't want to see me get my heart broken. Again." He smiled sadly. "So, let's not show her. It's cool. I get it. Learning you're dating someone with deep dark secrets, who has no problem killing people who hurt others, is jarring. If every time you look at me you see what I did, then we need to not see each other." His voice cracked, his tone thick and tight. He ran a hand over his bald head as he went into the kitchen. Then Nathen could hear him rummaging in the fridge as he called. "Yeah. So, that's that."

Nathen stayed silent staring off into the distance. He had barely heard Cameron and had tried hard to stay focused on what he was saying. But...Wednesday? Last night had been Saturday and he had woken up on the couch at work. Could he have slept that long at the office? Or did he sleep for a couple of days at his home? His missing time, coupled with the revelation that Cameron was unremorseful and didn't have any qualms at killing someone, disturbed him. Plus, he wondered if his mother knew where he was and was worried and then his mind started spinning because he hadn't checked in with her that morning. He had just gotten up and come when Cameron had called. His mind raced with too much to process and he realized he needed to slow down.

Finally, he looked up and saw that Cameron had returned to the living room and was sitting on the couch, drinking from a bottle of orange juice without a glass. Seeing Cameron anchored him in a strange way, and he was drawn back to an interesting longing. A desire to have the connection with him that he had never had with anyone in his life. "Well, but you did it to protect me and yourself. Yeah, I mean... You didn't do it for enjoyment, like Jacks did. He seemed to take perverse joy from hurting and killing people. I don't understand why someone would take pleasure in that." Nathen found himself slipping into the memories of the horrible things Jacks had done and shook his head. "You're not like that, right?"

Cameron opened his eyes and glanced over, then shook his head. "No. I don't take any joy in anyone's pain or in killing." His brow furrowed as he studied Nathen.

Nathen saw that Cameron seemed to be thinking about something because he wasn't talking. Then he took another long drink of juice and put his head back on the couch, closing his eyes again.

Relief massaged Nathen. "Okay. I haven't killed anyone and haven't known people that have. Well, I mean my grandfather said he killed Nazis in the war. I'm not sure what I am supposed to think and am feeling anxious about it, because I don't want to lose you over this. I really like you. I feel safe and relaxed in your company, but I'm also interested in you as a person. What are your thoughts? I can't feel you anymore. I think I must have used up all of your blood."

Cameron leaned forward, resting his elbows on his knees. "The blood?" he asked. "Yeah. I can't feel or sense you at all. It's..." He shook his head. "I think you need to arrive at your own conclusions. I love spending time with you and want to get to know you better. I love your outlook on things and that you know so much about a lot of stuff that I'm clueless about." He smiled half-heartedly. "I always thought Syn's tech ability made me feel safe and it was cool that you have that too." He shrugged, taking a deep breath. "There are bad people and creatures out there that want to hurt others. Children, those who can't protect themselves, my family and people I love. And I think that having read Jacks as he followed us all night, I came to the conclusion that in time it would come down to him versus us and had resigned myself to making sure it wasn't us. Which is why I guess when I had your blood, I channeled it into him. I don't know. It's even more disturbing to me that I was in no conscious control over that. Do you think you could be with someone who is a murderer? Who would rather protect than see people hurt? If any part of you doesn't know, then..." He took another deep jagged breath and offered a small sad shrug, looking away again.

Nathen dissociated from the whole topic as he often did when he found that he was becoming emotional about something. It was easier to observe an emotion, acknowledge it's there and dismiss it so he could think logically about loaded topics. He said impassively, "Murder and murderer are legal definitions and concepts. That part is not of concern to me. What concerns me is the act itself and the intent behind it. Your intent was to protect us, yourself, etcetera. And we know the type of man Jacks was. I grew up not thinking about this stuff. I mean I kill virtual 'bad guys' all the time in games, but that's not real. I don't know if I have it in me to outright kill someone. Their death would haunt me, seeing their face, their expression, etcetera. I would probably replay that in my mind over and over and drive myself insane. But you're not me and don't have my...issues. So, I don't know how you would react to that. I guess I can turn the question around. How do you feel about being with someone who might not have the grit to do what 'must' be done to stop someone from harming others? I mean I would be okay with incapacitating someone, but killing? I don't know."

Cameron coughed out a small laugh. "What? Now there is something one never thinks about. Or maybe I have. Syn talks about killing people sometimes—if someone broke in here and tried to hurt us, or the kitties. And she's a sharpshooter. But I don't think I ever thought about that. I see Syn's argument about not wanting to leave someone alive to come back after us. But I wouldn't think anything about that at all. I would never expect or want someone to kill for me. And I didn't see Jacks die either. So, actually, I'm not sure how I would react to killing someone close up." He grew quiet. "I did see someone die. And it does still haunt me. And I used to play it over and over, but between my first boyfriend and Syn, they kept me sane. But this isn't about me. It's about you and what happened last Saturday. I'm sorry that I scared you. Thank you for saving me. That had to have been so messed up. I saw it from your memories, and it freaked me out. I can only imagine what you were dealing with. Before I took off, I considered removing all memories of it, and me. I still can if you want, but you would have to have some of my blood."

Nathen considered, then shook his head. He didn't like the idea of having memories removed. Memories served as a record and having it removed would be a lie. He knew that as soon as you tell a lie, that later if you don't remember the lie then you're caught. He lived his life without having to deal with all of that, and as painful as it was, he would never want to live a lie. "No, I think I'm okay with the memory...But, umm, could we hug and get yesterday behind us? I do not want to think about it anymore."

"Nathen, it wasn't yesterday," Cameron said with a pained look. "This is *Wednesday*. The whole thing went down on Saturday. You...you only texted me this morning." He retrieved his phone and handed it to Nathen who looked at it and then back at his own phone.

Nathen's eyes narrowed as he began flipping through his phone, which clearly showed not only the time and his text to Cameron that morning but also a text to his mother on Saturday night. A text he had no memory of sending. "Just writing to let you know I'm working on a very important project at work and will be staying in the city for a few days. Not able to get or send texts but will call when I get a chance." There was a response from his mother Sunday morning thanking him, then two on Monday and two on Tuesday checking on him. He knew she had been asleep this morning when he left the house, but he berated himself again for having not woken her.

He sent a quick text to make sure his mom knew he was okay, then looked up at Cameron and showed him the phone. "What does this mean?"

Cameron glanced at the phone then asked, "What happened after I left you?"

Nathen shook his head. "I was in the garage, then woke up in my office upstairs. I got my stuff together and went home. I thought it was Sunday today."

Cameron's mouth dropped open with anguished guilt. He quickly moved to hug Nathen to him. "I'm so sorry. I should have never left you. I'm sure you went upstairs to sleep because you were so exhausted. You...had to grow back a hand after all."

Nathen nodded, curling up in Cameron's arms, his scent familiar and comfortable. Cameron let out a long-shuddered breath that he had been holding as he buried his head in Nathen's hair. He kissed the top of Nathen's head and remained like that for a long time before sniffling and wiping his face off on his sleeve.

"Um...Cameron..." Nathen said, looking up into Cameron's eyes. "I can also tell you are...uh...excited. Your heart rate is up and pupils are dilated, and there was a spike in hormone excretion. Or, at least I think that is what that was..."

Cameron's head dropped as a blush extended from his neck over his newly shorn scalp and he moved quickly back to the couch and strategically placed a pillow in his lap. "Sorry," he muttered. "Was thinking about you. Kissing...you. Heh. Keep forgetting you can, um, sense stuff."

Nathen smiled. "Well, we can kiss if you want. I would like that. And...maybe we should swap our liquids again, so we can 'talk' more...intimately?"

Cameron bit his lip and hugged the pillow a little tighter. Nathen could see the effect that his proposal had on Cameron with a large concentration of blood under that pillow. He saw Cameron squirm and grow quiet. Then Cameron grabbed his phone and texted someone. Having obviously arrived at a decision, Cameron hooked a finger and smiled when Nathen complied and moved to the couch. He leaned forward, cupping Nathen's face and searching his eyes before gently kissing him. Nathen realized that the proximity to Cameron had dissipated his anxiety.

Cameron said, "I have an idea. Can you bite my tongue as we kiss? Just a little?"

"I think so, yeah..." Nathen shrugged.

Cameron pulled Nathen to him again and Nathen slipped his hands up under Cameron's shirt so that he could trace the muscles of his back as their lips met once more. Cameron darted his tongue in to taste Nathen and Nathen could tell immediately that he was again a willing captive.

Cameron crushed Nathen to him, his kiss intensified, his tongue rolling around Nathen's before he came up for air, offering an almost apologetic smile. Nathen adjusted his pants, as his fangs extended, and he stared into

Cameron's brilliant blue eyes. Cameron smirked and returned to the kiss, sliding his tongue along Nathen's razor-sharp fang and shuddering with pleasure against him. The familiar sense of euphoria from a few drops of blood filtered through Nathen, and when their tongues met the wound was sealed. He realized that the peach flavor that now infused his senses was probably like heroin because he wanted more.

Chewing nervously on his lower lip, Cameron pulled back with a questioning look, silently asking Nathen if he was okay with their kiss. Emboldened, Nathen gave a small smirk: his extended canines and manhood told the same story.

Cameron grinned and laid Nathen back across the couch, following him down as their lips met once more. He positioned himself atop Nathen so he could grind gently while continuing to kiss him, continuing to play with Nathen's fangs, granting both of them small pleasurable slices that closed as their kisses grew more passionate and allowed just enough blood to trickle past Nathen's tongue. With each new drop, Nathen found himself more and more aroused, energized, alive. It was if he were tuning into a radio station, homing in on Cameron. He ran his hands down under Cameron's loose waistband so he could kneed his firm cheeks.

"Fuck," Cameron finally groaned, pushing up. "This isn't working. I can't hear you. Please bite me?" he begged, breathlessly.

Nathen blinked up at Cameron, readily agreeing. Swirling his tongue in small circles across Cameron's exposed neck, Nathen kissed it teasingly before slowly sinking his teeth into Cameron's flesh. There was no resistance as the supple skin gave way and his lover's sweet life blood trickled down his throat a sip at a time. The power of Cameron's blood was intoxicating, and he lost all negative emotions as he drank slowly, savoring, not wanting to drain Cameron too quickly, as he hoped to maximize the sexual pleasure he knew he was feeling.

Cameron's hand flexed against Nathen's scalp holding him to his throat as the other dug into Nathen's back. Moaning with the sensations that Nathen brought, soon an exhalation of release escaped Cameron as he came. Despite his continued sounds of desire, after a while Cameron physically relaxed when he *felt* Nathen. *"There you are..."* Emotionally overwhelmed, Cameron gently caressed Nathen, sharing and luxuriating as wave after wave of passion coursed through him. *"Don't go away again, please..."* he begged, cradling Nathen's head.

Nathen heard Cameron talking in his mind again, and he mostly understood the sentence, but he was still swimming in the pleasure of taking in his blood. He continued to gently suckle on the trickle of blood, secure in the knowledge through their link that Cameron enjoyed this as much as he did. He worked his hand into Cameron's pants and stroked his member, feeling the wet of his passion cover his hand, using it as a lubricant.

Cameron followed suit, swimming through the sensations to fumble with Nathen's jeans. Finally seeming to remember how to work buttons and zippers, Cameron snaked his hand under the elastic of Nathen's boxer-briefs, wrapping his fingers around Nathen and clutching him tightly, applying much more pressure than he might otherwise, but joyous to be able to read Nathen's desires. Cameron thrust into Nathen's hand in time, projecting the animalistic joy he felt back to Nathen. Nathen let out a pulse of pleasure from Cameron's touch: the sensation on his manhood and the pleasure he was getting from the blood were all encompassing. He projected the sensations he was feeling to Cameron and the feedback loop enveloped them both.

"*Come with me,*" Cameron begged, increasing his speed with Nathen and bucking as another climax threatened.

Silently agreeing, Nathen sped up his stroking and applied more pressure to the bite. He instinctively bucked into Cameron's hand, as his body was nearing the point of no return. Feeling Cameron come again, he licked the wound on his neck and joined him. A stream of thick blood flowed from his manhood onto Cameron's hand and shirt.

Sighing small moans as he was hit with pulses that flowed through him, Cameron clung to Nathen emanating a tide of positive emotions. He rested his head against Nathen's shoulder, breathing in his scent. "*I can't get enough of you.*"

Nathen relaxed into Cameron, feeling content and safe, all tension that had been there was released with his passion. "*I feel safe and right with you, and...I'm starting to...uh...feel stronger emotions. I didn't mean to hurt you, but I wasn't sure what I was supposed to be feeling, and I wanted time to process it. I had no idea so long had passed.*"

Cameron let out a small sad sound at Nathen's apology, trying to quell the tide of tears that welled up as a wave of gratitude and love filled him. "*It's okay. I'm so, so sorry that I scared you. I'm so sorry I left you! I didn't know what was going on. I mean, I would do anything to protect you.*" He chuckled, leaning back and gently cupping Nathen's face. "*What man wouldn't kill for you?*

But… I swear, unless it's immediate danger or I'm out of control, I'll get your permission before killing anyone. And I promise to try and remain in control again." He rested his head back against Nathen's shoulder. *"Before you…I never lost control. Now look at what you've done to me."* A good-natured reel of orgasmic memories played for Nathen of their two days together. With a playful smile, Cameron peeled himself away from Nathen, laughing at the mess they had made on each other. He helped Nathen strip and immediately threw their clothes into the washer after spraying the blood stains.

As they showered, Cameron reminded them, *"We still need to figure out everything that's been going on."*

Nathen rested his head on Cameron's shoulder as the water poured over them. He nodded finally and luxuriated in feeling Cameron's strong embrace tighten around him.

Chapter Thirty-Two

NATHEN

When they finished their shower, Cameron and Nathen walked out and found Syn in the living room working hard on her computer with a set of chopsticks propped up on takeout boxes.

"Do *not* tell me that you gave him my Gryffindor pajama bottoms!" Syn cast a glare over her shoulder at the pair and gawked at Nathen before turning on the television.

Nathen shrank away from Syn, back into Cameron's arms. Cameron gave a good-natured laugh, kissing Nathen on the cheek before saying, "His clothes are in the washer and if you'll recall, we are *both* Gryffindor. So, he's wearing mine and *I'm* wearing yours!" He stuck out his tongue, "I'm not sure what you're so annoyed about. All the pajama bottoms in the house are communal property anyway."

"His clothes are in the—?" Syn shot her hand in the air. "Whatever!"

The coffee table had several other boxes with the lids off and Cameron settled onto the couch and snagged sashimi for himself, handing Nathen a box. "One of the many great things about living in San Francisco was that you can have pretty much any kind of food delivered to your doorstep any time of day."

Nathen nodded. Even though he didn't *need* to eat food anymore, he marveled in the new sensations of everything. It was the most peculiar feeling to actually need to concentrate on "digesting" it, which was moving it through his new vampiric body, and he didn't think about having to move it *out* of his body. But the flavors that before used to be fairly bland were now somehow colorful. Before he was awakened, he used to gravitate toward foods that were extremely salty or spicy. He remembered his mother used to reprimand him for pouring salt on everything, even items that most people didn't put salt on. But it was so he could taste them. Otherwise, it didn't matter what was put in front of him. He would eat it all, methodically, one item on the plate at a time. In the forums with other people who had been diagnosed with Autism, he had learned that that was a common thing.

But now it was like every taste receptor on his tongue was sending signals that exploded with life as he mindfully savored the spicy tuna roll, wondering why he had never paid attention to the subtle nuanced taste of each ingredient: the spicy sriracha, salty soy sauce, heat of the wasabi, the earthy green onion, the undercurrent of seaweed, the fatty tuna, even the starchy rice all blending together in such a marvelous way.

Nathen had become distracted again by his experience of the food that he almost missed what Syn was saying. What had they been talking about?

"Don't you see, Cam? There's just so much more going on..." Syn shook her head, having flopped down in the overstuffed chair with one leg dangling over the side, her short cropped black hair resting against the back. She had a container of sushi perched on her belly and was spearing a sashimi with a single chopstick.

Nathen cleared his throat for effect, since he didn't actually have to breathe. "I also brought the drive I took out last night. I mean Saturday," he quickly corrected, having to remind himself that somehow he lost four days and today was Wednesday. He reached over and pushed the SSD they had recovered toward Syn.

Setting the food aside, Syn took the drive and turned it over in her hands, musing aloud. "So, I didn't want to tell you, but I've been looking at that flash drive that Statix, I guess his real name is Theo, gave us."

Cameron piped up, explaining for Nathen's sake. "The night you and I went into the hospital, a friend of Syn's, Theo, was also there. He's a mage who pulled down information and gave it to us on a flash drive. So, what'd you find?"

"There were a ton of documents and even a couple of video files. Apparently, Paradigm is behind the Sons of Discord."

Nathen interjected, "Paradigm? The huge corporation?" His mind started spinning with everything he knew about the corporate conglomerate.

"Yeah, so, see here?" Syn hit the power button on the remote that turned the large television monitor on. Remotely connecting her computer to the monitor, she started flipping through various documents. "So, two weeks before the Sons' made their announcement, there was a shift in security systems. But whoever did it was good enough to hide their tracks, so it wasn't obvious that there was a shift at all. It looks like Theo was somehow able to find it. None of this is that exciting..." Several windows shifted as she scrolled past various financial records. "It all goes to show that a new security group did go in. But here's where it gets wonky. They kept most of the old staff. Usually when a new security company comes in, they have their own people. For this one, the only thing that changed was where the security guards got their payment. I doubt if they even know there was a change at all since the only thing that changed was 'LLC' to 'Inc.' on their pay stubs. Same generic company name and everything. But Theo tracked down that corporate entity, which was owned by different corporate entity, and so on. Don't ask me how he did it, but he was able to trace it back to Paradigm."

"I don't understand," Cameron said. "So, what if Paradigm owns some security firm? Granted, it's fishy. But it's not a smoking gun."

"Wait...did you say 'most' of the old staff?" Nathen asked.

"You got a smart one." Syn winked at Nathen while grinning at Cameron. "Most, not all. There were four different people who went in after the change. But Theo pointed out something strange. Two still seem to work there. Are on the payroll. Two went in that don't seem to connect to the payroll. One was in and out the same day. This is him," she brought up a picture of a man with a crew cut wearing a blue security guard outfit.

Cameron began choking, setting aside his take-out box and gawking at the screen. Nathen sat silently staring.

"Umm," Syn said, looking from one to the other.

"That's the man from Impetus who was there the day I was awakened," Nathen said, his gaze swinging slowly to Cameron.

"That's Jacks..." Cameron's beat-red face slowly drained of all color as he stared in horror at the ghost of the man who he had murdered less than a week before.

"Oh...well, hell. But does that not complicate shit? If I'd have known, I would have saved that for the punchline instead of..." She shifted the picture to depict a blond dark-skinned woman wearing a security guard outfit. "This woman went in on the same day as...well, Jacks, though his name badge reads *Rellik*. But she has never come out. Du-du-dunnnn," Syn delivered this last with lack-luster enthusiasm.

"So...let me get this straight. There are two groups: Impetus and Paradigm who are both fairly renowned in the world for a ton of different holdings. Nathen works for Impetus who apparently in the 2000s started making vampires, and it seems like they also give their human employees injection that stops their aging."

"They're in cahoots apparently? Or maybe Jacks has a twin? Or maybe freelances? Whatever. Paradigm takes over security, which would make things a lot easier to take over a whole hospital. They masquerade as a cyber terrorist group, Sons of Discord. But, why? Both groups have more billions than they know what to do with. This makes no sense at all," Cameron said with a sigh, resting his head on Nathen's shoulder, which shook Nathen out of his mindful eating that he had started to fall back into. He found himself stiffening because he wasn't sure what to do. Should he put his arm around Cameron or...?

Before he was able to get a plan for how to act, Cameron pulled away and started talking again. "At the same time, Impetus makes Nathen into a vampire and tells him to go find shit out about the group Sons of Discord? Why would they want that? Perhaps Impetus caught wind that their greatest competitor is up to something with this hospital thing. Maybe that's why Jacks was there? There seems to be so many strange things going on. Especially that Impetus seems to be able to get information that Syn buried. Theo thinks the same thing about Paradigm. What do you think about all of this?"

Nathen observed, "I think we need to get the true motivations and specializations of both companies. Though they have many investments, they may all have a central theme. For instance, IBM would not invest in a food company unless it somehow involved technology, say an automated cook."

"I think that's a good point," Syn said. "And we should check that out. But...and I hate to say this... I think you guys need to go back in."

"What?" Cameron shook his head emphatically.

"Why?" Nathen asked, intrigued.

"Because of this..." Syn played a video that showed the tall attractive security guard with the blonde afro walk in the front door. It switched to another camera, and then another, following her through the hospital to a subbasement.

"As far as I can tell, that wing is just storage. And there's no way out. And though I haven't watched any other footage, Theo pointed out that she hasn't come out. At least she hadn't until we got the video a few days ago. If she's not there, there's still something interesting there that might help us figure something out."

"I don't know. I don't want to put Nathen in danger," Cameron said, shaking his head.

"Me?" Nathen said, chuckling. "Babe, I don't want you to be put in danger. I'll go in alone."

"That's ridiculous!" Cameron protested.

"The three of us are all going to go in, and we're going to figure out what's going on," Syn declared.

"No!" Nathen and Cameron both said in unison.

"Uh-huh. So, maybe we should spend a little time going through how Paradigm and Impetus might be connected. Then we can get a game plan."

"Syn, no. It's way too dangerous."

"For who, Cam? For my brother to go in and get himself blown up and have his boyfriend save him with blood? For our vampire muscle to go in and get taken by surprise or duped somehow? I'm good with a gun. I'm pretty good with technology. The three of us are going to go in and figure out what's going on. And, we're going to do it tonight because guess what. Midnight is our deadline. That's when the Sons of Discord gave. And I don't know exactly what that means."

Cameron looked at Nathen helplessly. He shrugged. "Maybe she's right? I mean, if they're in this together and Impetus already has a death watch on us, none of us is safe."

Grunting, Cameron acquiesced, "I'll get my laptop."

Returning from his bedroom, Cameron resumed his position on the couch beside Nathen and said, "Well, let's search." Nathen saw him tapping a few keys in a basic search engine and was about to offer a more efficient way of looking up information, but stopped himself as Camron said, "A quick search for Impetus indicates they have merged with companies in the: biomedical, pharma, research and development, business strategy consulting, identity management, database software, data sciences, IT services, business intelligence—" He looked up shaking his head. "—the list goes on and on." Cameron opened a new tab and typed in PARADIGM and read through, "Same thing. There are like a hundred different industries that all seem the same. Guess that's why they're competitors. Though…maybe not. Paradigm seems to also have a bunch of online stuff? So, it looks like while a lot of their stuff overlaps, I guess that Impetus would be more hardware and Paradigm would be more software, or an online presence?" He turned the computer around and offered it to Syn and Nathen with the search tabs open.

Syn groaned, grabbing her own computer as Nathen took Cameron's. Nathen glanced over the edge of the laptop and smiled awkwardly, finally saying, "I agree, it seems they're competing, but it almost looks like two monopolies colluding to corner the market in such a way as to not raise suspicion from regulators. Impetus is mostly in the biotech and high-tech sector. Paradigm is more about IT and data mining, though both have a lot of crossover."

Cameron groaned, laying out across the couch, his frame too long and his legs propped up against the edge as he laid his head in Nathen's lap. Nathen awkwardly set the computer to the side and pet Cameron's bald head. He could feel the ginger stubble starting to grow back and became distracted with the soft prickles against his fingertips. Cameron hadn't shaved and he found himself staring down at his gorgeous boyfriend, his fingers trailing down to the courser hair on his chin.

Syn interrupted, "So, are you two still meeting up with Theo and Robbie at the Snake Pit tomorrow?"

Cameron groaned, looking up into Nathen's eyes. The contact shocked Nathen for a moment. Before Cameron, he had never been comfortable with eye contact. Now he found himself being lost in Cameron's liquid blue gaze. "Nathen, I forgot to ask. They suggested meeting up. Syn won't go with me to Snake Pit. And I know you don't like bars, but…"

Nathen had never liked large crowds that he could get overwhelmed by. Despite this, he said, "Sure, we can meet them, but I have never been there. And I might be ...quiet. I normally don't go to bars of any kind."

Nathen was surprised again when he a shudder of revulsion echoed from Cameron. It was new, being able to read someone else's emotions. Nathen knew it was because he had Cameron's blood in him, but the sensation left him confused for a moment. He guessed Cameron probably didn't like the bar either.

Cameron said, "Well, we will plan to be there for a short while. I want to know more about other mages. Aside from my mom, I've never met another mage. I'm lucky he's willing to meet up."

Nathen studied Cameron and realized he *could* see more. He began flipping through the surface memories Cameron had of exactly what went on in the Snake Pit and with his ex-boyfriend.

Nathen heard Cameron, as if from far away, asking, "Nathen? Are you okay?"

Nathen blinked and shook his head, fixing Cameron with a look of pity. "I saw the times Frank made you go to the club. I'm sorry, what an...A-hole."

Cameron sat up and scooted back, his eyes wide. "What? How? I didn't...I wasn't projecting that."

Syn looked from one to the other, then took a swig of beer.

Nathen was confused. "Oh, I'm not sure. I felt you being uncomfortable about it and I wondered why. Then I got a flash of various memories from you where Frank was being inconsiderate and bullying you into going even when he knew you didn't like it."

Syn started snickering at Cameron. "Now, you know how the rest of us little people feel!"

"That is not funny!" Cameron emphasized, and Nathen could feel his emotions of vulnerability.

Syn laughed harder. "Sure, it is! Now, the question is how? Hey, Nathen, can you tell me what I'm thinking? Maybe it's a vampire thing?"

Nathen focused on Syn. "No, I can see your aura and heartbeat, and smell your scent, but can't read your mind. I would probably have to feed on you first."

"Check please." Syn waived to an imaginary waitress and laughed. She turned back to Nathen. "Thanks for the offer, honey, but you're not my type. Now, as I told Cam here, if you've got a little sister vampy hidden away somewhere, I'd definitely think about it considering what I've felt you do to Cam." Turning back to Cameron, she chastised, "Stop pouting. This could come in handy. You have a good time reading my mind, and everyone's. Now if there is something you need him to know he can know too."

Nathen was confused. He wasn't hitting on her. "I wasn't offering to bite you. I have a brother. No sisters."

Syn gave Cameron a perplexed look and he waved her off mentally, and Nathen could *hear*, almost as if Cameron had said it out loud, *"Remember, Syn? People with Autism are often literal."* Nathen could also hear Cameron's surface thoughts about how much of a violation being able to read minds was. Then Cameron turned his attention quickly to Nathen and started, mentally asking, *"Fuck! Did you read all of that?"* He then sighed heavily. *"It's okay. Just took me by surprise."*

Nathen wasn't insulted by Cameron's telling Syn that he was literal, because it was the truth. "For a long time, I didn't know I was taking things literally at all. I thought people were misunderstanding me. Sometimes it's obvious, and I get it, most of the time not. The psychologist explained that humor, sarcasm, and other stuff like that will usually go over my head." He studied Cameron. "I'm sorry. I didn't know that was going to happen. But it's usually how my mind works. I go off on tangentially related memories of mine all the time, only this time the information was coming from you instead of my mind."

"It's okay, Nathen, really. It's something I'm going to have to get used to. The trade-off is well worth it," Cameron offered a weak smile.

Chapter Thirty-Three

CAMERON

Cameron busied himself with cleaning up after lunch as Nathen read over the documentation that was on the flash drive.

He heard Syn ask, "What did you get at the train wreck last week?"

Nathen seemed confused momentarily, "I...oh...the explosion! I got an SSD. Thankfully it wasn't damaged. I brought a USB to SATA adaptor, will need to use your Linux box."

While Syn and Nathen looked at the information and talked in nerd code, Cameron finished cleaning, did chores, and hung out in Syn's room for a while playing with the cats that they locked away when Nathen was in the apartment because they didn't react well to him. After he emerged from her room and saw that Syn and Nathen were still at it, he announced he was going to the gym, which was in part to be alone with his thoughts and in part because he knew it would make Syn happy. Besides, now he had someone to stay in shape for. He leaned over to kiss Nathen before leaving but made the mistake of diving in for a little taste, only to have it last much longer, gently wrapping a hand around the back of his head as the kiss intensified and he found his sweats growing tighter. The kiss of his vampiric boyfriend never ceased to amaze and arouse him.

Turning away from the scene of the crime taking place between Nathen and Cameron's lip lock, Syn took the hard drive and dongle, plugged it in, and logged in. Cameron tore himself away only when Syn's unamused mental tapping at the back of his head became noticeable and flushed a brilliant tomato color that matched his facial hair, ducking away and out the door.

*

The gym was only a few blocks from their home and on the way, Cameron cranked XM Octane on his earbuds, enjoying Red Sun Rising and began to run over and over his relationship with Nathen. He knew it was apophenia to have songs like "Amnesia" playing at the most perceived opportune instant, as if it was playing just for him. But Cameron *was* afraid to love. Terrified in fact. He didn't want to feel like he did when his first boyfriend left after they were together for two years. Granted, they were seventeen and Tommy was returning home to the East Coast, but still. Nathen had been gone for several days and Cameron had not stopped thinking about him the entire time. He had all but convinced himself to stop being such a sissy. But being with Nathen made him relax in a way he had not realized he had been missing for almost six years. He found himself sitting close to Nathen and touching him often, savoring each stolen contact like a drowning man on his very last breath. He smirked at himself. Being with Nathen was like breathing. Maybe that was what he was really afraid of? Choking in the abyss of solitude he had gotten accustomed. He had Syn, his friends, his life. But he was always so alone. Perhaps that was why he had chosen someone like his last boyfriend to be with. He knew what Frank was before they even got together. He could read the guy. Or maybe he wanted to punish himself, knowing that Frank would do that for him with his narcissistic lashing out.

Cameron entered the Silver Stream gym and made pleasantries with the staff who he had come to know over the years. Hell, he had been there for each one of their interviews, positioned somewhere in the gym when Syn was doing her manager thing. He had sifted through those who would actually be reliable and gave Syn the mental thumbs up or down. He thanked them for setting aside the sheets from Nathen's home that he had brought there and left in the dryer, plucking the curiosity from their minds as easily as if he were plucking petals from flowers. As he took to the equipment, he was reminded that Nathen was now able to be in *his* head. How was that possible?

Cameron started going over the last week. Neither had been able to read the other at all, but once Nathen had Cameron's blood in him (arousal threatened with the memories and Cameron began working out harder) Cameron could sense him in every way, as if he were anyone else. Well, anyone else who wasn't another vampire or a mage who could block him! Cameron needed for vampires to have his blood in them for him to sense them. He replayed that thought. Blood was power, and if Cameron could get a little of his blood into all the vampires in Impetus, he could read them, learn all of their secrets. He filed that piece of information away.

Cameron's thoughts were everywhere. He brought it back to the main topic he had brought himself to the gym to ponder, and it was not to be ogled by other guys (who he mentally began making himself "invisible" to). Having

Nathen in his mind was a distraction. Cameron had too many secrets, regrets, hidden shames that he had to keep from surfacing. He had an undercurrent of terror, knowing that someday Nathen would be disgusted, at best; would hate him and leave him at worst.

The thought made Cameron choke and he decided he had had enough of a workout in only forty-five minutes. He found himself in the steam room, smirking with memories, his growing erection hidden only by a towel. He mentally suggested the old guy sitting in there had had enough and stretched out when he was alone. He usually didn't hog the steam room like this but needed to figure something out. Instead, he replayed the memory of Nathen leaning over, his mouth surrounding Cameron, his greedy tongue probing for...what had he said? *"Peaches and cream?"* Cameron laughed aloud, the sound a surprise as he realized he had been stroking himself wantonly. He let out a small sigh of relief that he was still alone and quickly pulled his towel over himself. What the hell had gotten into him?

Nathen's blood...When Nathen had saved him by giving him his blood—that was when Nathen had been able to hear him, read him, "see" him do things he didn't remember doing. How could he have surrendered so much control in only a few days? So much so that he had killed with someone watching? And in such a spectacular way. If he could somehow figure out how to harness Nathen's blood so he was in control... Perhaps it was because he was all but dead when Nathen gave it to him? What Nathen had experienced was confusing and Cameron assumed it was likely because Nathen himself couldn't actually process it. Hell, it took him years as a child to be able to process what he was capable of. But was it the blood link that now allowed Nathen to read his thoughts? Now that Cameron had Nathen's blood in him, had Nathen in his mind, would Nathen always be able to read his thoughts? No...Cameron realized it wasn't until Nathen had drank from him that morning that the link was re-established. But how deep did that go? Could Nathen probe? Learn more...Cameron hoped not.

Could he actually keep his surface thoughts neutral? Cameron didn't think so. He would have to accept that Nathen could read them. That might be helpful in the hospital tonight. Or when communicating. Speaking mentally was Cameron's preferred way anyway, if only with Syn. But to have someone who could always read what he was thinking? Syn was right! Cameron groaned with the irony that he would now have to deal with what he did to Syn and everyone else in his life. Though they didn't know he was doing it. The thought hit him. Chilled him. Did that mean Nathen could manipulate his thoughts?

Cameron took a long shower and changed into a clean set of clothes, bundling what he had come in wearing and replaced the set with a new one from his bag. He grinned at Nathen's shirt that had been part of the bundle and smelled it, imagining he could smell Nathen. He couldn't of course, just laundry detergent. In fact, Cameron realized, Nathen didn't have a natural scent at all. He didn't sweat. So, the only scents he had were soap, shampoo...and blood.

Chapter Thirty-Four

NATHEN

Nathen could feel a slight tickle in the back of his mind when Cameron was close. He and Syn were sitting on the couch playing World of Warcraft when the thoughts and emotions that were not his warmed him briefly. He pondered momentarily how interesting the sensation was before dismissing it, focusing again on the game that forever held his interest.

"Couldn't get anywhere. Nathen has a date with a guy he knows tomorrow to get it de-encrypted," Syn called over her shoulder.

"Oh?" Cameron asked.

Nathen frowned at the pang of jealousy that emitted from Cameron when Syn had used the word "date."

"Don't worry," Nathen soothed as Cameron rested his head on his shoulder. "It's nothing romantic. Just decrypting a hard drive."

"I know, gorgeous. She's trying to goad me. But tomorrow is going to be too late. We need to figure this out tonight."

Syn set aside the controller, turning her attention to Cameron. Nathen reluctantly followed suit.

"Well, Nathen and I were talking. I mean, we figured we should go in now. Well, as soon as we're all locked and loaded. We'll have a look around and see what we can see.

We might not figure it out tonight, and if we don't, that's okay. It may be that the deadline isn't met and the Sons of Discord, Paradigm, or whoever, is going to do whatever they're going to do. But if we do go in and find out something, maybe we can put a stop to it. Either way, tomorrow we'll start the process of decrypting the hard drive that might give us more information?"

Nathen began to excitedly explain technical things about the computer system. Picking up on the fact that Cameron didn't get most of what he was talking about, Nathen began to break things down for him, which Cameron seemed grateful for, though for the first time, Nathen realized that what he was talking about Cameron wasn't actually interested in.

The revelation shocked him. He had never before been able to read when someone wasn't interested in what he was talking about. Nathen's brother told him all the time to shut up because he was boring, but Nathen just thought it was Jake being mean. "I'm sorry. I didn't realize you weren't interested. I don't have to explain all this."

He smiled at Cameron's mental hug and guilt, as he followed with physically wrapping his strong arms around him. "I'm sorry, gorgeous. I don't understand all of that, and I don't have the same passion for it that you do. It's like when I go off on nerdy excitement about the validity and reliability of a new personality test. Syn gives me the look, but I can also feel that she has no interest at all."

"I'd be interested in it!" Nathen protested, slipping an arm around Cameron and settling against him. He'd be interested in anything having to do with science and research.

Cameron chuckled, "Well, I'll go off into all the nerdy stuff about psych testing then. But I'm sure there's stuff

I'm going to bore you with. That's just part of life." He kissed Nathen's head.

"Do I need to give you two a moment for a quickie?" Syn snorted.

"That's not a bad idea," Cameron countered. "But let's just go. Figure this out. What's the plan?"

"I think we simply walk in. You blind everyone to the fact that we're going to beeline to where that security guard went," Syn explained.

"We'll be caught on tape," Cameron pointed out.

"That doesn't matter," Nathen said. "Tonight's the last night for anything to be done. Maybe the government is planning on paying the ransom? Regardless, they haven't shut down operations and so we should go and see if we can't figure out what we can."

The trio readied for their infiltration into the hospital. A revving of excitement accompanied Nathen telling himself it was an adventure and trying desperately to remind himself not to be anxious. He failed and as they rode in the back of the Uber, he pulled Cameron down to kiss him, pricking his tongue with a fang and taking a drop of Cameron's blood, which somehow was a chemical means of relaxing. He moaned into Cameron's mouth when he slipped his hand behind Nathen's head and clasped him to him, deepening the kiss and obviously begging for more since that had just brought him to the edge of climax. The only thing that interrupted the moment was a whack from Syn who was sitting next to them.

They arrived in the Uber, and Syn remarked as they exited, "Remind me to wipe the record of us being in this guy's car, afterward if we survive." She laughed, though with a hint of uncertainty.

Nathen said, "Okay," and filed it away for later.

All three made their way to the hospital doors, with Cameron visually looking as though he was concentrating on his part of the plan.

Syn lead the way, holding out her phone as she had charted a course based on the video of the woman. Nathen held onto Cameron's arm, guiding them as they navigated through the hospital, to the elevator, and down. They had to snake their way through the labyrinth of corridors to find another larger elevator that took them further down into the hospital. As they exited, the din of hospital sounds that had greeted them on the previous floors was conspicuously absent and Nathen was momentarily distracted by the serenity of quiet. He considered that the tranquility could be taken as peaceful, but on the other hand could also be seen as ominous as it was so out of character for a busy hospital in the middle of San Francisco. He inhaled deeply and noted that there was also an absence of the smells that went along with ailing people. This floor didn't smell like it had people moving through it often at all.

As they followed Syn down one hall to the next, Nathen laughed. It was like a video game where at any moment hell hounds or zombies could be popping out. Nathen hadn't realized how much he had to tune out the stimuli around him at all times, but somehow the quiet was becoming oppressive.

"*I only feel one mind on this floor,*" Cameron imparted silently. "*But...it's different. Sleeping?*"

Nathen focused on his newfound auric sight to see if there was anything, or anyone he could see in the distance. There was a mild glow coming through the door at the end of the hall, though he couldn't tell anything else about it except it was a strong aura, closer to Cameron's.

"I see someone on this floor, though not sure how far away they are or who it is. We're walking toward them," he pointed.

"Well, whoever or whatever it is has to be on the other side of that door. This is where the camera feed ends." Syn gestured to the corner where a discrete security camera was mounted.

Nathen looked around and thought that the brightly lighted corridor didn't match the situation at all. In horror movies with abandoned hallways in a hospital there were flickering lights or halls were strangely lit by hidden bulbs. Everything seemed out of place. The floor was certainly not active and there was definitely someone behind the double door at the end of the hall. But the strange quiet, open lights, and unimpeded path was unexpected. It didn't fit. And that made Nathen nervous. His mind raced trying to fill in the gaps. He hated things that he couldn't anticipate or plan for. He had spent the afternoon planning for the unknown which had left him spiraling until he had suggested running quests with Syn in their online game so he was not so focused on what he had no control over. And now here they were.

He watched as Syn slid her phone into her pocket and patted her lower back, probably assuring herself the gun she had placed there was still there. Nathen didn't like guns, but he understood the importance for Syn to be able to protect herself. And maybe Cameron. Nathen's first priority was to make sure Cameron was going to be okay. Reminding himself of that priority gave him focus. Strength. He slid an arm around Cameron to assure him, and himself, and was rewarded when his boyfriend wrapped an arm around his waist.

"No time like the present, huh?" Cameron asked and tried to pull away and take lead.

Nathen was faster though. As much as he didn't want to do it, he couldn't let either Cameron or Syn go first.

He took a deep breath that only after he did it, he realized he didn't need to, and pushed both doors open stepping inside with his shoulders back and head up. His brother had taught him to walk with confidence and he borrowed on those lessons now. But what faced him on the other side of the door wasn't exactly something that demanded confidence.

Nathen glanced back over his shoulder at both Syn and Cameron who stepped in to either side of him.

The room was large and in the center was the security guard woman from the videos lying on a bed. This room was not as bright as the corridor had been. It had soft recessed lighting and smelled sterile, perhaps even recently cleaned. It might be any other patient lying in a hospital bed. She seemed to be peacefully sleeping. Nathen noted that it was strange that she didn't have an IV drip. When his mother had gone into the hospital for complications related to her MS, one of the first things they did was set up a saline drip. But this woman didn't have anything like that. She had an EEG cap on her head with bright purple electrodes all over it and leads going down under a blanket that he assumed were hooked to EKG pads. Nathen had once been interested in neuroimaging and brain scans and knew that the electroencephalogram read electrical energy in the brain. He remembered that it was used to diagnose sleep disorders, epilepsy, and other brain stuff. The electrocardiograph was for diagnosing issues with the heart. There was a bank of monitors set up that had all kinds of information displayed.

"Electrical energy..." Nathen said as he walked toward the bed. "That's what they're monitoring..."

Cameron stood back, staring at the woman on the bed as Syn began wandering the perimeter keeping alert.

Nathen went around the bed looking for anything out of place. The bed itself and the sheets and blanket all looked like standard hospital fare, nothing different from any of the other beds he had seen in the hospitals his mother had been in.

He bent down to check under the bed. "Hmm, that's strange."

"What?" Syn asked.

Nathen crouched down and came up with an open ornate keyboard not plugged into anything. He turned it to face the group and the dark screen had the message "PRESS ANY KEY TO CONTINUE."

"Well?" Syn chuckled.

Cameron opened his mouth in protest when Nathen exaggeratedly took his free hand and dropped it, forefinger extended so that he pressed a random key. The atmosphere in the room seemed to instantly change. It had lost its somber sense, as though the noise of the world was allowed to enter the room again. Nathen also lost, though didn't realize that it was there till it was gone, the sense of unease and being in the wrong place.

"Whoa!" Cameron's surprise was mirrored by Nathen.

The room was flooded with the sounds of the monitors and Syn started to say something when suddenly the woman on the bed sat up. All three jumped back. Nathen was immediately in front of Cameron, pushing him behind him as Syn drew her gun from across the room.

Beeping from the monitors grated on everyone's nerves before the woman calmly swung her legs over the side of the bed and hopped down. She was clad in a hospital gown, the back of which was open to reveal that she was naked beneath. Seemingly uninterested in modesty, the woman walked to the bank of monitors dragging with her cords that were hooked to the machines still attached to the leads on the cap on her head and under the robe.

Flicking a few switches, the sounds stopped, and the room returned to relative quiet, though not the unearthly quiet of a few moments before. Ignoring the group, the woman pulled the cap off her head and let the robe slide to the floor as she began to pluck the EKG pads from her chest.

Nathen didn't want to interrupt the woman, as she seemed to be taking her time removing the medical equipment from her body. The other two stayed silent as well. When she looked finished, Nathen finally raised his voice, "Hello Ma'am...uhh...What are you doing here? Who do you work for?"

"For god sakes, cover up," Syn added behind him. Nathen idly wondered if Syn was offended by the woman's nakedness or attracted to it.

The woman didn't respond, only went to a terminal, typed in a seemingly random string of letters and numbers, submitted it, and the monitor that had the ransomware background turned dark. She then turned to the group, "Congratulations, you have paid the Sons of Discord and released this hospitals data from being stolen and wiped."

"What?" Cameron asked. "We didn't pay anything. Who are you?"

"Simple," the woman answered. "You are looking at the Sons of Discord."

"But you're a girl," Nathen chimed in.

"What kinda sexist shit is that?" Syn asked Nathen.

"What do you mean?" Nathen asked. "She's a woman but is the Sons of Discord? That's kind of confusing..."

"I don't understand," Cameron reiterated. "What's going on?"

"What are you?" Nathen asked, looking close at the woman's aura. Now that she was no longer hooked up to the machines, he could tell there was something exceedingly different about her. Her blood moved differently, and she smelled more potent, like Cameron, but not the same.

The woman smiled at Nathen and the banter going on. "I'm like you, but have been enhanced beyond what you are. Keep being useful, as you have been to the company, and they will shower all kinds of rewards on you. Stray but a little and their sword will fall on you just as swiftly."

"Yeah. We know. Impetus kidnaps and murders people, turning them into vampires and slaughtering them if they don't get with the program. But if you're from Impetus, then how is Paradigm involved? What is this whole Sons of Discord thing? Have you gone rogue or are you doing this for them?" Cameron fired off questions too fast for Nathen to keep up.

The woman's smile was serene. "It's better to show, than tell..." She lifted her left hand, and using a nail of her other hand, pierced the skin and ran it to cut through her forearm along its length.

She winced as she was doing it but made no sound. Using her right hand, she lifted up the skin to expose silver metallic structures with light moving and blinking throughout it.

"I'm a conglomeration of Impetus and Paradigm." She looked at them, seemingly amused at the horror and disgust in their eyes.

"Umm...Nathen?" Cameron said.

He saw Syn quickly pull her gun back up to train it on the woman.

"That's fascinating," Nathen said. "How were they able to tie your nervous system to the electronics, if we're dead?"

She focused on Nathen. "By revivifying my mind enough to emit echoes of my conscious will into the physical world."

She turned to Syn. "There is no need for violence, I won't be hurting you and I would appreciate the same kindness. We can all walk away from here alive...well, relatively—" She winked at Nathen and continued. "— having gained information that you three are missing."

"That's why I'm able to sense you? At least when you were sleeping. I can tell you're still there, but fairly vague," Cameron said, stepping around the bed that he kept between them. He kept his eyes on the woman while putting a steadying hand on Syn who lowered her gun.

"That's right," the woman said.

"But what is this whole thing with the Sons of Discord? I don't get it. Why terrorize children and their families?" Cameron demanded.

"That, Sir, is actually above my pay grade. I was instructed only to remain here until midnight and report on who, if anyone, identified me. It wasn't any of the official agencies: FBI, law enforcement. It wasn't the hospital itself... I guess it was the ones hired by my makers. The wild card—" She nodded to Syn. "—and neonate—" She nodded to Nathen.

The woman then turned and picked up a pair of blue jeans that were neatly folded on the counter. Unfurling them, she slid one leg and then the other in. She next shimmied into a white T-shirt, before turning back to them. "We were testing how humans would respond to various threats with the least lives lost. To see how government agencies and law enforcement would act. The same way our bodies respond to infection, threat, and foreign bodies."

"I don't get it," Cameron said.

The woman rolled a shoulder.

"But Paradigm and Impetus are working together," Syn interjected. "And you're a product of both of them you said?"

"Indeed. Their innovations will revolutionize mankind. I can only assume that this most recent endeavor will assist in identifying and neutralizing threats." The woman flashed a smile. "And now it's time for a much-earned vacation. I'm thinking Greece."

Cameron gawked.

Nathen asked, "But... Why did you try to blow us up?"

The woman looked upset for the first time. "That was unfortunate. I, we, apologize. We were not trying to blow you up, per se. That was a safeguard, and it would be obvious to spot if a military or government agency had found that building. We purposefully made it easy to find. The place was a relay station that only held information important to the experiment. It was set up to go off if anyone tried to take the server from the premises without disarming the trap. If someone disarmed the trap, it would have wiped the server. Either way, it was meant to be destroyed. It seemed you set it off without first exploring the building. I'm glad to see everyone survived."

"So, let me get this right," Syn said, having stashed her gun. "You're some type of cyborg vampire who works for two big corporations who are fucking with society out of some experiment to see how they will respond? Corporations who, I might add, covertly hired us! And you're not going to kill us...why?"

The woman's laugh put Nathen at ease for some reason. He liked her.

"Because you're useful. Smart. Resourceful. Human interaction and responses are forever a quandary and one that they hope to quantify someday. Until then, it looks like you all have solved the puzzle, rescued the maiden, so to speak." She gestured to herself with a bow of her head. "If you check the news media, you'll see that a benefactor came along and neutralized the threat. Just so you know, though, there was no actual threat."

Cameron shook his head, annoyed and confused. The woman flipped a few switches and all of the machines turned off. "Good luck to you all."

Nathen saw her run out the door but realized the rest of the group probably hadn't noticed. He had barely caught it as she moved much quicker than he could even with his enhanced abilities. Part of him wanted to chase after her, to ask her questions. But he realized that if she wanted to talk any longer, she wouldn't have left.

"Where'd she go?" Syn asked.

"She ran out," Nathen explained.

Cameron harrumphed. "For the record, I hate Impetus. And now Paradigm, for that matter. If they didn't make the best cell phones I'd probably cut them out entirely."

"And laptops, and tablets, and…" Syn snorted. "Guess that's it. Food anyone?"

Chapter Thirty-Five

CAMERON

Moodily stuffing sushi into his mouth without tasting it, Cameron played over the alien surface thoughts that he had read from the blond-haired woman. Thinking back, he realized it hadn't been quite human thoughts he was reading, though it was there. Something. Just beneath the surface.

He saw that Nathen was lost in his own thoughts, quietly chewing with a faraway look. Syn was staring at him and Cameron offered an apologetic smile. "*Sorry.*"

Syn shrugged, "It's not a problem. I think we were all left with more questions than answers."

"Me too," Cameron sighed heavily, loving that Syn and he were of one mind most of the time.

"I wonder if they will want to add implants to me," Nathen interjected.

"Why would you want that?" Cameron stared.

"I don't want it, necessarily. But it's fascinating. Don't you think?" He looked from Syn to Cameron for confirmation which wasn't coming from either of them.

They ate in silence for a while longer until Syn suddenly said, "I just thought of something."

Both Cameron and Nathen tilted their heads in unison.

She stared at them for a second then shook her head and went on. "That woman. She thinks that the SSD was destroyed. She doesn't know that you have it."

Cameron searched his memory. "That's right. She said that the fire was to destroy all evidence and that she believed that it did."

"It probably doesn't matter," Cameron said. "Just more information that points to Paradigm and Impetus. She already tied that together for us. Probably want a monopoly. Come on, gorgeous. You wanna spend the night?"

"Let me text my mom. But yeah. Yeah, I think I'd really like that."

Cameron grinned at his *boyfriend*. The vampire. He glanced at Syn. His sister. It didn't matter what the future held with these huge organizations that seemed to hold a lot more secrets than anyone could realize. The only thing that mattered was right here in front of him.

Epilogue

"Will there be anything else, Sir?" Agnes asked, setting the tablet with the newest nightly report on the huge mahogany desk that dominated HR's office. She made sure to turn the handle of the coffee cup (always with black coffee) that she had also brought around to him so it would be easier to reach.

"Not at this time, Ms. Katz," HR responded in his normal stoic tone, his attention on the tablet. He was acutely aware when the woman quietly slid out of room and only then did he pick up the tablet to start reading.

MISSION: SONS OF DISCORD

Success

- Local, State, and Federal Agencies' tactics identified and evaluated.

    o Local law enforcement—not a threat.

    o State law enforcement—not a threat.

    o Federal law enforcement—not a threat.

- Independents' tactics identified and evaluated.

    o Independents—not a threat.

- Unexpected Independents identified and evaluated.

- o Mage "Theo"—a threat. To be monitored.

- o Mage Aaron Molina, AKA "Cameron Corazon"—a threat. Consider recruitment.

- Security Asset

  - o Todd Jacks—indisposed.

- New Asset Hale's tactics identified and evaluated.

  - o Acquisition of skills—rapid. Affected by blood of enhanced.

  - o Loyalty—adequate.

  - o Termination—not applicable at this time.

  - o To be monitored.

End Report.

About the Author

Connal Braginsky is a software engineer who lives in San Diego, California. Diagnosed with high functioning autism, Connal sometimes struggles in social situations, but has an inner world that is always incredibly rich. With an insatiable thirst for knowledge about many esoteric things, Connal brings a lot of personal philosophies and interests to writing.

Sean Ian O'Meidhir is a psychologist who lives in San Francisco, California. Sean is a hedonist who believes in living for today, living every day to the fullest, and enjoying as much as possible. They have been gaming since adolescence and have written about and played hundreds of lives, revelling in the chance to take on new personalities, dramas, even disorders.

Email: seanomeidhir@gmail.com

Facebook: www.facebook.com/SeanOMeidhir

Twitter: @SeanIanOMeidhir

Website: www.dreamersworkshop.com

Also Available from NineStar Press

Connect with NineStar Press

www.ninestarpress.com

www.facebook.com/ninestarpress

www.facebook.com/groups/NineStarNiche

www.twitter.com/ninestarpress

www.tumblr.com/blog/ninestarpress